DINEY COSTELOE

Miss Mary's Daughter

HEAD of ZEUS

Miss Mary's Daughter

DINEY COSTELOE is the author of twenty-three novels, several short stories, and many articles and poems. She has three children and seven grandchildren, so when she isn't writing, she's busy with family. She and her husband divide their time between Somerset and West Cork.

9 7 5 3 1 2 4 6 8

A catalogue record for this book is available
from the British Library.

ISBN (HB) 9781784976163
ISBN (XTPB) 9781784976170
ISBN (E) 9781784976156

Typeset by Adrian McLaughlin

Printed and bound in Great Britain by
CPI Group (UK) Ltd, Croydon CR0 4YY

Head of Zeus Ltd
First Floor East
5–8 Hardwick Street
London EC1R 4RG

WWW.HEADOFZEUS.COM

My heartfelt thanks go to Mike Rapps, solicitor, author and friend, who answered all my legal questions in great detail and with enormous patience. Also to the Cornish Andersons, Rosie and Ian, who offered me bed and board and drove me round Cornwall while I was doing my research.

Finally to my long-suffering agent, Judith, and editor, Rosie. Thank you both for your continued encouragement, your input and your patience, without which I might well have sunk beneath the wave.

•

Prologue

Trescadinnick 1860

In the pale dawn of her twenty-first birthday, Mary Penvarrow stole out of the house carrying a large leather bag containing her worldly goods. She skirted round the outhouses and set off up the track that led to the moor. As she approached a stand of trees she saw a figure waiting, holding the reins of two horses. She ran towards him, dropping her bag as he gathered her into his arms.

'You came!' he murmured into her hair. 'I was afraid you'd change your mind.'

'Never,' she replied as she returned his embrace.

'Did anyone see you leave?' he asked as he let her go and picked up her saddlebag.

'No, the house was still asleep.'

'Not even Miss Matty?'

'No, John. Not even Matty,' sighed Mary.

'Then it's time to go,' John said and lifting her up in his arms, tossed her into the saddle. He slung her saddlebag behind her and then mounted his own horse. 'There's an early train to Truro from St Morwen,' he said. 'We'll leave the horses at the inn.'

Together they rode out from the shelter of the trees and took the track that edged the moor. As they crested a rise, Mary drew rein and turned for one final glimpse of the house where she had lived for her twenty-one years... from now, no longer her home.

In wreaths of early mist, its tower jutting into a yellowing sky, Trescadinnick stood strong and solid, staring out across the pewter of the restless sea. In the distance, early-morning smoke rose from the hidden chimneys of Port Felec, the little fishing village and its harbour sheltered from the worst of the weather in a hollow of the cliffs. The church with its squat tower stood sentinel above the village, behind which a few sturdy cottages clung to the rising cliff, and beyond it all, etched against the pale morning, the tall finger of the copper mine pointed to the sky. It was a view Mary knew by heart, and as she gazed upon it one last time a shaft of sunlight pierced the mist, illuminating the home she was leaving. For a moment tears filled her eyes as she imprinted the view on her mind, but her decision had been made five days ago when her father had sent John Ross away, his suit unheard. She lifted one hand as if in salute and then turning the horse's head, she followed John over the hill, riding into the unknown that was the rest of her life.

Chapter 1

London 1886

Mary Ross sat down at her bureau and pulled a piece of paper towards her. The July sun streamed in through the window and for several minutes she put off what she intended to do. Instead she looked out into the familiar street. For nearly twenty years she had looked out at the plane tree rooted in the opposite pavement, casting its shade across the road, and at the modest houses lined up on the far side, all reflections of her own. She had lived nearly all her married life in this house, looking out at this street, and it was in this house that she would die... and soon. She had battled against the illness which was now consuming her and she knew it was a battle she had lost. Her own mother had succumbed to the same disease at a similar age and Mary had recognized the signs well before anyone else. She had been nineteen when her mother died, a year younger than her own daughter, Sophie, was now, but somehow she felt Sophie was younger than her remembered self. Brought up in a house where love flourished, Sophie seemed to her mother ill-prepared for the chilly winds of the outside world. Even as she was thinking these thoughts, the sound of the piano drifted up the stairs from the drawing room below; Sophie practising as she did every afternoon. 'For,' as she pointed out, 'I can't begin to take on more pupils, Mama, if I'm a stumbling pianist myself.'

Listening to her now, Mary was well aware that Sophie was

anything but a stumbling pianist. She played with a fluidity and expression that she, Mary, had never achieved, despite the encouragement and the long hours of practice demanded by her own mother. Sophie had surpassed her several years ago and was well able to instruct the two little girls to whom she gave lessons twice a week. Sophie's intention was to take on more pupils to help supplement their slender income.

'I'm sure if I asked Emma and Harriet's mothers they would recommend me,' she'd enthused. 'I shall build a list of pupils and start a music school.' Her mother had smiled fondly at these ambitious plans.

Dear Sophie, Mary thought now, as she listened to the melodies wafting through the house. So keen to help, to make life easier, but it would be no good. Since John had been killed, run over by a hansom in one of London's famous pea-soup fogs, they had been living off the small capital inherited from his mother, all that he had left behind. It was meagre enough, but as a younger son he was entitled to little of his father's modest estate. He might have inherited more but he had died before his father, and his share of the inheritance had returned to his brother, Harold.

With only a small annuity, a legacy from Mary's mother, and without John's regular income from his work in the City, Mary and Sophie had been left in decidedly straitened circumstances.

The annuity paid the rent, but Mary knew that it would cease with her death. When she died Sophie would have only the last of the dwindling capital to live on. When that had gone she would have to go out and make her own way in the world... unless.

Unless I eat humble pie and ask the family to look after her, Mary thought. That, she knew, was the situation in a nutshell, and it led her back to her decision.

Reluctantly she again turned her attention to the paper in front of her and, picking up her pen, began to write. She had delayed writing this letter for too long and now that she faced imminent death, she knew it had to be written before it was too late.

She hadn't been in contact with those at Trescadinnick for over nineteen years. Not since Sophie was born. She had written to her father then to tell him he had a granddaughter, but there had been no reply, not even an acknowledgement that her letter had been received. Now, though, she must either leave Sophie almost destitute or she must swallow her pride and beg the family to provide for her. Was her father even alive still? she wondered. He'd be an old man now. She knew her brother Joss had been killed in an accident, but what about her sisters? Surely they'd still be there; Louisa running Trescadinnick, Matty married to George Treslyn. Surely they would see Sophie was looked after. However, it was to her estranged father that she knew she must address herself.

Slowly Mary wrote, *Dear Papa...* More than once she tore the page across and started again before she was satisfied with the result. She had told him she was dying, explained the position in which this would leave Sophie and asked for his help. At last the letter was finished and having read it through once more, she slipped it into an envelope and sealed it. Would it be ignored like her last letter, when Sophie was born? Well, if it were, Sophie need never know it had even been sent. She put it in a pigeonhole in the desk and closed the lid. It was done.

Suddenly she was exhausted and with the familiar pain coursing through her, she crawled onto her bed and lay back, closing her eyes for a minute before she reached for the bell at her bedside and rang for Hannah.

Hannah she could rely on. She had been employed as a nursery maid when Sophie was a baby and somehow she had stayed on as cook-housekeeper, almost one of the family.

Moments later Hannah came into the room, opening the door softly and pausing on the threshold in case her mistress had dozed off again, as she did sometimes these days. But as she stood by the door, Mary's eyes opened and she beckoned Hannah inside.

'I want you to do something for me, Hannah,' she said. 'Without question.'

'Of course, ma'am. You just say what and I'll do it.'

'There's a letter in my bureau, in the right-hand pigeonhole, addressed to some people in Cornwall. When I die... and not before, mind... you're to post that letter immediately. But you're not to say a word about it to Miss Sophie, you understand?'

'Just post a letter for you? I could do that now if you want me to.'

'No, not till... after.' Realizing she had to give some explanation, she went on, 'It's just a letter to... to some friends that Sophie doesn't know about. A final farewell. They live a long way away and I don't want them to come visiting.' That much at least was true. She had set aside her pride to write and ask help for Sophie, but she would ask nothing for herself.

'Well, ma'am, if you say so,' Hannah said, pleased to promise anything that would ease her mistress's mind and happily unaware of the consequences of that promise.

Later that evening, Sophie sat by the bed, her mother's hand in hers no heavier than an autumn leaf, blue-veined, transparent, but an infinitesimal pressure from her frail fingers proved that she was not yet asleep. Sophie returned the pressure, knowing if she tried to speak she would break down and weep. As she sat there, watching the evening sun mellow the familiar wallpaper, Sophie found herself thinking about her father.

Unlike her mother's, his death was entirely unexpected. He had taken the omnibus to the City one dull, November morning – an ordinary morning, the start of anything but an ordinary day. He had dropped a kiss on his daughter's head as she sat eating her breakfast before she too left the house to go to school; he'd paused at the front door to tip his hat to his wife, a familiar gesture of respect given every day as he left, and stepped out into the street. They never saw him alive again. As he'd alighted from the omnibus and started to walk to his office, the morning fog had swallowed him. He had collided with another, unseen pedestrian and had been tipped into the path of an oncoming hansom. Sophie had not been allowed to see him. His coffin had been closed, the damage to his head making him almost unrecognizable. Now, Sophie's thoughts were of his funeral. She had not been allowed to attend that either. She had watched as the coffin was carried out of the house and laid in a hearse drawn by black-plumed horses. His brother, her Uncle Harold, attended, following the hearse in a black-swathed carriage, while other friends followed the cortege on foot. After the burial, with a brief handshake and words of condolence to Mary, Harold had returned home. The friends, with murmured sympathy, had dispersed and Mary had walked alone through the chilly November streets to the home where Sophie and Hannah awaited her.

Sophie had never seen her mother shed a tear, though on occasion a bleakness in her expression told of her private grief. Sophie gradually became used to her father's absence. Sometimes a jolt of reality hit her when she longed to tell him something, wanting to share some excitement or piece of news, and she had to accept again that he would never walk back through the door. But the ordinariness of daily life took over as she went to school, took her piano lessons, walked with her mother along the towpath by the river or across the common, and the fact of his absence became the ordinary.

Will that happen when Mother dies? Sophie wondered as she looked down at the frail form, now asleep in the bed. Tears sprang to her eyes and she bit her lip to stop herself from crying out. How will I manage when she's not here any more? How can I watch her simply fade away? Will living without her become ordinary?

The end came a week later in that same sunlit bedroom. Mary lay motionless in her bed, no longer aware of her surroundings. She had taken no food for two days; no water since the night before. Sophie was sitting holding her hand, hoping that Mama knew that she was there with her, that she was not alone, but with a gentle relaxation of her hand, Mary slipped into her final sleep.

On a hot August day, with sun burning in a cloudless sky, the coffin was carried in a plain black carriage pulled by a single, black-plumed horse, first to the church and then to the cemetery. This time it was Sophie who led the little knot of mourners who followed on foot.

Sophie had written to her Uncle Harold to tell him of her mother's death and had received a black-edged card of condolence, but he had not come to the funeral, pleading pressure of business. Mr Phillips was there, as was Dr Hart, but when they left the graveside, Sophie and Hannah walked quietly home and Sophie was left to mourn her mother alone.

Since the death of her father five years earlier, Sophie and her mother had only each other, and Mary's last illness had bonded them closer than ever. Now Sophie was left surrounded by an infinite emptiness, achingly alone. Her life seemed to stretch out bleakly in front of her, a grey wasteland full of pitfalls that she would have to negotiate by herself.

On the day after the funeral Hannah took the letter from Mary's bureau to the post. It was only a letter to some distant friends, she had reasoned. There was no hurry for them to receive it; they lived somewhere in Cornwall and would hardly be coming to the funeral. Sophie might hear from them some time in the future, but as far as Hannah was concerned the important thing had been to get the funeral over and consider what to do next.

Hannah was no fool and she knew well that they'd been living on a shoestring for the past couple of years, and there were certain things that needed to be decided upon, and sooner rather than later. She was relieved when the lawyer, Mr Phillips, came to see Sophie, bringing the simple will that her mother had left. Surely a man like Mr Phillips would know what they should do, Hannah thought as, having served them tea, she retreated to the kitchen and left them to it.

'Everything of your mother's is left to you,' Mr Phillips told Sophie. 'There's a little money and a few pieces of jewellery. She mentions a ring and a necklace.'

'I know about those,' Sophie told him. 'They were given to her by my father. I'm sure there used to be a bracelet that matched the necklace, but I can't find it. I think Mother must have sold it.'

'If that's the case,' he suggested gently, 'you might think about selling one of the other pieces, just to tide you over until...?'

Until what? wondered Sophie. Until I get a job? Until I get

married? Until I have to sell the next piece? But she gave utterance to none of these things, simply saying, 'I don't intend to sell those if I can help it, Mr Phillips.' She managed a smile. 'I know things are going to be difficult from now on. For a start, I shan't be able to last long on the money I've got now. Mama's illness was long-drawn-out, you know, and the doctor's fees mounted up. Then of course there was the funeral... We've been eating into capital, I'm afraid.' She smiled ruefully. 'And there wasn't much in the first place.'

'What about the house?' asked Mr Phillips. 'Not yours, I believe.'

Sophie shook her head. 'No, it's rented. We pay the rent quarterly. It's due in a month or so.'

'Well, let me know if you have any difficulties, my dear,' Mr Phillips said as he rose to leave. 'Only too happy to help. Good friend of mine, your father.'

Sophie saw him to the door and then sighed as she returned to the parlour. The rent of the small house in Hammersmith was indeed paid up until the end of the quarter, but that was only a matter of weeks away. Despite Mr Phillips's offer of help, Sophie knew she must move to a cheaper place and find some form of employment.

'There are two possibilities really,' she sighed to Hannah. 'Finding somewhere much cheaper to live and taking more piano pupils to pay the rent, or becoming a governess somewhere so I've no living expenses at all... unless, of course,' the thought struck her, 'I could get work in a shop.'

'A shop!' The redoubtable Hannah was horrified. Having come to look after Sophie as a baby and continued with the family ever since, she had very definite ideas of what was right and fitting for her beloved Sophie and she was never afraid to speak her mind. She did so now. 'That's not what your ma would have wanted, Miss Sophie, and that's a fact. A shop girl indeed, the very idea.'

'Well, I've got to do something,' Sophie pointed out reasonably. 'I can't afford to go on as I am.' Reaching out, she took

Hannah's hand and said gently, 'But whatever I do, Hannah, I'm afraid you'll have to find another position.'

Hannah stiffened. 'You're never turning me off, Miss Sophie? Not after all these years.'

'Oh, Hannah, dear Hannah, of course I'm not,' Sophie cried. 'It's just that I can't afford to pay you any longer, and from now on I'll have to fend for myself.'

'That you will not, Miss Sophie,' Hannah asserted hotly, 'not while Hannah Butts is here to look after you. It isn't proper for a young lady to live alone. Don't you worry about wages. We'll manage.'

'But, Hannah dear, I can't take you with me if I go for a governess,' Sophie said gently, touched by Hannah's determination.

'Then you'd better not go for one,' returned Hannah stoutly. 'We'll get by, Miss Sophie, you'll see.'

But Sophie was not so optimistic. She knew that despite Hannah's determination to do without wages, they would be hard pressed to live on the tiny income they had left, and secretly she began to scan the advertisement columns of ladies' magazines to find a suitable family seeking a governess.

'After all,' she said to Hannah, 'it's not as if I'm not well educated. Both Papa and Mama were determined that I should go to a good school, and even when Papa was killed and money was tight, Mama insisted I stay on. I could teach small children to read and write, to learn their numbers, perhaps a little history and geography. I love children. I know I could do it, if only someone would give me a chance.'

''Course you could,' Hannah said encouragingly, 'if you had to. But maybe it won't come to that. Never know what's round the corner, do we?'

Sophie was pretty sure she did know what was round the corner, and it wasn't very much. They certainly couldn't afford the rent of the little house where they'd lived ever since she could remember. Come quarter day they would have to move.

She set out to find lodgings of a cheaper sort, but the rooms she could afford were so dreary and depressing, she didn't commit

herself to any of them, though as the days dragged by, she realized
miserably that she must make a decision, and make it soon. How
she wished her mother were at hand to advise her, or that she had
a close friend in whom she could confide. She considered going
back to Mr Phillips with her problems, but hesitated, and finally
decided against it. He would tell her to sell Mama's necklace, or
worse, her wedding ring, neither of which she was prepared to
do... at least not yet. So, short of lending her money, there was
not a lot that Mr Phillips could do. Sophie was determined not to
get into debt, but unless she found work of some sort soon they
were going to be out on the street. With only Hannah for company
in those dark days, her spirits sank lower and lower.

She had answered several advertisements in ladies' magazines,
families looking for a governess, but had only been invited for
interview once. That interview had been extremely short. Lady
Carson of Ovington Square had taken one look at Sophie and
decided against her. Her fifteen-year-old son, Rupert, was at
such an impressionable age and here was Miss Ross, perfectly
acceptable from the answers she gave, but too attractive by far
with her dark auburn hair, her delicately clear skin and fine dark
green eyes. Her pale beauty, of which she seemed entirely
unaware, was set off by the severe black of her mourning. To
have such a person living in the house with Rupert, and indeed
her own husband, Henley, would be tempting providence. Lady
Carson looked down her aristocratic nose, bid Sophie good
morning and sent her away.

'Lady Carson didn't find me suitable,' Sophie told Hannah
when she returned from the unsuccessful interview. 'It looks as
if I may have to try and get work in a shop after all. I've got to
find something.'

'Woman must be mad not to give you the job,' sniffed Hannah,
secretly pleased that she hadn't. 'Can't see a good thing when it's
right in front of her, if you ask me. Any answers to your own
advertisements yet, Miss Sophie?'

Sophie shook her head. 'Not yet,' she replied. 'Still, as they
only went in this week, we must give them time.'

Sophie had advertised her services as a music teacher, offering to work in the pupils' own homes, teaching piano, singing and music appreciation. Her fees would be low, but with these to supplement her tiny income she and Hannah might just manage, provided they found the cheap lodging they'd been seeking.

It was Hannah who found a place eventually, two rooms in Putney, with a private parlour and the use of a kitchen.

'It's not much, Miss Sophie,' she said sadly. 'But at least it's clean and the woman there seems a decent sort of a body. A Mrs Porter. She tells me too that there is a seminary for young ladies down the road, which might need a music teacher.'

Sophie went to see the rooms and to meet Mrs Porter, who led her upstairs to view what might become her new home. The two tiny bedrooms, cramped and dark with small windows, looked out onto a backyard filled with an accumulation of junk and a privy standing against the wall. The parlour faced the narrow street and the blank wall of a factory opposite, but at least it was south-facing and blessed with sunshine for much of the day. The kitchen was downstairs and they would have to provide their own pots and pans, but there was a stove that could be used by arrangement.

'Don't you worry, Miss Sophie,' Hannah said as she surveyed what it had to offer. 'I'll arrange with Mrs Porter for our cooking. We'll manage.'

With great reluctance, Sophie agreed to take the rooms and paid two weeks in advance to secure them. It was the best they could do and they arranged to move in at the end of the quarter. Sophie also approached the girls' school Mrs Porter had mentioned, explaining to the rather formidable principal, Mrs Devine, that she was looking for work as a music teacher. Mrs Devine looked at her critically and with a sniff, regretted she was in no need of a music teacher at present, adding as she rang the bell to have Sophie shown out, 'You're too young for such a position, Miss Ross, scarcely older than my girls themselves.'

'I wouldn't mind if I couldn't do the job properly,' Sophie complained bitterly to Hannah over a cup of tea when she got home again, 'but they never ask me to play or anything, so they've no idea if I'm any good or not. They always use my age as an excuse.'

'Never mind, Miss Sophie. It's their loss, that's what I say. We'll manage, you'll see. Now you just relax over your nice cup of tea, and I'll run down to the market and find some good fresh vegetables to go with dinner.'

Hannah disappeared down the road and Sophie wandered from room to room, to make final decisions as to which of her parents' cherished furniture and other possessions she would have to part with.

'For we've no room in Putney for Mama's bureau or Papa's chair, or the grandfather clock. Still,' she had told Hannah, trying not to sound too depressed, 'I'll keep the piano because I'll need that, and if we sell the other things it'll give us a little more money.'

With the house silent, she stood motionless in her mother's bedroom. She'd known no other home and now she was about to leave it.

'What else could I do, Mama?' she asked aloud, and as misery and frustration overtook her, she flung herself onto her mother's bed and wept. Gradually her sobs subsided, and exhausted by the tensions of the last few weeks and her bout of weeping, there, on the bed, her head pillowed on her arms, Sophie drifted into an uneasy sleep.

Chapter 2

Trescadinnick was in turmoil. Thomas Penvarrow had had some sort of seizure. One minute he had been walking through the hall on his way to the stables and the next he had crashed to the floor, taking a chair and the chenille cloth from the hall table with him.

AliceAnne, aged six, who had been in her habitual hiding place beneath the table, found herself staring at her great-grandfather's red face only inches from her own. She let out a piercing scream which brought the housemaid, Edith, scurrying from the morning room where she had been clearing the breakfast table. Seeing the master lying on the floor, eyes closed, breath rasping in his throat, she added her screams to AliceAnne's.

Charles Leroy emerged from his office as his mother, Louisa, came rushing from the kitchen. He took one look at Thomas and shouted for Paxton who, having heard the commotion, was already running to the scene.

'Send Ned for the doctor,' Charles ordered, 'quick as you like. Then come back here and help me get Mr Penvarrow up off the floor.'

Paxton dispatched the stable lad for the doctor and then he and Charles managed to lift the dead weight of Thomas Penvarrow off the floor and carry him into the drawing room. They eased him down onto a sofa and Charles, reaching forward, pulled off the old man's cravat and loosened his collar.

'For goodness' sake, girl,' Louisa snapped at the still wailing Edith. 'Stop that dreadful caterwauling and take Miss AliceAnne to Mrs Paxton.' Then, turning to her granddaughter, she said more gently, 'No need to cry, AliceAnne. Be a brave girl and go to the kitchen with Edith. I'll come and find you in a little while.'

Her briskness had the desired effect and clamping her jaws on her screams, the maid took the child by the hand and led her through to the kitchen.

Summoned by Ned the stable boy, Dr Nicholas Bryan arrived not twenty minutes later. He had been about to set out on his rounds and the pony was already put to the gig. He strode into the house to be greeted by Charles Leroy, who held out his hand and said, 'Ah, Dr Bryan, thank you for coming so quickly.'

He led the young doctor into the drawing room, where Thomas was still lying on the sofa, his eyes now open though unfocused.

Dr Nicholas Bryan looked down at the old man for a moment, and then kneeled beside him to lay a hand on his forehead and to take his pulse.

Thomas stared up at him, his mind befuddled, and for a moment he thought he was looking at his son, Jocelyn.

'Joss?' he muttered, before his vision cleared and he recognized the young doctor who had recently taken over the practice of old Dr Marshall.

'Stay still now, sir,' Dr Bryan said, 'and let me look at you. Do you know who I am?'

'Of course I do.' Thomas's voice was a husky whisper. 'I'm not stupid, young man.'

'Now, Papa,' Louisa said, 'you had a fall and Dr Bryan has come to make sure you're all right.'

'I'm perfectly all right,' Thomas said, trying to sit up, but as he did so his head swam so violently that he lay back, gasping.

'Stay lying down for a while and then we'll get you up to your bed and make you comfortable.' Dr Bryan turned to Louisa and Charles and went on, 'He needs to be kept still and quiet for several days, with nothing to worry or alarm him. Once we've got him to his bed I'll give him something to make him sleep.'

'Don't discuss me as if I wasn't here,' Thomas growled, though he made no further effort to sit up. 'I'm not in my dotage.'

'Certainly not, sir,' agreed Dr Bryan cheerfully. 'And if you do as I tell you, you'll be up and about again in a week or two.'

With Paxton's help, they managed to get Thomas up the stairs and into his own room. Though not prepared to admit it, he was relieved to be in his own bed. With a bad grace, he drank down the draught that the doctor prepared for him and after a short while lapsed into sleep.

'Thank you for coming so quickly, Doctor,' Louisa said as they went back downstairs. 'Is there really no danger to my father?'

'It's difficult to tell,' replied the doctor. 'He's an old man, and these things happen as one gets towards his age. They are unexplained. Sometimes they recur; others they never happen again. It is important that you keep him quiet for the next week or so until we are sure that he has recovered. Light foods, broth, a little fish, but no meat or potatoes or puddings. Try not to let him get upset or angry about anything. That is always an added risk in such cases.'

Charles gave a wry smile. 'Easier said than done,' he murmured.

Louisa offered the doctor some refreshment, but he shook his head. 'Thank you, Mrs Leroy, but I should be getting out on my rounds now. I have several visits promised for today. However, I shall look in on Mr Penvarrow on my way home, just to reassure myself that there is nothing more I need to do at present.'

With a smile and a handshake, the doctor picked up his hat and walked out to his waiting pony and trap.

'He seems to know what he's doing,' Louisa said as she watched him drive away. 'Though I wish we still had Dr Marshall. He knew us all so well, and was always so reassuring.'

'He was an old man,' Charles said. 'Old-fashioned in his ways. We're very lucky to have Dr Bryan to take his place. Not many young doctors would want to bury themselves in a small place like Port Felec.' He smiled at his mother. 'I don't think we need to worry about my grandfather, but perhaps I'll send Ned over to Aunt Matty and suggest she comes over to see him.'

'You really don't think he's dangerously ill, do you?' Louisa sounded concerned.

'No, Mother, but even so I think we should let Aunt Matty know what's happened.'

Matty arrived at Trescadinnick before the morning was out. 'Tell me what happened,' she said to Louisa as she strode into the house, carrying a capacious bag which indicated that she'd come to stay. 'Ned gave me some garbled message about Papa, so of course I came at once.' She dropped her bag onto the floor. 'What happened?'

'We don't know exactly,' replied Louisa. 'He had some sort of seizure, and collapsed onto the floor. We sent Ned for Dr Bryan, but by the time he got here Papa was coming round. We got him into his bed and the doctor gave him a sleeping draught, so he's asleep now. He's to be kept quiet and not to be angered or upset.'

'That won't be easy for you,' Matty said, 'especially if the doctor insists on him staying in bed! So, he's going to be all right?'

'Dr Bryan thinks so, provided he doesn't have another attack.'

Matty looked across at her sister. 'What's he like, the new doctor?'

'Personable enough. He was very efficient, rather matter-of-fact. He doesn't have the comfortable bedside manner of Dr Marshall, but he's coming back again later, to see how Papa is doing. If you stay you can meet him then.'

'Of course I'm staying,' Matty replied, unpinning her hat. 'I plan to stay at least tonight.' She laid her hat down on the table and as she did so she saw an envelope lying on the brass plate where the delivered post was always placed. She stared at the letter for a moment and then said, 'Louisa, when did this arrive?'

'What?' Louisa had already turned to go to the kitchen.

'This letter. It's addressed to Papa.'

Louisa shrugged. 'This morning's post, I suppose. What about it?'

'I just wondered. He hasn't opened it.'

'It must have arrived while we were getting him to bed,' Louisa said. 'I didn't hear the postman. Edith must have taken it in.' Louisa disappeared to tell Edith to prepare a room for her sister, leaving Matty standing in the hall, turning the letter over and over in her hands. The address was right, *Thomas Penvarrow, Esq., Trescadinnick, Port Felec, Cornwall.* It was the handwriting that had caught her attention: Mary's... or very like Mary's. Could it really be from Mary after all this time? Matty hadn't seen or heard from her twin since the day of their brother Joss's funeral. Mary had returned to Cornwall on that sad day and though their father had ignored her presence, Matty had been delighted to see her. They'd had plenty of time to talk before Mary had to leave to catch her train back to London. Though she had given Matty an address to write to, none of the letters Matty had sent received a reply and at length she had stopped writing. Perhaps Mary had moved, or perhaps her father's attitude at Joss's funeral had decided Mary that the break was now complete.

Recently, however, she had found herself thinking more and more of Mary, wondering how she was. She'd had a sense of disquiet, a feeling there was something wrong; nothing definite, just a nagging worry at the back of her mind, and now, suddenly, here was a letter. How would her father react to a letter from Mary, the first for over twenty-five years?

Thomas Penvarrow was still asleep when the family sat down to luncheon in the dining room. When they had all been served, and Edith had returned to the kitchen, Matty said, 'There was a letter for Papa this morning.'

Louisa glanced up. 'Yes, you said so earlier. It can wait. We don't want to worry him with letters now. It can't be that important.'

'I think it might be,' Matty said. 'I think I know who it's from.'

Louisa looked shocked. 'How? You haven't opened it, have you?'

'No, of course not,' snapped Matty. 'It's addressed to Papa.'

'Then he can open it when he's feeling better,' Louisa said firmly. 'Dr Bryan was insistent that we shouldn't worry him with anything for the next few days.'

'I think it's from Mary.' There, she'd said it.

'From Mary?' Louisa stared at her with incredulity. 'What makes you say so?'

'It looks like her handwriting.'

'Looks like?'

'I think it is.'

'Well, if you're right, we certainly can't give it to Papa yet, if at all.' Louisa was adamant. 'That would definitely upset him.'

'Why would Aunt Mary write to my grandfather after all these years?' Charles spoke for the first time. He had no recollection of Mary, who had left when he was still a small child, and was intrigued.

Matty shrugged. 'We shan't know until it's opened, shall we?'

'Are you suggesting that we should open it ourselves?'

'No, Charles, I'm not, but I do think we should give my father the chance to read it if he wants to.'

'If it is from Mary, she's probably writing because she wants something,' Louisa said tartly. 'Though why she thinks he'll give her anything after the way she went against his wishes, I can't imagine.'

'She's still his daughter,' replied Matty, 'and our sister.'

'Papa doesn't regard her as such, and to be honest, Matty, neither do I. Mary walked out on this family, causing a scandal we all had to live down. She made her bed, so she must lie in it.'

Matty's lips tightened but she made no answer to this, simply pushed her plate away and got up from the table. What Louisa said was true, but even so, Matty knew she couldn't simply forget that she had a sister, and a twin at that.

'I'm going up to sit with Papa,' she said.

'He's asleep,' snapped Louisa.

'Perhaps he is, but I'm going to sit with him until he wakes up.'

'You're not to tell him about the letter,' Louisa said fiercely. 'It's not up to you, and I don't trust you.'

'I don't trust you either,' Matty retorted. 'I have the letter safely with me and it'll stay with me until the time comes to give it to Papa.' She hadn't really thought Louisa would destroy the letter, not until this moment, but now she was glad that she had tucked it into her bag.

Matty was still sitting with her father when Dr Bryan returned to have another look at his patient. Louisa brought him upstairs and having introduced him to Matty said to her father, 'Now then, Papa, here's Dr Bryan come to see you again.'

Thomas was propped up against his pillows, awake and already fretting at being confined to bed. 'As if I were some ninny of a schoolgirl.'

'I understand your frustration, sir,' Dr Bryan said. 'But it will speed your recovery if you follow my advice and keep to your bed for another few days.'

'They're feeding me pap,' growled Thomas. 'I want some bread and cheese and a glass of brandy. *That's* what I need to speed my recovery!'

'Certainly a glass of brandy will do you no harm,' the doctor agreed with a smile. 'But nourishing soups are the diet I would prescribe for a day or so. We don't want to put a strain on your digestion until you're quite well.'

When the doctor was leaving, Matty went downstairs with him. She liked the way he had dealt with her father; not many people could handle him so well. He had made Thomas agree to stay in bed for the next day at least, and then only to come downstairs for a while in the afternoons.

'You don't feel his condition is serious?' she asked as they stood together in the hall while Edith retrieved Dr Bryan's coat.

'One can never be sure,' replied the doctor, 'not with a man of his age. But he seems tough and I expect him to make a good recovery. He may have to slow down his pace of life, take things a little easier. This seizure today is a warning. If he heeds it there may be nothing further.'

Matty held out her hand. 'Thank you, Doctor, you are very encouraging.'

'What a charming man Dr Bryan is,' she said as they all sat down to dinner that evening. 'I think he'll be very popular in the village.' She smiled across at her sister. 'He's good-looking too, don't you think?'

'Maybe.' Louisa was dismissive. 'I haven't given his appearance much thought. It's his skill as a doctor I'm interested in.'

'So am I,' agreed Matty. 'But I'm sure he'll set a few hearts aflutter in the village.'

'Well, that has nothing to do with us,' returned her sister tersely, and gave her attention back to her plate.

Matty said no more. She and her elder sister did not get on well these days. Louisa resented the fact that Matty's marriage to George Treslyn had released her from Trescadinnick, leaving her, Louisa, to deal with their father. George's death several years ago had left Matty with a financial independence that Louisa envied. When her own husband, James, had died, Charles was just eleven and she'd been left, with little money, to bring him up alone. She always regretted she and James had no children, but she loved her stepson as if he were her own and had done her best to give him a happy childhood. They had remained at Trescadinnick, the only home Charles knew, and Louisa continued to run the household and care for her father as she had since her mother's death all those years ago. Thomas seemed fond of Charles and had paid for his education at Blundells School in Devon. Since leaving school Charles had worked with Daniel Treglyn, the estate manager, learning the ins and outs of the estate. When Daniel had retired and gone to live with his widowed sister in Truro, Charles had taken his place, and as Thomas grew older he became increasingly reliant on Charles. Since both his sons had died young, Thomas had no son to inherit the house and estate, and Louisa assumed that her father would leave it all to Charles when he died. But that was all in the future and it annoyed her when Matty breezed into the house, inviting herself to stay and telling Louisa how to look after their father.

The letter was a case in point. Matty still maintained that they should give it to their father to open straight away. Louisa refused to do so, feeling it might bring on another attack.

'But supposing it's from Mary,' Matty said, 'and he does die without reading it.'

'He's not going to die in the next few days,' snapped Louisa. 'We'll give it to him when he's on his feet again and not before.'

The argument was left at that. But, to Louisa's annoyance,

Matty elected to stay at Trescadinnick until Thomas was better and she could hand him the letter from London.

The day came a week later when Thomas came down to breakfast in the morning room. Charles had already left the house to ride to one of the outlying farms and AliceAnne had been sent up to the schoolroom. Matty and Louisa sat at the table with their father as he ate some scrambled egg and drank his coffee.

'Where's my post?' he suddenly demanded. 'I'm expecting a letter from my solicitor.'

'It's waiting for you, Papa,' Matty said. 'I'll fetch it.'

Several letters had accumulated over the past week and despite Louisa's frown of dissent, Matty slipped the envelope she'd been keeping in her bag in with the rest of his mail.

She saw her father put on his spectacles, then slit open the envelope to pull out the single sheet of paper that it contained. She watched as the colour fled from his cheeks and the letter fell to the table.

'Papa, are you all right?' Louisa was immediately on her feet. 'I knew we shouldn't have given you that.' She snatched up the letter, crumpling it in her hand.

Thomas recovered himself and said sharply, 'Give that to me.'

Reluctantly Louisa handed him the crumpled letter, and he smoothed it out on the table before handing it to Matty, saying, 'Read it to me, Matilda.'

Matty stared at the letter for a moment before she began to read. It was dated nearly three weeks ago and sent from an address in Hammersmith in London. She cleared her throat and began to read aloud.

Dear Papa
I'm dying. I have the same wasting sickness as poor Mama and it will only be a few days until it's all over. My husband died in an accident some years ago and with my death my beloved daughter, Sophia, will be left alone. Our small capital is all but exhausted and the annuity I have from my mother dies with me, so Sophie will have to make her own

way in the world. She is an intelligent girl and I have no doubt she will manage alone if she has to, but I am writing to you this last time to ask if you will provide for her in the way your only grandchild should be. I wrote to you when she was born and you ignored my letter, but as I am dying, I am prepared to beg you to look after her.

I may have wronged you, but she is your flesh and blood and she has not.

I have told her nothing of you or of Trescadinnick, so that if you decide to ignore my dying plea, she will not know she's been rejected.

I bid you farewell, Father, for when you receive this letter I shall be in my grave.

Your daughter,

Mary Ross

Silence descended on the room and then, with a groan of despair, Thomas Penvarrow took the letter from Matty's hand and getting unsteadily to his feet, left the room.

Louisa rounded on Matty. 'You see!' she cried. 'I was right. We should never have given him that letter. We should have burned it unopened.'

'We should have done no such thing!' said Matty, equally angry. 'Mary wrote to him and he was entitled to receive her letter. If he hadn't been ill, he'd have had it days ago.'

'I said she'd be asking for something,' Louisa reminded her.

'Yes, you did, but it wasn't for herself, was it? It was for her daughter, a daughter we didn't even know she had.'

'Well, now you've seen the letter delivered, you can go back home,' snarled Louisa. 'I hope you're satisfied with the effect it's had on Papa and can only pray that it doesn't bring on another attack. You saw how he looked!'

Matty had been shocked when she'd seen her father's face as she read the letter to him. But she wasn't prepared to admit as much to Louisa, so she simply got to her feet and followed her father out of the room, leaving Louisa alone with her anger.

Chapter 3

Sophie woke to an insistent knocking on the front door, and realizing that Hannah must still be out, she glanced into the mirror. Her eyes were red and her hair in disarray, but she sluiced some cold water onto her cheeks, patted the stray wisps of hair into place, and went down to see who should be demanding entrance so determinedly. She opened the front door with words about impatience on her lips, but those words died unspoken as she saw her mother standing outside on the step; her mother, not as she'd last seen her, sunken-eyed, her skin stretched tight across her cheekbones, translucent and paper-white, her hair thin and greying, but as she had been before her illness took hold, cheeks glowing with health, eyes bright with laughter and curiosity, hair thick, rich, dark, luxuriant. Her mother stood on the step, a question in her brown eyes, and said in her gentle voice, 'Sophia?'

Sophie didn't pass out, though she thought for a moment or two that she was going to. She simply stared at her mother, her head spinning and her body cold, as the shock hit her and the colour drained from her face. Her lips formed the word *Mama*, but no sound came and she continued to stare.

Her mother's expression changed from one of query to one of concern, and stepping forward she took Sophie's arm and guided her into the house. Sophie sank onto a chair in the hall and the visitor closed the door behind them. For a long, silent moment Sophie remained crouching in the chair at the foot of the stairs, her mind dazed. Diamonds of sunlight cast through the glass of the front door, patterning the floor, and the solemn tick of the grandfather clock emphasized the silence, rather than broke it. Her mother spoke again. Only it wasn't her mother, of course. Her mother was dead. But it was someone so incredibly like her that it took careful study of her face to notice the differences. When she did speak her voice was one of great concern.

'Sophia, my dear, are you all right?'

Sophia. Well, her mother had never called Sophie that, and anyway the voice was wrong. This was deeper and there was the trace of an unfamiliar accent, missing from her mother's voice.

The visitor continued. 'I'm sorry if I've given you a shock, my dear. I did write but perhaps you've not received my letter yet. I'm your Aunt Matilda and I've come to take you home.'

Sophie stared at her uncomprehendingly. 'Aunt Matilda?'

Her aunt said gently, 'Yes. Aunt Matty. I'm your mother's twin. She'll have told you about me, no doubt. Your grandfather wants you to come home.'

Still dazed, Sophie ignored the last part of what she'd said, but latched on to the first. 'Her twin? I didn't know she had a twin. I didn't even know she had a sister… or any family!'

Matilda knew from the letter that Mary hadn't told Sophie she was writing to Trescadinnick, but she'd assumed that Sophie had at least some knowledge of the family. Clearly not. She smiled and reached for Sophie's hand. 'Well, we've obviously got a good deal of catching up to do. Perhaps we could go into the parlour and have some tea.'

'Hannah's out. She's at the market.' Sophie was still unable to think straight.

'Then I'll make us some,' declared Aunt Matilda. And taking off her coat, she hung it on the stand in the hall. As if she'd known the place all her life, she found the kitchen and set the kettle to boil. She looked into cupboards to find cups and saucers, a teapot and the tea. Still bemused, Sophie watched her and then obediently led her through to the parlour where she set down the tray on the table and poured the tea.

'My father received a letter from your mother some days ago,'

Matilda began, after she'd tasted the tea. 'We were all heartbroken to hear she was dying.'

'A letter from my mother?' Sophie stared at her incredulously. 'I know nothing about a letter.' She replaced her teacup on its saucer and stared at the carbon copy of her mother, sitting across the hearth. How could Mama have posted a letter in the last weeks of her life? She hadn't left the house. Then she realized. Hannah! Of course it must have been Hannah.

'So...' Sophie spoke abruptly. 'What did my mother say in this letter?'

'She addressed it to your grandfather. Unfortunately, he'd just had a seizure and was very ill when it arrived so it wasn't opened for several days. If it had been I'd have come sooner.'

'My grandfather?'

'Thomas Penvarrow of Trescadinnick.' When Sophie looked blank, she added, 'That's in Cornwall.'

'Cornwall?' echoed Sophie faintly. She picked up the teacup again and took a sip. 'I don't know anything about any of you. I didn't think Mama had any family. She never mentioned you.'

'No. Well, I can understand that,' Matilda said sadly. 'She became estranged from our father when she left home to marry yours.'

The tea began its work and Sophie felt a little steadier. 'Why?' she asked sharply. 'Why were they estranged?'

Matilda sighed. 'That's a long story. I'll tell you all about it, but first I have to explain why I've arrived on your doorstep.'

'No!' Sophie interjected. 'Tell me the story first.' She felt a rising anger, both at her mother for not having told her about her family, even if she had nothing to do with them, and anger at this woman, this aunt, who assumed she could simply turn up in London and tell her what to do. She stared angrily at the woman across the room, seated in her mother's chair, a facsimile of her mother, and her anger burned inside so that hot tears filled her eyes.

'My dear Sophia,' began Aunt Matty, but Sophie interrupted her.

'I'm *not* your "dear" Sophia, I'm not your dear anything. It's obvious you're who you say you are, because you're so like...' her voice broke a little, 'like my mother, but other than the fact that you happen to be my aunt, there's nothing between us.'

Her aunt answered gently, ignoring her rudeness. 'No, I agree, there is nothing between us at the moment but an accident of birth. But that's something I want to change, something I've come from Trescadinnick to change. I was very close to Mary, your mother. You know, that often happens with twins; they feel each other's pain.'

'Do they?' Sophie's scepticism was clear. 'And did you know she was dying?'

'I knew something was wrong.' Her aunt spoke softly and wearily.

'Then why didn't you come? If you were so close, why didn't you come?'

'Because I didn't know where to come. Until her letter arrived, we didn't know where she lived.'

Silence closed round them. There was no answer to that.

'And when she died?' Sophie said at last.

'When she died I felt relief – the relief she must have felt at the end of her pain. I wept for her and knew part of myself was gone.'

'I don't understand.' Sophie sighed. 'If you were so close why did you lose touch? Your father, my grandfather, might have disowned her, but you didn't have to.'

'Did your mother tell you what caused the breach between them?' Aunt Matilda asked.

'No, she never mentioned any of you. I didn't know you existed till now. But *you* said she left home to marry my father.'

'And so she did.' Her aunt smiled ruefully. 'There was a little more to it than that. You see, Mary was Father's favourite among us, there's no doubt about that, and he had thought to marry her to a local landowner, George Treslyn. When she took up with John Ross it spoiled his plans.'

Sophie was incredulous, and staring at her aunt in amazement she interrupted. 'Just a minute, Aunt Matilda.' Sophie didn't even notice she had adopted this form of address, but her aunt did and smiled. 'You mean that's why he disowned her?'

'It's not as simple as that,' her aunt replied. 'Father had arranged Mary's marriage without consulting her, and she was never really reconciled to it, though she did agree in the end. George Treslyn was a much older man and extremely rich. His land is not far away from ours and Father considered it an eminently suitable match. Anyway, Mary finally agreed, provided she and I were allowed to come to London for the season first. Mary got her way and Father agreed to the bargain. Mother was already dead, of course, but a distant cousin of Mama's, Agnes Ross, invited us to join her family for the season as her daughter was being brought out. So, off we went with great excitement to have one glorious season of entertainments and parties before we settled down to the lives of country matrons.'

'Had he arranged your marriage as well?' demanded Sophie.

'Not by then, though I think he already had someone in mind. He'd decided to deal with Mary's first.' Matilda's laugh had a touch of bitterness. 'Mary always came first. Anyway, we went to London, and all went well until Mary met Agnes's younger son, John.'

'My father.'

'Your father. Mary and he fell in love and became engaged. I knew there'd be trouble, but Mary, glowing with happiness I remember, insisted that once Father met John, everything would be all right. Of course it wasn't. We came home at the end of the season and Mary told Father that she'd changed her mind; that she'd fallen in love with someone else and refused to marry George Treslyn. Father was furious and forbade the marriage. John travelled down from London and tried to speak to him, to obtain his consent, but our father wouldn't even have him admitted to the house.'

'What happened?' asked Sophie, wide-eyed.

'Father exploded with rage and sent John packing. He didn't go far. He stayed at an inn in Truro, while Mary tried to work on Father, but for once she wasn't able to talk him round. John came of a respectable Suffolk family, but he was a younger son and had no money of his own. He had to make his own way in the world. Not at all what Father had in mind.'

'What did Mama do then?' All Sophie's hostility to her aunt slipped away as she became embroiled in her parents' love story.

'Father told Mary that his decision was final and that John Ross wouldn't be coming back. He said that the date for her wedding to George Treslyn had been set and that she'd better put John Ross out of her mind.'

'He sounds very autocratic,' remarked Sophie.

'He always has been and he hasn't improved with age,' smiled Matty. 'But your mother had much of him in *her*, you know. She didn't like to be thwarted either. On hearing his pronouncement about her marriage, Mary quietly packed her bags and left. It was our twenty-first birthday, the day she came of age. Saying goodbye to no one, not even me, she went to meet him and they left for London.' Matty sighed. 'I'd never had Mary's courage, particularly in dealings with my father, and I couldn't defy him and go back to London with her. I had no one waiting for me there, so I stayed at home.'

'But your father? How did he take Mama's departure?'

'In ice-cold fury; far more frightening for the rest of us than his normal bellowing rage.'

'So you had to stay at home and face the music.'

'More than that,' continued Aunt Matty. 'I had to pick up the pieces Mary had left, and try to take her place.'

'Take her place? You don't mean...?' Sophie could hardly credit the idea that had slipped into her mind.

'Oh yes.' Matty confirmed the thought. 'I had to marry George Treslyn.'

'But didn't you mind?'

'Mind? Of course I minded.' Even after the passage of almost thirty years her tone still held a trace of bitterness. Then she smiled and said more gently, 'I hadn't much choice really, and there were things to be said for the match. I knew now I would never marry for love. I knew I'd never be allowed to return to

London and perhaps find a husband there. If I married George I would at least have some standing in the world. I'd no wish to stay at Trescadinnick at my father's beck and call for the rest of my life. So as soon as we heard that Mary had married John Ross and Father knew there was no going back, I became engaged to George Treslyn and was married on the day that had been arranged for Mary.'

'Didn't Mr Treslyn mind the change?' Sophie was fascinated by this whole tale, amazed at this strange introduction to her family. Her tea cooled unheeded beside her as she leaned forward in her chair to hear more.

Matty shrugged. 'He didn't seem to. He hardly knew us as people, and to his eye we were probably indistinguishable.'

'But why did you let your father bully you?' Sophie demanded.

'He was my father. I did as he wished.' She smiled wryly. 'I hadn't your mother's courage; I hadn't your mother's determination, and... I hadn't got John Ross.'

But you wanted him, Sophie realized, in the brief silence that followed her words. How sad that they'd both fallen in love with the same man. She looked with fresh eyes at her newfound aunt, her mother's twin. They were indeed almost identical; even their hairstyles were similar. But there was no way she would ever confuse the two of them again. It was the shock of finding Aunt Matilda unexpectedly on the doorstep that had blinded her to their differences; these were subtle, almost indefinable. And yet, conjuring up her mother's face before her, she knew that though the arrangement of the features was the same, with similarity of colouring and contours, and even at times the expression, the two faces were only alike, not identical.

Before the silence became awkward Matilda smiled up at Sophie and said, 'So, gradually we lost touch. Mary and I wrote to each other for a few months, but then the letters became less and less frequent. Then the time came that I had to break the news of Joss's accident. She travelled down to Trescadinnick for his funeral, but Father wouldn't speak to her, or even acknowledge that she was there.'

'Just a minute,' Sophie interrupted. 'Who's Joss?'

'Joss was our brother. He died in a tragic accident when he was still a young man. When Mary heard the news she came down to Trescadinnick.'

'And your father wouldn't speak to her, even then?' Sophie was incredulous.

'No. I'm sorry to say he ignored her, cut her dead in public.'

'But you? Didn't you talk to her?'

'Of course I did,' Matilda said. 'I think she'd hoped to make it up with our father, but after the way he treated her that day, well, she simply went back to London and disappeared from our lives.' Matilda sighed. 'She'd told me they were going to move, but I never heard from her again. I didn't know where she'd gone. I'd lost her.'

'How could your father treat her like that?' demanded Sophie. 'His own daughter!'

'It's how he is,' replied Matilda. 'And after Joss's death and Mary's marriage, he became more morose and dictatorial than ever, so woe betide anyone who crossed him, or set themselves against him. It was as if, somehow, he blamed himself for Joss's accident, though, of course, he had nothing to do with that.'

Sophie was about to ask what had happened to Joss, but Matilda went on. 'Life at Trescadinnick became even more bleak. In a way being married to George was a relief. It had given me an escape from the house and from… Well, anyway, it was pleasant to be my own mistress in my own home. George was always kind and generous, and we grew fond of each other. He was much older than I was and when he died ten years ago I was as sad and lonely as any other widow. Still, he left me well off and independent, and I've been happy enough. Now,' she went on briskly, 'no more of that. Tell me about your mother.'

Sophie was about to reply when she heard the back door bang. 'That'll be Hannah. I must tell her you're here. I don't want her to have the same shock as I did.'

She hurried from the room, to reappear almost at once with Hannah at her heels. 'This is Mama's sister, Hannah,' Sophie began. 'She's come from Trescadinnick in Cornwall, in answer to a letter from Mama.'

Hannah evinced no surprise when she saw Matilda seated in the parlour, but with a sniff she bobbed an infinitesimal bob, and said, 'How d'you do, madam? I hope you've come to see Miss Sophie straight in all her difficulties. It's not right that she should lose her home what she's lived in all her life and go out governessing when she's got family what's able to provide for her, and that's a fact.'

'Hannah—' began Sophie in dismay, but Matilda interrupted her.

'Quite right, Hannah,' she replied approvingly, showing little surprise or annoyance at being addressed in such a forthright manner by her niece's maid. 'Miss Sophie's troubles are over, I promise you. There is no question of her being a governess.'

'Well, I'm very glad to hear it, ma'am, indeed I am—'

'Hannah,' Sophie said quickly to stem the flow, 'I believe my aunt will stay for dinner. Please see to it straight away.' She glowered across at her and Hannah disappeared, shaking her head and muttering under her breath, apparently unrepentant.

'I'm sorry,' Sophie said as the door closed behind her. 'But she's looked after me ever since I was a baby, and she's very protective.'

'So I see,' said Matilda dryly. 'Still, she needn't worry about you any more. Now, tell me about your mother.'

So, as the afternoon faded into evening, they sat together in the little parlour while Sophie told her aunt about her life, of her father's death when he was knocked down in the fog, and of her mother's last illness and death.

'I don't know how she wrote to you,' Sophie said, as they lingered over the meal Hannah had prepared. 'I think Hannah must have posted the letter for her.' She suddenly remembered Hannah's remark about not knowing what was just round the corner. Had she been aware of what was in the letter?

'Your grandfather was very ill at the time. He'd had a seizure just before her letter came and it wasn't opened until he was safely on the mend. That's when he sent me to fetch you.'

'Fetch me?' Although her aunt had said this before, for the first time the meaning of her words really penetrated Sophie's brain. 'What do you mean, fetch me?'

'Your grandfather wants to see you, Sophie.'

'Why?' She spoke abruptly. 'He didn't want to see my mother.'

'He's no quarrel with you, Sophie. You're his only grandchild and he'd like to meet you. He's an old man and probably hasn't very long to live. Despite everything, he loved your mother, you know. When he heard of her death he broke down and cried. I've never seen him cry before, Sophie. It was a terrible sight. Then, a few days later, he asked me to come and find you.'

'If he loved my mother so much, you'd have thought he'd have asked her home.'

'He's a proud man, Sophie. His pride wouldn't let him admit his need to see her until it was too late. And remember, there are two sides to every argument. Mary could have made the first move.'

'She had her pride too,' Sophie said defensively.

'Exactly. Two pig-headed people each hurting themselves as much as the other. I think that was another reason he wept so bitterly, because he had left it too late to be reconciled. Don't carry on this feud, Sophie. Come and see him, for a short while at least.'

'I'll think about it, Aunt Matilda,' Sophie said, and stood up to bring the visit to a close. She wanted to be on her own now, to think things through and come to terms with everything she'd heard that afternoon.

Matilda got up too, saying as she did so, 'I'm sure this has all come as a great shock to you, my dear, but perhaps you'll think over what I've asked and if I may call again tomorrow we can discuss it further.'

They went to the front door and Sophie helped her aunt into her coat. 'Where are you staying?' she asked as she opened the door.

'I'm at Brown's,' Matilda replied, and seeing her niece's expression added with a cheerful smile, 'Don't look so surprised,

Sophie. I told you George left me very comfortably off. We've no children so I've no one to spend it on but myself.' She paused on the threshold. 'May I come and see you again tomorrow?' she asked. 'To hear your answer?'

'If you want to.' Sophie felt suddenly very tired and wished her aunt would go.

'I'll see you in the morning then. Goodbye, Sophie.' She held out her hand and as Sophie took it, Matilda reached across and kissed her cheek. Then she turned away and walked briskly down the path to the hansom, which must have been waiting for her ever since she arrived.

Sophie shut the door and stood leaning against it for a moment, her eyes closed, the silence crowding round her. Then the grandfather clock, her father's pride and joy, whirred noisily and struck nine. Her aunt had been there for just five hours, but those five hours seemed set to change her life.

Sophie didn't sleep easily that night. Despite her determination to put Matilda's story out of her head she found it impossible. It churned round and round, robbing her of sleep, and when at last she did doze off she dreamed of her mother, young and healthy, the mother of her childhood. They were walking on a cliff top. Sophie could hear the waves far below and the cries of the gulls wheeling above. Her mother stepped off the cliff, floating gracefully above the sea. 'This is where we belong,' she called as she drifted away from the cliff. 'Feuds are death to a family.' Sophie tried to reach out to her but found herself falling.

Her own cries of fear jerked her awake and she lay in bed trembling. In the grey of pre-dawn she could see the outlines of her own familiar room, but the dream stayed with her, vivid and disturbing.

There was no more sleep for Sophie after that and she soon gave up trying. She got out of bed and throwing a shawl over her nightgown, sat in the chair by her window watching the dawn rise over the street outside. As the sky began to lighten, colour came creeping back into the houses opposite, and shafts of early sunlight lit the undersides of the plane trees that lined the road. She saw the lamplighter walking slowly from street lamp to street lamp, extinguishing the yellowing flames. She watched the first signs of life as the neighbourhood began to awaken to another day, and yet her dream stayed with her, closer than the reality in the street outside. It didn't surprise her that she had dreamed of her mother; after all, she had been prominent in her thoughts throughout the previous day, but the powerful images of the dream did not fade and she could still see the cliff and the sea. Her tired brain must have confused her mother and her aunt as she slept, her mother's story muddled into her dream.

Chapter 4

'I'm very busy this morning,' Sophie said as Hannah showed her aunt into the room. 'All this has to go to the saleroom at the end of the week.'

'Why?' enquired Matilda gently.

Sophie glanced up angrily. 'You know perfectly well why, Aunt,' she said with some asperity. 'There's no room in my new lodgings to take all my parents' belongings. And anyway,' she added bluntly, 'I need the cash.'

'It seems a pity to move house if you don't have to,' remarked Matilda. 'Do you want to move?'

'No, of course not,' answered Sophie, preparing herself to turn down her aunt's offer of help. 'But I intend to make my own way now, and I can't afford to live here any more.' She picked up a crystal vase that had been a particular favourite of her mother's and began to wrap it; then on impulse she removed the paper again and set the vase aside. That should not go.

'There's no need for any of it to go,' Matilda said, as if she'd read Sophie's mind. 'I must tell you, Sophie, that I've seen the landlord's agent this morning and have paid the rent for another twelve months. The house is yours, at least until this time next year.'

Sophie froze and then slowly turned to face her aunt. 'Have you indeed, ma'am? Perhaps you'll allow me to say that I find that a gross impertinence and interference.'

'Now then, Sophie, come down off your high horse,' said her aunt, apparently unperturbed by her rudeness. 'I did it for your own comfort. I know how disturbing I should find it to have to move out of a house that had been my home for so long.'

'I don't want your charity,' snapped Sophie.

'I assure you it wasn't charity in the way you mean it,' replied Matilda calmly. 'I would prefer to think of it as a little of what I owe Mary.'

'I see. It's a sop to your conscience.'

'You can take it as that, if you wish.' Matilda remained unruffled. 'But whatever motives you impute to me, at least you may stay in your own home if you want to.'

'You will have wasted a great deal of money, ma'am, when I move to Putney and this house stands empty,' Sophie said haughtily.

'Perhaps,' agreed her aunt, 'but you will have cut off your nose to spite your face. I'm sure Hannah will not be at all pleased with you.'

'Hannah is my maid. She doesn't tell me how to run my life.'

Hannah came in at that moment with the tea tray and Sophie, looking across at her, felt a pang of remorse at dismissing her as just her maid moments earlier. How much more Hannah was to her than just a paid servant... not even paid at present. Guilt brought colour to Sophie's cheeks and she said softly, 'My aunt has paid the rent of this house for a twelvemonth, Hannah. We don't have to move to Putney if we don't want to.'

Hannah showed no surprise at this announcement; it was exactly what she'd expected of Matilda Treslyn. She nodded with satisfaction and said, 'It's no more that your due, Miss Sophie. I'll start unpacking the boxes in the hall.'

And so the decision was taken. Sophie would not move, and though she felt uncomfortable at having her obligations met by her newfound aunt, she had to admit to a great measure of relief at not having to leave her home, nor part with the familiar possessions of her childhood. But she would not agree to go to Trescadinnick, not at once, as if she were leaping to answer her grandfather's summons. Perhaps some time in the future...

Matilda left when she had taken her tea, and for a long while Sophie sat staring into the fire. Then she went across to the piano and for the first time since her mother had died, sat down and ran her fingers over the keys. Out in the hall, where she was restoring ornaments to their accustomed places, Hannah heard the music and heaved a sigh of relief. It had worried her greatly that since her mother's death Sophie had abandoned her piano, finding no solace in her music. Now, as she heard the soft trickle of notes expanding into an increasing flood of music, she knew that Sophie had at last turned the corner and would gradually re-establish her cheerful and determined grasp on life.

Hannah was right. Having found herself back in her music, Sophie spent much of the rest of the day at her piano and was playing again when Matilda came to visit her the next morning.

'You play beautifully, Sophie,' Matilda said when she finally stepped into the parlour. 'I've been out in the hall listening to you. Your grandmother was an accomplished musician, you know.'

'I didn't know,' Sophie said abruptly, but interest in her mother's family could not be denied and she added more easily, 'I know nothing about her. Mama never mentioned any of you.'

'Play something else,' suggested Matilda, turning the subject away from families. Time enough for all that, she thought as she set about regaining the confidence of her niece, trying to re-establish the beginnings of the rapport which had emerged that first evening.

Sophie continued to play, but when at last her hands came to rest on the keys, she turned to her aunt and said, 'Tell me about the others at Trescadinnick.' She hadn't meant to ask questions about them, in fact she was annoyed with herself for doing so now, and yet she couldn't help it somehow.

'It seems disloyal,' she said to Hannah later on. 'They cast Mama off, after all.'

'So they did,' Hannah agreed. 'But you have to remember it was her what wrote to them in the end, wasn't it? She didn't want no more feuding, did she? What's happening now is what she had in her mind when she wrote, isn't it?'

'I suppose you're right,' Sophie conceded reluctantly. 'But I don't like the way they think they can buy me back into the family.'

'As to that,' Hannah said, 'I reckon anything you get from them is no more than your due. Your poor ma had little enough from her relations!'

Sophie had never really noticed the lack of relations. They were a complete family, she and her parents; complete and fulfilled, each existing comfortably in the love and esteem of the others, needing no more extended family. But now she was adrift in the world, without connection, without commitment, perhaps she should find out more about her mother's family. On impulse she crossed to her mother's bureau and opened it. Sorting out the bureau was a job she'd been putting off, but now she was searching for anything connected with Trescadinnick and she set to with a will. She hunted through pigeonholes and pulled out drawers, finding several bundles of letters, some in dog-eared envelopes, tied with string. Bills, receipts and other papers she set aside to deal with later. At last she came across a tattered envelope in the bottom of one of the drawers, and in it she discovered two birth certificates, her own and her mother's, and her parents' marriage lines, proof positive of what Matilda had told her. Her mother had been born at Trescadinnick.

'There were four of us,' Matilda said. 'Well, five, actually, but my brother, Thomas, died in infancy. There was Louisa, my older sister, Joss, our brother, Mary and me. Louisa still lives at Trescadinnick with her son, Charles. He looks after what is left of the estate and tries to make it pay now that the tin mines are almost worked out. Louisa runs the house as she has done, really, since my mother died. She married a widower, James Leroy, who had a young son, Charles, and they all moved into a wing of Trescadinnick. Our brother, Joss, died years ago. He wasn't married, so there are no more Penvarrows. You are my father's only grandchild.'

'But surely, there's Charles,' Sophie pointed out.

'Charles is not Louisa's son. She's widowed now and has no

children of her own. Charles is her stepson. She's the only mother he's known and they are as close as any other mother and son, but as far as Father's concerned, well, he's not a Penvarrow.' Matilda sighed. 'I'm very fond of Charles myself. He was married too, but sadly his young wife, Anne, died in childbed, when their daughter, AliceAnne, was born. She's six now, but she's no blood-kin to the Penvarrows either.'

'They're closer to him than I am,' objected Sophie. 'They've known him all their lives.'

'Maybe,' conceded Matilda. 'But they're not family. Before he dies, your grandfather wants to meet you because you are part of the future he'll never see. Just come and visit him, Sophie. Stay a few days at Trescadinnick; it needn't be for long. You've got your home waiting here whenever you want to come back.'

Sophie had promised to think about it, and as she lay in the darkness later that night, she considered again a visit to Trescadinnick. Was that why her mother had finally decided to write to her family? Had she hoped that Sophie would visit her own childhood home? Perhaps, and despite herself Sophie was intrigued.

Well, she decided, I'll go. But not for long. Only for a few days. And with her decision made, she drifted off to sleep.

When Hannah heard of the proposed visit to Trescadinnick, she announced that she was coming too.

'But, Hannah,' cried Sophie, 'wouldn't you rather stay here in London and look after the house?'

'Certainly not, Miss Sophie, the house can look after itself. I'm not letting you go among them heathens in Cornwall on your own, and that's a fact.'

'But I'm only going for a few days,' Sophie laughed, 'a week at most.'

'That's as maybe,' Hannah declared darkly. 'But your ma left me to look after you, so if you're set on going there, then I'm coming too, and there's an end to it.'

Nothing would dissuade her, and secretly Sophie was pleased.

It would be very reassuring to have a loved and familiar face nearby when she faced the family she had never met, knowing they would be assessing her, perhaps criticizing her, searching her for signs of her mother.

Matty didn't seem at all surprised when she heard that Hannah was coming too. She simply nodded and said it was quite right that Sophie should have her companion with her; and so it was arranged.

The days before they left were well spent, refurbishing Sophie's rather shabby wardrobe. Apart from a few made-over garments of her mother's, Sophie had only her black mourning and two day dresses she'd almost outgrown. There had been little money for clothes in the last year and it had been a case of make do and mend. Looking at her aunt's stylish, well-cut clothes, Sophie realized she needed something other than her well-worn serge and her hastily bought black mourning dress. Reluctantly, she accepted the allowance Thomas had offered. Some new clothes would give her confidence and at least the unknown family would not find her lacking in appearance.

It may have been her grandfather who had provided the money, but it was Matty who took her to the dressmaker she always used when she came to London to update her own wardrobe.

Madame Egloff, in her discreet salon off Bond Street, was delighted when Mrs Treslyn came in with her niece. She saw immediately that with her neat waist, slender shoulders and delicate neck, this was a young lady well worth dressing. She stared in admiration at Sophie's abundant auburn hair and readied herself to supply hats and gloves, as well as gowns and under garments for this emerging beauty. She was horrified when Matty told her that they needed the clothes ready within the week.

'Ah, Madame Treslyn,' she cried, her accent very far from Parisian. 'That is *impossible*.'

'Difficult, I'm sure, Madame,' Matty agreed with a smile. 'But not *impossible*! I'm sure you have several dresses and gowns ready to show your customers that can swiftly and easily be adapted to our needs. On our next visit to London, I daresay we shall have more time at our disposal, but this time, please, bring out what you have and we shall make our selection.'

Realizing that this was the best she could offer, Madame Egloff sent her girls scurrying about the salon, bringing out day dresses, skirts and bodices, jackets and tea-gowns for Matty's consideration. No mention was made of the price of each garment; Sophie was simply dressed and undressed by eager helping hands as she tried on those Matty selected.

'I think, if my niece likes them, we should agree upon the plaid travelling dress, the woollen day dress, the stuff skirt and bodice...' Matty turned to Sophie. 'So practical for every day about the house, you know, and the green tea-gown.'

Sophie stared at her aunt in horror. 'I couldn't possibly have all those, Aunt. I love the plaid dress... so very Scottish. But as for the others, I'm sure I don't need them.'

'Your grandfather has instructed me to ensure you are suitably dressed, Sophie.'

Sophie's expression hardened at this. How dare her grandfather assume she would *not* be suitably dressed! But she knew, if she were honest, that without his generosity and Matty's help in choosing she might not have been.

Seeing Sophie's mutinous face, Matty softened the comment with a smile and added, 'And that is what I'm doing, Sophie. Don't you like the dresses I've chosen? If not, we can look again. Madame Egloff could show you plenty more, I'm sure. However, if you like these, then let us say we'll have them sent round once the alterations have been made, ready to leave next Monday.'

Sophie found herself lost for words. Still dressed in the tea-gown, she stared at herself in the mirror. She was amazed at how different she looked and felt in the soft mixture of silk and wool. She turned sideways, admiring the shape of the bodice and the drape of the skirt.

'That is my particular gift to you, Sophie,' Matty spoke gently. 'It suits you; that dark green is the perfect foil for your hair. It suits you and is very becoming and it is my pleasure to give it to you.'

What she said was true. It gave her great pleasure to be able to buy her newfound niece such a gift. Sophie was like Mary in so many ways that Matty's heart ached when she thought of the wasted years of estrangement. She was determined to make up for them now. In the few days she had known Sophie she had grown fond of her, not only for her mother's sake but for herself, but Matty was wise enough not to rush things. She had to win Sophie's trust before she could win her heart.

'It is beautiful, Aunt.' she breathed, 'but when shall I ever have occasion to wear it?'

'Don't worry about that,' Matty said cheerfully. 'We'll make occasions.' She turned to Madame Egloff, who stood, hands held out in front of her, expressing her admiration. 'Please make the alterations, Madame, and have the gowns sent round to Brown's Hotel by the weekend.'

Half an hour later, when they left Madame Egloff's salon, Sophie had been dressed and pinned into each of the garments Matty had chosen, and promises had been made to deliver the clothes to the hotel by Saturday morning at the latest.

Monday morning saw them at Paddington Station being conducted to a private compartment on the train. Sophie had never travelled in such style before, being more used to the uncomfortable rowdiness of a third-class carriage, but Matty had insisted.

'I always travel this way,' she said. 'The journey is quite tiring enough without being crammed in next to crying children and shrill women.'

Having directed the porter to place their luggage in the guard's van, Matty had settled herself into their compartment with a copy of the new *Murray's Magazine*, which she had bought from a news-stand at the station. Beside her on the seat was a hamper, provided by Brown's, with the food and drink they would need for the journey.

As the train drew out of the station and started its long journey west, Sophie felt keyed up with anxious anticipation and was grateful for the comforting presence of Hannah, ensconced on the other side of the compartment. Dressed in her new plaid travelling dress, with a matching hat perched on her head, Sophie knew she was a different person from the one who had sat at her dying mother's bedside, holding her hand. No longer a young girl on the brink of adulthood... but who? There had been too much change in her life in the past weeks that she still had to come to terms with. *Who am I?* she wondered. *I don't feel like me!* She looked across at Hannah, so familiar, so safe, huddled in a corner, her eyes shut as she dozed, and Sophie felt a wave of affection flood through her. *Dear Hannah*, she thought, *I'm so glad you came too.*

When they had left Madame Egloff, Matty had taken Sophie for afternoon tea at Brown's. Looking round the famous tea room, with its panelled walls, its alcoved fireplace and its windows giving onto Albemarle Street, Sophie had felt uncomfortable sitting in the luxurious room and was clearly ill at ease. A selection of little cakes and tiny sandwiches arrived on a silver stand, and when Matty had poured their tea from an elegant, silver teapot she looked across at Sophie and said, 'You look disconsolate, Sophie. What's the problem?'

Sophie sighed. 'It's just that Mama only passed away a month ago, and here I am sitting drinking tea in an expensive hotel; buying new clothes, not mourning, not even half-mourning. It feels wrong, as if I've already forgotten her, as if I didn't care.'

Matty reached for her hand. 'Of course you care, Sophie,' she said gently. 'You care on the inside, which is where it matters. You don't have to make outward show. You remember Mary with love, and that's as it should be, but she wouldn't want you to stop living your life to the full. That's what she always did and that's what she'd want for you.'

Sophie had nodded, appearing to accept what her aunt said, but not quite convinced. *And now*, she thought, as the train gathered speed along the track, *here I am, leaving London and off on an adventure.*

At last the train steamed into Truro Station and from there

they took the tiny branch line to St Morwen, the nearest stop to Trescadinnick itself. Sophie looked out of the window with ever-increasing interest as their destination drew closer.

'Can you see Trescadinnick from the train?' she asked her aunt.

'No,' Matty replied. 'It's a mile or two from St Morwen. That's our local market town... not much more than an overgrown village really. I live just the other side. Paxton should be at the station to meet us.'

Sophie stared out of the window. She was nearly there. Before long she would meet her unknown family. What would they be like? Well, she decided, they should not find *her* wanting. They'd be left in no doubt that she was her mother's daughter.

Chapter 5

Matty had been away for several days before the family at Trescadinnick had any news from her. Thomas was fuming with frustration by the time her first letter arrived.

'Thank goodness she's finally written,' muttered Louisa as she took the letter upstairs to her father. He was still in his bed, grumbling because the doctor had called again and continued to recommend that he take life more easily. That was all very well, but since he'd dispatched Matty to London to find his grand-daughter, Thomas could settle to nothing. When Louisa brought the letter to him he'd almost snatched it from her hand.

'Now then, Papa,' she protested gently. 'No need to get excited. Remember Dr Bryan's instructions to try and stay calm.'

Thomas didn't reply, simply slit open the envelope and pulled out its contents. Louisa waited as he scanned the letter and then, when he said nothing, simply folding it back into the envelope, asked, 'Well, Papa? What did she say?'

Thomas looked up, as if surprised that she were interested. 'It's from Matilda. She says she has found Sophia and is hoping to persuade her to come here for a visit. It would seem her mother,' Louisa noticed that her father still couldn't bring himself to name Mary, 'has left her in financial straits. Matilda has settled some debts and paid the rent on the house for another year. Now all she has to do is bring the girl down here.' He paused and added, 'She doesn't seem to like the idea at present, but Matilda is encouraging her to come, just for a short visit, so that we can all get to know her.'

46

'I think she sounds very ungrateful,' sniffed Louisa. 'After all, you owed her nothing. And having taken care of her debts, at least she should do as you wish and come and see you.'

'She'll come,' Thomas asserted. 'Matilda will persuade her. So you, Louisa, must prepare a room for her. We must make her welcome.'

'Of course, Papa,' Louisa said dutifully. 'I think I'll put her into Mary's room... if she comes.'

'Whatever you think best.' Thomas was happy to leave such decisions to her.

The decision was easy; Louisa felt no need to prepare one of the main guest rooms for Sophie. Matty and Mary had always shared a room at the back of the house, overlooking the walled garden, and Louisa considered it quite good enough for the daughter of her wayward sister; someone who, as far as she was concerned, had no place at Trescadinnick. All this fuss for a chit of a girl whom none of them had known anything about until a month ago. It was ridiculous! What had got into her father's head?

Matty's second letter arrived the following day and when he'd read it Thomas called Louisa back in to see him. 'Matilda's bringing the girl down with her,' he said. 'They'll arrive on Tuesday. Oh, and Sophia is bringing her maid with her.'

'Her maid?' Louisa sounded outraged. 'She has a maid? I thought she was a pauper! And anyway, what right has she to bring a servant without so much as a by-your-leave?'

'Matilda agreed she should come,' Thomas said. 'She thought Sophia would be more at home with a familiar face nearby.'

Sophia, Sophia. Everything was Sophia! Louisa pursed her lips but made no further comment, not to Thomas anyway. Later on, to her son, Charles, she said, 'I don't know why he's getting so excited about her. He wouldn't see Mary, even cut her dead at Jocelyn's funeral. And now, suddenly, he's wanting to meet a granddaughter he knew nothing about.'

'Perhaps that's the reason,' replied Charles. 'It is *because* he knew nothing about her that he wants to meet her now, before it's too late.' He smiled wryly at his mother. 'He's not getting any younger and she's the only grandchild he has. The only true Penvarrow heir.'

Louisa stared at him. 'He wouldn't,' she breathed as she took in the import of what Charles was saying. 'He wouldn't disinherit you for her... not after you lived here all your life, not after you've worked so hard to keep the estate running!'

'I'm not his grandson,' Charles pointed out.

'As good as,' cried Louisa.

'Not blood-kin,' Charles answered with a shake of his head. 'Not good enough for him.'

The sun rose in a clear blue sky over Trescadinnick the following Tuesday. To Louisa's surprise her father appeared in the morning room for breakfast. It was the first time he had reverted to his usual routine since he'd had the seizure and Louisa, who was already at the breakfast table, got to her feet at once.

'Now, Papa,' she remonstrated. 'What are you doing up so early?'

'She'll be here today,' Thomas replied. 'Sophia.'

'I know, but there'd have been plenty of time for you to get up later this morning. Their train doesn't get in until this afternoon.'

'Don't fuss, Louisa!' Thomas took his place at the table and Edith brought him tea. 'I'll have eggs and bacon, Edith,' he said. 'You can serve me and then you can go.'

Normally Thomas would have helped himself from the chafing dishes on the sideboard, but though he had no intention of admitting it to his daughter, his morning ablutions and getting dressed had taken more out of him than he could have imagined. He was pleased to be able to sit down again without drawing this to her attention.

Edith dutifully loaded his plate with what he'd asked for and then at a nod from Louisa, left the room.

'Is everything ready?' Thomas demanded when he'd made a start on his breakfast.

'Yes, Papa,' Louisa replied. 'You know it is. Edith has spring-cleaned the room and cleaned the windows. The bed is made up with fresh sheets and AliceAnne is going to pick a few of the late chrysanthemums and put them in a vase beside her bed.' She turned to the child who was seated on the opposite side of the table.

'If you've finished your breakfast, child,' she said, 'you can go up to the schoolroom and learn your Bible passage. I will come and hear you later on.'

'Yes, Grandmama.' AliceAnne slipped down from the table and left the room, pleased to get out of her great-grandfather's sight. He was kind enough when he paid her any attention at all, but she was terrified of him when he flew into one of his rages, and she never knew when that might happen. She wondered, as she stared out of the schoolroom window, what this new cousin would be like. She didn't like meeting new people; you never knew where you were with them, but the house had been so filled with talk of Sophia's arrival, both among the family and below in the kitchen, that she wanted to see who this special person was. Aunt Matty had gone to London to find her, but that had been ages ago. Now, all of a sudden, they were both coming down to Trescadinnick and this Aunt Sophia, as AliceAnne had been told to call her, was going to stay.

Louisa left her father finishing his breakfast in the morning room and went to ensure that all was ready for her niece's arrival. She knew it was not the girl's fault that Thomas had summoned her. No, as always, it was Mary's. Even from beyond the grave, Mary was the cause of trouble at Trescadinnick. But it didn't stop Louisa resenting Sophia, an interloper into their settled world, and she hoped that the girl's stay would be a short one indeed.

Charles had breakfasted early and had already left the house. He had business at the last copper mine on Felec Head and was not expected home again until the late afternoon, by which time Matty and Sophia would have arrived. Paxton was meeting them at the station with the pony and trap and bringing them home; there was no need, Charles had decided, to be waiting for their arrival. His absence was deliberate; his mother was not the only one who resented Sophia's coming.

*

When the train steamed into the station the three of them climbed down onto the platform where Paxton was waiting to meet them. He took immediate charge of the luggage, directing a porter to load it into the open carriage that waited outside.

'Paxton is our general handyman, Sophie,' explained Matty. 'He and Mrs Paxton have been with us for years and look after us all. This is Miss Sophie, Paxton,' Matty continued the introduction, 'Mr Penvarrow's granddaughter.'

'How d'ye do, miss,' said Paxton, nodding.

'And this is Miss Hannah Butts, Miss Sophie's maid,' Matty went on.

Paxton grunted and put Hannah's bag into the trap with the others. Then they were off, Paxton turning the horse's head for home.

They were soon clear of the town, following a narrow road that wound uphill to edge a windswept expanse of moorland tufted with heather, tussock grass and gorse and pocked with outcrops of weathered, grey stone. The road levelled out for a little and before it dropped down into relative shelter beneath jutting grey crags, far in the distance Sophie caught a glimpse of the sea. Sophie had never seen this country before, but something stirred in her, an awareness, not recognition exactly, but the strange expectation that recognition would come. She gazed round at the unfolding countryside; occasional patches of marshland where still, dark water had gathered amid the stones and grasses at the side of the track and reeds rustled in the wind; a patchwork of fields marked off with stone hedges spread out in the valley, an occasional farmhouse, sheltered by trees, but above it all, the rising sweep of the moor.

A pale autumn sunshine bathed the upland in mellow light, gilding the gorse to brilliance. The line of the moor rose, etched against a patchy blue sky; drifting clouds cast moving shadows across the high slopes and the valley spread beneath.

Sophie knew a mounting excitement, almost a singing in her

head. 'It's beautiful,' she breathed, turning with glowing eyes to her aunt.

Matty smiled. 'Yes,' she agreed, 'and you're seeing it at its best.'

Hannah did not agree. Sitting behind them in the trap, she stared round at the empty landscape. She had never seen so much space. Where were the houses? Bleak and no mistake, she thought dismally. If this is its best, I'd hate to see it at its worst!

They crested a rise and Sophie saw it: the house, standing on a sweep of the cliff top; the house and beyond it, restless in the afternoon sun, the sea.

Sophie didn't need Matty to tell her it was Trescadinnick; she knew it at once. It stood four-square, strong against the wind and the storms that so often attacked it from the south and west, looking out in four directions. At the north-west corner, a small squat tower rose above the roof to give a view out over the sea and the fishing boats that came and went from the harbour. Grey and strong, its austere lines were softened somewhat by the ivy which threatened to smother it. Other buildings gathered at one side; stables, outhouses and sheds, sheltered by an encircling wall.

'That's Trescadinnick,' said Matty, her hand raised towards it. 'That's the house and farm buildings. Port Felec, the fishing village, is over the headland.'

Once she could drag her eyes away from the house itself, Sophie gradually took in the fields, clawed back from bracken and gorse on the hillside, with wider pastures on the flat land below and a clutch of cottages crouching in a hollow, seeking shelter from the Atlantic winds. Beyond the houses stretched the slate-coloured sea, merging at an imperceptible horizon into the grey-blue sky. Of the fishing village, nestling, sheltered in the curve of the cliff, she could see nothing. Only a telltale drift of smoke from its hidden chimneys warned that it was there at all. Sophie heard Hannah sniff, clearly unimpressed by what she saw, but Sophie was enchanted. She raised her hand to the house. 'Is it very old?' she asked.

'Parts of it are,' replied Matty. 'Bits have been added over the years.'

As the pony pulled the trap down the hill, they passed a farm gate set between white gateposts. 'That's the home farm,' Matty said. 'A family called Shaw lives there. They've been here even longer than we have!'

The road swung round sharply and there before them were two enormous gateposts, white-painted stone, with a white, stone acorn set into a white, stone acorn-cup crowning each.

'Here we are at last,' said Matty cheerily as the trap turned in. It rattled up a short driveway and drew up on a gravelled sweep before the great front door. Already standing there was a gig, with a tired-looking bay waiting patiently in the shafts.

Matty looked worried. 'That's the doctor's,' she said. 'I hope Father hasn't had another attack.' She got out of the trap quickly and with Sophie at her heels said, 'Paxton, please take the luggage in and introduce Hannah to Mrs Paxton. Come, Sophie.'

She strode to the huge front door, which she opened, twisting the large ring handle to lift its heavy latch. Sophie followed more slowly, feeling suddenly afraid. Close to, the house was even more imposing with low-silled sash windows on either side of the front door and a similar row across the floor above. Ivy covered much of that side of the house, leaving the windows to peer short-sightedly between the leaves, and at one end the walls curved round to become the small round tower she had noticed from the hillside. For a moment she paused on the step by the front door and then, not knowing what else to do, she pushed the great door wider and followed her aunt inside.

It was not quite as she'd visualized it when her aunt had described her mother's childhood home, but it was not that different either. The walls were panelled and dark, hung with great portraits in heavy gold frames. Doors were let into the panelling and a wide staircase with an iron balustrade curved up to a landing above. The windows on either side of the front door let in the light of the autumn afternoon, but the hall was still gloomy. Sophie paused by a table covered with a chenille cloth, waiting, uncertain. Matty was above on the landing, speaking to someone Sophie couldn't see.

'Then why have you come?' she was saying. 'Did my sister send for you?'

'No, no.' The voice was reassuring. 'It's just a routine call. I hadn't been in for a couple of days and I like to keep my eye on him.'

'Well, that's very good of you, Doctor. You know how we all appreciate your concern.' Matty turned back down the stairs and the doctor, following her, came into view.

Sophie's first impression of him was one of height. He towered over her aunt, who herself topped Sophie by a head.

'Will you have a cup of tea before you go?' Matty was asking. 'I don't know where everyone is, but it'd only take a moment to have a pot made.'

The doctor shook his head, thanking her, but saying he still had calls to make. Then Matty realized that Sophie was in the hall, waiting, and cried, 'Oh, Sophie, there you are. I'm sorry, my dear, I didn't mean to leave you to find your own way in.' She hurried across the hall, saying to the doctor as she did so, 'Dr Bryan, come and meet my niece, Miss Sophie Ross. We've just come down from London. Sophie, here is Dr Bryan who looks after your grandfather.'

The doctor paused at the bottom of the stairs and said, 'I can see you're one of the family, Miss Ross.' Extending his hand, he crossed to Sophie, adding, 'I heard you were coming. Welcome to Trescadinnick. How d'you do? I'm Nicholas Bryan.'

Sophie's hand was firmly grasped and looking up to return his smile, she found herself looking into a young and handsome face, whose light blue eyes seemed to be assessing her and appreciating what they saw.

She felt the colour flood her cheeks at his appraisal, but managed to return his handshake and answer coolly enough. 'How do you do, sir?'

'I'm delighted to meet you,' he replied. 'What a charming addition you will be to the neighbourhood.' And before Sophie could think of a suitable reply to this compliment, he turned to include Matty and added, 'I'm sorry I can't stay, but I really must get on.'

'Of course,' agreed Matty, turning to the door with him. 'We quite understand.'

'I'll drop in again in a day or two,' he said. 'Just to see how he's getting on. Don't let him do too much.'

'You try and stop him!' Matty laughed.

'Well, I know it's difficult, but do try.' He turned back to Sophie. 'No doubt we'll meet again then, Miss Ross. Good afternoon.'

As Matty saw him out of the front door, Sophie heard a rustle behind her and turning sharply, she caught sight of a small figure creeping out from under the chenille-covered hall table. It was a little girl of about six, slipping out of the hiding-place from where she had been watching Sophie's arrival.

It must be AliceAnne, Sophie thought, and was about to call a greeting to her, when the child put an imploring finger to her lips and scurried away down a passage. Sophie bit back her words and turned round to find Matty closing the heavy front door behind the doctor.

'Well,' said Matty, who hadn't seen the child. 'No panic after all. Let's see if we can find the others.' She opened one of the panelled doors and looked inside. Sophie caught a glimpse of book-lined walls, but that was all before Matty closed that door and tried another.

This room too proved to be empty and she was just trying a third when the front door opened and a woman came in, shaking the dust from her cloak. She stopped in her tracks and stared at Sophie. Sophie returned her look, realizing that this must be her mother's elder sister, Louisa. She looked far older than Matty and was much less stylishly dressed. Her grey hair was drawn back tightly into a bun and her face was pinched and tired, etched with lines of sadness or, perhaps, Sophie thought, discontent; it was hard to tell.

Matty, emerging from the third room, saw the new arrival and cried, 'Ah, Louisa. There you are. We've arrived, as you see. Here's Sophie. Here's Mary's daughter.'

'So I see.' Louisa managed a smile. 'Welcome to Trescadinnick,

Sophia. I'm sorry I wasn't here when you arrived.' She crossed the hall, and taking Sophie's hand in hers, touched cheeks in a token embrace. Her words and actions were those of welcome, but they were belied by the look in her eyes. Her smile did not reach those and there was no warmth in them; rather, they scanned Sophie's face mistrustfully, as if searching out her secret thoughts and assessing her strength. As she drew back, Sophie felt the veiled hostility towards her and wondered at it, questions flitting through her mind. Had Louisa disliked her sister Mary? Envied her escape from their father and Trescadinnick? Was that why her outward show of welcome rang so false? Sophie knew an answering flicker of mistrust herself, but she pushed it aside, smiling, and said how pleased she was to meet her new aunt.

Apparently entirely unaware of the tension between them, Matty said, 'Where's Charles? Isn't he home yet? And AliceAnne, where's she?'

'I don't know. I've been out myself all afternoon, but Charles knows you're arriving today. As for the child, she could be any-where.' Louisa dismissed them from her mind, but she added sharply, 'What was Dr Bryan doing here?'

'He just came in to have a look at Father,' Matty replied easily.

'That young man is too free with his coming and going in this house,' snapped Louisa. 'He wanders in and out as if he owns the place.'

'Don't be silly, Louisa,' soothed Matty. 'He's the doctor after all. We should be glad he bothers so much about Father. He does have other patients to think about.'

'And he should remember it,' replied Louisa. 'Father didn't need him today. He was up and about this morning, looking forward to seeing Sophia. There was nothing wrong with him at all!' And with that Louisa turned down the passage along which AliceAnne had vanished a few moments before. 'You might as well take Sophia straight up if he's awake anyway,' she said over her shoulder.

'I didn't realize he was in bed,' Matty said, a note of anxiety in her voice. 'Dr Bryan said he was doing well.'

'And so he is, provided he rests in the afternoon,' Louisa answered. 'Anyhow, he said he wanted to see Sophia as soon as she arrived. I'll bring up some tea.'

'Yes, that would be nice,' agreed Matty. 'We've had a long journey. We'll go on up then. Come on, Sophie, time to meet your grandfather.' They shed their cloaks and then Sophie followed her aunt upstairs.

Matty led the way from the gallery landing along a corridor and opened a door at the end. Quietly, she entered the room, motioning Sophie to wait for a moment, and spoke softly to someone inside.

'Are you awake, Father? I'm back.'

Sophie heard an old man reply testily, 'Of course I'm awake, Matilda. Did you bring her? Has she come?'

'Yes, don't worry. She's here.'

'Then bring her up. Bring her up. I want to see her.'

'She's just outside,' began Matty. But Sophie had decided to make her entrance and pushing the door open, stood framed in the doorway. The room she had entered had a curved outer wall, with windows staring out across the cliff to the sea and watching inland across the stone-hedged fields to the moors. In the fading autumn light she could see a large, old bed, set so its occupant could see through either set of windows, and a log fire smouldering in a wide stone hearth, lending a little warmth to the chill of the afternoon.

Sophie's attention was drawn to the bed as a voice said, 'Come in, Sophia.'

She looked across at the old man propped up against the pillows and slowly moved forward into the room.

'I'll go and help Louisa,' said Matty, quickly leaving the bedside. 'I'll be back in a minute.' She left the room, closing the door behind her, and Sophie stood looking down at the frail husk of what had once been a strong and energetic man: her grandfather. His skin was the colour of parchment, wrinkled and dry. His hair, a thatch of silver, sprang unruly on his head, shaggy over his ears and curling at the back of his neck. But his eyes, bright and alert, drew her own and held them as they studied her face.

'So you're Sophia Alice Ross.' The name lingered on his tongue as he said it aloud for the first time.

Having already resolved not to be intimidated by her grandfather, Sophie said, 'They call me Sophie.'

'I shall call you Sophia.' He pronounced it with a hard 'I', Soph-i-a. 'It's a good strong name. I don't hold with soft nicknames.'

'I prefer Sophie. Sophia is harsh and doesn't feel like me.'

The old man sniffed disdainfully. 'Far too fanciful.' He waved a hand at the chair by his bed. 'Come and sit down here where I can see you.'

Sophie walked round the bed and sat down.

'You came then,' said her grandfather. 'I thought you might not.' Before she could reply he went on, 'You're not like your mother, but you could be her mother's twin. Did you know that? Did she ever tell you that you look just like your grandmother?'

'No, she never spoke of any of you.'

'Never?'

'I didn't know you existed.'

'She never once mentioned her family?'

'Why should she?' Sophie spoke more calmly than she felt. 'You'd thrown her out; you weren't important any more.' It was a harsh thing to say and Sophie knew it, but she felt defensive of her mother.

Surprisingly, Thomas Penvarrow laughed at this. 'Well done, Sophia, don't let yourself be bullied.'

'I won't,' promised Sophie. 'And my name is Sophie.' She looked him firmly in the eye and added, 'I'm not afraid of you and if I don't like what you say and do, I shall simply go home.' The old man nodded appreciatively and Sophie went on, 'How did you know my full name?'

'I've always known it,' her grandfather replied. 'Your mother wrote and told me when you were born.'

'Did you reply?' flashed Sophie. 'Did you write back?'

'No.'

'Why not? Why couldn't you forgive her?'

'She chose her own path. I didn't choose it for her.'

'You tried to,' said Sophie. 'You tried to run her life.' Colour flooded Sophie's cheeks and she clenched her fists in her lap, but the fight suddenly went out of the old man and he said, 'That was a long time ago, Sophia. There's nothing to be gained by dragging all that out again. I'm your grandfather; you're my granddaughter. Can't we start from there and begin again?' He reached out his hand to her, his eyes searching her face, compelling her to respond. And in spite of the antagonism that had grown within her ever since she had heard of her grandfather and his dictatorial ways, Sophie found herself reluctantly extending her hand to meet his. Her mother had written to him to ask for help, perhaps hoping Sophie might heal the breach in the family; having come so far, it seemed wrong to draw back now. So she took his hand in hers and said quietly, 'We can try, Grandfather.'

There might have been tears in his eyes, for he looked away, but if there were they did not fall. The old man simply said, 'Thank you, Sophia, thank you.'

In the brief silence that followed Sophie spoke briskly. 'Well, if we are to start again as grandfather and granddaughter, please may I remind you that my name is Sophie.'

Thomas looked at her for a moment, as if surprised at her temerity – then he sighed.

'I'll call you Sophie if you prefer,' he conceded, 'but Sophia was your grandmother's name and you're so like her.'

'My grandmother's name?' Sophie faltered. 'I didn't know.'

Thomas gave a brief smile. 'Sophia Alice, the same as yours. When you stood in the doorway just now you could have been she – just as she was when I married her, so beautiful she made me catch my breath. You will stay, won't you?' His voice was suddenly demanding again. 'You will stay here now that we've found you?'

'I'll stay a few days, Grandfather.' Addressing him as 'Grandfather' seemed very strange to Sophie, but she could see that he was pleased she'd done so.

At that moment the door opened again and Louisa came in carrying a tray, followed by Matty with another. 'Here we are, Father. We've brought you some tea,' Louisa said.

'Where's Charles?' demanded her father. 'I want to see Charles.'

'He's around the estate somewhere,' Louisa replied. 'He's been very busy after the storms last week. They caused a great deal of damage.'

'He's never here when I want him,' muttered the old man irritably.

'He works very hard on your behalf, Father,' said Matty severely, handing him his tea. 'You never give him enough credit for all he does. The place would fall apart without him, and you know it. You'd never get an estate manager who'd work as he does.' She turned to Sophie. 'You'll meet your cousin Charles at dinner this evening.'

'He's *not* her cousin,' grumbled Thomas to himself as he sipped his tea. 'That's the trouble.'

'Now then, Father,' Louisa said nervously. 'He's my son and that makes him your grandson and Sophie's cousin.'

'Of course it does,' agreed Matty heartily and then changed the subject by saying, 'Poor Sophie hasn't even seen her room yet. Where have you put her, Louisa?'

'In the cliff room,' replied Louisa. 'Where else?'

'That used to be our room,' explained Matty. 'Your mother's and mine. I'm sure you'll love it. It looks over the cliff top and out to sea. When you've finished your tea I'll take you up to see it.'

'There's no need for that,' Louisa said abruptly. 'I can show her. You'll be wanting to get back home, I've no doubt.'

Sophie felt dismayed; Matty suddenly seemed her only friend in a house full of strangers. 'Aren't you staying here, Aunt Matty? I thought...'

'I'm afraid not, Sophie. I did explain to you that I have my own home, Treslyn House, near St Morwen. Paxton will drive me home as soon as I've finished my tea. Don't look so cast down, my dear. I'm only a few miles away, and you're with your family now.'

She smiled encouragingly at Sophie. 'Now then, you must be longing to wash and change after the long journey, so if you've finished your tea, my dear, I'll take you along. Hannah will have unpacked for you by now I expect, so everything will be ready for you.' As if anticipating Louisa's objections, Matty turned to her sister and said, 'You don't mind if I show Sophie, do you? After all, it was my room as well as Mary's.'

'You must suit yourself.' Louisa shrugged. 'You always do. But don't be too long. Paxton will be waiting for you.'

Matty swept Sophie out of the room and along the landing. There were more stairs halfway along the gallery, leading to a half-landing from which two rooms jutted out from the back of the house. Matty flung wide the door of one and ushered Sophie inside.

'Here you are, my dear, and here's Hannah waiting for you.'

Sophie went into the room that had been her mother's as a child. It was large and had two beds covered with faded, rose-patterned quilts. It was comfortably if somewhat shabbily furnished, with a chest of drawers topped with a mirror, a heavy wardrobe, and a washstand complete with a rose-patterned bowl and jug. A cheerful fire leaped and crackled in the grate. Hannah had lit the lamp too, and in the warmth of its glow the room looked cosy and welcoming. Hannah was about to draw the curtains across, but Sophie stopped her and, going to the window, peered out into the September evening. The sun had gone and colour was fading to flat grey dusk, but she could still make out the line of the cliff and the expanse of sky beyond.

Immediately below the window was a walled garden full of shapes and shadows, surrounded on two sides by the house itself, and beyond it she could just discern the roofs of outbuildings, sheds or stables.

'Wait till you see the view in the morning,' Matty told her, smiling. Then she looked round the room. 'Well, Sophie, do you think you'll be comfortable in here?'

'I'm sure I shall, Aunt Matty.' She paused and then added, 'But I'm sorry you're going home straight away, Aunt.'

Matty smiled. 'Don't worry, Sophie. I'll be back to see how you're getting on in a day or so. You'll soon get to know them all. And don't worry about your Aunt Louisa. She'll get used to having you here and be pleased with your help and your company. It hasn't been easy for her these past years, running this place and taking the brunt of my father's ill-humour. There was no escape for her, even when she married, living here at Trescadinnick.'

'Tell me about my cousin Charles,' Sophie said, as much to keep her aunt with her a few minutes longer as because she was interested.

'Charles?' Matty smiled affectionately. 'You may find Charles a little cold at first. He's a very private person and it's sometimes hard to break through his reserve. Don't worry if you find him a little stiff to begin with, that's just his way. Life hasn't been that easy for him either. As I told you, Louisa's husband, James, was married before and Charles was the son of that marriage. James's wife died trying to give birth to their second child, and Charles and James were left alone. When James married Louisa, he and Charles moved in here. Trescadinnick is the only home Charles remembers, and we're the only family he knows. Louisa has no children of her own, but she loves Charles as if he were indeed hers; we all do.'

'Except for my grandfather,' remarked Sophie, thinking of his earlier comments.

'No, you're wrong there,' Matty said. 'My father is very fond of Charles in his own way and really regrets he isn't a true Penvarrow, but unfortunately he does remember that thin dividing line which the rest of us have long forgotten, and it's important to him.'

'How horrible for Cousin Charles,' said Sophie.

'It wouldn't matter if there was another male heir,' sighed Matty. 'But Father is reluctant to leave Trescadinnick outside the family. He's such a traditionalist at heart; he can't bring himself to accept that Charles is just as good as any other grandson he might have had.'

'What exactly happened to your brother, Jocelyn?' asked Sophie suddenly. 'You once said he was killed. I suppose he didn't have any children. He wasn't married, was he?'

Matty didn't answer the question immediately and Sophie felt the change in her as she searched for words to frame her answer. 'I told you before, Joss was tragically killed in an accident, and no, he wasn't married. He was hardly more than a boy when he died.'

'Oh, how dreadful,' cried Sophie.

'It was,' Matty said flatly and then added, 'We never talk about him now, it upsets my father too much. Don't mention him or ask questions while you're here, Sophie, your grandfather's not supposed to be upset. As for Charles,' she went on swiftly, returning to their original subject, 'he works very hard to make what's left of the estate pay, but it's not easy. Much of the wealth used to come from tin mining, but the mines are closing now and there's little profit to be made from farming this land. Since my father grew ill everything has fallen on Charles's shoulders. He works to provide for them all, to save Trescadinnick from being broken up. When he first married and brought Anne to live here, the whole house was filled with new life, infused with hope and happiness.'

'But she died having... Alice?'

'AliceAnne, yes,' confirmed Matty. 'It was as if a cloud descended on the place again, as it did when my mother died. Trescadinnick needs warmth and laughter to keep it alive. It used to be my home, but I'm always glad to leave it these days.'

As if suddenly realizing exactly what sort of picture she was painting, Matty laughed lightly. 'But enough of this gloomy talk,' she said. 'Now you're here, I'm sure everything will change. Perhaps you can even do something with AliceAnne. She's a quiet little thing and needs someone to take an interest in her. Charles is too busy and they've never been close.'

'She must be very lonely, living in a house full of adults,' said Sophie. 'Hasn't she anyone to play with? Children from the village?'

'No, she's a solitary child,' Matty said. 'Unfortunately, there are few suitable children of her age nearby, and playing with the village children is out of the question.'

Sophie was surprised at the vehemence of this last remark and said, 'Poor child, how sad to have no friends at all.'

'She's a strange little girl,' conceded Matty. 'I'm never quite sure about her. She's far too secretive and she's always watching, almost as if she was spying on the rest of us.'

There was a knock and without waiting for an answer, Louisa came into the room. 'Paxton's waiting for you, Matty,' she said. 'If you're going tonight you really must go.'

'I'm coming now,' replied her sister. She turned to Sophie. 'I'll be over again in a few days,' she said. 'Goodbye now, and remember you'll always be a welcome visitor at Treslyn House.' She presented her cheek for Sophie's kiss and then added warmly, 'I'm glad you've come to Trescadinnick; I think it needs you.' She left the room then, followed by Louisa, who paused only to tell Sophie when she would be expected downstairs for dinner.

Chapter 6

Sophie dressed very carefully, choosing to wear the simple black gown she had bought to mourn her mother. With her hair swept up and secured with her mother's tortoiseshell combs and the plain silver band of her mother's necklace about her neck, she looked pale but composed.

'Don't you worry, Miss Sophie,' Hannah had said as she saw her charge take one final glance in the mirror. 'Your ma'd be proud of you.'

It was a comforting thought and Sophie smiled at her gratefully. 'Thank you, Hannah, I'll remember that.'

Sophie went downstairs at the appointed time in some trepidation. She was not quite sure why she felt so nervous. She wanted to meet her cousin, Charles, after all, but from what she had heard he seemed to be rather a severe man, and she wondered if he would approve of her.

Not that it matters if he doesn't, she thought. After all, I'm not going to be here long.

There was no one in the hall when Sophie descended the stairs, and she paused for a moment, uncertain where to go. Then she noticed that one of the panelled doors was slightly ajar and there was light within, so drawing a deep breath, she crossed the hall and pushed upon the door. Hesitating in the doorway, Sophie looked round her. The room she had entered was large and high-ceilinged, with heavy furniture and a well-worn Turkey carpet on the polished floor. There were several portraits on the wall in heavy gilt frames and the windows were curtained to the floor with faded velvet. Three oil lamps made warm pools of light, but the edges of the room receded into shadow.

If it weren't for the fire crackling cheerfully in the grate, Sophie thought, it would be a very overbearing room.

To her surprise she found her grandfather already there, dressed for dinner and sitting in a chair beside the fire. She had not thought that he would leave his bed again that day. He looked up as she came in. 'Ah, there you are,' he said, as if they had all been waiting for her, though in fact there was no sign of Charles or Aunt Louisa yet. 'Don't stand in the doorway. Come and sit by the fire and talk to me.'

Sophie did as she was bid, settling herself on the plump tuffet he indicated at his side, and was thus in close conversation with him when Louisa came in. She too had changed her gown and after a long appraising glance at Sophie, she announced, 'Dinner is ready, Father.'

'Then Charles is late,' he remarked.

'I expect he's gone to say goodnight to AliceAnne,' Louisa replied wearily. She spoke, Sophie thought, as if she were tired of defending her son against his grandfather. But almost at once the door opened and Charles was on the threshold, apologizing for keeping them waiting. 'I hadn't realized you intended joining us for dinner, sir,' he added. But his eyes were on Sophie, sweeping over her.

Almost, thought Sophie, disconcerted, as if I were a horse he considered buying. That's the fourth time today I've been inspected to see if I pass muster and I'm getting tired of it. She raised her chin in a determined fashion, levelly returning his gaze.

'Well, let's not waste any more time now you do,' the old man was grumbling. 'Make your compliments to your cousin Sophia and then help me out of this chair.'

Sophie had risen at her cousin's arrival and they met, hands extended in greeting. Despite his appraisal she smiled at him as she said, 'I'm called Sophie, not Sophia. How do you do, Cousin Charles?'

He was not at all as she had imagined him. His dark hair was thick and slightly curling, and being of medium height, he did not tower over her as Dr Bryan had done, but he was broad-shouldered and strong and his grip was a firm one. Clear brown eyes met hers and a brief smile touched his lips as he heard her daring to correct her grandfather.

'It's a pleasure to meet you, cousin,' he said. 'I trust that the journey from London wasn't too tiring.' Then without waiting for her answer, he dropped her hand and turning to the old man, assisted him to his feet. Once he was standing, however, Thomas Penvarrow brushed the helping hand away and offering his arm to his granddaughter, led her into the dining room. This was another gloomy room, panelled in dark wood and lit this time by two candelabra on the dining table and two sconces over the mantelpiece. Logs glowed in the fireplace, silver and glass glinted in the flickering light, and the table was covered with a gleaming white cloth, but the corners of the room still lurked in shadow, where neither candlelight nor firelight could reach.

Not a welcoming room, Sophie decided as she glanced round it, nor a warm one. She was glad when she was seated in the place nearest the fire.

'You'll find we're very simple here, Sophie,' Louisa said as they sat down. 'Mrs Paxton brings in the dinner, but when we've all been served, we dine unattended.'

As she spoke Mrs Paxton came into the room carrying a large tureen which she placed on a serving table, followed by Edith with soup plates, and together they dispensed and served the thick broth the tureen contained.

Not yet having met either, Sophie looked at them with interest. Mrs Paxton was a small neat woman of middle years. With her hair drawn back in a bun topped with a white cap, she was dressed in a plain dark-blue stuff bodice and skirt, and moved with quick confidence about the table. Edith, on the other hand, was a short, dumpy girl of perhaps eighteen years, dressed in a black uniform dress, cap and apron. She seemed awkward as she served those at the table and Sophie could see that she kept an anxious eye on Thomas Penvarrow, and was clearly afraid of him.

'Thank you, Mrs Paxton,' Louisa said in dismissal when they had all been served. 'I'll ring when we're ready.'

Once Mrs Paxton and a relieved-looking Edith had left the room, Sophie turned to Charles who had been seated next to her. 'I still haven't had the pleasure of meeting your daughter yet, Cousin Charles. How old is she?'

'Six,' he replied shortly.

'That's a lovely age,' Sophie said. 'Children of that age are so eager to learn, aren't they? Does she do well at her books? What does her governess think?'

'She's still too young to have a governess,' Charles said.

'At six?' Sophie was surprised. 'Surely that's just the right age to—'

'You're an expert on the education of children, are you?' Charles asked coldly.

'No, but—'

'Well, in that case, I'll thank you to mind your own business. I think I may be relied upon to know what is best for my child.'

'Certainly,' agreed Sophie, clinging to the rags of her temper, 'but in fact I have taught children her age with great success.'

Charles looked at her coolly. 'You were yourself a governess until you learned of your inheritance here, were you?'

'No, I was not,' Sophie flashed back. 'But I did teach children to play the piano. And as for my inheritance, as you call it, as far as I know I have none. I am simply carrying out the dying wishes of my mother. I am paying a visit, and when it is over I shall return to my own home.'

'This is your home now, Sophie,' said her grandfather, who had been listening to their exchange.

Sophie turned at once. 'No, Grandfather, it is not. I have come here to heal the breach between my mother and you, and when I have finished my visit, I shall return to my home, in London.'

Charles's eyes flashed a look of appreciation when he heard her stand up to their grandfather, and seeing it, Sophie wondered if she had perhaps found an ally after all. He made no comment, but adroitly turned the conversation.

'Do you ride, Cousin Sophie?'

'Do you think we could drop the "Cousin", Cousin Charles? We are not cousins, you know, and I'd much prefer you simply called me Sophie.'

'As you wish. Do you ride, Sophie?'

Sophie smiled. 'I used to,' she answered. 'My father had relatives in Suffolk, and we used to go and stay with them sometimes. I learned to ride there.'

'I see. That's a pity.'

'What is?' demanded Sophie.

'Well, if you haven't ridden since you were a child...'

'I didn't say that,' retorted Sophie. 'I learned in Suffolk at my Uncle Harold's home, but when I grew older my father used to hire horses on occasion and we'd ride in the park. It was something special we did together.'

'Hhrumph.' Thomas looked annoyed. It was clear that he didn't want to hear anything about Sophie's father.

'If you'd like to ride while you're here, Sophie,' Charles said, 'we must find you a suitable horse. It's the perfect way to see the countryside.'

'Thank you, Charles, I'd love that,' she said, smiling at him with genuine pleasure.

The meal progressed slowly. When Louisa rang the bell Edith appeared to clear the plates and Mrs Paxton brought in baked meats, and for dessert there was a syllabub. Sophie enjoyed the food. It was simple, well-cooked and tasty, but throughout the meal there were long and awkward silences. Sophie wished more than ever that Matty had stayed at least one night. Louisa contributed almost nothing to the conversation, and the two men spoke only occasionally, speaking of local affairs of which Sophie knew nothing. Her own efforts at conversation were answered shortly, and Sophie was soon wondering if all mealtimes at Trescadinnick would be as dull and as difficult as this.

If so, she thought, it certainly won't be long before I go home.

Even so, it gave her a chance to observe her newfound family. Her grandfather, irascible, used to having his own way, tended

68

to make statements, which no one questioned. Charles seemed dour and distant, as if his mind were elsewhere and interruption of his thoughts was a nuisance. Louisa also seemed withdrawn. Some years older than her sisters, her face was lined and tired. She seemed afraid of her father, shock and something akin to fear registering on her face when Sophie answered back to him. But at last it was over and Louisa led her from the table into the drawing room, where Mrs Paxton brought them tea.

'Aunt Louisa,' Sophie began, deciding it was time to make an effort with her taciturn aunt, 'it's very kind of you to have me here.' It seemed a lame beginning, but she could think of nothing else.

'Your grandfather wanted to see you,' Louisa replied, her voice devoid of expression.

'But you didn't?' Sophie asked, softening her question with a smile. 'I am your niece after all. Weren't you curious?'

'Mary left a long time ago,' Louisa said. 'She cut her ties with us. She chose not to belong here.' Her eyes flashed at Sophie as she added, 'You don't either.'

In the face of such hostility Sophie felt at a loss, so she simply said, 'As I said to my grandfather, I'm only here for a visit. My home is in London.'

An awkward silence fell and they drank their tea without further conversation. Sophie was relieved when Charles and her grandfather joined them and there was some desultory discussion about what everyone planned to do the next day.

Suddenly Thomas turned to Sophie and said, 'You mentioned you played the piano, Sophie. There's the piano.' He waved a hand towards the corner of the room. 'Play us something now.'

Sophie looked across at the piano that stood in an alcove and then back at Thomas. 'Of course, Grandfather, if you want me to. But I haven't any music with me, so I'll have to play something from memory.'

'Plenty of music in there,' replied Thomas, gesturing to the piano stool.

'Even so, I think I'll play something I know.' Sophie smiled, crossing to the piano and lifting its lid. 'Perhaps you could bring the lamp over, Charles.'

He did as she asked and Sophie settled herself down on the stool and ran her fingers over the keys. 'It's a bit out of tune,' she remarked. 'When was it last played?'

'It hasn't been played for years,' Louisa said. 'Not since... since Anne died.'

Sophie turned to Charles, who had remained beside the piano. 'I'm sorry. Did she play often?' she asked.

'Yes,' he replied shortly. 'She was a good pianist.'

Sophie chose a Beethoven sonata that she knew well and then a folk song, which she sang in her clear soprano voice, shakily at first but steadying as she grew in confidence. Then she closed the piano and turned back to her grandfather. 'I'll practise something else for tomorrow,' she said. 'I'd love to look through the music here. If you don't mind, that is.'

'Play whenever you like,' Thomas said. 'Charles, arrange to have the piano tuned at once; it sounds terrible. Now I'm going to bed and I suggest you do the same.'

They all moved into the hall where candles were set out on a side table. 'Do you know your way up to your room?' Thomas enquired as Sophie picked up a candle and Charles lit it for her. 'Louisa, take the child up to her room.'

'It's all right, really, Grandfather. I know my way and Hannah will be waiting up for me.' She reached up to him and to the amazement of both Charles and Louisa, kissed his cheek. 'Goodnight, sir. I hope you sleep well.' She turned back to see Louisa watching her coldly, and changed her mind about offering her a goodnight kiss. Instead she said, 'Goodnight, Aunt. Goodnight, Charles. I would love to go riding some time if it's possible.'

Then, with a smile that encompassed them all, she lifted her candle high and went upstairs to her room.

'Thank goodness that's over,' she said to Hannah as she closed the door behind her. 'What a dreary evening. Do you know, Hannah, none of them seems happy. They never smile. We're not staying here longer than we have to, or I shall go mad.'

'Now then, Miss Sophie, you're just tired, that's all. Things'll look different in the morning, you mark my words. Come on now, it's time you were in bed.'

Later, when Hannah had gone to her own room, Sophie lay in bed listening to the wind whining round the house and rattling her window. The banked-up fire gave a faint glow, but as her eyes grew used to the dark, it was enough to make out the shapes of the furniture in the bedroom. How often had her mother lain here in the fire glow, listening to the wind before she fell asleep, Sophie wondered.

She thought back over her day; the journey, her arrival at Trescadinnick and the people she had met there, and decided the only one she really liked was Dr Nicholas Bryan.

Chapter 7

When Sophie had gone up to bed, Thomas bade his daughter goodnight, but instead of following her upstairs he turned to his grandson and said, 'Before you go up, Charles, a word.' Without waiting for Charles to reply, he opened his library door and led the way inside.

Charles followed his grandfather into the room, wondering what he wanted to discuss at this time of night. Of course Thomas was *not* actually his grandfather, though Charles had always thought of him as such and even addressed him as Grandpapa as a small boy. That was the trouble. Charles had always known that Thomas Penvarrow was disappointed that he had no living son or grandson to inherit Trescadinnick, but Charles always assumed that when the time came the estate would pass to him, the step-grandson. Thomas had never said so, but until a few weeks ago there had been no one else. Now there was this Sophie girl, daughter of the erring Mary. Charles knew very little about either of them. He had only the vaguest recollection of Mary, from when they had been living together at Trescadinnick. He had been four years old when she left to marry John Ross, and he'd been told nothing about why she had gone. He was considered far too young to understand such matters, and the memory of another aunt, so like his Aunt Mary who had gone away, soon mingled with the reality of the aunt who was still there, so he had given her little further thought. Certainly, no one had actually mentioned her name for years. No one had dared. Now though, she had died and left an orphan daughter, a grandchild for Thomas, and Matty had been dispatched to fetch her.

Charles had not been party to much of the heart-searching that had gone on before Matty had left to find Sophia. When told of Mary's letter he felt a mild curiosity about her daughter, and agreed with the decision already taken that it was right for Matty to visit her, but he was surprised at his stepmother's reaction to the idea.

'Why did you encourage them?' she asked tersely. 'Why did you agree that they should ask the girl here?'

Charles shrugged. 'Why shouldn't I? Clearly my grandfather wants to see her. What difference does that make to me?'

'You really aren't very bright sometimes, Charles,' Louisa said, exasperated. 'Don't you see that she stands between you and your rightful inheritance? It doesn't seem to matter to my father how hard you work on his behalf; you are not his own flesh and blood. He will make *her* his heir and everything you've worked for will become hers.'

Charles looked at her and said simply, 'If that's the case, Mama, there is very little I can do about it.'

'You could talk to him. Before she comes, you could talk to him and tell him how you feel. You and AliceAnne belong here far more than she does. She may be Mary's daughter, but Mary chose to leave this family and so her daughter has no place here. You've been brought up here and Trescadinnick is your home. You deserve to inherit when your grandfather dies. It's your right. You must demand your right.'

'I can't start demanding rights before I even know what my grandfather intends, Mama,' Charles pointed out. 'I think you're worrying unnecessarily. He's not an unjust man, and you can't blame him for wanting to see this girl.'

'If that's all he wants,' said Louisa darkly.

'As to that, we shall have to wait and see,' Charles replied. 'It'll do more harm than good if I start making demands.' But Louisa's angry comments had started him thinking.

'Well, I can demand for you,' Louisa stated. 'I'm not prepared to stand by and watch while he sets you aside for some slip of a girl we don't even know. *I* shall speak to him if you're too afraid.'

That stung Charles and he retorted angrily, 'I'm not afraid of him, Mama. I simply do not see the necessity for creating problems before they occur. Nor,' he added with a grim smile, 'do I want to put ideas into his head. I hope you won't say anything yet, because there may be nothing to worry about. We'd be much better to hold our fire for the time being and just wait upon events.'

Louisa was not convinced. She still wanted to tackle her father while she had the courage. She had always been afraid of him and his explosive temper, but when it came to fighting for what she considered the rights of her son, she was determined to face up to him, and win. Why should some young girl arrive on the scene and charm her way into the old man's heart, taking away the chance of Charles inheriting Trescadinnick? Thomas had recently been coming round to the realization that Charles had earned the right to Trescadinnick. Indeed, he'd sent for his solicitor, Mr Staunton, and Louisa had got the idea that he'd been told to draw up Thomas's will. If so, it could only be in Charles's favour. It was, after all, Charles who was putting the estate back on its feet; Charles who had looked into new methods of farming to obtain a higher yield from the land; Charles who had invested some of his own meagre inheritance from his father in a seine net and two fishing boats, paying local fishermen to crew them when the vast shoals of pilchards followed the warm currents into Cornish waters, in the late summer and early autumn, to provide a new source of income. He knew only too well that the days of the tin mines were over, the tin worked out and the price at rock bottom. The mines had been the foundation of the Penvarrow family fortunes, and it had taken Thomas time to accept that now they were worthless; though the family was not penniless, certain retrenchment had been necessary. They no longer employed all the servants they had when Louisa was a girl: the cook, the housemaid and parlour maid, the valet and the groom, two gardeners and a boy. Now they ran the house with the help of the Paxtons, Edith, the maid-of-all-work and a kitchen skivvy; Davies, the gardener, and Ned, the stable lad, worked outside. Louisa left Mrs Paxton in charge of the kitchen, but she supervised the housekeeping, was her own dairymaid and also saw to the few hours' schooling AliceAnne needed. There was no governess for her as there had been for Louisa and her sisters. Most of the time Louisa did not mind the life she led. She was used to it now, and at least the running of the household was left to her and she was her own mistress. She had been sure that in the end her father would see the rightness of leaving everything to Charles, but now that was all put in jeopardy by the appearance of Mary's daughter. However, Charles had asked her not to approach her father on the subject of inheritance and for the moment she had, against her better judgement, acquiesced.

'But if we discover that he plans to cut you out, Charles, I *will* speak to him,' she declared. 'He has no right to do so.'

Of course, they both knew that he had every legal right, but Louisa was adamant that he had no moral right, and if necessary she would take her courage in her hands and tell him so.

As Charles wondered now what his grandfather was going to say, he could only hope that his mother had held her peace.

'Put another log on the fire, Charles,' Thomas said as he settled himself in his chair. When Charles had done so, and poured two glasses of brandy, also at Thomas's bidding, he sat down opposite him and waited.

'Well, she's come,' Thomas began. 'My only grandchild, Charles. Pretty girl, eh? Looks like her grandmother, don't you think?' He glanced up at the portrait of his wife that hung over the fireplace and with a sigh said, 'You'll think I'm getting senti-mental in my old age.'

Sentimentality was the last accusation Charles would have levelled at his grandfather. He could see the likeness between the woman who smiled down from the painting and the girl who had sat next to him at the dinner table, but he made no comment, simply waited for Thomas to go on.

'Well,' snapped the old man. 'What do you think of her? Pretty enough for you?'

For a moment Charles thought of Sophie as he'd first seen her, dressed in her simple black dress, her chestnut hair swept back off her face, her dark green eyes shining in the candlelight, and replied cautiously, 'She seems a likeable young girl, but we hardly know her yet.'

'We will, soon enough,' answered Thomas. 'She won't be going back to some hovel in London. I shan't allow it.'

'She said she was only here for a short visit,' Charles reminded him.

'She'll change her mind,' said Thomas. 'I'll tell you straight, Charles, I intend to make her my heir.'

'I see.' Charles managed to keep his voice level, despite the abruptness of this announcement.

'And that being the case,' Thomas went on as if he hadn't been interrupted, 'I've decided you'd better marry her.'

'Marry her!' ejaculated Charles, this time unable to control his reaction.

'Certainly marry her,' said the old man testily. 'Why ever not? That'll make everything right and tight. I know you've worked hard for this place, specially over these last few years.' He spoke gruffly, finding it difficult as always to express his thanks to anyone. 'You marry the girl and you'll get the reward you've earned.'

Charles was dumbfounded. He stared at Thomas for a moment before repeating incredulously, 'Marry her? Marry her! I only met the girl this evening. I don't know her and more to the point, nor do you.'

Thomas was unrepentant. 'What does knowing her matter? She's family. You need a wife. That daughter of yours needs a mother. It seems to me to be the perfect solution to all your problems.'

Charles felt the anger rising up in him and did his best not to let it overwhelm him. 'I wasn't aware, sir, that I had any particular problems,' he said tightly. 'And if I had, I would find my own solutions. If, and I repeat *if*, I felt in need of a wife I am perfectly capable of choosing one for myself. I certainly wouldn't marry some young girl scarcely out of the schoolroom just to ensure I inherit this estate.'

'Your daughter needs a mother,' Thomas reminded him.

'If that is the case, and I dispute it, I would choose a woman of good sense, experienced with children, not a chit of nineteen.'

'She's twenty, getting on for twenty-one, and it's the only way you'll get your hands on Trescadinnick,' Thomas said flatly. 'Now send Paxton to me. I want to go to bed.'

Charles downed the last of his brandy in one gulp and stood up. 'I will indeed send Paxton to you, sir, but before I do, allow me to say that if you make marriage with Miss Sophia Ross a condition of inheriting Trescadinnick, I tell you straight away that I'm not interested. There are plenty of other estates in the country, which I could run a great deal more efficiently than this one, and if necessary I will apply for the position of estate manager on one of those. And,' he added with a vicious smile, 'get paid for what I do. I wish you goodnight, sir.'

With this parting shot, Charles left Thomas alone in the library, and having called Paxton as requested, he went out into the cold night air, to cool his temper and to calm his seething thoughts. For long minutes he paced up and down, his fists clenched in fury. How dare he! How dare his grandfather dictate to him on such a matter? How dare he decide to marry him off simply to suit himself! To ease his own conscience! And to a schoolroom miss.

Well, he thought, as he paced the garden, the old man can think again. I have no intention of marrying her.

He wondered what Sophie herself would think of Thomas's plans for her. Certainly she'd had enough spunk to stand up to him this evening, and Charles allowed himself a rare smile as he remembered how she had corrected her grandfather on his assumption that she would now live at Trescadinnick. That had surprised Charles as much as it had the old man himself. Not many people held their own against Thomas Penvarrow, and Charles wondered if she would continue to do so when she heard she was to be his heir. But I will stand against him, Charles thought to himself. He will not dictate to me and I won't be coerced into marrying Sophie Ross... or anyone else, for that matter.

His mother had been right about her father's intentions, he thought ruefully, but even she hadn't imagined the extent to which he would go to carry them through. He decided not to tell her of the conversation in the library yet. Perhaps, as a result of his reaction, Thomas would reconsider the ultimatum he'd laid down once he realized that Charles would not, now or ever, accept his demands.

At last he turned back to the house and, resolutely setting aside thoughts of Sophie, locked the great front door behind him and went upstairs to bed.

Chapter 8

Sophie awoke the next morning to the sound of a rooster crowing and to the far-off murmur of the sea. For a while she lay in bed, listening to the unfamiliar sounds. She thought again about Trescadinnick and its inhabitants, and a wave of tingling expectation came over her. She got out of bed and crossing the room, threw back the curtains to look out on the view her aunt had promised her the previous evening. Throwing up the sash, Sophie kneeled with her arms on the sill, sniffing the crisp air and drinking in the sights and sounds around her. Autumn sunlight played on the garden immediately below her window, giving a pale imitation of the warmth which would invade that sheltered spot in summer. The garden was enclosed on three sides by the house, the fourth opening out onto a wider expanse, sheltered by a wall at the far end. A huddle of outbuildings lay to the side of the house, the dairy and a hen house perhaps, where the rooster still announced the day. She could see stables and what must be the stable yard; even as she looked, Sophie saw Paxton emerge from the house with clattering buckets, which he filled at the pump and carried back into the kitchen through some unseen back door. And beyond it all, dipping and curving to a jutting headland at the end of the bay, was the sweep of the cliff. It was bleak and windswept, its grey-green grass tufted and coarse, and in the distance, restlessly sighing, was the slate-grey sea.

This is the view that Mama looked at all through her child-hood, thought Sophie. This won't have changed at all.

She looked down into the sheltered garden where neat flower-beds bordered the lawn. Though they were brown and empty now, Sophie knew they would be full of colour in the early summer. Shading one corner of the grass stood a huge old apple tree, its bare boughs stretched out, waiting for spring. She could imagine a swing hanging from one of those spreading branches; indeed, Sophie thought it strange that none hung there now for little AliceAnne to enjoy. Built against the wall of the house were two stone benches, each set into an alcove to catch the afternoon sun.

That's where they played, Mama and Aunt Matty, or sat and read, Sophie thought. And she tried to visualize her mother seated on the bench with a book in her hand, or playing under the tree with her sister.

A knock and the immediate opening of the door brought Hannah into the room and Sophie sharply back to the present.

'Oh, Miss Sophie, you'll catch your death sitting there at the window with nothing over your nightgown,' scolded Hannah. 'Close it at once and come back here by the fire.'

Sophie did as she was bid, turning back into the room as Hannah busied herself poking the fire into life and putting on more coal.

'I've brought you up some tea,' Hannah went on, 'and when you've drunk that I'll bring your hot water.'

'Is everyone else up?' Sophie asked as she sat by the fire and sipped her tea.

'Yes. Mr Penvarrow had his breakfast on a tray. Mrs Leroy and Mr Charles finished theirs half an hour ago, but Mrs Leroy said to let you sleep after your long journey.'

'Then I must get dressed at once,' cried Sophie, jumping to her feet. 'Please fetch the water now, Hannah. I can't wait to explore this place.'

Within twenty minutes Sophie came down to the hall. For a moment she paused uncertainly, then went into the dining room where they'd had dinner the night before. It was cold and dark, with no sign of occupation this morning. As she backed out again, she heard a movement behind her and turned to find AliceAnne standing at the mouth of the kitchen passage, solemnly regarding her.

Sophie smiled at her. 'Good morning, AliceAnne,' she said. 'Can you tell me where we have our breakfast?'

'In the morning room,' replied AliceAnne.

'Will you show me where that is?'

The child nodded and led her through another door into a snug room, flooded with sunshine and a view out over the garden. The table was laid for breakfast with bread and butter and jam, and on a small sideboard was a chafing dish with kidneys and bacon in it.

'Mrs Paxton says will you take coffee or tea, and will you have two eggs?' AliceAnne's words all came out in a rush as she discharged her message.

'Coffee, please, AliceAnne, and just one egg,' answered Sophie. And as the child turned to leave the room, she added, 'If you're not busy, will you come back and talk to me while I have my breakfast? I don't like eating alone.'

AliceAnne nodded again and disappeared on her errand. Sophie went to the window and looked out. She was looking over the sheltered garden she had seen from her bedroom, but from a different direction. The morning-room window faced east and was at right-angles to her bedroom.

AliceAnne came quietly back into the room, hovering inside the door as if she expected to be sent away again.

'Come and sit with me at the table,' Sophie suggested with a smile and having helped herself to bacon from the dish, sat down and pulled out a chair beside her. 'I want you to tell me all about Trescadinnick, and yourself, and all the people who live here.'

AliceAnne came shyly across and slid onto the chair, but still said nothing.

'Your name is AliceAnne, isn't it?' Sophie tried again. 'Mine is Sophie, and I've come all the way from London. Do you know where London is?'

The child shook her head.

'Well, it's hundreds of miles from here and it's the capital city of England. It's where the queen lives.'

'Do you know the queen?' AliceAnne asked.

Sophie shook her head, laughing. 'No, but I saw her once, driving through the park in her carriage. My father took me when I was a little girl, and we all waved and cheered, and the queen waved back.'

The door opened and Mrs Paxton came in with Sophie's egg and a pot of coffee. She was followed by Louisa, who said briskly, 'Good morning, Sophie. I trust you slept well. When you've had your breakfast, your grandfather wants to see you.'

'Of course, Aunt. Where will he be?'

'In his room, where you saw him yesterday. He's decided not to get up this morning. Now, AliceAnne, don't be a nuisance to your Aunt Sophie.'

'Oh, she's not,' put in Sophie quickly. 'I asked her to come and talk to me while I had my breakfast.'

'I see,' said Louisa stiffly. 'We don't usually encourage her to talk at the table. Still... just this once, AliceAnne.'

'Yes, Grandmama,' whispered the little girl, shrinking back into her chair.

'Is there anything else you'd like me to do?' Sophie asked, to turn Louisa's attention back to herself.

'Spending time with your grandfather is the most help to me,' Louisa replied. 'The papers should be arriving from London today. Paxton will pick them up from the post office at St Morwen, later, then you can take them up and read them to Father. This is a working household,' Louisa went on. 'We have a meal at midday in the dining room, tea later in the afternoon for those who want it, and dinner in the evening. Oh, by the way, Matty is coming over to join us for dinner this evening. I'm going to the village now and then I shall be in the dairy. I'll see you at luncheon.'

When Louisa had gone, Sophie ate her breakfast quickly. 'What are you going to do today, AliceAnne... or do you prefer to be called Alice?' she asked.

'AliceAnne, Aunt Sophie,' answered the little girl.

'I'm not really your aunt, you know,' Sophie said gently.

'No, but Grandmama said I was to call you that.'

'That's fine then,' Sophie agreed quickly, not wanting to make any further difficulties for her. 'So what are you going to do today?'

'I don't know, Aunt Sophie.'

'Well, in that case,' Sophie said, 'when I've seen my grandfather and done whatever it is he wants of me, perhaps you'd like to show me everything.' She smiled cheerfully at AliceAnne. 'I don't even know my way round the house, so perhaps you could show me? And the garden too?'

'Yes, Aunt Sophie.'

'Good.' Sophie was on her feet and heading for the door. 'Where will I find you when I need you?'

'In the kitchen with Mrs Paxton.'

Sophie watched her scurry down the kitchen passage and then went up the stairs to her grandfather's room, and knocked on the door.

'Good morning, Grandfather,' she said cheerfully. 'How are you this morning? Did you sleep well?'

'No, I didn't,' grumbled the old man. 'Never do. Is Paxton back with the newspapers yet?'

'No, not yet. Aunt Louisa said that he would be fetching them later. Now what did you want to see me about?'

'I wanted some company,' he replied, and then added after a pause, 'I wanted to hear about your mother.'

'What do you want to know?' asked Sophie, sitting down on a chair by the bed.

'Was she happy?'

'Until my father was killed, she was very happy,' answered Sophie. 'After that we had each other. Then she became ill. The doctor couldn't do anything for her; she just wasted away before my eyes.'

Sophie still found it difficult to speak of her mother and she fought back tears as she told Thomas about her mother's last illness, her pain and her courageous fight against it.

'Well, you're here with us now,' he said gruffly when she fell silent. 'This is where you belong. I have plans for you here.'

'I'm only visiting for a little while, Grandfather,' Sophie reminded him, but he seemed not to hear her.

'I've changed my mind,' he announced suddenly. 'I'm going to get up. Send Paxton to me, please, and tell Mrs Paxton I shall be down for luncheon.'

Sophie took this as her dismissal and hurried down to deliver the messages. She went into the kitchen where she found both the Paxtons and AliceAnne. Paxton went straight upstairs and Sophie said to AliceAnne, 'Well, AliceAnne, would you like to show me the house now?' She held out her hand and the little girl took it. 'And later, perhaps, we could go to the village.'

AliceAnne took her job seriously, and beginning where they were, the kitchen, she led Sophie through to the pantry and into the dairy. With Mrs Paxton's permission, she showed Sophie the snug little sitting room where the Paxtons sat in the evenings.

'I like this room,' AliceAnne confided, looking round it. 'It's warm and cosy and full of... things.'

Sophie looked round, too, at the comfortable clutter and agreed that indeed, it was full of things.

From there they inspected the rooms off the hall; dining room, drawing room, rather imposing and not at all comfortable, both of which Sophie had seen the previous evening. Next, the morning room, and then AliceAnne paused before another door and knocked. There was no reply and after a moment's hesitation she opened the door and stood aside for Sophie to enter. She found herself in a library, its walls lined from ceiling to floor with books. Sophie had never seen so many, and she exclaimed with delight as she saw them. Its long windows faced west, waiting for the evening sun. From them Sophie looked out across a lawn, over a low wall to the cliff top beyond. There was a fire laid ready in the grate and Sophie could imagine the room, curtains drawn, lamp-lit and snug, with her grandfather in the huge leather armchair beside the chimneypiece, reading or playing chess on the chess table which stood beside it. It was much the most welcoming room she'd been into so far.

'I like this room,' she said to AliceAnne. 'So many books.'

'Only Grandfather and Papa come in here,' AliceAnne replied. She hovered uneasily at the door, and Sophie, seeing she was worried they would be found in the room uninvited, led the way back to the hall.

'And that's Papa's study,' AliceAnne said, waving a hand at the last unopened door but making no effort to open it. 'He does his work in there. Shall we go upstairs now?'

'Yes, you can show me your room.'

AliceAnne led the way up the stairs and pointing at closed doors on the landing, said, 'That's Papa's room, and that's Grandmama's. Grandfather's is along there, but you know that.' Turning back along the landing, past the few stairs that led up to Sophie's room, she opened another door at the far end, revealing a twisting staircase. At the top another door stood open and AliceAnne took Sophie through.

'This was the nursery, where I used to sleep,' she said. 'But it's my schoolroom now, where I do my lessons.'

Sophie stepped into the room and looked about her. The room was large with two dormer windows jutting out from under the sloping eaves. Beneath one was an old schoolroom table and beneath the other was a cushioned window seat.

'Oh, AliceAnne, this is lovely. What can you see from your window?' Sophie kneeled on the window seat and looked out. 'You can see the sea like I can. It's a lovely view!' She turned back to admire the rest of the room, though it was clearly furnished with cast-offs from the rest of the house. At the far end was a closed stove giving off gentle heat, flanked by two easy chairs. An aged sofa stood along one wall beside which was a shelf of rather dilapidated books.

'Are these your books? Which stories have you got?' Sophie moved to the shelf, but AliceAnne was already opening a door in the corner, leading to another, much smaller room; her bedroom.

'I sleep in here now,' she said, and crossing to the bed, she picked up a very elderly and obviously much-loved rag doll, holding her against her cheek.

Following her into the room, Sophie smiled and said, 'Who's that?'

'Mary-Jane,' whispered AliceAnne. 'She belonged to my mama.'

'Did she now? Well, d'you know, I have a doll a little like Mary-Jane, who belonged to *my* mama. Would you like to see her?'

'Yes, please,' AliceAnne replied, and for the first time Sophie saw the glimmer of a smile on the little girl's face.

'Come along then,' said Sophie, holding out her hand. 'Bring Mary-Jane and I'll introduce you both to Emily. She's in my room.'

They went down to the gallery landing and then mounted the few stairs that led to the half-landing and Sophie's room. As they reached it, Sophie pointed to the other door on that landing and asked casually, 'Whose room is this, the one next to mine?'

'That's Uncle Jocelyn's room,' answered AliceAnne. 'He died. We don't go in there. It's locked up.'

'Oh, I see,' replied Sophie and said no more, but she didn't see. Why should Jocelyn's room be kept locked? He died in an accident, she knew that, but that was years ago, before she was born. Why close up his room? Perhaps I'll ask Aunt Matty, she thought.

Opening the door to her own room, she took AliceAnne in to see her doll, Emily, the one that had belonged to her mother.

As they went back downstairs they were met by Hannah, about to come and find them. 'Ah, there you are, Miss Sophie. Mr Paxton's been for the newspaper and your grandfather wants you to go and read it to him.'

'Of course,' Sophie said at once. 'Where is he, Hannah?'

'In the library, Miss Sophie.'

'I'll go at once. AliceAnne, I'd love to see the garden and maybe we could go to the village later on. Perhaps after lunch while my grandfather has his rest.'

Hannah said, 'You come with me, Miss AliceAnne, and we'll see what Mrs Paxton's been baking, shall we?'

Sophie watched, as together they went off hand in hand down the kitchen passage to find Mrs Paxton, before entering the library to find Thomas. She spent the rest of the morning in the library reading to him. The fire had been lit and they sat, one either side of it, while Sophie picked out pieces of news that she thought might interest him.

'I used to do this for Mama when she was too ill to read the paper for herself,' Sophie told him. 'Is there anything particular you want to hear about?'

Thomas shook his head. He was content to hear what she chose to read, and when at last she fell silent he said, 'Thank you, Sophie, that's enough for now.'

At that moment the gong went for lunch and they left the library to join the others. Apart from breakfast, it turned out to be the only meal at which AliceAnne was allowed to join the adults, but even so she was not included in the desultory conversation and Sophie could see that she was glad to be released from the table when she had finished. Sophie would have liked to be released too, but she had to stay while her grandfather drank a glass of brandy. When they finally left the dining room, Thomas, at the insistence of Louisa, went grumbling to his room for a rest.

'Now you know what Dr Bryan says, Papa,' Louisa said sternly. 'If you're going to get up in the mornings you must rest in the afternoons.'

'Takes too much on himself, that young man,' muttered Thomas.

'Not at all, Papa,' replied Louisa, though Sophie had heard her say much the same herself the previous day. 'He's an excellent doctor and takes very good care of you.' Seeing her granddaughter hovering in the hall, waiting for Sophie, she called, 'AliceAnne, run and tell Paxton your grandfather needs him upstairs.'

AliceAnne disappeared to the kitchen, and Louisa and her father set off up the stairs. It was the first time Sophie had heard Louisa speak up to Thomas, and it made her realize that her aunt did have a streak of the Penvarrow determination in her.

Charles, who had remained silent through most of the meal,

turned to Sophie and asked, 'What are you going to do this afternoon, Sophie?'

'AliceAnne has promised to take me to the village,' Sophie replied eagerly. 'I want to see everything.'

'Don't let AliceAnne be a nuisance to you.'

'She's not a nuisance,' Sophie assured him warmly. 'I'm pleased to have her company. She seems a lonely child.'

Charles made no comment on this, but simply nodded and said, 'I'll see you this evening then,' and went out to the stables. Moments later Sophie saw him, mounted on a fine black horse, trotting down the drive and disappearing through the gate. It was so long since she'd had the chance to ride and she knew a moment of envy as she watched him ride away. With a sigh, she went to find AliceAnne and suggest they take their walk to the village.

As they were leaving the house, both wrapped up well against the strong wind, Sophie saw Hannah and called her to join them on their walk. 'AliceAnne is going to show me the village, Hannah. Why don't you come with us and learn your way about too?' she suggested.

Hannah looked a little uncertain about the idea. 'I'm not sure—' she began.

But Sophie cut in briskly. 'Come on, Hannah, I want you to come. We often walked together in London. What's the difference down here?' She insisted that they would wait while Hannah found her coat and hat, and then all three of them set off along the footpath that led to the little fishing village of Port Felec.

'There's the road down that way,' AliceAnne had said, 'or we can go by the cliff path.'

'Let's make it a round walk,' suggested Sophie. 'We'll go along the path and come back on the road.'

The path ran across the cliff top, and in places skirted the very edge of the cliff, where steep, narrow paths ran down to the little coves below. Standing at the top of one of these, Sophie looked down at the sea, grey and restive below her. She could hear the waves pounding on the rocks and the sound excited her.

'Let's go down to the beach,' she cried. 'AliceAnne, does this path go right down?'

'Yes, Aunt Sophie, but it's very steep. There's a better one from the end of our garden. It's not so steep and there's a rope to hold on to. I'm not allowed to go down this one.'

Sophie stood looking down, the wind whipping her hair and tugging at her cloak. Far below her she could see a tiny, rocky cove, a crescent of sand in its midst. The sound of the waves breaking over the rocks and smoothing the patch of sand echoed up the cliff in rhythmic rumble. She longed to go down and stand on that glossy sand and was tempted to try the path anyway, but seeing the look on her face, Hannah took charge. She had no wish to go scrambling down steep and dangerous cliff paths, so she said briskly, 'Come along, Miss AliceAnne, let's get to the village.'

Reluctantly, Sophie turned away from the intriguing path and followed the other two along the footpath towards the ridge. She could always go back and explore the rocky cove another time, when she was on her own, without AliceAnne to consider.

When they reached the ridge, they stopped and looked down at the fishing village of Port Felec, which lay in a bowl beneath them. From their vantage point they could see the tiny harbour, partially enclosed by a harbour wall, and the houses clustered round the main quay, with a few more straggling up the hill towards them. On the far side of the houses, above a stretch of sandy beach, stood a squat grey church, sheltered from the westerly wind by a ring of yew trees, and next to it stood a bigger house which was, Sophie presumed, the parsonage. She could see a narrow road passing these, zigzagging its way down the opposite side of the hollow until it disappeared amongst the cottages. The path *they* had been following ended up as a flight of stone steps that gave onto one of the narrow streets leading up from the quay. Beyond the village the cliffs swept away, curving to form a headland at the end of the bay, with the sea sucking and swirling at the jagged rocks below. Atop this headland, silhouetted against the sky, the tall finger of a disused mine chimney, rising amid the derelict mine buildings, pointed to the sky.

AliceAnne led the way down the steps and into a steep, narrow street that ran between cottages that faced out to the sea, watching for their fishermen to come home. When they reached the harbour they saw that the tide was out, leaving small boats grounded on the shingle of the harbour floor. The air smelled of salt and mud and fish, and the cry of the gulls which soared above rose eerily on the wind.

Few people were about, and those that were paid scant attention to the three standing by the harbour wall.

For a long moment Sophie stood and stared out over the harbour, drinking in the sights and sounds. Hannah sniffed and looking round her said, 'Not much to this place, Miss Sophie, and that's a fact. Look at all them dirty stones... little better than mud!'

Sophie laughed. 'You won't see that when the tide's in, Hannah.' She swung round to look back at the houses that stood above the beach and climbed the hillside. 'Just look at the way they've made little gardens, cut them out of the hill. Everyone grows their own vegetables. And look, Hannah, there's the village shop. Shall we go in?'

Before they could walk over to the little general store that fronted the main quay, there was the sound of hooves, and a pony and trap came down the road from the opposite direction. As it rounded the corner the driver saw them and waved, drawing his pony to a halt and jumping down to greet them. It was the tall figure of Dr Nicholas Bryan.

'Miss Ross,' he cried in pleasure. 'How delightful to see you again. Hallo, AliceAnne, how's your grandfather today?'

AliceAnne didn't reply, edging behind Sophie, but the doctor didn't seem to notice and beaming at them all, shook Sophie by the hand. 'And who's this?' He looked enquiringly at Hannah.

'This is Miss Hannah Butts,' Sophie replied, returning his smile. 'Hannah has looked after me ever since I was a baby. Hannah, this is Dr Bryan, who attends my grandfather.'

'How do you do, Hannah.' Nicholas extended his hand, but Hannah simply gave him a little bob and said, 'Nicely, thank you, sir.'

'So, Miss Ross, you've come to look at Port Felec. What do you think of it?'

'I haven't seen very much of it,' Sophie said with a laugh. 'But I'm looking forward to exploring the whole area while I'm here. It couldn't be more different from where I live in Hammersmith.'

Beside her, AliceAnne shivered in the wind, and immediately Nicholas was all concern. 'You mustn't stand here in this cold wind,' he said. 'You'll catch your deaths, and I've enough patients as it is. Why don't we go into The Clipper.' He waved his hand in the direction of the inn across the little square. 'We can sit in the parlour window and watch for the boats to come in with the tide. Maggie Penlee will give us a cup of tea and some home-made cakes. Allow me.' Taking her acceptance for granted, he offered Sophie his arm, and led her towards the inn, followed by AliceAnne and a rather unwilling Hannah.

As they reached the door, Hannah said, 'I won't take tea, thank you, sir. I'd like to look in the shop, if you don't mind.'

'Good idea,' agreed Nicholas. He turned to AliceAnne. 'Why don't you take Hannah in and introduce her to Mrs Howard, AliceAnne? You can come and find us in Mrs Penlee's parlour afterwards.'

Sophie caught the look of relief on AliceAnne's face as she turned to go with Hannah, and noticed with pleasure that the little girl took hold of Hannah's hand as completely naturally as she herself had done as a child.

Nicholas led the way into the inn, opening the door to the parlour and calling, 'Maggie, Maggie, we'd like some tea and cakes, please.'

At his call, a grey-haired, motherly woman came into the room, greeting him with a wide smile. 'Ah, Doctor,' she said, 'the kettle's on the hob. I'll be bringing your tea directly.'

'Thank you, Maggie. But first let me introduce you to Miss Sophie Ross, Mr Penvarrow's granddaughter.'

Maggie wiped her hands on her apron and came forward to meet Sophie. 'Mr Penvarrow's granddaughter? You're Miss Mary's daughter!'

Clearly the news of her arrival had reached the village and Sophie agreed that she was.

'Well now!' exclaimed Maggie. 'Very nice to meet you, miss, I'm sure. Miss Mary's daughter! Fancy!' She paused a moment and then added, 'I was sorry to hear that your mother had passed away, miss.' Sophie gave a nod of acknowledgement and she went on, 'She was such a lovely lady. Please accept my condolences.' When Sophie made no reply, Maggie Penlee drew a deep breath and continued. 'So you've come to live at Trescadinnick.'

It wasn't a question but Sophie answered it as one. 'No, Mrs Penlee. I'm just spending a week or so with my grandfather, and then I shall be returning to my home in London.'

Nicholas, apparently feeling that Sophie had had enough of questions, drew out a chair at the table in the bow window and said, 'Have you any muffins, Maggie?'

'Of course I have, Doctor. I know how you like your muffins. I'll just set them to toast and then I'll be in with your tea.' Maggie scurried from the room and Nicholas smiled across at Sophie.

'Sorry about the inquisition,' he said. 'I should have realized. Still, there's one good thing about it. No one else will have to ask you anything about yourself. If Maggie knows something at four o'clock, the rest of the village will know it by five. Won't you sit down, Miss Ross?'

Sophie sighed as she took the offered chair. 'It doesn't really matter. I still find it difficult to speak about Mama sometimes, and I'm not used to having a big family yet. Up until last week I didn't know any of them.'

'Didn't you? How strange.'

'My mother left Trescadinnick to get married in London and...' Sophie said awkwardly, '... and we never saw them.'

'But now you've come to Trescadinnick and have to get to know them all at once,' said

Nicholas sympathetically. 'It can't be easy.'

'No, it isn't,' Sophie found herself admitting. 'My grandfather keeps saying I've come home, but I don't feel that I belong there. And,' she added with determination, 'I don't intend to stay. I agreed with my Aunt Matty to come for just a week or so to visit my grandfather, but then Hannah and I will go back home.' Even as she spoke Sophie wondered why she was telling Nicholas all this. Somehow she found him easy to talk to, and she began to tell him about her mother. He was a good listener and encouraged her to go on talking with occasional comments or questions, and by the time the door opened, bringing in AliceAnne, followed by Maggie with the tea tray, Sophie felt completely at ease with him, as if she had known him for a long time.

Seeing AliceAnne on her own, she said, ' Come in and sit down, AliceAnne. Where's Hannah?'

'Still in the shop, Aunt Sophie,' replied AliceAnne. 'She said she'd wait there till we've had tea. There's lots to look at.'

A scattering of raindrops hit the window as they were finishing their tea and Sophie looked anxiously at the sky.

'Don't worry, Miss Ross,' Nicholas said. 'I'll take you all back to Trescadinnick in the trap. I'm going in that direction anyway,' adding, as she seemed about to refuse, 'It'll be quicker than walking.' He smiled at her so warmly that Sophie, who had indeed been going to turn down his offer, found herself smiling back at him and accepting it. She had never met anyone quite like Nicholas Bryan, never seen such open admiration in any man's eyes as she saw in his, and as he helped her from the table and his hand brushed hers, she knew an unfamiliar tingle of excitement and felt warm colour flood her cheeks.

They went out to the waiting pony and trap, and at once Hannah appeared from the shop. With her was a man of about forty, small but wiry with strong shoulders. His tanned face, that of a man who worked on the land, was topped with an unruly head of dark hair streaked with grey, and his eyes were wide and honest. He smiled at Hannah as they parted and then turned away and disappeared between two houses.

'Who's that?' Sophie asked.

'That's Will Shaw from Home Farm.' It was Nicholas who answered. 'His daughter, Lizzie, works in the kitchen at Trescadinnick.'

'Dr Bryan has kindly offered to drive us home, Hannah,' Sophie said. 'We want to get back before it really starts to rain.'

One by one, Nicholas handed them into the trap and the little party set off at a brisk trot for Trescadinnick. When they arrived at the house, Sophie sent AliceAnne in with Hannah to get dry, while she thanked Nicholas for driving them home.

'It was no trouble,' he assured her. 'I have to visit one of the farms out towards St Morwen anyway.' He paused and then said, 'Perhaps you'd like to come on my rounds with me one day. It would give you a chance to see more of the countryside and to meet some of the people.'

'Well, I don't know...' began Sophie doubtfully.

'You don't have to decide now,' said Nicholas easily. 'But when I'm next passing this way, perhaps I could call in and take you for a drive. I should very much enjoy your company.'

Sophie could feel herself blushing again and said hastily, 'That would be very kind of you, Doctor. I should like to see something of the neighbourhood.'

'Splendid.' His eyes smiled into hers. 'I shall look forward to it. Good afternoon to you, Miss Ross.' He shook her hand, his grasp firm and warm in hers, and then with a wave he stepped up into the trap and drove away.

For a moment Sophie stood in the drizzle and watched him go. She had never met with such a charming man before. How comfortable she had felt with him as they chatted across the teacups in the window of Maggie Penlee's parlour; how easy he had been to talk to, listening and drawing her out in a way no one had ever bothered to do before. How kind he'd been to bring them all home before the rain started in earnest. She could still feel the warmth of his hand in hers as he had said goodbye, and the remembered warmth of his smile gave her a glow of pleasure that she carried with her as she turned and went indoors.

Chapter 9

Dinner that evening was a much easier affair. Matty had arrived soon after Sophie had got home and was to stay the night. Having her at the dinner table made the conversation flow a great deal more easily.

'How was your day?' she'd asked as they sat in the drawing room waiting for Thomas to appear. 'What did you do with yourself?'

Sophie told her about the walk into the village. 'We met Dr Bryan there,' she said, smiling. 'He gave me tea at The Clipper and then, as it was starting to rain, he very kindly drove us home in the trap. If he hadn't been there, we'd have got awfully wet.'

'That was kind of him,' Matty agreed. 'I think he's a good man and a good doctor. He's very conscientious about coming in to see your grandfather. He often just drops in to see how he's doing. The problem is that we can't always get Father to take his advice.'

'What's that? What are you saying?' Thomas had walked into the room and overheard Matty's last remark.

'I was just saying, Father, that Dr Bryan is a good doctor.'

'Always fussing,' muttered her father as he crossed the room to sit by the fire. 'Where's Charles?'

'Just coming, Father,' answered Louisa, who had followed him into the room.

'We're lucky to have him,' Matty said to Sophie. 'Old Dr Marshall died suddenly last year, and we were without a doctor for several months before Dr Bryan came to take his place. Not everyone would want to come to such an out-of-the-way place as Port Felec.'

Before Sophie could ask any more, Charles came into the room, apologizing for keeping everyone waiting. 'I was just saying goodnight to AliceAnne,' he explained, and Sophie found she was surprised. Somehow she couldn't visualize Charles going up to kiss his daughter goodnight. Then she rebuked herself for the thought and wished she'd done the same thing.

'Well, you're here now,' grumbled Thomas as he got to his feet and offered his arm to Sophie, before leading them all into the dining room.

During the meal Charles mentioned that he'd ridden over to one of the outlying farms on the estate. 'John Hever's having trouble finding this quarter's rent,' he said.

'Then we should have him out,' snapped Thomas.

'No, I think not,' returned Charles. 'If we wait he should be able to pay his arrears in the spring, or the summer at the latest. After all, it wasn't his fault that the storm laid waste his crop.'

Thomas opened his mouth to argue, but Sophie, hoping to avert an argument, spoke first. 'I saw you riding out earlier today, Charles,' she said. 'What a beautiful horse you have.'

Louisa glanced across at her father to see how he would react to being interrupted. Surely, her eyes said, he'll slap her down for such rudeness, but Thomas did not. He looked over at Charles and said, 'What did you do about finding a horse for Sophie, Charles?'

'Nothing as yet, sir,' Charles replied. 'I'll look into it tomorrow. Perhaps Will Shaw has a suitable mount at the farm that we can borrow.'

Thomas sniffed. 'Don't want Sophie on any old nag,' he said. 'And you must ride out with her until she gets to know her way around. Make sure she's safe on the horse and knows where she's going.' He gave Charles a meaningful look, but only Charles knew its true significance and his lips tightened.

'I could bring Millie over,' suggested Matty. 'Millie's my horse,

Sophie. She's a brave little mare,' she went on, 'but I hardly ride her any more, and she could do with the exercise.'

'Don't know why you keep her at all,' sniffed Louisa.

'Because I'm fond of her,' replied Matty. 'She'll do very well for Sophie while she's here and if she needs a better mount later on, well, that will be the time to worry about it.'

'She'll do for now,' conceded Thomas.

'What do you think, Charles?' Matty asked. 'Shall I bring her over in the next couple of days?'

'If you have the time, Aunt, I think it would be an excellent idea,' Charles replied, though in fact he was less than delighted. He recognized his grandfather's ulterior motive in suggesting that he should ride with Sophie, realizing that this was a way to throw them together. After the old man's revelation of his plans for the two of them last night, Charles had already decided his own course of action. He was determined to stay well away from Sophie whilst she was in Cornwall, and could only hope that she would remain true to her original plan of returning to London after a short visit to Trescadinnick. The sooner she left, the happier he would be. He glanced across at his mother and saw from her pinched expression that she was unhappy with the idea too, but there was nothing either of them could do.

'That's settled then.' Matty smiled across at Charles. 'I'll bring her over in the next couple of days.'

Everything seemed to have been decided without reference to Sophie, but Sophie was delighted with the outcome. She longed to ride again. There had been no opportunity since her father's death. How exhilarating it would be, she thought, as she imagined herself cantering across the cliff top, the wind in her hair, the sun on her face. She didn't like the idea of Charles having to keep an eye on her, as if she were a child, but once everyone realized that she knew how to handle a horse, she would surely be allowed to ride out on her own.

Charles had not told Louisa what Thomas had said the night before. He didn't know how she would react; if she would also see it as the answer to the inheritance question, or whether she would consider it another example of Sophie's intrusion into the Penvarrow family. Whichever it was, she would put him under pressure. Charles felt sure that Thomas had not yet broached his plan for their marriage to Sophie herself. Looking at her across the table, her auburn hair gleaming in the candlelight, her eyes alight as she talked with Aunt Matty, he recognized the Penvarrow strength of character and knew that she would not simply accept the old man's dictates.

At the end of the meal Thomas announced that he was tired and was going straight to bed, whereupon Louisa and Charles also excused themselves, leaving Matty and Sophie to return to the fire in the drawing room and wait for Mrs Paxton to bring tea and sweetmeats.

'Thank you, Aunt, for the offer of your horse,' Sophie said when they were comfortably seated before the fire. 'It's so long since I've had the chance to ride.'

'I'm only too happy to bring her over,' Matty assured her. 'But your grandfather's right, you shouldn't ride out alone until you're comfortable on her.' She smiled, adding, 'Though I'm sure you'll love her.'

A companionable silence fell between them and then Sophie said, 'Aunt, may I ask you something?'

'Of course, my dear,' replied Matty cheerfully. 'Anything you like.' She looked at Sophie expectantly. 'What do you want to know?'

Now the time had come, Sophie wasn't quite sure how to ask questions about Jocelyn; but, she reasoned, he was her uncle after all, so why shouldn't she ask? It was natural that she should wonder what had happened to him, and she was intrigued by the locked room. So she drew a deep breath and took the plunge. 'Aunt, I hope you don't mind me asking, but what really happened to your brother, Jocelyn, and why is his room locked?'

For a moment Matty didn't answer. She seemed disconcerted by the question. It clearly wasn't one she'd been anticipating. Sophie watched the emotions fleeing across her aunt's face as she waited for her to answer.

At last Matty sighed. 'Jocelyn? After your mother left Trescadinnick my brother, Jocelyn, was the light of my father's life. He was an only son and heir since our elder brother died as a baby. We don't know exactly what happened the night Joss died. For some reason he'd gone to the village one winter's evening, though we never really knew why. Possibly to meet someone? The weather can change very quickly here, you know, and while he was out, a sea mist rolled in. It happens from time to time and when it does it can be very thick. You can't see your hand in front of your face. Joss was coming home from the village along the cliff path and he must have been caught in the mist.'

'But surely he knew his way home, even if it was foggy,' said Sophie.

'In a mist like that you can get very disorientated; a sea mist, it alters everything. It's thick and swirling and you can lose your sense of direction. Landmarks disappear, pathways become invisible. If you get caught in a mist like that, well, you could wander for hours, sometimes simply going round in circles, often going in completely the wrong direction.' She paused, a distant look in her eyes. 'That must have happened to Jocelyn that night. He must have become disorientated... must have walked too close to the cliff edge.'

'And he fell?' whispered Sophie.

'And he fell. The most dreadful, dreadful accident. My father became an old man overnight.'

Sophie shuddered, thinking how close she had gone to the edge of the cliff that very afternoon. Of course it had been a sunny afternoon; she had been in no danger as she'd stood at the top of the steep path that twisted its way to the tiny beach she could see below.

Had that been where Joss had fallen, she wondered, and the thought made her feel slightly sick. How terrifying to feel yourself slip, to clutch at grass, gorse, thin air, as you tumbled through the darkness to be smashed on the rocks below.

'It was a terrible day,' Matty continued. 'Poor Joss. He wasn't missed until next day when Annie the maid brought up the hot water and found that his bed hadn't been slept in. Search parties went out, but they only found his body later in the day. It was still lying where he'd fallen, caught among the rocks. It was a miracle that it was above the tideline and hadn't been washed away.'

Poor Joss! Sophie closed her eyes as if to blot out the imagined sight of a young man lying broken upon the rocks.

Silence fell round them and when it was clear that her aunt would say no more, Sophie said gently, 'How awful it must have been for all of you.' A thought struck her. 'You said my mother came to his funeral.'

'Yes, I still had an address for her then, and I wrote and told her.' There was a break in Matty's voice as she went on. 'That was the last time I saw her, at Joss's funeral. The last time any of us saw her.'

'His room was next to yours, wasn't it? The room I'm in now?'

'Yes.'

'And now it's all locked up. AliceAnne told me it's never opened. Why's that, Aunt?'

For the first time Sophie saw a flash of hostility in her aunt's eyes.

'I'm not sure that's any of your business, Sophie,' Matty said. 'But if you must know, my father had it sealed off the day Jocelyn was... found. No one has entered it since.' She gave Sophie a sharp look, adding, 'And nobody will.'

'No, Aunt Matty,' Sophie said hastily. 'Thank you for telling me. I just...' She paused to find the right words. 'I just wanted to know, so that I didn't say the wrong thing to my grandfather.'

Matty's face softened and she smiled. 'Don't worry about it, Sophie. What happened to Jocelyn, happened twenty-five years ago. We miss him, of course, but he's never, never,' she fixed Sophie with a penetrating look as she repeated the word 'never', 'mentioned in front of your grandfather.'

Sophie returned her look and replied, 'I understand, Aunt.'

Matty smiled at her and said, 'Of course you do, my dear.' Making it clear that the conversation was over, Matty got to her feet and said, 'Well, I'm off to my bed. Sleep tight, my dear, and don't dwell on the past. It's all so long ago. It's the future that matters now.'

Carrying her candle up to bed, Sophie paused for a moment outside the door of the room next to hers. Twenty-five years, she thought. That door has not been opened for twenty-five years, and the memories of poor Jocelyn are locked away behind it. Shut away and forgotten. When will someone open that door and let him out? Who will look at his things and remember him with love? Poor Jocelyn.

Sophie got ready for bed and then lay watching the candle alight on the dresser, its flickering flame reflected in the mirror. What a day it's been, Sophie thought. How much I've seen and done in such a short time.

She considered each of her new family. Grandfather Thomas, still its autocratic head, trying to deny his advancing years. She could see how much it frustrated him occasionally to accept help from other people. Next, there was Aunt Louisa, who clearly resented her arrival at Trescadinnick, though Sophie wasn't quite sure why she should. Had she disliked her mother? Or envied her? And then there was Charles, reserved and cold. He treated her with punctilious courtesy, but there had certainly been no warmth in his welcome either. None of the adults seemed to have any time for poor little AliceAnne. What a lonely life the child must lead. True, Charles had been up to say goodnight to her this evening, but was that usual? Sophie wondered. And last was Aunt Matty, seemingly always bright and cheerful. She didn't live in the house, of course, but she came and went as she always had. Was that why there was obvious resentment between her and Louisa?

Ah well, Sophie thought as she snuffed the candle and climbed back into bed, I suppose I'll get to know them all better in the next few days.

Warmed by the fire that Hannah had banked up before she left the room, Sophie drew the bedclothes up to her chin and with a sigh, drifted off into sleep.

Chapter 10

The next morning, when Sophie awoke, the view from her window could not have been more different from that of the previous day. She threw back the curtains to be greeted with a blanket of white. Gone was the walled garden, the spreading cliff top and the polished gleam of the sea. All was shrouded in dense, grey, shifting mist, smothering the land, the sea and the sky in thick, drifting fog. Sophie stared out at the colourless day beyond the window and with a jolt, realized that this was the mist Matty had been describing the night before. It must have been a mist like this that had descended on Joss the night he died. Until this instant, Sophie had not been able to accept that someone who'd lived here all his life, and knew the countryside like the back of his hand, could have got lost simply because it was foggy. But now she realized it would have been all too easy to become disorientated, as Matty had suggested. Sophie shuddered at the thought and having poked the fire back into life, she went back to the warmth of her bed and waited for Hannah to bring her morning tea.

Moments later Hannah was coming in with a tea tray, saying, 'This is a gloomy place, Miss Sophie, and no mistake.'

'It certainly is grey outside, Hannah,' Sophie agreed. 'But it's no worse than a London fog really, is it? So,' she went on, 'unless it suddenly clears, it'll be an indoors day today. Still, I'm sure there'll be plenty to do.' She sipped her tea and smiled at Hannah's long face. 'Cheer up, Hannah, it won't be long before we go back to our own London fog, and you can feel more comfortable.'

'Now then, Miss Sophie, there's no call for such talk as that,' Hannah replied placidly. 'It might be a day when you could help Miss AliceAnne with her schooling.'

'That's an excellent idea, Hannah,' Sophie cried. She set down her teacup and swung her legs out of bed. 'Can you bring my hot water, please, and then I'll get dressed. I was late for breakfast yesterday; I'd better not be so again today.'

It was only half an hour later that Sophie went downstairs to start her day. As she reached the hall, Charles was leaving the morning room and walking across the hall to his study.

'Good morning, Charles,' smiled Sophie. 'Am I late again?'

'Not at all, Sophie,' he replied. 'Aunt Matty and my mother are still at table with AliceAnne.' Then, with a brief nod, he went into the room that AliceAnne had told Sophie was his study, and closed the door behind him. Sophie shrugged. He hadn't been rude, but there was no warmth in his greeting.

Oh well, she thought, if that's how he feels, there's nothing I can do about it. When she opened the morning-room door, she found AliceAnne about to leave the table. Louisa and Matty looked up as she came in.

'Good morning, Aunt Louisa, Aunt Matty,' Sophie said. 'Good morning, AliceAnne.'

'Good morning, Sophie,' said Aunt Matty with a smile. 'Did you sleep well?'

'Yes, thank you,' Sophie replied, but before she could say more Louisa got to her feet and said, 'If you'll excuse me, I have to see Mrs Paxton. AliceAnne, go up to the schoolroom and make a start on the sums I've left written out for you there. I'll be up in a little while to see how you're getting on.'

'Yes, Grandmama,' whispered AliceAnne and scurried out of the room.

As Louisa moved to follow her, Sophie said, 'Would it be useful, Aunt, if I went up to the schoolroom and helped AliceAnne?'

Louisa looked at her in surprise. 'Do you want to? The child is perfectly able to get on by herself, and you'll have your grandfather to consider. He should be your priority.'

'Oh, you don't need to worry about him this morning,' Matty said, suddenly joining in the conversation. 'I'll go to him this morning.'

'Won't you be going home?' said Louisa pointedly. 'I thought you were leaving this morning.'

'My dear Louisa, anxious as you are to get rid of me, even you can't expect me to get Paxton to drive me home in weather like this.' She shook her head. 'No, I shan't go home until this lifts, so I'm quite happy to spend the morning with my father, and that'll give Sophie a chance to get to know AliceAnne.'

Louisa compressed her lips and with a sharp 'As you will!' left the room.

'I think it will do AliceAnne good to have someone to take an interest in what she's doing,' Matty said. 'She gets little enough attention in this house. Why don't you go up and see her when you've had your breakfast?'

Sophie did as Matty suggested, climbing the stairs to the day nursery as soon as she'd finished eating. AliceAnne was sitting at the table in the window with a sheet of paper in front of her. She was sucking the end of a pencil and looked up anxiously when Sophie came in. When she saw who it was, her whole body relaxed, though she still looked anxious.

'Hallo,' said Sophie. 'I thought I'd come and see how you were getting on. Your grandmama is busy with Mrs Paxton just now, but I expect she'll be up later.' She crossed the room and sat down at the table opposite the little girl. One glance at the paper showed that she had done none of the sums that had been set out for her.

'What sums are you doing?' Sophie asked.

'Take away,' AliceAnne whispered.

'Are you stuck?'

'A bit. I know how to do take away, but these ones are all wrong. You can't take eight from nothing, can you? So how do you do it?'

'Let me help,' Sophie said, and moved round to sit next to her. 'Now, the sum says ninety take away seventy-eight. Which is bigger?'

'Ninety, of course,' said AliceAnne.

'Right, so you know that you can take seventy-eight away from ninety and have something over. I mean, if you had ninety bullseyes, you could eat seventy-eight and still have some over.'

'I'd be sick,' AliceAnne said solemnly and they both laughed.

'You certainly would,' said Sophie. 'But if you want to know how many you'd have over, you can set it out as a sum, like these,' she pointed to the sums Louisa had written on the paper, 'and work it out. Let me show you how.'

Together they worked through the sums that had been set and by the time they reached the end of the page, AliceAnne was able to work them out on her own. Sophie watched her as she completed the page. Hadn't Louisa shown AliceAnne how to do subtraction when it required borrowing?

When the little girl had finished, Sophie checked that she'd got them right and then said, 'What would you like to do now?'

AliceAnne gave the question some thought and then said, 'Reading.' She chose a book from the bookshelf. 'It's a bit difficult to read,' she said, 'but I like the pictures.'

'How about if we read it together?' suggested Sophie. 'I'll read a page and then you read one.'

'Not all by myself?'

'More fun to do it together, don't you think?'

AliceAnne nodded enthusiastically. 'You start,' she said.

When Louisa came upstairs a little later she was surprised to find Sophie and AliceAnne sitting on the window seat, their heads bent over a book. 'AliceAnne! You're supposed to be doing arithmetic,' she said. 'What about the sums I left you?'

'Please, Grandmama, I've done them.'

'What? All of them?'

'Yes, Grandmama.' AliceAnne picked up the paper from the table and handed it to Louisa. She glanced through it and then, turning to Sophie, said, 'Did you do them for her?'

'No, certainly not,' Sophie replied. 'Once I'd shown her how to do them, she did them all by herself. She's a clever girl and soon got the hang of them.'

Louisa nodded and said, 'Well, that's good, AliceAnne. Now run along downstairs and have your milk. Mrs Paxton's in the kitchen.' AliceAnne made for the door, only to be halted again.

'Don't forget to thank your Aunt Sophie for her help.'

'Thank you, Aunt Sophie,' came the dutiful reply, before AliceAnne disappeared down to the kitchen for her milk and a slice of cake.

Sophie got to her feet. 'I think I'll go down and sort out some music now,' she said. 'I want to practise something to play for my grandfather after dinner.'

'He doesn't always come down for dinner,' Louisa said, her lip curling. *She* knew what Sophie was up to, trying to curry favour with her grandfather in the hope he'd change his will and she would inherit Trescadinnick.

'Well,' Sophie said, aware of Louisa's hostility but unable to account for it, 'I shall enjoy practising anyway.' With that, she left her aunt in the nursery and went back downstairs to the drawing room.

The room was cold and dull, with only grey light filtering through the windows, so Sophie lit the lamp and carried it over to the piano. She found the music Thomas had mentioned and there was plenty of it, some stored in the large piano stool, some in a large polished wooden chest that stood to one side. She lifted out the sheets, and was soon engrossed in what she found. Some pieces she knew well, others she'd heard but never tried to play, and yet more were entirely new to her. Selecting several of her favourites, she sat down and began running her fingers over the keys. The piano still needed tuning, but that didn't spoil her enjoyment. For some time she was immersed in the music, but gradually she became aware that she wasn't alone in the room, and turning she found AliceAnne standing awkwardly by the door.

'AliceAnne,' she said gently, 'don't stand in the doorway. Come in and listen properly.'

The child didn't move for a moment and then she edged her way into the room, still cautious and uneasy. Sophie held out a hand to her and the little girl crept closer.

'Did you like the music?' Sophie asked.

AliceAnne nodded.

'Shall I play some more?'

AliceAnne nodded again, and edged a little nearer.

Sophie picked out a simple nursery rhyme, a tune that she thought AliceAnne might recognize, and was rewarded with one of AliceAnne's rare smiles.

'Would you like to have a try?' Sophie asked.

AliceAnne glanced anxiously over her shoulder, and then shook her head. 'Grandmama says I'm not to touch.'

'I see,' said Sophie thoughtfully. 'Well, I don't expect she'd mind if I'm with you. You mustn't touch the piano when you're on your own.' She took the child's hand and drew her to her side. 'Now,' she said, 'just press down some of the keys and see what sound they make.'

Tentatively, AliceAnne touched one of the keys.

'That's right,' Sophie said encouragingly, 'and another.'

Half an hour later AliceAnne could, with one careful finger, pick out the tune of the nursery rhyme.

At luncheon, when they were all assembled round the dining table, Sophie turned to Charles and said, 'Charles, if you have no objection, I would like to teach AliceAnne to play the piano.'

'AliceAnne?' He sounded surprised at the suggestion. 'Isn't she a little young for that sort of thing?'

'No, not at all,' Sophie disagreed. 'She's the perfect age, and I think she'd like to learn.'

AliceAnne sat silent, watching her father and awaiting his decision. To her surprise he turned to her and said, 'Would you like to learn, AliceAnne?'

'Yes, please, Papa,' AliceAnne whispered, her eyes bright. 'Oh yes, please.'

Charles shrugged and said to Sophie, 'If you want to spend the time, you may do as you please. I have already sent to Truro for someone to come and tune the piano.'

Sophie was surprised he had remembered, and she thanked

him for his kindness. Charles brushed aside her thanks and excusing himself, disappeared into his office.

'The mist is lifting,' Matty said. 'If you have no need of him this afternoon, Papa, I'll ask Paxton to drive me home.'

Thomas gave a nod of indifference. 'Do as you please.' And rising from the table he went into his library, leaving the three women sitting in awkward silence at the table. Then Louisa got to her feet saying, 'I'll tell Paxton you need him, Matty,' and strode out of the room.

Matty gave Sophie a wry smile and getting to her feet said, 'It sounds as if I'm leaving straight away.'

Ten minutes later Paxton had brought the trap round to the front door and carried out Matty's bag. Sophie followed her aunt outside to say goodbye.

'I'll bring Millie over tomorrow,' Matty promised. 'Or if I can't, I'll get my groom, Timothy, to do so.' She presented a sweet-scented cheek for Sophie to kiss and climbed up into the trap. Paxton shook up the reins and with a wave she was gone.

Sophie turned back into the house, wondering if her grand-father needed her. The house was quiet; there was no sign of AliceAnne. Louisa had disappeared into the kitchen and Sophie felt completely at a loose end. Though the weather was still dull and grey, the mist had lifted and she decided that some fresh air would do her good, and she'd go for a walk.

Collecting her cloak, she wandered out into the garden. She'd had no chance to explore it yesterday and she walked slowly out from the sheltered garden that lay below her bedroom, and turned towards the outbuildings she had seen from her window. The back door of the house opened, as she'd thought, into the stable yard. Beyond that, unseen from the house, was a kitchen garden where Sophie saw an elderly man planting out cabbages.

That must be Davies, she thought as she raised a hand to wave to him. Whether he saw her or not, she received no acknowledgement and so she continued along a path that led through a shrubbery to the wall at the far end of the garden.

Reaching it, she found there was a wooden gate set into the wall, which gave access to the cliff. It was bolted on the inside, but it was only the work of moments to slide the bolts and pull the gate open. The wind that had dispersed the mist had continued to freshen, and as Sophie stepped out from the shelter of the garden onto the cliff top she was buffeted by a blast of cold air that made her clutch her cloak more firmly around her. A rough path led away from the gate, twisting through the coarse grass and scrubby heather, following the contour of the cliff. Sophie paused to look out across the sea, a shifting mass of grey topped with white caps of foam. From here she could see that the path ran all along the cliff edge until it joined another, emerging from the other side of the house; the one she, Hannah and AliceAnne had taken to the village the previous day. It was cold out here in the wind, so Sophie decided she would only walk as far as that and then perhaps return the other way, to the front of the house. That would be enough fresh air for today. She set out, keeping carefully to the pathway. She remembered AliceAnne had said there was a path down to a beach from the end of the garden, and sure enough she saw it almost at once – not a path, but rather a series of rough-hewn steps cut into the rock. Posts had been driven into the ground and attached to these was a rope, offering a handhold to anyone who might choose to descend. Taking hold of the rope, Sophie edged her way down the first few steps. Though little more than a footstep wide, the rocky stairs didn't seem particularly steep. Sophie could hear the pounding of the waves at the foot of the cliffs and, gripping one of the posts, she peered over the edge to see a strip of sand gleaming dully below. Holding tightly to the rope, Sophie made her way downwards. Halfway down, the steps levelled out into a pathway for a few yards before there were more steps leading finally to the beach below. It was rough underfoot, but as she'd realized, nothing like as steep as the path she had seen the day before. When she finally reached the bottom she found herself in a small cove, its strip of beach protected by two arms of rock that jutted out into the sea. The cliff itself had been eroded over time and there was a hollow under an overhang, providing shelter from the prevailing wind. Standing under this arch, Sophie felt a finger of sunshine that had pierced the cloud warm her upturned face. In the summertime it must be a lovely place to come and have a picnic, she thought. It would be sheltered from the wind, and there was even a flattish rock at the side where you'd be able to lay out food, or sit in the sun.

Sophie sat down on it now and looking out across the water, wondered how often her mother had sat in this exact same spot. It was then that she noticed the ring; an iron ring, old and rusty, set into one of the rocks at the foot of the arch. It must be for tying up a boat of some sort, Sophie thought. But who would bring in a boat here? It would have to nose its way through a narrow, rocky passage in from the sea and would be in danger of being holed on the razor-sharp rocks. Smugglers perhaps? But surely they didn't still sneak into such coves to offload their contraband. That was years ago. Who would be bringing a boat in now? It was then that she noticed the waves had begun to encroach on the sand. The tide must be coming in. Quickly she got to her feet and retraced her steps across the little beach to the path leading back up the cliff. As soon as she stepped out from the shelter of the hollow she felt again the wind whipping her cloak and realized how strong it had become. The weak sunshine that had broken through for a few moments had vanished and dark clouds stained the horizon. It was definitely time to leave the cove. She grabbed for the rope and using it to help her climb, began the clamber back up the path. Going up, it seemed much steeper than coming down, and by the time she reached the steps at the top and hauled herself out onto the cliff path, she was flushed and out of breath with exertion. Glancing back out to sea, she could see storm clouds scudding in over the water. With no time to walk her planned route, she turned and hurried back to the gate in the wall, anxious to be indoors before the rain arrived. When she reached the gate she found to her dismay that it was closed and would not open. Someone must have bolted it on the other side. With a cry of frustration, Sophie turned and hurried back along the path to its junction with the path leading to the front of the house. It only took her just over ten minutes to reach the front door, but by then the rain was already falling steadily and when she opened the front door she was greeted by a horrified Louisa.

'Sophie! Where on earth have you been? We've been searching the house for you. Your grandfather is up from his rest and wanted to speak with you.'

Feeling bedraggled and knowing she must look an absolute fright, she pushed her damp hair from her forehead and said, 'I'm sorry, Aunt Louisa, but I got caught in the rain.'

'But where have you been?' demanded her aunt again.

'Nowhere much,' Sophie replied, finding that she did not want to admit going down to the cove on her own. 'I was in the garden, and when I reached the gate to the cliff I went out and walked a little on the cliff path. When it started to rain I went back to the gate, but it had been shut and locked, so I had to come all the way round. By then,' she added ruefully, 'as you can see, it was raining quite hard and I got soaked.'

'Of course the gate was locked,' snapped Louisa. 'We seldom open it and if Davies found it open he would certainly have shut and locked it.' She gave Sophie an exasperated look and said, 'Well, you'd better get dry and changed. There'll be tea in the drawing room directly.'

Feeling like a scolded child, Sophie simply said, 'Yes, Aunt,' and went upstairs to her room.

After tea, at which AliceAnne made a short appearance, Sophie went with her back to the schoolroom where they settled down to play some of the card games Hannah had been teaching the child. Outside, the storm had swept in from the sea and had intensified in fury. The rain continued to fall in torrents and the wind had strengthened, howling round the house and rattling the windows.

'I don't like storms,' AliceAnne said shakily. 'I'm scared. Can we pull the curtains and shut it out?'

'Yes, of course we can,' said Sophie, pulling the drapes across the windows. 'But there's no need to be scared, you know. You're quite safe in here.'

'Not me, Papa.'

'But, AliceAnne, Papa is safe indoors as well.'

'But sometimes the bangs happen and Papa goes out into the storm. I don't like it when he goes. Suppose he doesn't come back!'

'The bangs? What are the bangs?'

'Big bangs. And when they go off, Papa goes running down to the village because it means there's a wreck.'

When Sophie sought elucidation from Charles at dinner later on, he smiled and said, 'She means the maroons. When they see a signal flare from a ship in distress out at sea, they set off a gunpowder charge down on the harbour to summon the lifeboat men. As soon as they hear the bang, they drop whatever they are doing and come running down to Anvil Cove to the boathouse to launch the lifeboat.'

'But you don't go, do you?' asked Sophie in astonishment.

'I go to the harbour, but I'm not one of the regular men, no,' Charles replied. 'There are others far more experienced on the sea than I am, but there have been occasions when someone can't turn out and I've taken his place. Most of the men are local fishermen, but there are several others as well. Will Shaw from the home farm is a regular and Martin Penlee from The Clipper. Fred Polmire, the postman, is another. They all turn out.'

'But where's the lifeboat?' Sophie said. 'I've never seen one in the harbour.'

'You couldn't launch it from the harbour at low tide,' Charles explained. 'It's kept in a stone boathouse at Anvil Cove further round the head. It's a little more sheltered and they can pull it down to the sea on its carriage and launch it from there. This coast is very treacherous, with hidden reefs and rip tides, and very often there's a strong sou'wester, like the one blowing tonight. That can drive a ship seeking shelter from the storm onto a lee shore where she will break her back on the rocks below the cliffs.'

'And the lifeboat goes out to rescue them?'

'Always,' replied Charles. 'If a distress flare is seen, the maroons go off and the lifeboat is launched. There've been too many wrecks on this coast, too many lives lost and men drowned. Once a ship is cast up on the rocks or holed and sinking, the lifeboat is their crew's only chance. We can't save the ship, but we can save the men.'

'There was a time,' Thomas said reminiscently, 'when wreckers used false lights to lure ships onto the rocks during a storm, without any thought for the crew. Then, when the storm had passed, they'd steal what they could from the wreck. Whole villages would go down to the beach to pass goods back from the ship.'

'Indeed, Papa, so they say,' Matty said. 'But that was a hundred years ago. Nothing like that happens today.'

'But now it's the lifeboat that goes out to the rescue,' said Sophie.

'Sometimes several go,' Charles said. 'There are others further north, but it's the Port Felec boat that's launched first on this part of the coast.'

'It's ridiculous that you go, Charles,' said Louisa, entering into the conversation for the first time. 'What do you know about sailing?'

'Enough to be useful, Mama,' returned Charles. 'The coxswain, Joe Fraser, knows I'll take orders like any other hand, and they need a full crew. So, yes, I have been a few times when they've been a man down.'

Listening to the wind still howling round the house, and the clatter of hail on the windows, Sophie shuddered. 'It sounds terrifying. The sea must be so rough. Aren't you afraid?'

'It is,' Charles admitted. 'The waves are enormous and of course I'm afraid. We all are. But once you're out at sea there is so much to be done, you haven't time to think about it.

No wonder AliceAnne is frightened if there's a storm, thought Sophie later, as she lay in bed listening to the continued shrieking of the wind. There had been none of the 'bangs' that had so worried the little girl, but the storm continued unabated. The long curtains drawn across the windows against the darkness, stirred by a draught from somewhere, whispered on their poles. Sophie, seeing this, crept out of bed again to make sure that the windows were tightly shut. But when she pulled the curtains back and looked out into the impenetrable blackness of the night, she found that both were firmly closed and no current of air was coming from there. Intrigued, Sophie closed the curtains again and watched as they began their gentle motion once more. The candle flame was flickering too. She had noticed that as she'd sat in bed, but hadn't linked the two. There was, definitely, a draught coming from somewhere; she could feel it on her bare feet now, but from where? She retreated to the bed, but as she passed the old mahogany armoire she realized that the breath of air was coming from there, from under the wardrobe. Sophie picked up the flickering candle and opened the wardrobe door. There, carefully hung from a rail, or folded onto shelves, were her few clothes. She parted the hanging clothes and peered inside, but there was nothing else to see.

Closing the door again, she stood, staring round the dimly lit room. There was nothing, and yet still Sophie could feel cool air about her feet. Holding her candle high, she moved round the side of the wardrobe, looking at the solid mahogany of which it was made. It had a flared cornice with a decorated wooden top, extending outward in an exuberant flourish. To accommodate this extending sill, the wardrobe stood out an inch or so from the wall and as Sophie approached, she realized this was where the cool air was coming from. She held the candle nearer, put her eye to the gap, and at last discovered the source of the draught. The wardrobe stood, not against a wall as she had assumed, but in front of, and concealing, a door... a connecting door to the next room: to Jocelyn's room. In the dancing light of the candle Sophie could just make out the dark panelling of the door. She tried to slide her fingers into the space between the wall and the back of the wardrobe, but her hand was too big. All she could feel, with the very tips of her fingers, was the edge of the door frame. She went round to the other side of the wardrobe and peered through the tiny gap there, but could see even less. She needed light, and all she had was one feeble candle.

It's no good, she thought in frustration. I can't see anything. I'll have to wait for the morning.

She went back to bed, glad to creep in under the covers, for the fire had died down and the room was getting cold. Once in bed, she blew out the candle and lay listening to the wind moaning round the house, and the distant sound of the waves pounding on the rocks at the foot of the cliff – the rocks where poor Jocelyn's broken body had been found.

And now there was a door; a door from her room into Jocelyn's. When they were all children, her mother, Matty and Jocelyn, they must have wandered at will from one room to the other, the door seldom closed as they played together. Tomorrow, Sophie decided, she would try and move the wardrobe a little and see if the door was locked.

Chapter 11

Sophie wasn't sure why she was so determined to open the door and to look into Jocelyn's room, a room which no one had entered for twenty-five years, but the idea consumed her. Of course she knew that the door was probably locked, that she wouldn't be able to open it, but until that proved to be the case, well, it was an exciting prospect. She would need time, uninterrupted, in her room with enough daylight to see what she was doing; but what reason could she give for retiring to her room during the day?

The sound of Hannah outside her bedroom door brought Sophie sharply away from the wardrobe, so that when Hannah came into the room with the heavy jug of hot water, she was once again at the window, a picture of innocence, looking out over the wind-tossed garden below.

After breakfast Sophie spent an hour with AliceAnne in the schoolroom, before she was summoned to the library to read to her grandfather, and when the gong rang for lunch the rain was still streaming from a leaden sky. As they crossed to the dining room, Sophie heard someone striking notes on the piano in the drawing room and thought for a moment that it might be AliceAnne, but as the child came downstairs at that moment she guessed that the piano tuner must have come. She was delighted and said as much to Charles when he joined them in the dining room.

'I shall look forward to hearing you play,' he replied in his stiff and formal manner.

During the meal, Louisa asked Sophie what she planned to do that afternoon and she replied, 'If you have no need of me, Aunt, I think I may rest in my room for a while and then, if the rain eases, perhaps I'll take a walk to get some fresh air.'

Louisa looked surprised at this. 'Really?'

'Certainly,' Sophie replied, 'and I could take AliceAnne with me if you would like me to.'

'No,' Louisa replied firmly. 'It's too cold and damp for AliceAnne. She has a weak chest and mustn't be allowed out in such weather.'

'In that case, since the piano tuner has been, perhaps AliceAnne would like another piano lesson.' She turned to the little girl sitting beside her. 'Would you like that, AliceAnne?'

'Oh yes, please, Aunt Sophie.'

'Good,' returned Sophie as she left the table. 'I'll come and find you a bit later on.'

Within moments of Sophie reaching her room and closing the door, there was a knock and Hannah entered. 'Now then, Miss Sophie,' she said, standing, hands on hips, just inside the door. 'What's all this about having a rest? Are you ill? Do you have the headache?'

'No, no, Hannah,' Sophie assured her. 'I'm not ill. I'm fine. It's just that I didn't sleep very well last night, with the storm raging outside, you know, so I thought, as it's still raining, I'd have half an hour on my bed.'

Hannah, unconvinced, looked at her suspiciously. 'Well,' she said, 'if you're sure...'

'I am sure,' Sophie said again. 'I'll be down again in a little while, really. I've promised AliceAnne.'

Hannah gave her a nod. 'I'll leave you to sleep then.'

When Hannah's footsteps had faded down the stairs, Sophie got off the bed and turned the key in her bedroom door. At least no one could walk in unannounced and surprise her and if Hannah came back, well, she'd say she locked the door so that AliceAnne wouldn't come and disturb her. Now, finally, she could turn her attention to the wardrobe.

The old armoire was heavy. Sophie had known it would be, but by bracing herself against the wall, she was able to edge it a little way forward, just enough at least to slide her hand in behind. The sound of it scraping across the wooden floorboards seemed incredibly loud, and for several anxious moments Sophie waited, but hearing no one coming to investigate, she turned again to the wardrobe. The draught she'd noticed during the night was still in evidence, definitely coming from under the connecting door, though perhaps less strongly now that the wind had dropped somewhat.

Sophie pressed herself against the wall, her cheek against the faded wallpaper, and extended her arm into the gap. She could feel the smooth wood of the door panels now, but still couldn't reach the handle. Cobwebs curtained the space between wardrobe and door, and a grey sticky web was clinging to her hand when she withdrew it.

I have to move this thing further, she thought, pulling at the cobwebs that filmed her skin. I have to ease it out far enough for me to get in behind.

Once again she strained at the heavy piece of furniture, and was gradually able to inch one end further away from the door. Picking up a towel from the dresser rail, she wrapped it round her arm and, using it as a makeshift duster, she cleared most of the cobwebs away. Tossing the now dirty towel aside, she turned sideways and edged into the space she'd made. She was squashed between the wardrobe and the door, her cheek against its smooth wood, but at last she could take a firm grip on its handle. The handle was stiff but, exerting all her strength, she managed to turn it. The door remained stubbornly closed. It was locked.

Well, thought Sophie, ruefully, I suppose I knew it would be.

Bending down, she tried to put her eye to the keyhole, but she couldn't bend low enough in the confined space to reach it. Determined that all her effort should not be wasted, she put her hands flat against the wall and with her back against the wardrobe, strained with all her might to lever it further away. At first she thought she wasn't going to be able to shift it, but then suddenly, with an ominous creak, it slid another few inches from the wall. For one dreadful moment Sophie thought it was going to topple over. But although it shuddered a little and its door swung open with a crash, allowing some of her clothes to tumble out onto the floor, it remained upright.

At last, there was enough room and, heedless of whether anyone might have heard the noise, Sophie turned back to the door and bent over, placing an eye to the keyhole. A breath of air escaping through the hole made her blink, but when she applied her eye a second time, she found she could see daylight. There was no key in the other side, nothing to block the narrow view she now had of the room.

A chair, she could see a chair, and... was that part of a desk? The corner of a bedstead? A finger of pale sunlight struck the back of the chair, and she could see that it was covered in a thick film of dust. The dust, she thought, of twenty-five years.

She was brought sharply back to the present by a rap on the door, and the sound of Hannah's voice on the landing. 'Miss Sophie? Are you all right, Miss Sophie? I've brought you some tea.'

Tea? Whatever time was it? Sophie glanced at the little watch pinned to her bodice and saw with amazement that an hour had passed since she'd come upstairs. She'd been so determined to get to the door she'd been entirely unaware of the passage of time.

'Just a minute, Hannah,' she said, and looked round the room in dismay. There was no way she could move the wardrobe back against the wall without a great deal of effort; her disgorged clothes lay on the floor and the cobwebbed towel hung on the back of a chair. A glance in the mirror showed her that she was as be-cobwebbed as the towel. Grey strands lay across her hair and her face was streaked and grubby. No, there was no way of hiding what she'd been doing from Hannah; she'd just have to take her into her confidence.

Reluctantly, Sophie crossed the room and opened the door. Hannah was outside on the landing, a tea tray in her hands. When she saw the state Sophie was in, Hannah nearly dropped the tray.

'Come in quickly,' Sophie hissed, and as Hannah came into the room, Sophie hurriedly closed the door behind her and turned the key.

Hannah put the tray down on the dresser and said, 'What on earth have you been doing, Miss Sophie?' She ran her eyes over the wardrobe, its open door, the clothes on the floor. 'No resting, and that's a fact! I knew you was up to something when you said you wanted a nap. You! Resting in the afternoon... in broad daylight? Never, I said, or my name's not Hannah Butts.'

'Yes, and you were right,' conceded Sophie with a rueful smile. 'But if I tell you what I've been doing, you mustn't say anything about it downstairs. Promise?'

'Well...' began Hannah cautiously.

'Come on, Hannah,' pleaded Sophie. 'I want to tell you all about it.'

'Well, if you say so, Miss Sophie—'

'I do, Hannah. Look, I've found a door. Behind the wardrobe. A connecting door to the next room. That was Jocelyn's room.'

'Yes,' Hannah said. 'But what are you doing?'

'My grandfather had the room closed up when Jocelyn died. Aunt Matty says that no one has been into it in twenty-five years.' She looked a little sheepishly at Hannah and said, 'I just wanted to see into it, that's all. I found the door by accident. But when I had found it, well, I just wondered if it was unlocked.'

'Miss Sophie, you should be ashamed of yourself,' said Hannah hotly. 'What right have you to go poking your nose into things what don't concern you?'

'I wasn't poking my nose in, Hannah,' snapped Sophie, angry that Hannah should have pricked her conscience. For a moment they confronted each other across the heap of clothes on the floor, and then Sophie continued more calmly. 'I'm not being nosey, Hannah. I'm interested, that's all. Jocelyn was my mother's brother, my uncle. Why has he been shut up here for twenty-five years? Why is he never mentioned? What did he do wrong?'

'It's just your grandfather doesn't want to have sad memories of losing his son,' responded Hannah gently. 'It makes him sad to think of his son dying so young. Talking about him would open old wounds.'

'But he talks about my grandmother, and she's dead,' Sophie pointed out. 'No, Hannah, I'm sure there's something more to it than that. He's cut Jocelyn off. It's what he does when someone has angered him, or gone against his wishes. He cuts them off... just like he did with Mama.' She glanced at the wardrobe, still at an angle to the wall, its door hanging open. 'But, anyway, I can't get into Jocelyn's room, because this door's locked too.'

'Did you really think it wouldn't be?' asked Hannah as she began picking up the clothes from the floor and hanging them up again.

'No, not really, I suppose,' replied Sophie. 'But I thought it was worth a try.'

Hannah was now complicit in Sophie's exploration and together they eased the old armoire back against its wall, concealing again the door behind it. Then, as she drank the tea Hannah had brought, Sophie suffered Hannah to brush out her hair again, so that when she descended the stairs half an hour later there was no sign of the cobwebs that had so lately turned it a premature grey.

The drizzling rain had stopped at last, giving way to occasional shafts of watery sun, and Sophie decided to take a walk to the village. AliceAnne was nowhere to be seen, and so Sophie set off across the cliff path by herself. She had no particular aim in her walk; she just needed to get out of the house and stretch her legs. It was still windy, but the gusts were now scurrying the clouds across the sky, ragged wisps of white against the sombre grey. With the wind in her face Sophie strode out, following the path to the cliff edge. Once again she saw the tops of little paths that disappeared down the cliff face to coves below, but with the wind buffeting her, she had more sense than to try and clamber down a path that was probably both steep and slippery. It had been hard enough yesterday when there were steps and a rope to help her. Pausing at the top of one such, she leaned over as far as she dared, to look down on the beach below. She could see a curve of sand, gleaming dully in the afternoon light, embraced by two rocky arms stretching out into the sea, very similar to the one she had explored the previous afternoon. The grey sea, its waves white-capped, pounded the vicious black rocks, exploding with spray and sending fountains of spume up high into the air. Some of the spindrift was carried on the wind, and Sophie found that she was getting wet, even this high above the breaking waves. The cliff itself had been undercut by the weather, and the thick grasses which overhung the eroded edge thrashed in the gusty wind.

Was it this path? Sophie wondered. Was it here that Jocelyn fell to his death? Had he, disorientated by the swirling sea mist, stepped on the unsupported grass and tumbled, flailing, to the rocks below?

Sophie shuddered at the horrible death he had suffered and stepped hurriedly back onto the pathway, well away from the cliff edge.

It was a relief to reach the steps leading down into Port Felec. Here it was a little more sheltered, and she had less of a struggle against the wind. She followed the narrow street down to the quay and stood for a moment on Fore Street, looking out at the low-tide expanse of muddy shingle enclosed by the harbour wall. Small boats lay canted on their sides, waiting to be refloated by the rising tide, and one or two larger fishing vessels were tied up along the outer side of the harbour wall where the water was deeper. So much of life in Port Felec depends on the sea, Sophie thought.

Across the square she could see lights beginning to flicker in the windows of The Clipper; the evening was closing in. Sophie knew she ought to be going back home, and so she turned her steps to the road that led back out of the village. She had no wish to take the cliff path again today. As she climbed the steep hill that led up towards Trescadinnick, she paused to catch her breath and, turning back, looked down once more on the little village below. The church stood in solid, grey darkness as the twilight closed in around it, but there was a light shining out through one of the windows of the Parsonage.

I wonder what the rector's like, Sophie thought. Is he an old man? Hannah had said that he was a widower, looked after by his daughter, Sandra. Had he been the incumbent when her mother and Jocelyn were still at Trescadinnick, she wondered. Had he known them? Was Jocelyn buried in the little churchyard that surrounded the church and looked out over the sea?

Tomorrow, I'll come again, Sophie thought. I'll go into the church and I'll look in the churchyard; see if I can find Jocelyn's grave.

When she finally got back to Trescadinnick there was still an hour before she needed to dress for dinner. She could hear AliceAnne's voice in the kitchen with Hannah and so Sophie went back into the drawing room to practise the piece she intended to play for her grandfather this evening. The fire had been lit, and a lamp stood on the corner of the piano. Almost, she thought, as though someone had been expecting her to come in and play. She lit the candles in the sconces attached to the piano itself and sat down. She looked through the sheets waiting for her on the stand and then, flexing her fingers, started to play. This time it was not AliceAnne who interrupted her, but Charles.

'You are an accomplished pianist, cousin.' Despite their agreement to dispense with 'cousin' and address each other by their Christian names, Charles seldom did so. It was, he decided, another way to keep her at arm's length. Sophie had noticed, but she shrugged it off. She had made the suggestion as an offer of friendship. If he didn't want to take it, it was no skin off her nose. She'd be returning home soon and could forget all about his antipathy.

Now he spoke from just behind her and, unaware that he'd come into the room, Sophie jerked her hands away from the keys, startled.

'I'm sorry, cousin,' he apologized. 'I didn't mean to make you jump.'

'It's all right,' replied Sophie, turning from the keyboard. 'I didn't hear you come in. Have you been there long?'

'Long enough,' Charles said with a smile. 'You really do play beautifully.'

Sophie smiled back at him, amazed at the way his smile swept years from his face, lighting his eyes and transforming his normal gravity of expression to one of attractive animation. 'Thank you, Charles,' was all she could think of to say.

'Will you really be able to teach AliceAnne to play?' he asked, as she rested her hands once more on the keys.

'Certainly,' Sophie told him, 'provided she wants to learn. Just a short time each day, so that she doesn't get bored. I think,' she added with a speaking glance at him, 'that any individual attention she gets will do her good.'

The smile faded from Charles's eyes, but he didn't look angry. 'I expect you're right,' he sighed. 'But I have to rely on my mother for her schooling. I haven't time to teach her, and there's been no one else.'

'Charles,' Sophie took her courage in both hands, 'she needs other children to play with.'

'There are none suitable,' replied Charles flatly.

'There must be some, somewhere around. What about the Parsonage?'

'Dr Phineas Osell is a widower, and Miss Sandra Osell is unmarried.'

'What about the people who live in that house just above the village?' suggested Sophie. 'Surely they'd be the right sort of people for her to mix with.'

'So they might be,' acknowledged Charles. 'But their children are older, and we have no contact with them,' adding by way of further explanation, 'My grandfather does not know them.'

'You must have a very small circle of friends, Charles,' said Sophie, adding almost without thinking, 'You must be as lonely as poor AliceAnne.'

Charles stiffened and Sophie recognized at once that she'd spoken too freely.

'I'm perfectly happy with my life, thank you, cousin,' he said stiffly, 'and I think you can trust me to look after my own daughter's best interests.' With this he turned away, saying, 'It's time I dressed for dinner.'

Sophie remained at the piano for several minutes after he'd gone, feeling suddenly dispirited. She had, for a fleeting instant, seen another Charles, hidden beneath his formal, outward self. She'd had a glimpse of his rare smile, and suddenly she knew she wanted to see it again. There had been a brief moment of harmony, a moment when they'd been completely at ease in each other's company.

But now I've spoiled things by seeming to criticize how he's bringing up AliceAnne, thought Sophie gloomily. 'But I'm right,' she announced to the empty drawing room as she rose to go upstairs. 'AliceAnne needs children of her own age to play with, or she'll grow up as dour as her father.'

Thomas did not leave his bed next morning and Sophie spent the first part of the day with her grandfather. Paxton had collected the newspaper and it was while she was reading this to him that the doctor arrived. Louisa brought him up to the bedroom where Thomas was still lying in bed.

'Dr Bryan's here, Father,' she said, and when she saw the look of annoyance on her father's face she added sharply, 'I didn't send for him, Father. He simply decided to call.' It was clear to Sophie that Louisa was no more pleased to see the doctor than Thomas was. Louisa stood aside and Nicholas Bryan came into the room, a broad smile on his handsome face.

'Good morning, sir,' he cried before Thomas could speak. 'And how do I find you this morning?' Not waiting for a reply, he turned to Sophie and continued, 'Good morning, Miss Ross, what a beautiful day. Such a change from yesterday.'

'What have you come for?' grumbled Thomas. 'I'm not ill.'

'No, indeed,' agreed Nicholas cordially, 'and that's the way we want to keep it. But you were ill, you know, sir, so I just want to keep an eye on you and make sure there's no relapse.' He glanced meaningfully at Sophie and Louisa, saying, 'So, if you would excuse us, ladies?'

Louisa nodded and turned for the door. 'Come, Sophie,' she said. 'We must let the doctor make his examination.'

'But come back, Sophie, when he's gone,' instructed her grandfather. There was a slightly wavering note in the old man's voice and Sophie smiled at him reassuringly. 'Of course I will, Grandpapa. I'll be waiting downstairs.'

'I don't like the way that young man arrives uninvited and unannounced,' muttered Louisa once they were out of the room.

'But surely, Aunt, he has my grandfather's best interests at heart,' said Sophie.

'Has he?' replied Louisa. 'Or is it that the more he visits, the higher his bill?'

Sophie was shocked. 'How can you think so?' she asked. 'Truly, Aunt Louisa, I think you must be mistaken in him.'

'We shall see.' Louisa sniffed, and walked through to the kitchen, leaving Sophie standing in the hall.

Sophie turned to the drawing room, intending to play the piano until Dr Bryan left. But as she reached the door, she heard a scuffle behind her, and once again saw AliceAnne emerging from under the chenille cloth on the hall table. The sight of the little girl creeping out from her hiding-place made her smile and she said, 'AliceAnne, what are you doing under there?'

'Hiding,' whispered AliceAnne, glancing anxiously around her.

'Hiding? Who from?'

'From the doctor.'

'From the doctor?' Sophie cocked her head. 'Why would you hide from the doctor?'

'Because I don't like him.'

'I see.' Sophie didn't see, but she thought there was no point in continuing this particular conversation. Perhaps Dr Bryan had attended the little girl and given her some foul-tasting medicine. It would be enough to frighten a child of her age. Sophie decided to try and turn the child's mind in a different direction.

'Would you like to begin your piano lessons, AliceAnne?' she suggested. She was rewarded with a dazzling smile, like the sun breaking through on a cloudy day; a smile reminiscent of the one Sophie had seen on AliceAnne's father's face the previous afternoon.

What a difference a smile can make, she thought, as she led the way into the drawing room. She threw back the heavy curtains and sunlight flooded into the room. Dr Bryan had been right when he said it was a beautiful day.

She seated AliceAnne at the piano and pulling up a chair beside her, began to explain the keys. AliceAnne was a good pupil and keen to learn, and they spent the next twenty minutes or so, heads together, bent over the keyboard.

'What an enchanting picture,' came a voice from the door, and they both jerked round to see the doctor standing, framed in the doorway. 'Is your pupil a diligent one, Miss Ross?'

Sophie felt AliceAnne shrink against her, as she replied easily, 'Indeed she is, sir.'

'I was wondering, Miss Ross, as it's such a beautiful day, whether you might like to accompany me on my rounds this afternoon. I know your grandfather requires you this morning, but I have to go out to Tremose this afternoon, to visit an elderly patient, and I wondered if you'd care to come with me? It would give you a chance to see something of the country hereabouts.'

Sophie got to her feet, and taking a firm hold on AliceAnne's hand said, 'That's a very kind invitation, Dr Bryan, and one I'd love to accept, if my grandfather has no objection.' She looked down at the little girl at her side and said, 'And perhaps AliceAnne would like to come too.'

A fleeting look of annoyance crossed the doctor's face, but his smile returned immediately and he said, 'What a good idea.' He glanced at AliceAnne and said, 'Some fresh air will do you the world of good, young lady.'

AliceAnne said nothing, but she slipped her hand out of Sophie's and darted away down the passage to the safe familiarity of Mrs Paxton's kitchen.

'I shall look forward to our outing this afternoon, Dr Bryan,' Sophie said, as she offered him her hand in farewell.

'I too, Miss Ross,' he replied with a smile, 'or may I presume to call you Sophie? I hope we shall become great friends.'

Sophie felt the colour rise in her cheeks. 'If... if you wish, Dr Bryan.'

'And you must call me Nicholas.'

'Nicholas,' she repeated dutifully.

Together they went outside and as they stood by the doctor's gig in the bright winter sun, a man trotted up, with another horse on a leading rein. As he dismounted, Paxton appeared round the house and greeted him.

'Morning, Timothy. You brought the mare then.'

'Aye,' agreed Timothy. 'Brought Millie over for Miss Sophie.'

Sophie looked in delight at the small bay mare standing quietly in the sun. She was saddled and bridled, and as Paxton took her head to lead her away, Charles emerged from the house.

'Timothy,' he said, 'good morning. My aunt is not coming?'

'No, sir,' replied Timothy, touching his cap as he spoke. 'She sent her regards, sir, and says she'll be over in a day or two, but she wanted Miss Sophie to have the mare straight away.'

'Take her round to the stable,' Charles said to Paxton, 'and ask Ned to have her ready this afternoon at three.' He turned to Sophie. 'I trust that will suit you, cousin, to ride with me this afternoon.'

'Oh yes, please, Charles,' cried Sophie, and then with sudden remembrance of the doctor's invitation, said, 'Oh, that is, Dr Bryan has offered to take me and AliceAnne out with him, this afternoon. Perhaps we could postpone our ride until tomorrow?' And as she saw Charles's face harden, she repeated Nicholas's remark. 'It will do AliceAnne good to have some fresh air on such a lovely day.'

'Whatever suits you, cousin,' came the tight-lipped reply, and with that Charles turned on his heel and went back into the house. At the door he almost bumped into Louisa, who was coming out to find Sophie.

'Sophie, your grandfather wants you,' she announced abruptly, and then she too went back inside.

Sophie gave an apologetic smile to the doctor. 'I'm sorry... Nicholas.' She hesitated over the use of his Christian name. 'But I'm needed indoors.' She extended her hand again and he gripped it in his own.

'Don't worry, Sophie,' he said, smiling as always. 'I'll look forward to your company this afternoon. Yours and AliceAnne's,' he amended. And climbing up into his gig, he waved a hand and drove away.

When Sophie went back into the house there was no one to be seen. All was quiet, and so she went straight upstairs to her grandfather's bedroom and knocked on the door.

When the old man called her in, she went to his bedside. 'Do you want me to go on with the newspapers, Grandpapa?' she asked.

'No,' he replied. 'I want to talk to you. Sit down.'

Sophie resumed her seat by his bed, and with an enquiring look on her face, waited.

'I'm an old man,' he began, 'and I may not have long to live.'

'Oh, sir,' Sophie interposed, leaning forward to take his hand. 'You're getting well again. The doctor just said so.'

'Don't interrupt, girl,' snapped Thomas, pulling his hand away. 'Just listen to what I have to say.'

Sophie drew back and folding her hands in her lap, waited.

'I'm an old man, and I may not have long to live,' he repeated. 'I've sent a message to my lawyer in Truro and he'll be coming out to see me in a few days' time, so that I can make a new will.' Thomas looked at Sophie now, as if to see the effect his words were having on her, but Sophie, whilst dreading what he was going to say next, managed to keep her expression one of polite interest.

'I've decided to make you my heir,' he said. 'You will inherit Trescadinnick and its estate. It will be your home from now on, and when I die it will all be yours.'

Now Sophie could no longer maintain the polite interest. 'But, Grandfather,' she burst out, 'that's not fair!'

'What do you mean, girl?' he demanded angrily. 'Don't be ridiculous.'

'I mean,' stated Sophie, 'that you should be leaving everything to Charles. He's the one who's grown up here. He's the one who has kept the estate together. He's the one who's worked so hard for Trescadinnick. It should all go to him.'

Thomas's face stiffened at her outburst. 'Charles is not

family,' he retorted. 'He knows what I'm planning to do, and he knows why.'

'But you're wrong,' insisted Sophie angrily. 'It's wrong to cut him out like this.'

'That's enough!' roared her grandfather. 'I won't be spoken to like that by a chit of a girl. How dare you, miss? How dare you! My own granddaughter!'

'I wasn't even acknowledged as your granddaughter until a few weeks ago,' snapped Sophie, determined to remain uncowed by his anger. 'You disowned my mother. You can disown me and I'll go back to London and make my own way in the world. Do you think I want Trescadinnick? No, I don't. I'm not part of it and it's not part of me.'

Thomas stared at her for a moment and then broke into a harsh laugh. 'You'll do,' he said. 'Whoever your father was, you're a true Penvarrow. Now, go and tell Paxton I need him. I'm getting up.'

It was Sophie's turn to stare. Her anger still boiled inside her, and here she was being dismissed as if nothing had happened, as if there had been no disagreement, no argument. She stood up, and with a defiant lift of her chin said, 'Dr Bryan is taking me and AliceAnne out this afternoon. He has to visit a patient at Tremose, and we're going with him.' She had planned to mention the invitation at luncheon, and gain her grandfather's approval for the excursion, but now she simply announced that she was going, and even if he forbade her, she knew she would go anyway. Perhaps Thomas knew it too, for he simply said, 'I'm sure the outing will do you both good.'

Sophie sent Paxton upstairs and then returned to the piano. As always, the music cascading from the keys began to work its magic. When Charles paused in the hallway, listening to her playing, he thought of his wife, Anne, the last person to conjure music from that piano. In the six years since her death he had learned to live without her. Her face had receded to the depths of his memory, and though he had loved her, the hurt left by her death had dulled, so that now it was no more than a faint ache.

He looked through the door, watching Sophie's graceful movements as her hands flew over the keys, and he was jolted with
the recognition of an all but forgotten emotion. Young as she
was, more than ten years his junior, the sight of her at the piano,
concentration on her lovely face, stirred him in a way he'd thought
he would never be stirred again. He watched her for a moment,
and then as the recollection of the old man's demands that he
marry Sophie flooded into his brain, he turned away. How could
there be any future in that idea? Even if he allowed himself to
entertain it, Sophie, once she heard of her inheritance, would
immediately think that it was the reason for his attentions. How
could she believe otherwise?

Luncheon was a very quiet affair. The tension was almost
tangible. Sophie looked at the two men at the table. Thomas was
eating his lunch and treating her as if nothing had happened
between them, and Charles seemed particularly morose. In an
endeavour to put things right between them, Sophie said, 'I'm
sorry that I'd already made an engagement with Dr Bryan, cousin,
and wasn't able to ride with you this afternoon.'

'It's of no consequence,' Charles replied stiffly. 'Tomorrow
will do as well.'

Sophie smiled at him. 'I'm so looking forward to it, but I have
to admit I am a little nervous. It's so long since I was on a horse.'

'Your mother rode well,' remarked her grandfather. 'I'm sure
you do too.' He glanced across at Charles as he added casually,
'You need to be able to ride well when you live in country like
ours.'

Charles made no comment, but he knew what Thomas was
telling him. Sophie was to stay at Trescadinnick, and he should
be doing everything to encourage her to do so. Well, he would
take her out and make sure she knew how to handle Millie. At
least then she would not need to drive round the countryside
with Dr Bryan.

As if reading his mind, Sophie said, 'I'm looking forward to
seeing a little more of the countryside this afternoon. It's very
kind of Dr Bryan to take us out with him, isn't it, AliceAnne?'

AliceAnne, sitting silent as usual at the table, turned crimson at thus being applied to. She turned an anxious face to her father and whispered, 'I don't want to go, Papa. Must I go?'

Surprised at this temerity, Sophie said cheerfully, 'Come now, AliceAnne, it'll be a great treat, you'll see.'

Charles, though surprised at his daughter's dislike for the excursion, was about to say that she need not go if she didn't want to, when it struck him that, though only six years old, she would act as a sort of chaperone for Sophie. She would not be jaunting around the country alone with the doctor, and there could be no whispers when all three were seen to be out together.

'I think you should go, AliceAnne,' he said. 'Aunt Sophie will be disappointed if you don't, and so will Dr Bryan.' He doubted this last remark, but no one else seemed to think it strange.

'I don't like him,' AliceAnne averred.

'Why ever not?'

'Just because he made her drink his special linctus when she had that cough in the spring,' said Louisa dismissively.

So I guessed right, thought Sophie. That's why she's afraid of him. Then she corrected herself, no, not afraid of him, but why she doesn't like him much.

'Well, I'm afraid doctors give us all medicine we don't like from time to time,' Charles was saying to AliceAnne. 'Even poor Grandpapa.'

AliceAnne stared in amazement at Thomas. She had a healthy fear of him too, and couldn't imagine anyone making him take medicine he didn't want.

The sun was still bright when Nicholas returned, and Sophie and AliceAnne, warmly wrapped against the chill, climbed up into his gig. AliceAnne seemed to have resigned herself, and when she was settled with Sophie under the blanket the doctor had provided to keep them warm, she looked about her with interest.

Hannah came out to see them off, and knowing AliceAnne's disinclination to go, she said, 'Now, Miss AliceAnne, you look after your Aunt Sophie for me, won't you? Make sure she brings you home well before it gets dark, and Mrs Paxton'll have muffins ready for your tea.'

AliceAnne gave her a smile. 'Yes, Hannah,' she said earnestly. 'I will.'

'Good girl,' Hannah said and watched as they drove away. Charles had not been the only one to wonder at the propriety of Sophie driving around unaccompanied with a single young gentleman. Hannah was sure that Dr Bryan was respectable and Sophie didn't really need a chaperone, but she too was happier that AliceAnne was with them, even if she was only a child.

Chapter 13

Once they were trotting at a brisk pace along the road, AliceAnne brightened up. She had seldom been far from Trescadinnick, only once or twice going into Truro with her grandmother to buy shoes. All her clothes were made at home, and outings were restricted to walks into the village, or the occasional excitement of a ride in front of her father on his big black horse, Hector. Sophie relaxed again as Nicholas kept up an easy flow of conversation, pointing out landmarks and points of interest as they clopped along. They passed several small hamlets, each little more than a clutch of cottages, but he made no stops at any of them.

'I promised old Mrs Slater that I'd come back and see how she was getting on this afternoon. The poor lady has great difficulty breathing with water in her lungs, and it's difficult for her to manage when her son is away at sea.'

'Is there no one else who can help her?' asked Sophie, touched at the thought of an elderly woman struggling on her own.

'Oh yes,' Nicholas Bryan said airily. 'In villages like these they all look after each other. And of course your Aunt Louisa visits from time to time.' He glanced at Sophie and seeing the look of surprise on her face, spoke with a lift of his nose. '*Noblesse oblige*!' And then, to soften what he'd said, he added, 'These hamlets all lie within the Trescadinnick estate. Mrs Leroy does her duty visits, and they're appreciated.'

When they reached Tremose the doctor drew up outside a

small stone cottage, showing only one door and one window beneath a grey slate roof, and standing a little apart from the others. The village was hardly worthy of the name, being little more than another cluster of houses, grouped round a small inn; there was no church, no shop and no meeting hall. Though it was situated a good half-mile inland, Sophie could see the cliff jutting, dark against the sky, and she could still hear the faint sound of waves breaking on the rocks below. Some of the nearby land was cultivated; small fields marked out with stone hedges, each being a holding for one of the village families in a bid to supplement their meagre diet with home-grown potatoes and vegetables. Beyond the patchwork of walls and tilled land stretched open moorland, and on a rise above the village she could see the stark finger of a mine chimney pointing upward amid a shamble of disused mine buildings.

Was that why this village, in the middle of nowhere, was there at all? she wondered – the home of the miners who, not so long ago, climbed down ladders a hundred feet long to work in the underground levels of the tin and copper mines? Miners who had now moved away to sell their skills elsewhere, leaving empty cottages to fall into disrepair.

'Will you come in?' suggested Nicholas, bringing her attention back to him. 'I'm sure Mrs Slater would love to meet you.'

Sophie looked doubtful. 'I think you should ask her first,' she said.

Nicholas went into the cottage, and after several minutes came out again to say that Mrs Slater would indeed like to meet her. 'What about AliceAnne?' asked Sophie, thinking of the risk of infection in such an unsavoury-looking cottage. 'I don't think she should come inside.'

'No, better not,' Nicholas agreed. 'You go on in. I'll wait out here with her.'

Glancing back at AliceAnne, still huddled under the blanket, her face pale, her eyes wide, Sophie said, 'Stay out here with Dr Bryan, AliceAnne. I won't be long.'

With some trepidation, Sophie knocked on the stout wooden

door. A voice called to come in, and she pushed the door open, wondering what sort of squalor she might find inside.

There was none. The cottage consisted of a single room with a tiny staircase leading upward from a corner at the back. Much of the room was taken up with a scrubbed wooden table, a chair to one side and another tucked neatly under it. Beside the fire that smouldered on the hearth was an old wooden rocking chair, and half hidden in a tiny alcove beyond the chimneypiece was a truckle bed. Though small, the place was clean and tidy. Mrs Slater was sitting at the kitchen table and as Sophie entered she tried to stand up.

Sophie held out a hand and said, 'No, no, please, Mrs Slater, don't get up. I was outside in the gig, and I just popped in to say hallo.'

'You're Miss Mary's girl,' she said.

'Yes, that's right,' answered Sophie, and indicating the spare chair she added, 'May I?'

Mrs Slater waved a hand by way of invitation. 'Would have knowed you anywhere,' she said.

Sophie smiled. 'Am I so like my mother?'

Mrs Slater shook her head. 'No, not like your ma, like your uncle. Like Jocelyn.'

'Jocelyn?' Sophie was startled. 'Did you know my Uncle Jocelyn?'

''Course I did, bless you,' wheezed the old woman. 'Everyone knowed Jocelyn.'

'And I look like him?' Sophie found she could hardly breathe, she was so excited.

'Well, you got his colouring, that dark red hair and them green eyes. Oh, he was a looker, I can tell you, your Uncle Jocelyn. Many a local girl lost her heart to him.' She looked at Sophie with interest. 'They must have told you, up at the big house, must have said you was the image?'

'No,' replied Sophie. 'No, they didn't say. They...' she hesitated, 'they don't talk about him much.'

'No,' Mrs Slater sighed. 'No, I suppose they wouldn't. Not

when he committed suicide and all... must have been a dreadful shock to them, that must. Well, it was to everyone. Not the sort of man to take his own life, wasn't Jocelyn Penvarrow...' She broke off as she realized that Sophie was staring at her in consternation.

'You didn't know, did you?' she asked softly. 'They ain't told you?'

'They said it was an accident,' murmured Sophie. 'They said he'd got lost on the cliff in a sea mist and fallen to his death.'

'Well, that bit's right,' Mrs Slater said. 'Certainly he fell to his death, but he knew them cliffs like the back of his hand, did young Jocelyn. He wouldn't have fallen. No, it were suicide all right, but of course the family hushed that up. Well, they would, wouldn't they? Think of the disgrace! He wouldn't have been allowed to be buried in the churchyard, would he? Not if he'd killed hisself. Rector wouldn't have stood for that.'

'And he's buried in the churchyard?' Sophie's voice was almost a whisper. She could not believe what she was hearing. Jocelyn had committed suicide? 'But why? Why did he do it? And in such a dreadful way!' She shuddered as she thought of his body flailing through the air on its death-dive to the rocks below. In the eternity of that fall, had Jocelyn regretted the leap he'd made? Had he, for one split second, changed his mind? Sophie felt sick at the thought.

'Why?' echoed Mrs Slater, pleased with the effect her news was having on Sophie. Nothing like a bit of drama to brighten her dull existence. 'No one knows for sure, but the word was he got a local girl into trouble and thought it was the only way out.' She shrugged and gave a gap-toothed grin. 'Penvarrows wouldn't have liked that scandal to come out.'

Sophie could think of nothing to say. Even if Jocelyn had disgraced himself, surely his family would have stood by him. Then she thought of her mother, and knew that they would not. Thomas Penvarrow would cast off any of his family whom he thought had disgraced them, and he was the only Penvarrow who mattered.

The door opened and Nicholas put his head into the room. 'We should go,' he said.

Still dazed, Sophie stood a little shakily. 'Yes, of course,' she said dully.

'Now, don't you forget,' Nicholas was addressing himself to Mrs Slater, 'you're to mix one of those powders I've left you with a little water, night and morning, and drink it down. It should ease your chest and help your breathing.'

'All right, Doctor,' wheezed the old woman. 'Miss Sophie and I've been having ever such a nice chat, haven't we, Miss Sophie? You come and see me again. Any time you want. I like having visitors.'

'Yes.' Sophie had herself under control now and smiled at the old woman. 'Yes, I will. Good afternoon, Mrs Slater.' And with that she walked out of the tiny cottage into the chill of the winter afternoon. The sun had disappeared, and early twilight was creeping across the sky. It was definitely time to go home.

Nicholas followed her out and handed her up into the gig. She pulled AliceAnne against her and he tucked the blanket around them both.

On the way home he asked casually, 'What did Mrs Slater have to say? You seemed to be getting on very well in there.'

Sophie, who had been reliving her conversation with the old woman, jerked back into the present. 'Sorry, Nicholas, I was miles away. Oh, nothing in particular. She was just telling me a bit about the area, the mines and the fishing.' Sophie tried to think of something else that they might have talked about; she was certainly not ready to share the intimate family history that had been revealed with anyone just yet, and certainly not with Nicholas, a newcomer to the area. If Jocelyn really had committed suicide, it had been hushed up at the time, and clearly that's how it should stay.

It was a chilly drive back to Trescadinnick, and there was little more conversation between them. Sophie and AliceAnne stayed huddled together under the blanket trying to keep warm, and Sophie was never more pleased to see the lights of Trescadinnick gleaming out across the fields.

At the door Nicholas handed her down and then reached up

to lift AliceAnne. The little girl shrank away from him, but he lifted her from the blanket and stood her down beside Sophie. Sophie had seen her reaction and sent her running indoors to get warm, then she turned to Nicholas and smiled. 'Thank you for taking us out,' she said.

'It was a pleasure,' Nicholas replied, returning her smile. 'Give my regards to your grandfather, and remind him to take the powder I left him, every morning. I don't think he always remembers.'

'He may not,' Sophie laughed. 'But rest assured, Aunt Louisa does.'

As soon as she was inside, Sophie hurried upstairs to change her dress for dinner. When Hannah brought up her hot water, Sophie related the events of the afternoon.

'I can't believe it, Hannah,' she said, still in a state of agitation. 'She said Jocelyn had committed suicide. He didn't slip off the edge of the cliff – he jumped!'

'Now then, Miss Sophie,' Hannah said soothingly, 'don't worrit yourself about that. Happened a long time ago. All forgotten now.'

'But don't you see, Hannah, it isn't. They never mention Jocelyn, and his room is all shut up. It's as if they've shut him up in there, in his room in disgrace! Even Aunt Matty won't talk about him.'

'Folks deal with death in different ways,' pointed out Hannah as she handed Sophie a clean towel. The cobwebbed one had disappeared, and had she been less caught up in the mystery of Jocelyn, Sophie might have wondered how Hannah had explained the state of it when she'd taken it down to be washed. 'Some folks need to talk about the person who's died. Others feel too sad and mention of the name brings the sadness back again.' She smiled at Sophie. 'We're all different, as God meant us to be.'

'I suppose so.' Sophie sighed, seating herself so that Hannah could brush the wind out of her hair. 'But you know...' she said, turning round so suddenly that Hannah nearly brushed her face.

'Oh, Miss Sophie, will you sit still!' admonished Hannah. 'How can I make you presentable when you're spinning about like that?'

'Sorry, Hannah. But listen, the old woman in the cottage, Mrs Slater, she told me that I look just like Jocelyn. She knew him, and she said I have his colour hair and his green eyes. Why didn't Matty tell me that? She didn't, not even when I was asking about him. And,' she said with sudden recollection, 'Grandfather said I looked just like my grandmother. So Jocelyn must have looked like her too, don't you think?'

'What I think,' replied Hannah, finally laying aside the brush, 'is that you should get yourself downstairs, before you're late for dinner and keep your grandfather waiting.'

Sophie gave a rueful smile. 'All right, I know you're right, but you can't help wondering, can you?'

'I can,' answered Hannah stoutly, beginning to tidy the room. That made Sophie laugh, and she left the room, her laughter on her lips.

Moments later, she was back through the door. 'Hannah...'

'Yes, Miss Sophie?'

'Is AliceAnne all right? I forgot to ask you. She didn't get too cold on the way back?'

'No, a little while by the kitchen fire and a hot drink'll set her right.'

'You will look after her, won't you, Hannah?'

Hannah's face softened. ''Course I will, Miss Sophie, she's a dear little girl. Wouldn't say "boo" to a goose, mind, but who can blame her, living in this household. She'll be all right with me. I've promised her a game of Snap before she goes to bed.' Hannah paused before adding, 'She'd never played it before I taught her... can you believe that?'

'Thank you, Hannah.' Sophie gave her old nurse a quick hug and ran downstairs to the drawing room.

That night, as she came back upstairs to bed, Sophie again paused outside Jocelyn's room. Had Jocelyn really committed suicide because he'd got some local girl into trouble?

Perhaps there was a girl, but surely he needn't have killed himself. Had he loved her, or had it just been a youthful fling? Had the girl truly loved him? Mrs Slater had said that lots of local girls had lost their hearts to him. Was the girl concerned simply another in a long line of flirtations? And what had happened to her? Sophie knew she could not discuss these thoughts with Hannah. Hannah would have been horrified to think that Sophie might be interested in such happenings. She would probably, if she heard the story, side with old Thomas about keeping the room locked, the disgrace sealed safely inside.

Later, Sophie lay in bed, watching the steady flame of the candle. Tonight there was no draught to make it flicker; no movement of the curtains. The night outside was cold but peaceful, and the only sound Sophie could hear was the distant whisper of the sea. It must have been the direction of the wind that caused the draught, that or its unusual strength, Sophie decided, looking across at the wardrobe.

Only the wardrobe and a door between me and Jocelyn's room, she thought. Had any secrets been locked away in there for twenty-five years, or was it simply the bedroom of a desperate young man, who had finally given way to his despair?

Chapter 14

Next morning Sophie was up early and shared the breakfast table with AliceAnne and Charles.

'Will you ride today, cousin?' asked Charles, when she'd joined them at the table.

'I'd love to,' replied Sophie, adding, a little embarrassed, 'but I've no riding boots. I'll have to go to Truro first.'

'So Aunt Matty told me,' remarked Charles. 'She suggested Anne's might fit you. I've looked them out and given them to Hannah to clean.'

Sophie was astonished. 'But...' she stammered, 'don't you mind? I mean, if they were Anne's...'

'Not in the least,' snapped Charles. 'You can't imagine, cousin, that I should feel sentimental about an old pair of boots. The only problem will be if they don't fit you.'

When a hurried note from Matty had suggested that Sophie might be in need of a pair of riding boots, and that Anne's might fit her, Charles had indeed wondered how he felt about it. But when he'd pulled them out of the wardrobe, where all Anne's clothes still hung, he found he wasn't thinking about Anne at all, but Sophie.

He'd been kept busy with estate business ever since she'd arrived, partly because there were always problems that needed sorting out, but partly by his own design. Even so, he caught Sophie slipping into his mind, settling quietly into a corner, and creeping to the forefront when he was at rest. Since she'd come to Trescadinnick the house seemed more alive than he ever remembered it. Music drifted on the air, a laugh echoed in the hallway, conversation filtered into the dining room. And AliceAnne? AliceAnne, though still a quiet little thing, seemed to have blossomed in Sophie's company. Charles had watched her with Sophie, and realized what the difference was. Sophie spoke to AliceAnne as an equal, not as a child. She listened to what AliceAnne had to say, and held real conversations with her. He listened to her now, asking AliceAnne about her lessons that day, and whether she'd like to have another piano lesson later, and he heard liveliness and enthusiasm in the little girl's replies, nothing like the one-word answers she would have given him had he asked such questions.

Had he ever asked such questions? he wondered. Did he ever really talk to AliceAnne about the things that might be important to her, or did he simply fire questions at her and expect her to... what? Love him? He loved her, of course he did; she was his daughter. But did she love him, or was she simply afraid of him? Had he earned her love, or had he left that to the others who had the day-to-day contact with her?

Sophie had been right, he thought with a stab of guilt as he listened to their chatter. AliceAnne needed children to play with or, if not other children, at least adults who took a real interest in her, rather than simply supplying her physical needs and then leaving her alone, considering their duty discharged.

'Perhaps I could have a piano lesson too,' he offered. His remark was greeted with a shriek of laughter from AliceAnne, something which would have been unthinkable only a few days ago when the child was expected to eat her meals in silence.

'You, Papa?' she cried. Then suddenly realizing the enormity of laughing at her father, she turned scarlet and covering her mouth with her hand, muttered, 'Sorry, Papa.'

But Sophie had laughed too, and Charles found himself grinning at them both. 'Why not?' he demanded. 'Men play the piano.'

'Indeed they do, cousin,' Sophie conceded. 'But while they are learning, they have to practise every day.'

'And you'll have to ride every day,' he stated firmly. He stood up. 'I'll be in the stable yard in half an hour,' he said.

Half an hour later Sophie came downstairs dressed in her mother's riding habit, packed at Matty's suggestion the last minute before they left London. It was a little large round the waist, and the bodice not as close-fitting as it was designed to be, but, nevertheless, when she'd looked at herself in the mirror she had been pleased with what she saw. The shape of the jacket showed her waist to advantage, and she had gathered the long, sweeping skirt into her hand, afraid that she might actually trip over it. Anne's boots were a reasonable fit; Hannah had polished them to a mirror shine and once she was wearing them, Sophie managed to put out of her mind the last pair of feet that had been thrust into them. Giving Hannah a quick hug, she ran downstairs to find Matty's mare.

When she reached the yard, Paxton was standing, waiting, holding Millie's bridle.

Sophie went over to the mare and stroked her velvety nose. 'Hallo, Millie,' she said softly. 'You and I are going to be great friends.'

Charles appeared a moment later, and taking the bridle from Paxton, led the horse to the mounting block. Once she was in the saddle, Sophie gathered the reins in her hands and waited while Charles swung himself up onto Hector. Her legs gripped the familiar pommels of the saddle, and though out of practice, she found that her body remembered the feel of the horse beneath her, her foot in the stirrup, and she began to relax.

Charles looked across at her and said, 'Ready?'

'Ready,' she replied. They exchanged smiles and he led the way out of the yard, onto the track across the cliff. Once they were clear of the house, Charles allowed Hector to trot and then canter along the grey-green turf of the cliff top. Sophie followed him easily, moving comfortably to the rhythm of the mare's gait. It was as she'd imagined it, sun on her face, wind snatching at her hair, and the remembered feeling of amazing freedom as the horse carried her forward. Charles drew rein and for the next few minutes they trotted companionably, side by side.

'Enjoying it, cousin?' Charles enquired.

'Oh, Charles, yes.' Sophie's eyes were alight with excitement. 'I'd forgotten...'

Words failed her, and she simply raised her arms to embrace the world about her.

Charles led her through a patch of woodland, where the sun filtered through the tangle of branches above their heads, dappling the ground with dancing shadows. Beyond was a stretch of open meadow, and as they turned onto a green pathway, Charles touched Hector with his heels and they were off at the gallop. Sophie kicked Millie into action, and though she was no match for Hector, she galloped gamely along behind him. When they reached the end of the green trail, Charles again drew rein and waited for them. Sophie's cheeks were glowing with excitement and exertion.

'You're going to be stiff tomorrow, cousin,' Charles remarked as she pulled Millie up beside him. 'But you ride very well.'

'Well enough to be allowed out on my own?' she asked archly, and he laughed.

'Well enough,' he agreed. 'But it isn't just the riding, cousin. It's knowing where it's safe to ride. Some of this ground is extremely rough. It'd be very easy to cast a shoe, or for the horse to go lame. If you're not sure of the ground, always let the mare pick her own route. She'll not let you down.'

'Thank you for the lesson, cousin,' Sophie said with a grin. 'I'll remember.'

'The other thing is the weather,' Charles said, his voice suddenly serious. 'It can change very quickly in this part of the world. Sun one minute, thick mist the next. If that happens seek shelter if you can. If not, let the mare bring you home.'

'I'll remember,' she promised.

As they walked the horses companionably back along the road, she turned to him and said, 'You know, you should get a pony for AliceAnne. You're never too young to start learning to ride.'

Charles looked at her sharply. 'Are you telling me how to bring up my daughter?' he demanded.

'Not at all,' responded Sophie 'But you yourself know that when living in such a place, being able to ride is essential. She'd love it... especially if you were the one to teach her.'

'You would have to teach her, Sophie,' he said. 'I wouldn't have time.'

'You would have to make time, cousin,' Sophie replied. 'As you're so quick to point out, she's your daughter.' With that she touched Millie with her heels and trotted ahead of him, leaving him staring at her back. No one had ever taken him to task in such a way; not his mother, not Anne. Certainly not Anne. She had been quiet and submissive to his wishes, seldom asserting an opinion of her own, and definitely not one in opposition to his. Sophie's direct manner of speech still surprised him, but it didn't upset him, as he knew it did his mother. Indeed, Charles found it quite refreshing. He clicked his tongue to Hector, and trotted on to catch up with his extraordinary cousin.

The next day was Sunday. When Sophie woke up she found that Charles's prophecy had proved only too right. She was extremely stiff after her ride, and her legs ached as she went downstairs, but she was determined that she would never admit as much to anyone but Hannah.

'We all go to church in the morning,' Louisa had told Sophie as she'd bid her goodnight the evening before. 'Be ready to leave at half past ten. You and AliceAnne will walk to the village. I shall bring your grandfather in the trap.'

And Charles? wondered Sophie, but she didn't voice the question. It was answered next morning when Charles strode into the hall where she and AliceAnne were donning their cloaks ready to set out. AliceAnne stared at him in amazement before asking, 'Are you coming with us, Papa?'

'Yes,' he replied shortly, and then added, 'if you'd like me to.'

AliceAnne broke into a huge smile. 'Oh yes, Papa,' she cried. 'We'd like you to, wouldn't we, Aunt Sophie?'

Sophie, thus applied to, also smiled. 'Yes,' she agreed. 'The company would be most welcome.' She reached out to the little girl and said, 'Stand still now, AliceAnne, so that I can straighten your hat. Your papa won't want to be seen walking with a ragamuffin.'

Together they set off to the village. Today they took the road, not the cliff path. Dressed in their Sunday clothes, Sophie was reluctant to follow the muddy path across the cliff. As they walked she noticed that Charles was making a definite effort to talk to his daughter, asking her what she had done the previous day, suggesting she might like to read to him after luncheon.

AliceAnne, who had been walking sedately between them, gave a little skip of delight, and seeing this, Charles went on, 'Aunt Sophie thinks it's time you learned to ride, AliceAnne. Would you like that, if I find you a pony?'

The child stopped dead in her tracks and spun round to look up at him. 'Oh, Papa,' she breathed, 'do you really mean it? And will you teach me, so that one day I can ride Hector?'

Charles met Sophie's enquiring eyes across AliceAnne's head and giving her a wry smile, turned back to AliceAnne and said, 'Yes, I will. But I shall be a hard taskmaster.'

'What's a taskmaster?' AliceAnne asked Sophie, looking confused.

'Your papa means that you'll have to listen to him carefully and do exactly what he says.'

The little girl's face cleared and she beamed up at her father. 'Oh,' she said, 'that's all right then.'

As they reached the village they met Nicholas Bryan coming out of his house, which was set back among trees on the seaward side of the lane. He called a greeting as he strode out to join them walking down the hill towards the church. They paused for him to catch up, and as he reached them his eyes swept over them, apparently a family group. For a second Sophie saw his lips tighten, but then his usual smile was back.

'Beautiful morning,' he cried. 'Good morning, Sophie, AliceAnne. Good morning, Mr Leroy.'

Sophie felt Charles stiffen beside her at Nicholas's use of her

Christian name, but she held out her hand to Nicholas and said, 'A beautiful morning indeed.'

As they stood at the side of the road, they heard the sound of a pony and trap coming along behind them and turning, saw Louisa with her father beside her, a rug about his knees.

'Goodness,' said the doctor, looking at them in some alarm. 'I hadn't realized that your grandfather would be venturing out in this cold weather.' He turned to Sophie. 'I really don't advise such a thing, Sophie. His state of health is far more delicate than I think you realize. He should be at home in the warm.'

'I hardly think my cousin is in any position to dictate to my grandfather when he may or may not go out,' said Charles coldly, watching as the trap went past. 'Come along, AliceAnne,' he added. 'Walk up, or we shall be late for church.' Reaching for his daughter's hand, he set off at a brisk pace.

Sophie turned to Nicholas. 'I'm sorry my cousin is a little abrupt,' she said, 'but don't worry. I'll try and keep Grandfather indoors if you think it best, but Aunt Louisa believes in the benefits of fresh air.'

'And generally I would agree with her,' Nicholas said, falling into step beside her. 'But in your grandfather's case it could prove the opposite. He must not take cold, Sophie. It could go to his lungs. You know he already has some trouble breathing and I've left him powders to ease his chest, but I sometimes wonder if he takes them as he should.'

'Oh,' replied Sophie cheerfully, 'you don't have to worry about that. Either Aunt Louisa or I insist.'

'That's good,' Nicholas smiled, and standing aside, allowed her to pass through the lychgate into the churchyard ahead of him.

Inside the church, Sophie walked down the aisle to join the rest of the Trescadinnick party where they sat in the front pew. Nicholas stepped aside into another pew, halfway back.

During Dr Osell's long and very dull sermon, Sophie's eyes wandered round the memorials that lined the grey stone walls. Several commemorated the lives of earlier Penvarrows, but one, newer than all the rest, simply said: *In loving memory of Sophia Alice Penvarrow, wife and mother 1805–1855.*

My grandmother, thought Sophie. Nothing of course for Jocelyn, but, as she read all the memorials, she wondered where he was buried. Mrs Slater had said that his grave was in the churchyard, as his suicide had been accepted as a dreadful accident, and Sophie decided to wander round the churchyard after the service and see if she could find it. She glanced across at the rectory pew on the other side of the aisle. Sitting alone was a woman dressed severely in black coat and bonnet, and Sophie remembered that Hannah had told her that the rector was widowed and his daughter, Miss Sandra Osell, kept house for him. At first sight Sophie took her for a lady approaching her forties, but when Miss Sandra turned her head and looked back at Sophie, Sophie could see that despite her old-fashioned mode of dress, the rector's daughter was only in her early thirties. Sophie smiled at her, but Miss Sandra simply looked away, returning her attention to her father's rambling discourse.

After the service the congregation gathered outside in the pale October sun, chatting to one another, before dispersing to their Sunday dinners. Sophie realized from the covert glances that came her way that she was the topic of many a conversation; Miss Mary's daughter come home to Trescadinnick.

It was Nicholas who introduced Sophie to Miss Sandra, as she came out of the church. 'I don't think you've met Miss Ross,' he said, 'Mr Penvarrow's granddaughter?' He turned to Sophie, saying, 'Here is Miss Sandra Osell, our good rector's daughter.' His tone was gallant, but it sounded insincere to Sophie's ears. Miss Sandra, however, coloured at his attention, and it was clear to anyone with eyes that she looked at the young doctor with something akin to adoration. He, apparently unaware of his effect on Miss Sandra or indifferent to it, was smiling at Sophie.

Sophie held out her hand to Sandra and said, 'How nice to meet you, Miss Osell.'

Miss Sandra took the proffered hand and answered, 'A pleasure, Miss Ross. Will you be making a long visit to Trescadinnick?'

'I don't know how long I shall be here,' Sophie answered, smiling, 'but I shall be returning to my home in London in due course.'

Miss Sandra nodded and turned her attention back to Nicholas. 'It's always nice to see new faces here, isn't it, Dr Bryan?'

Nicholas agreed, absently, that it was, but it was clear that his attention was elsewhere as he looked over her shoulder and watched Thomas and Louisa coming slowly out of the church.

Sophie excused herself and moved away from those gathered by the church door. Beside the path that led up from the gate there was a large sarcophagus tomb, and she'd guessed, rightly, that it was the Penvarrow family grave. The single name *Penvarrow* was engraved on the capstone, and then on each side were the names and dates of departed Penvarrows. Sophie walked round the big stone tomb, looking at the names of her ancestors. As in the church, the latest was her grandmother, Alice. There was no mention of Jocelyn. While she was reading the inscriptions Charles came up beside her.

'I see my mother's brother, Jocelyn, isn't buried here,' she said. 'Why's that?'

Looking startled at the directness of her question, Charles said, 'He's buried over there.' He pointed to a quiet area at the edge of the churchyard, where under the spreading branches of an oak tree, there was a single grave.

'But why?' asked Sophie. 'Why isn't he with the rest of his family?'

'I was a small child when he died,' said Charles, as if that answered her question.

'But you know why?' asserted Sophie, and before he could reply she walked away from him and, threading her way between old grey gravestones, crossed to the solitary stone under the tree. When she reached it she stared down at the inscription carved into the stone: *Jocelyn Thomas Penvarrow 1838–1861* – his name and the date, that was all.

'It's time to go home, Sophie.' Charles was standing beside her.

Sophie turned, startled. She hadn't heard him approach across the grass. 'It's sad, isn't it,' she said, 'that that's all there is left of him.'

Charles took her hand. 'It's all that's left of any of us in the end,' he said gently, 'a name on a stone.'

Sophie looked at him quickly, realizing that in all probability his wife Anne must be buried somewhere in this churchyard under a similar stone. Wishing she had said nothing, Sophie allowed him to draw her hand through his arm as together they walked to the gate where AliceAnne stood, waiting for them.

'All that's left of him' she'd said. But as Sophie walked back along the road with Charles and AliceAnne, she thought about the locked room and said to herself, *But that isn't true.*

As the days passed, Sophie gradually became absorbed into the pattern of life at Trescadinnick. In the mornings, after breakfast, she gave AliceAnne her piano lesson. Then, while the child sat in the schoolroom to do her other lessons with Louisa, Sophie went upstairs to be with her grandfather. Sometimes she read the papers that Paxton collected twice a week from St Morwen, occasionally she read to him from a book or magazine, and at others they simply talked. But very often they just sat; the old man lying in bed, Sophie sitting beside him doing some mending her aunt had given her. Thomas did not mention his will again, and as his lawyer had not come out from Truro to visit, Sophie was happy enough that Charles had not, after all, been displaced as her grandfather's heir.

Towards the end of the morning Thomas would send for Paxton to help him dress, and Sophie was at leisure to go into the drawing room and play the piano. She had worked on several new pieces, and had already been able to lighten the after-dinner evenings with music and the occasional song.

If the weather was fine her afternoons were usually spent with AliceAnne, either walking to the village, or exploring the countryside that surrounded it; if wet, they went into the schoolroom and Sophie read to her, or they played some of the simple card games she had loved herself as a child. She encouraged AliceAnne to draw, and entertained her with sketches she made of other members of the household.

Aunt Matty was a regular visitor to the house, and Sophie recognized a growing closeness between them. They were comfortable in each other's company, probably, she admitted to herself, because Aunt Matty was so like her mother; alike in many ways, and yet different in so many others.

So far she had not ventured out on Millie by herself, but once or twice Charles suggested they ride together, usually when he had to visit an outlying farm, and she'd enjoyed these outings immensely. She loved the feeling of freedom as they rode through country that was gradually becoming familiar to her. She found she enjoyed Charles's company too. There was little opportunity for conversation as they cantered across the open countryside, but as they walked the tired horses home at the end of the day, they talked comfortably together. She told Charles about her life in London, about her father's accident and her mother's last illness. He was a good listener and she found it comforting to talk about her parents, to bring them back to life again in her heart as she tried to bring them to life for Charles. Charles himself was more reticent; he spoke only a little about his wife, Anne.

'She was the daughter of one of the tin-mine owners, Sir Francis Shelton, over towards Camborne. We'd met on and off during our childhood and always got on well. We didn't see much of each other while I was away at school, just occasionally in the holidays, but when I left I met her again.' He spoke of his life at Trescadinnick, but only in generalities. Once Sophie had asked him if he remembered his Uncle Jocelyn, and he shook his head.

'Not really,' he replied. 'Well, I remember incidents, you know, as you do as a child. One day he built me a sandcastle that was taller than me, and dug a moat round it.' Charles smiled at the memory. 'He had me digging the moat deeper and deeper as the tide came in to wash the castle away and we tried to keep it out.'

'But his accident?' prompted Sophie.

'No, not really. I was only six or seven. I do remember being shut away in the nursery for several days. I didn't really know what was going on, and when it was all over everything went back to normal. Only of course it didn't. Uncle Jocelyn was never mentioned again, and I was warned by my mother not to ask about him. So, as I imagine children do, I soon forgot about him.' He looked across at Sophie, riding easily at his side. 'And I suppose one way and another, Trescadinnick's remained rather a sad household ever since... until now.'

'And now?'

'And now we shan't be in before dark unless we hurry,' he said. And urging Hector into a smart trot, he moved ahead of her, a strong, dark figure in the gathering gloom.

It was about a week later that Charles told her he'd heard of a child's pony that was for sale and suggested that she might like to go with him to look at it. 'I think you should come and see him too,' he said. 'I shan't tell AliceAnne, in case it's no good. I don't want her to be disappointed. Will you come this afternoon, cousin?'

It puzzled Sophie that, although an easy friendship was developing between them, Charles still tended to use 'cousin' to address her, and she realized she'd slipped back into using it too.

'I'd love to come,' she said, and was rewarded with one of his rare smiles.

Together they'd ridden companionably out of the yard. As they emerged into the lane, they met Nicholas turning in through the gates. He pulled the gig to a stop when he saw them.

The slight frown upon his face cleared to a smile as he greeted them. 'Good afternoon,' he said. 'I'm just looking in to see your grandfather, Sophie. Is he up and about today?'

'Yes, indeed,' Sophie assured him. 'He's having a rest now, but he came down for luncheon. He usually does, you know.'

'Ah, good. I was sure he must be feeling better if you felt able to leave him.'

'My aunt is with him,' Sophie said, sensing an edge of criticism in his remark. 'He's not alone, and I am not his nurse.'

'Of course,' Nicholas agreed easily. 'Well, I mustn't hold you up; it's a lovely day for a ride. I'll bid you good afternoon, Sophie. Mr Leroy.' He shook the reins and the gig moved on.

'I find that young man insolent,' Charles said as they too rode on. 'I don't like the way he presumes to address you as Sophie.'

'He takes good care of my grandfather,' Sophie said soothingly. 'And as for calling me "Sophie", he asked my permission first.'

'Did he? Well, I still don't like it.'

'I'm not sure that's of any consequence, cousin,' remarked Sophie airily.

Charles glanced at her sharply, but catching the sparkle in her eye, he gave a reluctant grin.

'That's better,' she said to him approvingly. 'Your smile suits you.'

'You're incorrigible, cousin,' Charles said with a shake of his head. 'I never know what you're going to say next!'

'That's just as it should be,' Sophie replied, as she nudged Millie into a trot.

Chapter 15

O n his last visit to Trescadinnick, Louisa had been out and Nicholas had been let in by Edith, who told him that Thomas was resting on his bed.

'I'll find my own way up,' he said cheerfully, and leaving her watching him wistfully, he set off up the stairs. As he reached the bedroom door which stood ajar, he heard voices and paused on the landing to listen. Thomas was giving Paxton precise orders about the delivery of a letter.

'Take it to Whitmore and Staunton, the lawyers in Castle Street,' Thomas said. 'Give this letter to young Mr Staunton and tell him that I shall expect him to call on me here next Thursday at two in the afternoon. Tell him I shall also expect the documents to be drawn up as I've instructed, and ready for signature.'

Nicholas stepped back hurriedly to the top of the stairs as Paxton emerged, tucking the letter into his pocket. 'Oh, Paxton,' Nicholas greeted him with a pleasant smile, 'I didn't realize you were in there with Mr Penvarrow. I'll come back another time.'

'That's all right, Doctor,' Paxton replied in his easy voice. 'He only wanted me for a moment, just to do an errand for him. He's ready for you now... did he know you was coming?'

'No, I just looked in to see how he was getting on.'

'Well, you go on in, sir. He's wide awake, so you needn't fear to waken him.'

Nicholas had moved along the landing and, knocking on the door, walked into the room. 'Good afternoon, sir,' he said. 'Just come in to take a quick look at you. I shan't keep you long.'

*

The following Thursday, he rang the bell at ten minutes to two and was admitted by Edith.

'I'm sorry, Doctor,' she said when she saw who was there, 'but I think madam's gone to the village.'

'Don't worry, Edith,' said Nicholas, treating her to his most disarming smile. 'It's Mr Penvarrow I want to see. I'll go on up, shall I? No need to show me the way.'

He's such a lovely gentleman, Edith thought with a sigh, as he left her standing in the hall.

Nicholas walked swiftly upstairs. He knocked on Thomas's door and went straight in. Thomas was sitting up in bed, propped with pillows.

'Good afternoon, sir.' Nicholas spoke breezily as he entered the room. 'And how are we today?'

Thomas glowered at him. '*I'm* perfectly well,' he growled. 'I couldn't possibly say how *you* are.'

'That's good to hear,' replied Nicholas, ignoring Thomas's ill-temper.

'Why are you here?' demanded the old man. 'I didn't send for you.'

'No, but as I was passing on my rounds I thought I'd just come and take a look at you.'

'It isn't necessary,' grumbled Thomas. 'If I need you, I'll send for you.'

Ignoring this, Nicholas said, 'Shall I have a listen to your chest now I'm here? Just to check that your lungs are back to good working order?'

'If you must,' Thomas grumbled. 'But you'd better be quick about it. I'm expecting a visitor.'

Nicholas opened his bag and pulled out the antiquated ear-trumpet stethoscope he had found in the late Dr Marshall's surgery. 'Not the latest equipment, I'm afraid,' he said as he placed the end of it on Thomas's chest. 'But it works pretty well.'

For a minute or two Thomas submitted to Nicholas's

ministrations, then he pushed him away. 'That's enough for today,' he said. 'Anything you haven't heard through that contraption can wait until another day.'

As he spoke there was a peal on the front doorbell. 'Here,' he said, 'get me back into my shirt.' Nicholas did as he was asked and was still putting his stethoscope away when Edith tapped on the door. At a bellow of 'Come!' she crept into the room, staying beside the door as if to beat a hasty retreat, and said, 'Please, sir, Mr Staunton is here to see you.'

'Show him into the library,' ordered Thomas, 'and tell him I shall be down directly.' Edith bobbed a 'Yes, sir,' and was just escaping the room when he shouted again. 'And tell Paxton I want him.'

Edith finally made her escape and Thomas swung himself out from under the covers, revealing, to Nicholas's surprise, that he was still dressed.

'You there, help me with my coat.' Thomas held out his arms and Nicholas helped him to shrug on the coat. 'Now, young man, give me your arm downstairs.'

Together they traversed the landing and went cautiously downstairs. As they reached the bottom, Paxton appeared from the nether regions of the house.

'Paxton, take Dr Bryan into the drawing room and wait there with him. I may need you both.'

Relying on Thomas's dictatorial manner, Nicholas made a faint protest that he had his rounds to finish, but his protests were brushed aside.

'Since you're already here, you can spare me another fifteen minutes,' Thomas said. And leaving Paxton to show Nicholas to the drawing room, he went into the library and closed the door.

At last the door opened and Edith came in. 'Please, sir,' she said to Nicholas with a bob, 'Master says will you join him in the library.'

Nicholas rose at once, saying to Paxton, 'I do hope Mr Penvarrow won't detain us for long. I really should be on my rounds again by now.'

Paxton made no reply, but simply knocked on the library door and opening it, stepped aside to allow the doctor to precede him into the room.

Thomas Penvarrow was seated at a desk in the window, papers laid out in front of him. Another man, Mr Staunton the lawyer, Nicholas supposed, was standing next to him, a briefcase open on a chair alongside.

'Ah, Dr Bryan,' said Thomas, looking up as they entered. 'Sorry to keep you waiting. I had a little business to discuss with Mr Staunton, but now it is all settled, I should like you to be a witness to my signature, if you please.'

The document in front of Thomas was covered with a blank sheet of paper, except for the place where Thomas would sign and the space for the signatures of the two witnesses.

Mr Staunton handed Thomas the pen, saying, 'Now then, sir, if you would be so good as to append your signature here.' The old man took the pen and having dipped it carefully into the inkwell, leaned forward to sign his name. As he did so, Nicholas saw the words:

Signed by the said Thomas Jocelyn Penvarrow of Trescadin-
nick Port Felec Cornwall
  In our presence and attested by us in the presence of
each other.

Thomas inscribed his name and then scattered sand across his signature.

'Now you, Paxton,' said Thomas.

Paxton stepped forward and signed his name above where his name and address had already been filled in. As he moved away from the desk, Nicholas stepped forward and was handed the pen. He took his time dipping the nib into the inkwell, before leaning over to sign his name in the prescribed place. As he steadied his hand on the paper, his fingers edged the blank sheet a little further from the document. Little was revealed from this, just the single phrase *set my hand to this my*, but it was enough for Nicholas Bryan to be certain that this was indeed Thomas's new will. When he'd signed he stepped away, apparently unaware that he had disturbed the covering paper, and said, 'And now, sir, if you have no further need of me, I'll bid you good afternoon as I must continue on my rounds. Patients will be expecting me.'

Thomas barely acknowledged his farewell, muttering to himself, 'Well, at least there was some use in your coming here this afternoon.'

As Nicholas was about to leave, Louisa came walking up the drive. She called his name, looking concerned. 'Dr Bryan. Did my father send for you? Is all well?'

'No, Mrs Leroy,' Nicholas said, smiling. 'I was passing on my rounds and I just looked in to see him.'

'And?'

'And I listened to his chest. I think he has a congestion of the lungs. He should rest more and if you can persuade him to take the powders I left with you before, I think it may ease him.'

'I'll do my best, Doctor,' replied Louisa. 'But he dislikes being told to rest.'

Nicholas laughed. 'I'm sure he does,' he agreed. 'Even now he has his lawyer with him.'

'His lawyer!' exclaimed Louisa, raising her hands in despair. 'I must go in.'

Nicholas watched her scurry into the house and smiled as he drove away.

Indoors Paxton had returned to the kitchen, and Thomas poured himself and Mr Staunton a glass of brandy.

'I shan't ask where this came from,' Mr Staunton said as he sipped his drink. 'But I do have to say it's exceedingly good.'

Thomas smiled. 'And I shan't tell you. But it's good enough to celebrate a new heir for Trescadinnick,' he said.

'And you say Miss Ross is going to marry Mr Leroy?' queried the lawyer. 'At least that way everything's tied up right and tight, and he's not entirely cut out.'

'Oh yes,' Thomas agreed nonchalantly. 'It suits everybody, but of course, nothing announced yet.'

Mr Staunton took the hint and said, slightly affronted, 'I never discuss my clients' business, Mr Penvarrow. Never.'

'Get down off your high horse, Staunton,' snapped Thomas. 'I wasn't suggesting you did. I was simply pointing out that it isn't common knowledge yet, you understand?'

Young Mr Staunton, the third of that name, knew it would be damaging to the firm to lose Thomas Penvarrow as a client and he bit back any further comment, wondering as he did so, how his father and more so his grandfather had managed to have dealings with this autocratic old man, without having a catastrophic quarrel. As soon as he'd finished his brandy, Staunton called for his horse, ready to take his leave.

'A good afternoon's work,' Thomas said, shaking his hand. 'An excellent afternoon's work.'

Is it? wondered his lawyer. I'm not so sure.

Chapter 16

Sophie and Charles had ridden to a farm several miles beyond Port Felec. The farmer had taken them to the stables and led the pony out. He was small, almost black, with a white blaze on his nose and bright, intelligent eyes. Looking him over, they both agreed that he would be perfect for AliceAnne to learn on. As Charles was in the yard negotiating the price with the farmer, Sophie stood holding their two horses and watched him. She had been surprised how quickly Charles had moved, once he'd decided that he would teach AliceAnne to ride, but she was delighted when he'd asked her to come and look at the pony with him. Watching Charles haggling over the price of the pony, she felt a rush of affection for him.

It must be hard being left with a daughter to bring up, she thought, even though he had his mother there beside him. It was clear that he found it very difficult to express his love for the little girl, but buying the pony and promising he'd teach her to ride was, Sophie decided, a very practical expression of that love.

Money changed hands and the pony was led out to where Sophie waited. The farmer held it on a leading rein while Charles, in the absence of a mounting block, put his hands round Sophie's waist and tossed her up into the saddle. The action took Sophie's breath away, and she could still feel the strength of his hands as they'd lifted her, long after he'd mounted himself, taken the pony's leading rein, and led them out into the lane.

When they returned to Trescadinnick, and AliceAnne saw what her father had brought her, nothing could curb her joy.

When he'd dismounted and helped Sophie from Millie's back, Charles turned to AliceAnne, and smiled.

'He's called Oscar,' he told her, 'and he's hoping you'll look after him.'

Impulsively AliceAnne flung her arms round her father's waist. 'Oh thank you, thank you, Papa,' she cried into his waistcoat. And Charles, unused to such displays, slipped his arms round her and held her tightly to him.

Nothing would do for her but that she should start her lessons now this very minute. Charles had bought Oscar's tack as well as Oscar, and so, with a smile, he lifted his daughter and placed her gently in the saddle.

'We'll have to get you a proper riding habit,' Sophie said, as Charles, still holding AliceAnne firmly in place with one hand, led Oscar slowly round the yard.

And this was how Matty found them when she arrived, being driven by Timothy in her pony and trap. As Paxton ran to take the pony's head, Timothy helped his mistress out of the trap.

'Hello,' she cried, looking at them gathered round the pony. 'What's happening here?'

'Oh, Aunt Matty,' cried AliceAnne from her perch on Oscar's back. 'Look what Papa has given me. Isn't he beautiful?'

'He certainly is,' agreed Matty, surprise showing for a moment upon her face. 'What a lucky girl you are!' She turned to Charles and Sophie and said, 'Good afternoon, Sophie, Charles. I believe you're expecting me for dinner.'

Louisa had told Sophie that Matty was coming over for dinner and staying the night, but with the excitement of the pony she had forgotten. 'Good afternoon, Aunt,' she said with a smile. 'You see what excitement there is here. But it's getting cold. Do let me bring you indoors where you can get warm after your journey.'

If Matty wondered at her niece taking on the role of hostess, she didn't show it, but tucked her hand through Sophie's arm and allowed herself to be led into the house. 'How is Papa?' she asked Louisa, who'd met them in the hall. 'Is he in good spirits?'

'He seems so today,' she said. 'Dr Bryan came this afternoon to see how he was doing, and while he was here Mr Staunton came from Truro.'

'Mr Staunton?' said Matty, taking off her bonnet and cloak and handing them to the waiting Edith.

'Yes, apparently my father sent Paxton to his office with a letter last week, and Mr Staunton came by appointment this afternoon.' Louisa sighed. 'I wish when Papa invites his lawyer to visit, he'd let me know in advance. I would have stayed at home to greet him and I would certainly have sent the doctor away.'

Sophie had been listening to this exchange with growing alarm. 'Is this Mr Staunton my grandfather's lawyer?' she asked.

Louisa looked at her sharply. 'He is,' she said brusquely, 'if that's any of your business, miss.'

Matty placed a hand on her sister's arm. 'I'm sure the child intended no rudeness, Louisa,' she said soothingly.

'No, Aunt, I did not,' Sophie agreed. 'But neither am I a child.' She dipped a bob to her aunts and went on, 'If you'll excuse me, I must go up and change after my ride.'

'And I must go and see my father,' said Matty, apparently unmoved by Sophie's outburst. 'How does Dr Bryan find him?'

'I saw him just as he was leaving,' Sophie heard Louisa say as the two sisters followed her up the stairs. 'He's worried about him. He says he has a congestion of the lungs, and certainly Papa seems to have trouble breathing at times.'

'And what does he prescribe?'

'He says Papa must rest more. He said Papa should take the powders he left before, but he doesn't like them and makes a dreadful fuss. Says they taste bitter and make him feel sick. But as you know only too well, Matty, he's not an easy patient at the best of times.'

Sophie heard the knock on Thomas's bedroom door, and Louisa announcing, 'Here's Matty to see you, Papa.'

She heard no more after that, but later before dinner in the drawing room, Matty confided, 'I was really shaken when I saw him, Sophie. It's only ten days since I was here, but the change in him is quite startling.'

'He's not good today,' Sophie agreed, 'but he has been better lately. Most days he gets up for lunch and stays up until after dinner.'

'Well, I'm glad he isn't coming down to dinner tonight,' said Matty. 'He looked completely exhausted and must certainly rest.'

'Perhaps the visit from his lawyer tired him,' suggested Sophie.

'Perhaps,' agreed Matty noncommittally, looking up as the door opened and Louisa came in.

'Ah, Sophie,' she said. 'Your grandfather would like you to go up and sit with him after dinner.'

'Yes, Aunt Louisa,' Sophie replied, but her mind was racing. Her grandfather's lawyer had been. Did that mean he had done as he'd said and changed his will, making her his heir?

As soon as the meal was over, Sophie excused herself and went up to her grandfather's room. When he answered her knock and she went into the room, she was assailed by a sickroom smell that she hadn't noticed before. Her grandfather was propped up in bed and his gaunt face seemed scarcely less white than his pillows. It was as if, since she'd been with him in the morning, he'd been attacked by some new disease. His breathing was laboured, but his eyes, when he turned them on Sophie, were bright and piercing.

'There you are,' he said, his voice impatient.

'I came as soon as dinner was over, Grandfather,' Sophie said, pulling up a chair to the bedside. 'I see you haven't eaten any of yours.' She nodded to the tray that sat on a table by the bed.

'Not hungry,' grumbled Thomas.

'But you must eat, sir,' Sophie said. 'You must keep up your strength.'

'Oh, so you're a doctor now, are you?' snapped the old man. 'One doctor a day is enough for any man. Sit down. I want to talk to you.'

Sophie did as she was bidden, and reached for the old man's hand. It lay bony and thin in her own and she had a sudden vision of her mother's hand as she'd held it just before she had died. She looked up sharply into her grandfather's face. Matty was right; he looked extremely ill.

'Mr Staunton came to see me today,' Thomas said without preamble. 'He's my solicitor. He brought my new will in which you are named as my heir.'

'Oh, Grandpapa, you can't—' began Sophie, but he silenced her with a scowl.

'Don't you tell me what I can and can't do, young lady,' retorted the old man. 'I've made my will and there's an end to it.'

'You've made it today?'

'Sent Staunton a letter last week, telling him what I wanted,' Thomas told her. 'He drew it up and brought it here today for me to sign.'

'And you signed it?' whispered Sophie.

'Of course I signed it,' said her grandfather. 'That's why he came. All signed and sealed. Called in Paxton to witness my signature, and that doctor was here, so he witnessed it as well. All done, right and tight, and Staunton's taken it safely back to his office. When I die, that's where you'll find it, safe and sound, and Trescadinnick will be yours.'

Sophie didn't know what to say. She gazed, unseeing, at the floor. He had done it. He had left Trescadinnick to her. 'I can't believe you've cut Charles out,' she said at last.

'Charles was never in,' snapped Thomas. 'He's not a Penvarrow.'

'He's a Penvarrow in everything except the blood in his veins,' cried Sophie.

'And it's the blood in his veins that matters,' answered Thomas. He closed his eyes and was instantly asleep, his rasping breath becoming rhythmical, his hand lying relaxed in Sophie's own. Gently, she replaced it under the covers and turning down the lamp till it was no more than a glimmer, stole quietly out of the room.

Chapter 17

Back in the seclusion of her own room, Sophie lay on her bed, thinking about what her grandfather had told her. Trescadinnick was to be hers. She found it almost impossible to take in the gravity of it. She thought of her home, cosy and familiar, waiting for her in London, but that now seemed far away, part of another life, when she had been another person.

When Hannah had come to help her prepare for bed, she had almost told her what had happened, but at the last minute had stopped herself. Until she had decided herself what she might do about it, Sophie wasn't going to let anyone else know about her inheritance. Did Charles know? she wondered. How would he react when he heard he'd been cut out of the will? How would his mother react? Had she suspected something of the sort? Was that why Louisa was so cold towards her?

Restlessly Sophie got off the bed and paced the floor. Despite the glowing embers in the fireplace, the room was chilly, so she went to the chest of drawers to find a shawl to wrap about her shoulders. The drawer was stiff and she had to jerk hard on the handle to pull it open. As she drew the shawl out, something else came with it, clattering to the floor. Glancing down, Sophie couldn't see anything at first, but when she had the shawl wrapped safely round her, she kneeled down, feeling about with her hands to find whatever it was. When she did find it she sat back on her heels and stared. In her hand was a key: a door key, similar to the one in the lock of this very room. Slowly she got to her feet, and crossing to the door she removed the key from the keyhole and compared the two. They were different. It was not a spare key for this bedroom. Holding the key she'd found tightly in her hand, she moved across to the wardrobe. Could this be the key that she needed? Could it really be the key to the connecting door, the door to Jocelyn's room? She'd never thought of searching the drawers for such a key. She'd simply assumed the door had been locked from the far side and the key removed.

Or perhaps, she thought, it would open the outer door to Jocelyn's room. Rather than struggle with the old armoire again, she would go out and try that first. She opened her own door and stepped out onto the landing. Unwilling to show a light, she had brought no candle out with her and she had to feel in the darkness for the keyhole of Jocelyn's door. When her fingers found it, she inserted the key. It fitted into the keyhole, but it would not turn. Sophie pulled it out and tried again. Again it fitted into the keyhole but it was impossible to turn. Not the key to this door then.

At that moment Sophie heard a cough and saw the flicker of light from a candle being carried along the main landing. Louisa was making her way to her bedroom. Sophie froze, hardly daring to breathe. The slightest flicker of movement might draw her aunt's attention to her, and how would she explain standing in her nightdress, in the dark, outside Jocelyn's room, holding a key in her hand? Thank goodness she hadn't brought out her own candle to give her away.

Louisa shuffled along the landing and it struck Sophie for the first time that dancing attendance on her father, and running the household, Louisa was slipping into an early old age herself. She had none of the zest that accompanied Matty into the room.

Sophie remained absolutely still until she heard Louisa's bedroom door close. Then, with a sigh of relief, she returned quietly to her own room.

Well, thought Sophie with a flash of excitement, it's not the key to my door, nor Joss's door, so it must be the connecting door, mustn't it?

There was only one way to find out and it meant shifting the wardrobe again. She put the key down on the dresser and went to lock her own door. Probably unnecessary, she told herself as she turned the key, but she was determined that no one should interrupt her in what she intended to do. Quickly she got dressed again. A nightdress and shawl, she decided, were not the attire for moving furniture. Remembering how she'd manoeuvred the heavy wardrobe before, she braced herself against it and edged it away from the wall. Puffing and red-faced from the exertion, Sophie at last managed to angle it so that she could slide in behind. She took the key from the dresser and squeezing herself into the gap, inserted it into the lock. It fitted. A wave of excitement filled her. It was the key. The right key. She tried to turn it, but the lock was stiff. Surely it must be the right key.

'Come on!' she urged it in frustration. 'Turn, will you!' She jiggled the key and tried again. Nothing. The lock refused to budge. She pulled the key out again and looked at it. It was old and rusty. Creeping back out into the room, she picked up her towel and rubbed at it. She needed oil, she realized, to help release a lock unused for so long, but she had none. She returned to the lock. Perhaps if she could use two hands, it would open. She set to work to move the wardrobe a little further out, and then tried again. This time, using both hands, she managed to get better purchase on the key, and finally, reluctantly, with a loud scraping noise, it turned and the lock released. Sophie reached for the handle and pushing open the door that had been closed for twenty-five years, let herself into Jocelyn's room.

It was dark and she could see nothing but the faintest outline of the window, so she retreated to her own room and picked up the lamp. Taking it through the door, she held it high and, at last, looked round the room that had been Jocelyn's. It was the mirror image of her own and equally simply furnished. There was the bed, the corner of which she'd seen through the keyhole. Beside it, was a nightstand on which lay a book, face down to mark the page Jocelyn had been reading. A wardrobe, the twin of the one in her own room, stood against the adjoining wall and opposite was a chest of drawers, and a washstand, complete with bowl and jug, beside which a razor was laid out ready for use. In the window was a desk, its chair at an angle as if its occupant had risen hurriedly to his feet. All were covered in a thick layer of dust. Grey silk cobwebs hung from the ceiling, festooning the curtains and walls in filigree grey lace.

Placing the lamp on the dresser, Sophie went first to the wardrobe and peered inside. It was full of clothes, some hanging, others folded on the shelves that ran down one side. All Jocelyn's clothes were here, as they had been the day he'd walked out of the room for the last time. She closed the wardrobe door, picked up the lamp and turned her attention to the desk.

It was made of oak with a leather inlay; a flat writing desk, with a central drawer. Laid out on the top of it were a steel-nibbed pen and a silver inkwell. Sophie lifted its lid, but the ink had long since dried up. Turning the chair back to the desk, Sophie sat down and pulled open the drawer, revealing a jumble of items: writing materials, papers, a pencil, a small penknife, sealing wax, the stub of a candle and several letters, some loose, some folded together. For a moment she looked at the letters. Her fingers itched to pick them up, but what right had she to read Jocelyn's private correspondence? She stared at them.

Jocelyn was long dead, she reasoned; nothing she saw could affect him now. Thus, Sophie allowed her curiosity to overcome her scruples. She lifted the papers out of the drawer and spread them out on the desk. The letters were old and the ink faded, and she had to peer at them in the yellow lamplight to make out the writing. As she turned them over, her hand suddenly froze. There, amongst them, was a letter written in a hand she'd never forget. It was her mother's careful writing. There was an address on the top, and a date, *4 October 1861*. The letter had been written five years before Sophie herself had been born, written from an address in London where Sophie had never lived. She stared at the familiar writing and then she started to read.

My dear Joss
What a scrape you've got yourself into! No doubt my father has taken it quite as badly as you say. Of course I'll help you if I can. I have given the situation great thought and

think you should encourage Cassie to stay with her sister, if she'll have her, until we can get things sorted. If the child is not due until December, by then you at least will have come of age and can marry without Papa's consent. You say that Cassie's father is a Methodist minister, so I assume he will willingly give consent to escape the shame that her giving birth to an illegitimate child would bring him.

We haven't much room here, but John, bless his generous heart, is quite agreeable for you to be married from here and so we will arrange it. In the meantime, I will look round for somewhere suitable for you to live once you are married and the baby is born. I know you have an annuity from our mother's will, so even if our father cuts you off with a shilling, you will have money to live on until you can find some sort of employment.

So, my dear brother, don't despair. I'm sure if you love Cassie, I will too. You can be married from here, the baby will be born in wedlock and all will be well. How I long for a baby to hold. There are days when I fear I shall never have one of my own.

When you come you'll be able to tell me all the news from Trescadinnick, how they all go on and how little Charles is growing. How I long to see you, Joss!

In the meantime, tell Cassie that we are waiting to welcome both her and the baby when it arrives.

Your loving sister, Mary

Sophie read and reread the letter. Who was Cassie? A Methodist minister's daughter? She must be the girl that old Mrs Slater had told her about; the local girl whom Joss got into trouble. It was clear from this letter that Joss and Cassie were to be married and, thought Sophie, how like Mama to have offered the disgraced Cassie a home. How like Papa to have allowed it. Such a very brave thing to do; if it ever leaked out to their friends that they had allowed an unmarried couple to stay under their roof, their reputation would have been ruined as well.

Thoughtfully, Sophie laid the letter aside. If her parents had been going to stand by Jocelyn and Cassie, why had Jocelyn given way to despair and thrown himself over the cliff? What could have happened to cause such despair?

She laid the letter aside and picked up another. Not recognizing the handwriting, which was tall and slanting, she looked straight at the signature. It was signed *Cassie* and dated a couple of weeks earlier than her mother's. The only address at the top was a scrawled *Truro*.

My dearest Jocelyn
Please don't worry so. I am quite well here with Henrietta, and though she is mortified at my disgrace, she will not throw me out like my father and Edwin. (Edwin has since been to see me but was extremely disagreeable and I told him to go away!)

Hetty's husband, Albert, is not happy with the situation (I am not allowed out of the house or even out of my room if there is company), but he has agreed to let me stay until my confinement, after which, I understand, the baby will be given away. I had thought it would be better for him... or her, do you mind which? to be born here among family rather than in lodgings somewhere, so I've been behaving as Albert and Hetty require, but, as I have now learned their plan, dear Joss, do come and fetch me as soon as you can. I will not

—Sophie paused when she saw how the *not* was underlined three times—

give up our child to strangers. I am determined that we three shall be together as a family. Surely your father will eventually come round to our marriage, but if not, well, you will be of age in November, and I am already cast out by my father, so we should be able to marry before the child is born without anyone gainsaying us.

If it's a boy I would like to name him after my father. It might make him look on his grandson with more favour than he does in prospect. If it's a girl, perhaps we could call her Emma, after my grandmother. I loved her dearly and it's such a pretty name. I long to hear from you, Joss, and for the time when we'll be together again.

I send you all my love, and that of the little creature that is kicking away inside me.

Your Cassie

Cassie hadn't heard of Mary's offer of a home when she'd written this letter, thought Sophie as she read this letter through again. A plan had been in place, but was now being altered. Cassie was safely with her sister and could stay there until Jocelyn could fetch her away and bring her to Mary in London. They would be married and when the baby was born they could live as a perfectly respectable family.

What changed? Sophie wondered. Did something happen to Cassie? Did she die? Is that what changed and brought Jocelyn to despair? And the baby, had that died too? A third letter was not in the bundle, but pushed underneath the others. It was only half finished, undated and unsigned, but addressed to Cassie, and as Sophie held it up to the light and read it, tears sprang to her eyes as she guessed why that was. *My darling girl,* it began.

It is all arranged. As I told you, my dear sister Mary has offered us a home, at least for a short while, and we can be married from there. She is already cut off from Trescadinnick as she married someone of whom my father disapproved, so she understands our situation very well. Her home is not big enough for us to stay for more than a few weeks, but the baby can be born there, so still among family. And once you have recovered from the birth we should be able to move into our own home.

I shall come and fetch you from Truro as soon as I

am twenty-one and can obtain a special licence for our
marriage. What a wonderful day that will be.
   I think

But whatever it was that Jocelyn had been thinking, Sophie
would never know, for here the letter broke off as if he had
been interrupted. He had not even finished his sentence. It was,
Sophie thought as she looked at the abrupt end to the letter, as
if he'd been afraid of being caught writing it. Had he pushed it
hurriedly into the drawer when someone had knocked on his
door, or even walked unannounced into his room? Had he been
writing it when for some reason he'd had to go to the village,
and on the way back he'd been caught in the mist? Surely he
had no intention of committing suicide when he'd begun to
pen that letter. He was optimistic about their future; plans had
been made, and it was only a question of time until all would be
well. Surely Jocelyn's death had indeed been a dreadful accident.
Sophie felt suddenly cold as she knew the terror he must have felt
as he slipped and found himself falling, wrapped in a shroud of
mist, to his death on the rocks below.

There were other letters in the drawer, most of them in Cassie's
distinctive hand, but Sophie did not want to read any more. She
knew now the story of Jocelyn and his love, Cassie, his 'Cassie',
and she was suddenly desperately tired. Everyone thought they
knew that Jocelyn had killed himself, and it had been hushed up
to hide the further disgrace, but it had indeed been the terrible
accident that they pretended it was. She ought to set them right;
but even as she had this thought, she knew it was impossible.
How could she explain, even to someone as sympathetic as Aunt
Matty, that she had, against an express prohibition, let herself
into Jocelyn's room and having rifled his desk, read his private
letters?

Slowly, carefully, she folded the letters and placed them back
in the drawer. Jocelyn's secret plans would remain secret, known
only to her. She rose to her feet, picked up the lamp, and with
one final look about the dust-covered room, slipped back

through the connecting door. It took several minutes and the last of her strength to ease the heavy wardrobe back against the wall, concealing the door once again, but at length it was done. She undressed, doused the lamp, and with only the candle's light for company she crept into her bed. Her little watch told her it was twenty to two in the morning. Had she really been in Jocelyn's room all that time? She reached up and blew out the candle, but try as she might, sleep did not come. She lay in the darkness, thoughts of Jocelyn and Cassie and her mother churning in her head. She remembered the letters she'd found in her mother's desk and set aside to deal with another day. Were Jocelyn's letters amongst those? Explaining about Cassie?

I'll have to look as soon as I get back home, she thought.

Back home. Suddenly she knew she ought to be returning to London. She'd stayed far longer than she'd intended and if she went back to London, perhaps refusing to come back to Cornwall, maybe her grandfather would recognize that it was Charles who had given his life to Trescadinnick, that he was more of a Penvarrow than she would ever be, and perhaps he would change his will yet again.

Part of her wanted to get away, to break free from the intensity of life at Trescadinnick and to go back to the familiar home in which she had lived most of her life. But there was another part of her, almost unacknowledged, that looked to the mundane life she'd led there, and which would reclaim her, with dismay. She pushed that thought aside. Home was home. Home was the little house in Hammersmith where she'd been brought up, not this great barn of a place in Cornwall. She had promised AliceAnne that she would be here to celebrate Christmas with them. She could at least keep that promise and stay till then, but after that, when 1887 crept over the threshold, she knew she should leave. As Thomas's heir, acknowledged or not, her position in the house would become untenable.

I shall go home soon, she decided. I can always come back for Christmas and so keep my promise to AliceAnne. And with some sort of decision made, she finally drifted off into an uneasy sleep.

Chapter 18

Next morning, when Sophie was summoned to her grand-father's bedroom, she had decided she would tell him of her determination to go home. She knew he would be angry and had readied herself for his reaction.

'To go home?' he spluttered in indignation. 'You *are* at home, girl. This is your home now, not some hovel in London.'

'No, Grandfather, it is not,' replied Sophie sharply. 'And,' she went on angrily, 'I do not live in a hovel. I live in a perfectly respectable house in a perfectly respectable neighbourhood.'

'It may be respectable,' Thomas grumbled, 'but you are a Penvarrow of Trescadinnick, and your place is here.'

'I am not a Penvarrow,' retorted Sophie. 'I am a Ross, whether you like it or not.'

'You're my granddaughter and that's the same thing,' said Thomas.

'No, it is not,' returned Sophie. She sighed and reached for his hand. 'I need to go home, Grandfather. I will come and visit you all again. Indeed, I've promised AliceAnne that I'll be here to celebrate Christmas with you, so I shall only be away for a few weeks.'

'And then you'll stay,' asserted the old man, adding, as if as an inducement, 'Your aunt isn't getting any younger. She needs help with the house.'

Knowing how much Louisa would resent any interference in the management of her household, this almost made Sophie laugh out loud, but any laughter died in her throat as her grandfather was seized by a paroxysm of coughing. Sophie leaped to her feet, and grasping the old man by his shoulders, heaved him more upright in the bed. As she tried to hold him steady, she could feel his thin shoulders shaking as the coughs racked his chest. When at last his coughing stopped and he lay back exhausted on the pillow, Sophie wiped his mouth with a linen handkerchief and was horrified to see that it was flecked with blood. She reached for the jug of water that stood at his bedside and pouring him a glass, held it to his lips.

'Here, Grandfather,' she said gently. 'Have a sip, and then I'll make you up one of the powders Dr Bryan left you. That should help.'

Thomas, whose hand had been gripping hers as she guided the glass to his mouth, suddenly pushed her away. 'No!' His voice was little more than a gasp, but there was no doubt about the ferocity of the word.

'But you must have your medicine,' soothed Sophie. 'It'll make you feel better.'

'Makes me feel worse,' murmured the old man. He allowed her to give him a little more water, but was obdurate in his refusal of the glass when she'd mixed one of the powders the doctor had left, so she set the glass aside. Aunt Louisa can try and make him take it, later, she thought.

They did not return to the subject of her departure again. Sophie picked up the newspaper Paxton had brought the previous day, and began reading aloud. But when she had finished, Thomas still felt too weak to dress and come down for luncheon, and she left him resting, ensuring his room was warm enough before finally closing the bedroom door. So he was not there when Sophie broke the news of her intended departure to her aunt, Charles and AliceAnne.

'But you said you'd be here for Christmas,' cried AliceAnne. 'You promised!'

'AliceAnne!' reproved her grandmother. 'That is no way to speak to your Aunt Sophie. You only speak when you're spoken to.'

AliceAnne closed her mouth, but she looked at Sophie with imploring eyes.

'I promised I'd be here, AliceAnne,' replied Sophie, 'and I will. I'll come back for a visit over Christmas... that's if you'll have me.'

Ignoring Louisa's earlier admonition, AliceAnne burst out, 'Of course we will, won't we, Papa? Aunt Sophie can come back, can't she?'

For the first time Sophie turned to look at Charles, who was calmly eating his lunch.

'Your Aunt Sophie will always be welcome here if she wants to come,' he replied. 'She may come and go as she pleases. Now, AliceAnne, I don't want to hear your voice again until your plate is empty.'

Sophie returned her attention to her own plate, but not before she'd seen a gleam of satisfaction in Louisa's eyes. She for one would not be sorry that Sophie was planning to leave.

The meal progressed in awkward silence. No one quite knew what to say after Sophie's announcement and they were all pleased when the meal was over. As they were getting up from the table Paxton appeared and said, 'The master wishes to speak to you, Mr Charles. You too, Miss Sophie. He says he'll expect you both upstairs in ten minutes' time.'

'I have an important letter to write,' Charles said. 'It won't take long. I'll be up in a minute or two.' And with that he disappeared into his study.

Sophie also wanted a little time to herself before braving her grandfather's wrath again. She went to her room and tidied her hair. As she looked at the wardrobe, she suddenly wished that she'd taken all the letters from Joss's desk. If she had the whole correspondence, Joss's letters and those waiting in her mother's desk, she might be able to piece together what had really happened. Perhaps, tonight, she'd struggle with the wardrobe just once more and collect them. After all, no one knew they were there, so no one would know they were missing.

As she opened her bedroom door and stepped out onto the

landing, Sophie met Charles coming up the stairs. She smiled at him, but her smile wasn't returned. He simply preceded her along the landing and knocked on the door of Thomas's bedchamber.

At the shout of 'Come!' he held open the door for her and they went in. Thomas was dressed and sitting in a chair by the fire. He waved them in, saying, 'Shut the door, Charles, there's a draught.'

Two chairs were set on the other side of the fireplace and he said, 'Sit down, the pair of you. I want to talk to you.'

Sophie perched on the edge of one of the chairs, a bird poised for flight. She knew what her grandfather was going to say and she didn't want to be there when he told Charles that he had been cut out of the will.

Charles, seemingly unaware of what was coming, closed the door and took the other chair.

Thomas looked at him and then across at Sophie. 'Now,' he said, 'you'll no doubt know why I want to talk to you.' He raised an enquiring eyebrow, but neither answered him; Sophie because she did know, and Charles because he could guess and had no intention of making it easier for the old man.

'Yesterday,' Thomas went on, 'Staunton, my lawyer, called at my request. I'd written to him and asked him to draw up a new will.' This statement was also greeted with silence, so he continued. 'He brought it yesterday for me to approve and sign. I'm telling you now that I did both.' He glanced across at Charles's stony face and said, 'I told Sophie this last night, that she is now my heir, the heir to Trescadinnick. But I see from your face that she hasn't shared the news with you, Charles.'

'Because I was hoping you'd change your mind, Grandfather,' interjected Sophie. 'I think it is quite wrong of you to cut Charles out. I've done nothing to deserve Trescadinnick. I have no right to inherit. It's Charles who has kept the estate running these last years, so he has every right.'

'I'm not going to argue the toss with you, Sophie,' snapped Thomas. 'I've done what I've done and I have no intention of changing my mind, now or in the future. Charles knew I was going to make you my heir and I told him what he should do about it.'

'Do about it? What can he do about it if you're refusing to change your mind?' demanded Sophie.

'He can marry you.'

Sophie stared at him, stunned. 'Marry me? Marry me? But I don't want to get married and I certainly don't want to marry Charles!'

'I'm glad we are of one mind about that!' Charles said with a harsh laugh. 'I've already told your grandfather, if that's what's necessary to inherit Trescadinnick, I'm not prepared to do it. I shall leave and make my own way in the world.'

'You mean you knew about this preposterous idea before... before now?'

'Your grandfather told me of his plans the night you arrived. I told him then that if marrying you was the price of Trescadinnick, I wasn't prepared to pay it.'

Sophie felt the colour flood her face at the starkness of his words, anger at their arrogance.

'Be reasonable, both of you,' barked Thomas. 'If you marry each other it solves all the problems at a stroke. Charles is able to stay and manage the estate as he's been doing so capably these last years. He has a charming and beautiful wife to run his home and provide him with more children. Sophie is set up in a suitable marriage and has a wonderful house to call her own, a place to bring up a family of her own; and little AliceAnne has a new mother who she already loves.'

'Have you quite finished, sir?' Charles spoke through gritted teeth. 'I told you then and I'm telling you now, if and when I wish to remarry, I shall choose my own wife and it will not be a chit of a girl scarce out of the schoolroom, who is foisted on me by my *step*-grandfather as payment for services rendered and as a sop to his own conscience!'

'And when the time comes when I want to marry,' Sophie retorted, 'I shall choose my own husband.' She fixed her grandfather with a baleful eye. 'Just as my mother did. I shall choose someone handsome and charming, someone I can love and with whom I long to spend the rest of my life, not a sour-faced, middle-aged man looking for a mother for his child and an inheritance for himself.'

'I thought I'd made it quite clear to both of you,' snapped Charles. 'I am not looking for a wife, or a mother for my daughter, or, for that matter, the Trescadinnick estate.'

'Oh yes, cousin, or should I say *step*-cousin, you've made that abundantly clear. And as you say we are of one mind.' She turned to face her grandfather and said with chilling calmness, 'You have our answers to your proposal, sir, and mine at least is irrevoc-able. I would not marry Charles if he begged me on bended knee!'

'There is absolutely no danger of my doing any such thing,' countered Charles. 'That I can promise you.'

Sophie got to her feet and mustering all the dignity she could, she turned her back on both men and walked, ram-rod straight, to the door. There she turned and said, 'I told you this morning, sir, that I intended to go home to London very soon. That has changed. I intend to leave Trescadinnick at the first possible opportunity.' And with that she left the room.

By the time she reached her own room, she found she was shaking with rage. How dare they? Either of them! It was her grandfather who had come up with this crackpot scheme, but it was Charles who had rejected her in no uncertain terms. She didn't want to marry Charles; she had said as much, but there were ways of saying so. When Charles had spoken of her as a schoolroom miss, the vehemence of his rejection had been echoed in her own.

When she had calmed down a little, she rang for Hannah, who had been waiting for her call. Sophie had warned Hannah that morning of her plans and was surprised when Hannah had said, 'If you're sure that's the best thing, Miss Sophie.'

Now, after the confrontation with her grandfather and Charles, Sophie knew that, definitely, it was the best thing. She still had money from that given to her by Matty, enough for their fares home and if necessary for an overnight stay along the way.

'I shall consult Bradshaw and find the times of the trains back to London. I intend to leave tomorrow. Paxton can take us to the station in the morning and at least we shall get as far as Truro. In the meantime, please will you pack and have us ready to leave first thing.'

'What does your grandfather say to your sudden departure?' asked Hannah.

'He's furious, but he should have expected it when he started telling me whom I should marry,' snapped Sophie. 'It didn't work with my mother and it isn't going to work with me!' Then, immediately repentant, she said, 'Dear Hannah, I'm sorry. I didn't intend to take it out on you. My grandfather is demanding that Charles and I should marry. Neither of us wish it and so it's better that I quit the house as soon as possible.'

'Could you not consider such an idea?' Hannah said gently. 'Marriage with Mr Charles?'

'No, I could not,' declared Sophie, adding, 'And nor could he. We are of one mind.'

Sophie stood up and walking to the wardrobe, pulled out her riding habit. 'I'm going out for a ride to clear my head,' she announced.

'By yourself?' Hannah said nervously.

'Certainly by myself,' said Sophie. 'I have no need of an escort and I'm sure my cousin has better things to do with his time than to play nursemaid to a schoolroom miss. When I get back I shall not go down for dinner. Perhaps you would ask Mrs Paxton if I might have a tray here in my bedroom.'

Hannah knew there was nothing she could do or say to Sophie when she was in this mood, and she simply nodded and said, 'I'll ask Paxton about the train times. I'm sure he'll know.'

'Yes,' agreed Sophie as she pulled on her riding boots... Anne's riding boots. 'That's a good idea. I'm sure he'll know.'

Once changed, Sophie took herself down to the stable yard and asked Ned to saddle Millie for her.

'Will Mr Charles be needing Hector?' Ned asked.

'No, I don't think so,' Sophie said casually. 'I'm sure he'll tell you if he does.'

Sophie mounted from the block and was just riding out of the yard when she saw Charles coming out of the front door. He stopped short, his face rigid, as he saw her set off down the drive. Determined that he shouldn't stop her and equally determined to show him that she was entirely her own mistress, she gave him an insouciant wave and broke into a trot.

Once she had reached the open cliff top, Sophie edged Millie into a canter. Winter was creeping in and the afternoon was cold and grey, but Sophie didn't care. She needed to get away from the house, to feel the freedom of riding alone. She looped round and, slowing, followed a cart track up and under the moor. She had been that way with Charles once and knew it led eventually back to Port Felec. She decided that she'd go that way into the village and perhaps visit Jocelyn's grave again before she left for London.

As she came down the lane that led to the church she heard someone call her name, and glancing round saw Nicholas coming out of one of the small stone cottages, his doctor's bag in his hand. She drew rein and waited for him to come up beside her.

'Sophie!' he greeted her with a wide smile. 'What a surprise! It's a cold afternoon for you to be riding out.' He looked back at the cottage he'd just left and added, 'Mrs Pennell was my last call of the day and I'm on my way home. Will you join me at The Clipper for a cup of tea and a muffin to warm you up before you return home?'

Sophie was sorely tempted to accept his invitation. That would show anyone who happened to be watching that she could do as she chose; that she didn't care that she should not be alone in public with a gentleman who was not family and to whom she was not engaged. She was about to say yes, but common sense prevailed, making her shake her head and say regretfully, 'Thank you, Nicholas, that's a very kind invitation, but I'm afraid I'm really on my way back to Trescadinnick. I'm leaving tomorrow for London and have much to do before I go.'

'To London?' he said. 'Is this a sudden decision? I thought you were making an extended visit to Trescadinnick.'

'I have to go back unexpectedly,' Sophie said.

'But you are coming back?' Nicholas asked anxiously.

'I may be back for Christmas,' Sophie replied. 'I have promised AliceAnne to try and come back then.'

'And you leave tomorrow? How very strange that you should be going just now,' he said. 'I too have business in London and will be there in a week's time. Perhaps I may come and call upon you there.'

Sophie saw his handsome, smiling face, looking up at her enquiringly, and found herself returning his smile. Here was a man who regarded her with admiration in his eyes, who always treated her with a warmth that brought an answering glow to her own heart. She reached out her hand and he took it in his.

'That would be delightful,' she said, 'if you can spare the time.'

'Oh, that will be no problem,' Nicholas said as he took her hand. 'If you just tell me where you live, I shall pay you a visit as soon as I have concluded my other business.'

His eyes held hers for a moment, making the colour seep into her cheeks, and then he raised her hand to his lips before releasing it.

'I had better go,' Sophie said in confusion, as she felt the warmth of his lips on her fingers.

'Of course,' Nicholas agreed. 'Perhaps I may walk into the village with you.'

Nicholas took hold of Millie's bridle and they walked down the hill past the church and into the centre of the village.

Few people were about, as the winter evening was closing in, and the lighted windows of The Clipper looked warm and welcoming. But though tempted to spend half an hour with the charming doctor, Sophie again turned down his invitation to step inside.

'Perhaps another time,' she said. 'But I look forward to seeing you in London.' And she told him where she lived before she left him outside his own house and rode back up the lane to Trescadinnick.

When she reached the stable yard, Ned was waiting to help her dismount and to deal with Millie. 'I'm glad you're back safe and sound, miss,' he said. 'Mr Charles said I shouldn't have let you ride out alone on a day like today.'

'I'm sorry if I got you into trouble, Ned,' Sophie said, another wave of irritation sweeping through her at Charles's presumption. 'But I am quite safe riding Millie and he need not have worried.'

There was no one in the hall as she entered and she went straight up to her room, where she found Hannah folding the last of her clothes into her trunk.

'Now, Miss Sophie, I'm right glad to see you back safe and sound,' she said, her relief all too obvious. 'Mrs Treslyn is here and wants to have a word with you when you've changed your dress.'

'Aunt Matty?' Sophie said in surprise. 'I didn't know she was coming again today.'

'Mr Penvarrow sent Paxton to fetch her,' Hannah explained. 'She's in the drawing room with Mrs Leroy.'

Sophie nodded. 'Did you tell Mrs Paxton that I'd like my dinner on a tray in my room?'

'I did, Miss Sophie. Mrs Leroy wasn't best pleased, but Mrs Treslyn suggested that it wouldn't hurt if you were tired.'

'Did you find out train times from Paxton?' Sophie asked.

'Yes, and he'll take us to St Morwen first thing in the morning to catch the train to Truro.'

'Good,' said Sophie. 'That's settled then.'

Chapter 19

Matty had been startled that afternoon by the arrival of Paxton in the pony and trap with a summons from her father to come at once to Trescadinnick. She had no idea what he wanted and not knowing if she would be expected to stay the night, brought an overnight bag with her.

When she walked in through the front door, she was greeted by Louisa in the hall.

'I'm glad you've come, Matty,' Louisa said as Matty removed her cloak. 'Papa is in a furious rage. He's had a great argument with both Charles and Sophie. Charles is refusing to go back and apologize; indeed, he's not even speaking to him. Sophie, stupid girl, has announced she's going back to London tomorrow, and in the meantime has ridden off alone on that horse of yours.'

'Gracious!' said Matty. 'What on earth sparked that off?'

'Father's made a new will and named Sophie his heir. It's she who'll inherit Trescadinnick when he dies, not Charles… And when I think of all the time and effort Charles has put into keeping the place running and solvent…' Louisa's face contorted as she fought for words. 'If it weren't for Charles, there wouldn't *be* anything for anyone to inherit except a crumbling house and a stack of debts.'

'And Father told them all this today?'

'He told Sophie yesterday, but she, little minx, kept it to herself,' said Louisa bitterly. 'She didn't warn Charles what Father had done.'

'Well, I think you have to agree it wasn't her place to do so, and it's hardly her fault that Father has changed his will.'

'Of course it's her fault,' snapped Louisa, 'ingratiating herself with the old man. Sitting with him, reading to him, playing the piano for him.'

'Don't be so ridiculous, Louisa,' Matty retorted. 'She did as she was asked. And,' she went on, 'both you and Charles must have known that it was on the cards that Father would change his will once he'd sent for her and brought her down here.'

'You were the one that brought her down here,' Louisa pointed out angrily.

'I was the one that was sent to fetch her,' Matty said patiently. 'It was Father who sent me, as you well know.'

'Well, she's leaving for London tomorrow,' said Louisa. 'And as far as I'm concerned it's not a moment too soon.'

'Tomorrow!' exclaimed Matty. 'No wonder Father's in a state.'

'Well, you'd better go up and see him,' Louisa said. 'He's waiting for you in his bedchamber.'

Matty knew there was nothing further to be learned from Louisa, so she went upstairs and knocked on her father's door. When there was no reply she softly opened the door and found him dozing in his chair by the fire. As Matty paused in the doorway, looking at him, she was struck yet again by how much he had aged in the last few weeks, perhaps even in the last few hours. She crossed the room and pulling up a chair beside him, took his hand in hers.

'Papa? Are you awake?'

The old man jolted upright and snapped, 'Of course I'm awake, Matilda. I've been sitting here waiting for you.'

'I came as soon as I could,' Matty said placatingly. 'Now then. Tell me what's happened.'

'What's happened is that I've made a new will in favour of Sophie. She, ridiculous child, says she doesn't want Trescadinnick. Can you believe that? Says it's not fair on Charles! What has fairness got to do with anything? She's blood-kin. He's not.'

'And you think that it's right to cut Charles out, after all he's done?'

'Charles was never in,' growled Thomas. 'You and Louisa were to have equal shares.'

'You mean you were never going to leave Trescadinnick to Charles?' Matty was incredulous. 'After all he's done?' She stared at her father. 'Louisa says he's not speaking to you, and I have to say, Papa, I'm not surprised!'

'I suppose he'd have got it in the end.' Thomas sighed. 'Louisa's share anyway. But this way he can have it all much sooner.'

'Sooner? How do you mean?'

'I told him, when Sophie first arrived, that I was going to leave the estate to her, but all he had to do was marry her and it would be his as well.'

'Marry her?' Matty shook her head in disbelief. 'You told him to marry her. And did you say the same to Sophie?'

'Not then,' Thomas admitted. 'I told them both again this morning of these arrangements.'

'You told them they were to marry each other?'

'Obvious thing to do,' grumbled Thomas. 'Sorts everything out right and tight.'

'Papa,' Matty tried to keep her voice calm, 'I'd have thought by now you'd have learned that you can't dictate to people how they're to live their lives, whom they're to marry, where they're to live. Look what happened when you refused Mary permission to marry the man she loved. You lost her. You banished her for not falling in with your wishes and you lost her. Do you want to do the same with Sophie? She's leaving for London tomorrow.'

'Tomorrow?' Thomas cried in agitation. 'So soon? I shan't allow it!'

'You can't prevent it, Papa,' Matty said, 'short of you locking her into her room. Sophie is her own woman, like her mother. If you try and force her to do something she'll simply walk away, and you can't stop her.'

'I can cut off her allowance,' muttered Thomas. 'What's the chit going to live on if I do that? Eh?'

'That's your *problem*, Papa. You still regard her as a chit of a girl when she's actually a woman grown. She'll be twenty-one very soon and able to look after herself. And Papa,' Matty spoke slowly and clearly, 'with regard to finances, I shall make sure she has no worries about money. I have plenty and will simply replace your allowance with one of my own.'

'How dare you interfere!' snapped the old man.

'How dare I?' Matty got to her feet and looked down at her father, still hunched in his chair. 'Because I'm no longer afraid of you, Papa. You can't bully me any more. I didn't dare stand up to you before and lost my sister. I wasn't in a position to help Mary then, and I lost her, but I'm not going to lose Sophie in the same way. I will look after her until she finds someone she does want to marry, and you can't stop *me* either.'

'It comes to something when a man isn't master in his own house!' growled Thomas.

'You can be master in your own house, Papa, but you can't be master of other people's lives! Now,' Matty continued, 'I'll wait till Sophie gets back and see what I can do to retrieve the situation.'

'Gets back? Where's the girl gone?'

'She took Millie out and went for a ride.'

'Alone? Didn't Charles go with her?'

Matty sighed. 'Papa, I don't think Charles and Sophie are speaking at the moment.'

'Ridiculous!' expostulated Thomas. 'And so I shall tell them!'

'Papa, I think you've told them enough,' retorted Matty, and with that she left the room. Downstairs she related her conversation to Louisa, who couldn't believe that Charles had never been in her father's will.

'But we always assumed everything would go to Charles!' she exclaimed.

'Did Papa ever say so?'

'No, but it seemed obvious. Admit it, Matty, you thought so too.'

'Yes, I did,' conceded Matty. 'But we should have known Papa better.'

Louisa sighed. 'Well,' she said a little unwillingly, 'I suppose if he did marry Sophie, it would...' She searched for the words. 'It could possibly be the answer.'

'Except,' Matty said, 'perhaps for Charles and Sophie.'

Next morning Paxton carried Sophie's trunk out to the waiting trap, while Sophie said goodbye to the family. She had breakfasted alone in her room, but she knew that she couldn't avoid making her farewells, especially to AliceAnne.

She went first to her grandfather, who had not yet risen from his bed. 'I'm returning home now, Grandfather,' she said. 'I have come to say goodbye.'

Thomas, propped against his pillows, said, 'But you will come back again?'

'Maybe,' Sophie conceded. 'But I'm not sure when. AliceAnne has asked me to come and spend Christmas with you.'

'I should like that,' Thomas said simply. 'We shall miss you, Sophie. Will you come?'

Sophie reached out and took his hand. 'That depends on you, Grandfather. I think it is wrong of you not to make Charles your heir. And I think it is wrong of you to tell him... and me, whom we should marry.'

'I shall not change my mind,' the old man said.

'Then it is unlikely I shall come back,' returned Sophie.

Thomas's lips tightened and he turned his head away from her. Sophie released his hand and with the murmur of 'Goodbye, Grandfather,' quietly left the room.

When she reached the hall, she knocked on Charles's study door and without waiting for an acknowledgement, went in. Charles was sitting at his desk, apparently writing a letter. He looked up and said, 'Good morning, cousin.'

'Paxton is waiting outside,' Sophie said, stretching out her hand. 'I've come to say goodbye.'

'So you really are going back to London?'

'Of course. I told you so yesterday.'

'But so soon?'

'The sooner the better,' Sophie replied. 'The sooner we can all get back to our normal lives.'

'Will you come back?' Charles asked.

'Not as things stand. There seems to be little point, don't you think?'

Charles had been regretting his outburst of the previous day. He knew it had been unfair of him to take his anger at Thomas out on Sophie. It was hardly her fault that the old man had changed his will and made the outrageous suggestion that everything would be fine if he just married her, but he'd said words he could never unsay and now he was at a loss.

Sophie still burned with humiliation at his harsh dismissal of her and faced him now, her expression set.

'What about AliceAnne?' began Charles.

'What about her?' snapped Sophie, for she too had been thinking of the little girl and the promise she had made. 'As you never fail to remind me, she's your daughter. You look after her. You spend time with her. You make her Christmas special. You're her father.' Then, without pausing to see how Charles had received this salvo, Sophie turned on her heel and walked back into the hall where her two aunts were waiting to see her off.

Louisa simply said, 'Goodbye, Sophie. I wish you well.'

'Where's AliceAnne?' Sophie asked. 'I haven't said goodbye to her.'

'She's in the schoolroom, learning her Bible passage. I will tell her you said goodbye.'

'Tell her I will write to her,' said Sophie, sad that Louisa's hostility had sent the child away before they'd had the chance for a proper farewell.

'I'll tell her,' said Louisa. 'Now, if you'll excuse me, I have work to do in the dairy.' And unaware of a muffled sob, she disappeared down the passage to the kitchen.

As soon as she had gone Sophie crossed to the table and peeped under its chenille cloth. There was AliceAnne, curled up on the floor, tears streaming down her cheeks. Sophie held out her arms and the little girl crawled into them. 'Don't cry, AliceAnne,' Sophie soothed. 'Don't cry, dearest.'

'B-b-but you're going away,' stammered AliceAnne. 'I don't want you to go. I like it when you're here.'

'But your papa is here with you,' Sophie said gently. 'He's here to look after you.'

'But I want you... and Hannah. I don't want Hannah to go.'

This brought Sophie up short. It wasn't that she minded AliceAnne wanting Hannah to stay, but it was the first time she had actually considered what effect her taking Hannah with her to London would have on AliceAnne. As their stay at Trescadinnick had lengthened from days into weeks, Hannah had taken over much of the child's care, looking after her clothes, sitting with her as she took solitary meals in the schoolroom. It was often Hannah who took her out for her afternoon walk, played with her, read to her, taught her parlour games, and helped her get ready for bed. Sophie, with her piano lessons and help in the schoolroom, had become part of AliceAnne's life, but Hannah had become central to it.

Sophie pushed these thoughts aside and giving AliceAnne a hug, said, 'I have to go now, AliceAnne. We have a train to catch. But we will come back and see you, I promise. I'm just not quite sure when. Come on now, there's a good girl, stop crying and come out to say goodbye to Hannah.'

AliceAnne gulped hard, her tears subsiding, and together they walked out to where Paxton waited with the pony and trap. Hannah was waiting with him and immediately AliceAnne broke free and ran to hug her. Hannah put her arms about her and held her close for a moment and then, holding her away a little, looked down into her tear-streaked face and said, 'Now then, Miss AliceAnne, no need for tears. You heard your Aunt Sophie say we'll be back. That's something to look forward to, isn't it?'

AliceAnne nodded, not able to speak without crying, and Hannah gave her one more hug before climbing up into the trap where Sophie was already waiting. Paxton flicked his whip and the pony set off down the drive. Sophie looked back at the house and was surprised to see Charles had come out of the front door and had lifted AliceAnne in his arms, holding her close against him. For a few minutes they stood there, Charles, AliceAnne and Aunt Matty, bathed in the pale winter sunshine, watching until the trap turned the corner and was out of sight.

Neither Sophie nor Hannah spoke as they travelled along the road to St Morwen, each deep in her own thoughts. Hannah had been very dubious about this sudden flight from Trescadinnick, and had said so the previous evening as they sat by the fire in Sophie's bedchamber while Sophie ate the simple supper that Mrs Paxton had sent up.

Sophie had been adamant. 'I can't stay here, Hannah,' she said. 'It's bad enough that Grandfather has made me his heir. I can't do much about that; he's made up his mind. But he's cut Charles out and that makes it very difficult for us to remain under the same roof.'

'I see that, Miss Sophie, but couldn't you at least stay a few more days and leave in a more dignified manner?'

'We might have managed that,' Sophie answered. 'But when Grandfather demanded that Charles and I should marry, without, as far as I knew, consulting either of us, it turned out that he'd already told Charles that was his plan. Charles had his answer ready and made it abundantly clear he doesn't want to marry me, and I certainly don't want to marry him.'

Hannah had to accept Sophie's decision and here they were on their way to the station, and by the end of the day they would be back in their own little house in Hammersmith. If Hannah had been given the opportunity to go back to London in the first few weeks of their stay at Trescadinnick, she would have jumped at the chance to return to the bustle of the city, but now they were actually going, her heart was heavy and she had no wish to leave. She had gradually slipped into the routine of Trescadinnick and though she looked after Sophie's few needs, it was her care of AliceAnne that gave her a definite place in the household. Louisa had been happy enough to relinquish the daily care of the little girl and Hannah had grown to love the lonely child who was growing up, almost overlooked. It wasn't, however, AliceAnne who filled her thoughts as they drove away that early morning, but someone else she had come to love: Will Shaw.

From their first meeting outside The Clipper, Hannah and Will had become friends. Will, a down-to-earth farmer with an outdoor face and an open smile, had never married. He'd never seen the point. His elder sister, Molly, lived in St Morwen with her husband, Jack, and her three young children. Their widowed mother, Grace, kept house for Will and his two younger sisters, Maggie and Lizzie, and they were a comfortable, loving family. Introduction of another woman into the household had, until he'd met Hannah, seemed to Will entirely unnecessary. He was forty now, and no one expected him to marry, least of all himself. Meeting Hannah outside The Clipper that afternoon in September had turned his world upside down. There was something about her that made her, well, different, and he wanted to meet her again, to get to know her. Here she was, a good-looking woman with a strong streak of common sense, who took life as she found it; the woman he thought he'd never meet, who was suddenly making him reassess his ideas. Clearly unafraid of hard work, Hannah had a kind and generous heart, and when his sister Lizzie came home from Trescadinnick with stories of her kindness, his mother sent a message inviting her to visit next time she had a free afternoon. Hannah accepted, and from then on had been spending what little free time she had at the farm.

She was made welcome by all the Shaws, but as they got to know each other, her friendship with Will had deepened to one of great affection, and great satisfaction to them both. Neither of them was of a demonstrative nature, but each had found contentment in the other's company. This was accepted by his mother and sisters as the most natural thing, and it was in the farmhouse kitchen where Hannah now felt most at home. She had never expected to have a husband or a home of her own. She had imagined that she would remain with Sophie for the rest of her life, acting as nursemaid to Sophie's children as she had to Sophie herself. She would never leave Sophie, at least until she was happily established with a home of her own, and Will knew and understood that, but their lives were filled with new possibility, a new future.

Now, suddenly, she was leaving, with no more than a brief note of explanation sent home with Lizzie and as the pony and trap carried her further and further away from Will, Hannah had to fight the tears of heartache.

Sophie's thoughts were altogether different. She knew a great feeling of relief at leaving the strained atmosphere of Trescadinnick. Had Mama known a similar feeling, Sophie wondered, when she had slipped away to marry John Ross?

When Hannah had finally left her to sleep, Sophie had yet again moved the great wardrobe and made her way into Joss's bedroom. Quickly, she went to the desk and scooped up all the letters in the drawer. No one else wants them, she told her stirring conscience. No one else cares about Joss any more.

She'd taken them back to her own room and they were now tucked into her bag, waiting for further perusal in the quiet of her own home. Home! she thought. She would have to find some form of employment, but she knew that thanks to dear Aunt Matty she had her home for as long as she wanted it.

'I shall continue to pay your rent, my dear,' Matty had said when she'd also accepted that Sophie was returning home. 'No ifs or buts; you're my niece and if the circumstances had been reversed I know Mary would have done the same for a child of mine.' Sophie had accepted her aunt's generosity and they had agreed to write to each other regularly.

But it wasn't Aunt Matty and her kindness that was at the forefront of her mind as they clopped along the lane to St Morwen; it was Dr Nicholas Bryan. Would he really come and visit her when he was in London? She had seen the admiration in his eyes, and the thought of his lips on her hand made her heart quicken. There was a man who… who what? Sophie didn't know, but she found herself smiling at the thought of seeing him again.

She was to see him far sooner than she had anticipated, for

when they arrived at the little station at St Morwen, Dr Nicholas Bryan was sitting in his gig in the station yard. As Paxton drew in beside him, he got out and came round to hand Sophie down from the trap.

'I thought you were probably catching the morning train to Truro, Sophie,' he said, smiling down at her and still continuing to hold her hand. 'I had business in the town and so I thought I'd come and wish you a safe journey home.'

Sophie felt herself blushing at the warmth in his voice and gentle pressure on her hand. 'How very kind of you, Nicholas,' she said, returning his smile.

'Let me escort you to the platform,' Nicholas said, offering her his arm as they walked into the station. Hannah, following, bought their tickets, and Paxton called the porter to take their luggage.

As the train pulled into the station, and stopped with a squeal of brakes and an explosion of steam, Nicholas stepped forward and opened a compartment door. Paxton saw their luggage into the guard's van, while Nicholas saw Sophie and Hannah settled into their seats.

'I shall look forward to seeing you in London,' he said as he stepped back down to the platform. 'In the meantime I hope you have a safe and comfortable journey home.'

Standing at the open window of the carriage, Sophie reached out her hand to him and as he had the day before, he raised it to his lips before releasing it again. Sophie felt her heart skip a beat and smiled up at him with brilliant eyes. 'I hope you will come,' she said.

'Of that you can be sure.' Nicholas smiled. 'It's a promise!'

Chapter 20

Sophie and Hannah were exhausted when they finally climbed down from the hansom that brought them from the station to the little house in Hammersmith. The journey had been long and this time there had been no private compartment; no overnight stop in Exeter. They had travelled in a third-class compartment from Truro to Paddington, accompanied at various stages of their journey by an assortment of other passengers, including a woman with a basket of hens, a family with two small children who squabbled most of the time and an elderly man who promptly went to sleep and snored loudly until he awoke. They'd had no time to prepare food for the journey, but Hannah went into the market in Truro before the London train came in and returned with a pasty each and some apples. Though they felt uncomfortable eating these with others in the compartment watching them, they'd found them both tasty and filling and were glad to have them.

Sophie turned the key in her own front door and it was with relief that they both stepped into the familiar hallway. The house was cold, but they didn't mind. They were home and as she closed the door on the dark street, Sophie felt her home wrap around her like a comforting shawl.

Hannah was immediately all busyness, hurrying first to the kitchen to light the range and then to the parlour to light a fire there.

There was no food in the house and so they went to bed hungry, but as Sophie lay in the familiarity of her bedroom, the bedclothes pulled up round her ears for warmth, she knew she had made the right decision. She was home, comfortable with the trappings of her childhood around her.

When she awoke the next morning, it was to find Hannah in the kitchen making breakfast. She had already been to the shops at the end of the road and come back laden with provisions.

It wasn't until some days later that Sophie had the time to take out Joss's letters and sort through them. She still set aside, unread, those that bore Cassie's distinctive handwriting, but looked through others to see if there was anything further relating to their plans to marry. She reread the letter from her mother, but decided she needed to look at the letters she'd found earlier in the bureau to see if any of those came from Joss and threw light on what had happened. She went back to her mother's desk and taking the letters out, spread them across the table. To her delight there were several from Joss, and she sorted them into date order.

30th September 1861

Dear Mary
You'll be surprised to hear from me no doubt after so long, but I am in great need of help and don't know where else to turn. I have fallen in love, and of course as far as Father is concerned, with the wrong woman. Her name is Cassandra Drew and she is the daughter of the Reverend Nicholas Drew, the Methodist minister in St Morwen. They have very little money and Cassie keeps house for her father and brother, Edwin.

When I told Father about her he forbade me to have anything more to do with Cassie or her family. Running true to form he has other plans for me and my marriage, I know you'll understand how that feels.

I'd best come straight to the point, Mary, Cassie and I have already consummated our love and now Cassie is expecting our child.

Her pious father has thrown her out, as a dire warning

to his flock. Fornication cannot be tolerated by anyone, especially that of his own daughter.

Well, perhaps he's right, but as it's too late to worry about that, we have to find the best way forward.

Father, of course, condemns Cassie for being a loose woman while simply proclaiming me a fool to have been so taken in. All blame falls on Cassie, a conniving girl who is trying to trap me into marriage, looking for the social position I can give her. He accuses me of stupidity, but not wrong-doing, saying that all young men have amorous adventures before they settle down. I'm told to pay her off and forget about her.

That of course is ridiculous. I love her dearly and am determined to marry her as soon as I can. I would never desert her and our child.

My problem is that I'm still under age and my father can prevent the marriage.

At present I have appeared to abide by his prohibition and have made no further mention of Cassie or our proposed marriage. I am saving all my allowance to give us a little money to start our married life. If Father knew this he would cut off my allowance now and I would have nothing to save.

Cassie's sister and her husband have taken Cassie in and though her brother-in-law is not happy with the situation, her sister, Henrietta, has talked him round. Poor Cassie is shut away and allowed no contact with me, but we have managed to correspond through her friend Nan Slater, so she knows that I haven't abandoned her.

The baby is due in December and as I come of age in early November, that should give us time to get married before the child is born.

I would like to arrange our wedding as soon after my birthday as possible, when I would remove Cassie from her sister's house and bring her to you.

I know this is asking a great deal of you, Mary, and

John, but I don't know where else to turn. I know you will
understand the situation only too well and hope you'll feel
able to give us a home for just a few weeks.
   Your loving brother, Jocelyn

Sophie read the letter through twice. What a dreadful situation, she thought, for both Cassie and Joss. How on earth had
they got into such difficulties? How had Cassie, the daughter of
a Methodist minister, allowed Joss to take advantage of her?

Mary had ensured that Sophie was not completely ignorant
of the facts of life. She had some idea of what went on in the
marital chamber, but the idea of it happening anywhere else was
incomprehensible. Surely Cassie must have tried to stop him.
Had he overpowered her? Sophie knew that girls in the lower
classes sometimes 'got into trouble' but not the sort of people she
knew; not her own family... and Jocelyn was her family. She
wasn't surprised to read of her grandfather's reaction, but how
calmly her mother had accepted what had happened. She had
not criticized Joss; she had been ready to help him out of his
difficulties. Even her father seemed to have accepted that it was
too late to do anything but help them make the best of things
and try and avoid a scandal.

She reread her mother's reply to this letter and then turned to
the next letter Joss had written.

11th October

My dear Mary
What a wonderful and loving sister you are. You and
John are so generous to offer us a home from which to be
married. I will be writing to Cassie to tell her about your
generosity. I don't want to burden you with our presence
for too long, so while Cassie is safe and comfortable living
with her sister, I have suggested she stays where she is until
I am of age and can fetch her away. It's only another few
weeks, but I am afraid of alerting my father to my plans

while he would still be in a position to stop them. For that reason, too, I haven't told either Louisa or Matty of the situation. I know they would probably be as scandalized as my father. Louisa anyway. Neither of them have followed their hearts as you and I have done. Of course I am hoping that all the family will accept Cassie once we are married and the baby is born, but if not, well, we shall have each other, just as you and John have.

Please give my heartfelt thanks to John. I know we have placed him in a difficult position and will be eternally grateful for his kindness.

I remain, your loving brother,

Jocelyn

So Matty and Louisa knew nothing about Joss and Cassie, thought Sophie. Did they ever hear about Cassie, she wondered, or did they still not know that their brother had been not only on the point of marriage but also of becoming a father?

There was only one more letter from Joss, obviously in answer to one of Mary's. It was dated four days before Joss died.

My dear Mary

You ask what Cassie looks like. My simple answer: an angel. She is quite beautiful with shining, fair curls and eyes the colour of cornflowers. She is not tall, only coming up to my shoulder, and delicately made with fine, slender hands. But the best is her smile. Her smile lights up my world. You see, Mary, I am indeed in love; besotted if you will.

I had hoped to come up to London and visit you last week, but my father demanded my attendance that day and as you know I am doing nothing to arouse his suspicions about my movements. He believes that I have done as he instructed and paid Cassie off, and that she has gone from my life, but as you can imagine he wouldn't approve of my coming to visit you either. I have told him that I have an invitation from a fellow student at Oxford, so should be

able to stay away for several days in the next week or so.
How I hate all these lies, but until Cassie and I are married
there is no escape from them.
   I look forward to seeing you very soon and getting to
know your John.
   Jocelyn

Sophie carefully put all the letters into the bureau drawer.
Though she was tempted yet again to read what Cassie had
written to Joss, she put her letters, unread, with the others and
closed the drawer. Then she sat down by the fire and thought
about what she had read. She knew, now, more of what had been
planned, but she still had no idea of what had happened next. So
many questions flooded her mind. Had he made the promised
visit to London? Was that why there were no further letters? Why
had Joss been out that cold October night? What had happened
to Cassie? What had happened to the baby? Had her mother
tried to find Cassie? Where had she been living as she waited for
Joss to come and fetch her? Truro was the only indication she'd
given in her letters. Had she mentioned her sister's name? Yes,
Henrietta, but Henrietta what? Sophie was almost certain there
had been no mention of her surname. She longed to discuss it all
with someone and very nearly told Hannah all about it as they
shared their supper that evening. But then she would have to
admit breaking into Jocelyn's room and stealing his letters, and
her own conscience was troublesome enough about that without
adding Hannah's inevitable comments.

Knowing that she must earn some money, and determined not
to be totally reliant on Matty's generosity, Sophie had contacted
the parents of her former piano pupils, Emma and Harriet, to
see if they wanted to resume their daughters' lessons. Emma's
mother replied that they already had found a replacement
teacher as Miss Ross was away for so long, but Harriet's mother
had not been satisfied with the replacement she had found and
agreed that Sophie should come twice a week and pick up where
she had left off.

It was when she had just got in from Harriet's lesson a week later and was drinking a cup of tea that the doorbell rang. She heard Hannah go to the door and then an exclamation of surprise as she saw who was standing on the doorstep. She heard a man's voice and then the parlour door opened and Hannah came in to say that Dr Bryan had called.

'Well, don't leave him standing in the hall, Hannah,' cried Sophie, colour flooding her cheeks. 'Bring him in.'

Hannah turned back to the hall, but Nicholas had heard Sophie's answer and was already stepping past Hannah, into the room.

Sophie greeted him with outstretched hands which he clasped in his own. 'Nicholas!' she exclaimed. 'You came!'

'Of course I came, Sophie. I told you I would.' For a moment his eyes roved over her, taking in her flushed cheeks, her neat figure, the glorious colour of her hair. But seeing Hannah waiting at the door, he dropped her hands and said, 'What a delightful welcome.'

'Hannah,' Sophie turned to her companion, 'please will you make a fresh pot of tea and bring some of those scones you made this morning?'

'Certainly, Miss Sophie.' Hannah changed from being close companion to being paid servant and with a bob left the room.

Now, she thought, as she brought the kettle back to the boil and laid out scones, butter and jam on a tray, what on earth has brought *him* here? And how did he know where to find us?

But when she thought about it, it was plain as a pikestaff why he was here: because Miss Sophie had invited him. The way she had greeted him made that very clear. She had seen the look of delight on Sophie's face... and what? Something like a flash of triumph in the eyes of the doctor.

What have I missed, down at Trescadinnick? wondered Hannah in dismay. Did I spend too much time with AliceAnne and not notice what was happening in front of me? What will Mr Charles think when he hears that Dr Bryan has been visiting up here? Well, I suppose he'll never know, for I shan't tell him.

He's already turned Sophie away. But, she decided, I shall keep my wits about me from now on. Then another thought struck her. Miss Sophie is still under age, so who is responsible for her? Who must be her legal guardian? Her grandfather? Probably, as he was her closest living relative.

Hannah sighed and picked up the tray, and took it into the parlour where she found Sophie and the doctor sitting on either side of the fire, deep in conversation.

'Why, Hannah, what delicious-looking scones,' said Dr Bryan with a smile.

Hannah set the tray down and asked, 'Shall I pour the tea, Miss Sophie?'

'No thank you, Hannah. We can manage now. I'll call you if we need anything else.'

When Nicholas left, Hannah came back into the parlour and asked, 'Did you know the doctor was coming, Miss Sophie?'

'Sort of,' admitted Sophie. 'When I told him I was coming home, he said he had business in London soon and asked if he might call.'

'And you gave him your address.' Hannah spoke flatly. 'Oh, Miss Sophie, you shouldn't have done. How can we allow him to call when you have no chaperone? It's not right for you to receive him alone. People will talk.'

Sophie laughed at this. 'But, Hannah,' she replied, 'I have no chaperone but you, and you were here in the house with me. Nothing improper took place, as you well know.'

'I do know, Miss Sophie, but it's not what I know that matters. It's what people think.'

'What people, Hannah? Who takes any interest in me and what I do?'

'Any right-thinking person,' Hannah answered. 'We have to protect your reputation.'

'My reputation is my own concern,' Sophie said briskly. 'And if I choose to receive Dr Bryan here in my own home, I think it is no one's business but mine.' She fixed Hannah with a hard stare and then, relenting, said more gently, 'Hannah, if Mama were here, of course she would be in the room with me, but she isn't. You would feel uncomfortable sitting in the corner while Dr Bryan and I talk, and I don't think he would like it either.'

'Whether he likes it is neither here nor there,' replied Hannah roundly. 'It's not proper.'

'I know what you're saying, Hannah, but in that case I'll never be able to meet any man who isn't a relative. At least you know Dr Bryan and know that he's accepted at Trescadinnick. They find him respectable. No one complained when I took tea with him at The Clipper, or when I went out driving with him.'

'No,' sighed Hannah. 'No, they didn't, but on both those occasions you had AliceAnne with you. You wasn't seen to be alone with him.'

Sophie laughed. 'AliceAnne was my chaperone?'

'You wasn't alone with him,' repeated Hannah doggedly.

'Hannah, I know you have my best interests at heart, but I'm not a child.'

'No, indeed,' Hannah agreed, 'and that's the problem. You're a grown woman and an heiress at that.'

'Well, as for being an heiress, Nicholas doesn't know that, does he?'

'Doesn't he? Maybe not, but he might well think it is likely.'

'Why should he? Everyone else thinks it's Charles who's the heir, as by rights it should be. Why would Nicholas think any different?'

'And that's another thing,' Hannah said, moving on. 'His use of your Christian name. He's much too free with that.'

'He asked if he might use it,' Sophie said patiently, 'and I agreed. He then asked me to use his, and so I do. We're friends, Hannah, that's all.'

'Are you?' said Hannah. 'I've seen the way he looks at you and I'm not the only one.' It was a mistake and Hannah realized it at once.

'Have you?' Sophie said, blushing. 'I thought I might be mistaken.'

'If he has honourable intentions towards you, Miss Sophie,

and you want to encourage them, he should approach your grandfather. Since both your parents are dead, he must be your natural guardian.'

'I doubt if he'd get far there,' countered Sophie. 'My grandfather is determined I shall marry Charles. He would never give Nicholas permission to address me.' She reached out and took Hannah's hand. 'I know you worry about me, dearest Hannah, but you don't have to. If anyone is going to give Dr Bryan permission to address me, it will be me.'

For an instant she thought back to Joss's letters to her mother and added, 'I shall be of age in March, and I shall require no one's permission to marry whomever I choose. And,' she added with steel in her voice, 'if Dr Bryan comes to call again I shall receive him as I did today, alone. He's a gentleman and will take no advantage of such licence.'

Hannah knew when she was beaten and she said, 'You must suit yourself, Miss Sophie, but I know your grandfather would not approve.'

'I care nothing for his approval,' said Sophie and getting up to indicate the conversation was over, crossed to her piano. She raised the lid and said, 'I think I shall practise now for a while, Hannah.'

Rightly taking this as her dismissal, Hannah left the room and went to the kitchen to prepare the evening meal. As she peeled potatoes she heard the flood of music coming from the parlour. I hope she knows what she's doing, Hannah thought. I know Dr Bryan seems quite respectable, but there is something I don't quite trust about him. He's too forward, too forward in every way.

If she'd known the truth of where he was at that moment, she'd have been even more worried.

Chapter 21

When Nicholas left Sophie, he took an omnibus across the river to a small house in Southwark. He walked up Clayton Street and paused briefly outside the familiar front door before reaching for the knocker. The door was opened by a small blonde-haired woman, who took a step backwards when she saw who was standing on her doorstep.

Nicholas treated her to a wide smile. 'Hallo, Dolly,' he cried. 'Surprise!'

Dolly began to close the door, but Nicholas was too quick for her and putting his foot in the way said, 'What's the matter, Doll, aren't you pleased to see me?'

'Pleased to see you?' sniffed Dolly. 'Why should I be?'

'Thought you might've missed me.'

'What? Like a pain in the 'ead?'

'Come on, Doll, aren't you going to let me in?'

'No.'

'Don't you want to know what I come round for?'

'No. You only comes round when you want somefink.'

'Not this time, Dolly. This time I got something to offer *you.*'

'Oh yeah? What's that then?'

'Fifty quid.'

'Fifty quid?' echoed Dolly, her eyes widening.

'Interest you, does it?' asked Nicholas with a grin. 'Thought it might!'

'Suppose you better come in,' Dolly said, stepping back into the house and allowing him to follow, closing the door behind him.

She led the way into the kitchen and as soon as she turned back to face him, he reached for her and pulled her roughly into his arms. For a moment he felt her body stiff, resisting him, but ignoring her resistance as usual, he slid his hands lower. And cupping her buttocks, he lifted her up against him so that she could feel his need, and murmured, 'You always did have a lovely arse, Doll.'

'Bastard!' she muttered, and squirmed against him, making him gasp.

Somehow they got upstairs to the tiny bedroom and Nicholas pushed her down onto the bed, pulling her blouse away and rubbing himself against her breasts. Reaching up, Dolly unbuttoned his trousers and released him, quivering, into her hands.

It was a quick coupling, full of pent-up energy, forceful and rough, as it always had been with Nicholas. When he rolled away, spent, Dolly lay beside him, still aroused, yet angry with herself for allowing him to take her so easily.

Why can't I resist him? she thought angrily. Why is it every time he comes back we end up like this?

Almost as if she had spoken her thoughts aloud, Nicholas said, 'You liked that, Doll, didn't you? You always were a good lay. Miss me, do you, when I'm not here?'

'No,' snapped Dolly, 'always glad to see the back of you.' And that was true too. She was far happier when Nicholas wasn't there. Sometimes she didn't see him for months and she'd think she'd finally seen the last of him, and then he'd turn up again, like today, and within minutes he'd have her gasping for him. And she hated him for it.

Even as she was thinking these thoughts, Nicholas reached over and ran his finger down between her breasts, teasing the still erect nipples.

'Ready for more?' he laughed. He placed her hand between his legs and said, 'Oh! Look at that! So am I!'

'So,' he said, later still, 'all right, are you, Doll?'

'As if you care,' muttered Dolly.

'Don't be like that, Dolly. Don't you want to know what I've come round for?'

'Thought that was pretty obvious!' Dolly replied bitterly.

Nicholas grinned. 'Well that too,' he admitted. 'But I just thought you might be interested in making a nifty fifty, that's all.'

'Yeah? An' how do I do that then?' demanded Dolly suspiciously.

'Our marriage lines,' he replied easily. 'I want them, you've got them and I'll give you fifty for them.'

'You mean our marriage certificate?' she repeated incredulously. 'What you want that for?'

'Well, you don't want to be married to me any more, do you?'

'No,' Dolly said flatly. 'Never does me no good, does it? Never see you, do I? Never get nothing off you.'

'Exactly,' Nicholas said. 'An' I 'spect you have other blokes when I'm not here,' continuing as Dolly began to protest, ''Course you do, Doll, stands to reason, a good-looker like you. *I* don't mind, but us being married when we don't want to be, well, it stops us getting on with our lives, doesn't it?'

When Dolly didn't answer, just looked at him with narrowed eyes, he went on. 'So what I thought was, it'd only be fair to give you a bit of cash for yourself, so's you can have a fresh start. You can give me our marriage certificate which I tear up and then we won't be married any more. What do you think? Fifty pounds says we never been married, and we never see each other again. I'll disappear from your life, you'll be a rich woman and can take your pick of the blokes.'

'A hundred,' said Dolly.

'Hey, Doll, that's a bit steep!' Nicholas complained.

'No, it ain't,' she drawled. 'I didn't come down with the last shower, Nicky boy. If you want to get shot of me, no questions asked, you must have a good reason. Yeah? Then a ton's cheap at the price, don't you fink?'

Nicholas did think, but he didn't trust her. 'Maybe,' he said coolly. 'I might manage that at a push. But it wouldn't be wise to come back for more, Dolly.'

Dolly looked at him, into the pale blue eyes that had once enchanted her and later terrified her, and nodded. She knew better than to cross Nicholas Bryan, but somehow she couldn't break free of him. Perhaps this would be her chance.

'You got plans then?' she asked, idly running a fingernail across Nicholas's stomach, making the flesh quiver and clench. 'Good in the sack, is she?'

'Who?'

Dolly shrugged. 'Whoever she is. Has to be someone.'

Nicholas laughed. 'Hardly. She's straight from the schoolroom. But by the time I've finished with her, she'll know what to do.'

'Poor girl,' murmured Dolly.

'I've some scores to settle,' was the enigmatic reply as he reached for her again.

'So, where's that certificate?' demanded Nicholas when he lay back, sated.

'Where's the money?'

'I'll get it,' Nicholas promised. 'But it'll take time. A hundred'll take time. Don't you trust me?'

'No,' said Dolly. 'You bring me the money. When I see that, then maybe I'll find the certificate. I'll fink about it, but I want to see the cash with my own eyes first.'

As she had known he would, Nicholas stayed the night, and as she lay beside him in the darkness Dolly thought about his proposition and considered the reason for it. They had met and married while he was at St Thomas's Hospital learning his 'doctoring'. Dolly had been the barmaid in The Falcon, a pub Nicholas and the other medical students liked to frequent, and when she had fallen pregnant with Nicholas's child, her father, with three other large dockers, had marched them off to St John's Church, Waterloo, for Nicholas to make an honest woman of her. They had lived together until the baby was born, a stillborn girl, and then the marriage was over. For Dolly it was a relief when, tired of married life in two rooms in Southwark, Nicholas had disappeared. In the following three years, he turned up occasionally, demanding his marital rights, and Dolly was too afraid to refuse. Now he clearly wanted to be shot of her, and with the promise of so much cash all at once, Dolly thought perhaps she really could put her miserable marriage behind her and start again.

When he'd gone the next morning, Dolly discussed the idea with her brother, Luke.

'What's he up to, I wonder?' said Luke, scratching his head. 'Somefink's up if he's gonna pay you a hundred quid for a bit of paper. Stands to reason, don't it? Has to be worth a looksee, don't it?'

'He's found someone he wants to marry,' answered Dolly. 'Don't envy her, poor cow!'

''Zactly,' said Luke. 'So, it must be worth finding out who she is.'

'What d'you mean?' demanded Dolly.

'What I mean is, there should be money here for all of us, innit?'

'Us?' queried Dolly. 'That money's for me, bro. I'm the one what's put up with him.'

'Yeah. But what if we could get more, much more?'

Dolly looked interested. 'How?'

'Simple, me old darlin'. Is he coming back here tonight?'

'Yeah, 'spect so. Said he was in London for a week and he ain't got nowhere else to go for a free shag.'

'What's he up to, here in London, anyway?'

Dolly shrugged. 'I dunno, do I?'

'P'raps he's getting the money,' said Luke. 'You got this certificate what he wants?'

'Yeah, 'course I have.'

'Well, Doll, if he's coming back here, I fink I'll take that certificate wiv me, so's he can't get his hands on it without paying up, all right?'

Dolly nodded. She certainly didn't want to be cheated of all that money.

'Then tomorrow,' Luke went on, 'I'll follow him, find out where he goes and who he's seeing, right?'

'Told you, he wants to get married again.'

'There you are then,' Luke continued. 'Should be worth our while, that should. Whoever she is, bet she'll pay well for a sight of them marriage lines, don't you?'

'Why would she?'

'Come on, Doll, fink about it, the girl's got to be rich for him to bother, yeah? But if she marries him she's gonna lose all her money, ain't she? Never mind the odd black eye. Your Nick'll bleed her dry. If we go and tell her he's already married, she'll cough up to see the proof.'

'Suppose she might,' conceded Dolly. 'But I wouldn't want to be around when Nick finds out. He'll come after us an' it'll be the worst for me. I been on the end of his fists too often to want it to happen again. No, Lukey-boy, I'm happy to settle for what Nick gives me to keep me mouth shut.'

'We don't *give* her the certificate, Doll. If she pays us, then we let her *see* it. It's Nick we *give* it to, when he coughs up the hundred. That way we gets paid twice, see.'

'An' if he finds out?'

'By the time that happens we'll be away on our toes where he can't find us. The only thing I don't understand is why he's come to you at all.'

'Cos I've got the marriage lines,' Dolly said. 'That's what he wants. Till he's got them, I got a hold, ain't I?'

'But you wouldn't have knowed he was getting married again.'

'I might have.' Dolly nodded judiciously. 'Word gets about with things like that. That old uncle of his is still about, what's he called? Edwin? I seen him sometimes. The thing is,' Dolly went on, 'if I'd heard about it after Nick had married this bird, I could've gone to the law and he could've ended up in clink. He weren't gonna risk that.'

'And 'spose you give him the certificate and then he don't pay up?' Luke said. 'Are *you* gonna risk *that*?'

'No,' Dolly said. 'You and some of your mates'll be here with me for the exchange. You'll be my protection. If we don't see the money he don't get the certificate. Nick'll pay up.'

'Still,' Luke said. 'Fink I'll keep an eye on him while he's here. Wouldn't hurt to know who she is and where she lives, now, would it? When we know who she is, well, we can decide what to do about her.'

With some reluctance, Dolly agreed. 'But for Gawd's sake don't let him see you, all right?'

Luke grinned. 'Don't worry, Doll, he won't.'

Chapter 22

On the day before Nicholas's return to Cornwall, he and Sophie spent a chilly afternoon at the zoo and were pleased to be back in the warmth of the parlour; Sophie, seated in an armchair at the fireside, Nicholas standing with his back to the fire. Silence surrounded them and then Nicholas stepped forward and reaching down, took Sophie's hands in his.

'Sophie, look at me.'

Sophie looked up into his face and her heart missed a beat. He was looking at her with such intensity that she felt almost afraid. She could feel the colour rushing to her face and knew that the moment had come.

'Sophie, my dearest Sophie, you know how I feel about you, don't you?' When she didn't reply he went on, 'How I've felt about you ever since the first day I saw you?'

Sophie found she couldn't speak, but she nodded.

'I haven't much to offer you,' Nicholas said, 'but I love you more than anything in the world. Will you marry me, my dearest girl? Marry me and be my wife?'

She looked away, hesitating. Gently pulling her to her feet, Nicholas slipped his arms round her, and held her close against him. He could feel her heart thumping against his chest, the pliant warmth of her body against his, and he was seized with a desire to possess her so strong that, for a second or two, he had difficulty restraining himself and thus undoing all his careful, gentle wooing. After a moment he relaxed a little and cupping the back of her head he tilted her face to his and simply murmuring the word 'Sophie', kissed her on the lips.

For a second she froze, but as his kiss was simply the gentle brushing of lips, she relaxed against him. She felt the strength of his arms about her, warm and protective.

This is how it must be, she thought as he held her close and she slipped her arms round him, feeling his breath on her neck. This is what it means to love and be loved. She had never received a kiss from anyone who was not a relative before; the only man had been her father, who would kiss the top of her head as he wished her goodnight. She had no brothers, no cousins, and until she'd met Nicholas, so tall and handsome, no man had paid her any attention at all. Now here she was, folded into his embrace, her whole being bursting with happiness, and she raised her face to him again, her eyes brilliant with tears of joy.

Nicholas looked down at her. 'Is that yes, my darling girl?' he whispered.

'Oh yes, Nicholas. Oh yes.' And his second kiss was as gentle as the first.

'Let's get married soon,' he said as he led her to the sofa and sat down at her side, her hand still grasped in his. 'There's no reason to wait, darling girl, is there?'

'No, Nicholas. I long to be your wife,' Sophie said. 'But I shall have to tell my grandfather. I believe he is my guardian and will have to give his permission for my marriage while I am still under age.' She smiled shyly up at Nicholas. 'I'm sure he won't refuse it, but if by any chance he should, well, we shall only have to wait until the end of March. I'll be twenty-one on the twenty-fifth.'

'I am a professional man; surely he can have no objection,' said Nicholas.

'I don't know,' Sophie replied. She hesitated, wondering if she should tell him her grandfather had made him her heir, but bit back the words. Hannah had suggested he might be after her fortune and if she didn't tell him, no one could accuse him of being a fortune-hunter. 'You know how difficult he can be!'

Nicholas forced a smile. 'Yes, your aunts have been in despair.'

'I think…' Sophie said carefully as she sorted her thought in her mind, 'I think it would be best if I tell him. I said I might go back and spend Christmas with them at Trescadinnick. If I do that it would be the perfect opportunity to tell him, to tell them all.' And Charles will know once and for all that there is no question of my marrying him, she thought with quiet satisfaction; but she didn't say that either. No need to spoil the perfect evening.

Later, having kissed gently her once more, Nicholas took his leave. 'I'll come round in the morning to say goodbye,' he promised.

Returning to the house in Clayton Street, he spent one last enjoyable night of energetic sex with Dolly, and when he got up in the morning he knew a moment of regret that this would probably be for the last time. He certainly wanted no further connection with her, but there was no doubt that she knew how to please a man in bed.

As he crossed the town for his final visit to Hammersmith, he was entirely unaware of the figure still sloping along behind him. Luke had followed him each day and had watched Nicholas squiring Sophie about the town. He knew what she looked like and where she lived. It didn't look like a rich woman's house, and she didn't look like a rich woman, but if Nicholas Bryan was investing so much time and money in her, Luke thought, surely there must be something in it for Dolly and him, and once again he settled down to keep watch.

Chapter 23

Charles Leroy got off the overnight train at Paddington and walked out into the street. He was at once assailed by the noise of the city; he had forgotten how noisy the capital could be with its thousands of inhabitants rushing about their daily lives. The road in front of him had come to a near standstill; a waggon had lost a wheel and was canted over at the roadside, its load of fruit and vegetables sliding into the street. The shouts and oaths of other drivers mingled with calls of the street vendors, the cries of ragamuffin children escaped from school, who darted fearlessly amid hooves and wheels to snatch apples from the tilting waggon, and the bellows of the waggoner as he tried in vain to stop them.

For a while Charles stood there, appalled at the uproar. How could people live in such a turmoil of sound and bustle? Even Truro, a city he knew well and which he was always glad to leave at the end of a day, was quiet compared with the clamour of London. What on earth am I doing here? he thought as he surveyed the chaotic scene. I must be mad.

He had come because AliceAnne had asked him to. Two months ago such a thing would have been unthinkable. He would have been unlikely to ask what she wanted, let alone listen seriously to her reply. The change, he realized, was due to Sophie's influence. She had taught him to pay attention to his daughter, to treat her as a real person with likes and dislikes, interests and ideas, rather than a child who should be seen and not heard; his mother's view. Since Sophie had left Trescadinnick almost three weeks ago, the house had seemed cold and dark, as if someone had quenched a light, leaving only lingering gloom. The music had ceased, there was little laughter and conversation in the dining room was stilted and stiff.

Charles had come to a truce with Thomas, each treating the other with the uneasy courtesy necessary for living under the same roof, and Charles knew how much Thomas missed Sophie. Several times he'd heard him hopefully asking Louisa if there was a letter from his granddaughter. There had been one, announcing her safe arrival in Hammersmith, but since then there had been no word to any of them. Once AliceAnne had also heard him ask and she too had waited with hope as her grandmother looked through the post that had just arrived, before shaking her head and saying, 'No, I'm sorry, Papa, nothing today.'

'I wish the stupid girl would write to him,' Louisa grumbled to Matty when she came to visit her father one afternoon. 'He really does miss her, and it's all a storm in a teacup.'

Hardly, Matty thought with some bitterness. You've never been told to marry someone you don't want to! But she didn't speak her thought aloud. After all, it wasn't Louisa's fault that Thomas had tried to force her sisters into marriage. Louisa had been allowed to marry her James and been very happy for the seven years they'd had together before a sudden seizure had carried him off, leaving her a widow with a stepson to bring up. Louisa had never wanted to remarry; she had transferred her devotion from her husband to his son.

Charles had seen how his daughter blossomed under the attention given her by both Sophie and Hannah, and gradually realized how neglected the little girl had been previously. Recognizing it was his fault for leaving her to the care of Mrs Paxton and a strict and elderly grandmother, he started to spend more time with her and was surprised how much he enjoyed her company. It wasn't a chore, or a tiresome demand on his time, and he began to take pleasure in discovering his AliceAnne. He found he could make her smile and that he loved doing so. Her smile, so reminiscent of Anne's, always brought an answering one of his own.

He kept his promise and began teaching her to ride Oscar, and to the delight of both of them she was unafraid and learning fast. As the evenings closed in, he would go up and find her in the schoolroom, and there they played the card games Hannah had taught her. But what AliceAnne enjoyed most was to curl up beside him on the old sofa before the schoolroom stove and read with him, turn and turn about, as she had with Sophie.

It was when they were sitting like this one evening that AliceAnne had suddenly asked, 'Papa, is Aunt Sophie coming back?'

'I don't know, AliceAnne,' Charles replied with a sigh.

'She said she would at Christmas and it's nearly Christmas now, isn't it?'

'She did, but I'm not sure if she's going to come after all.'

'But, Papa, I do miss her...'

'Yes, I know,' said her father.

I miss her too, he thought, and realized it was the first time he had admitted this to himself. He missed Sophie in a way that he hadn't thought possible. He missed her cheerfulness at the breakfast table, a time when previously he had insisted on quiet while he drank his coffee and contemplated his day. He missed her ready wit, always having an answer, and her refusal to be bullied by anyone, even the indomitable Thomas. He missed seeing her seated at the piano after dinner, the lamplight gleaming on her hair as she played, and the brilliance of her dark green eyes when she glanced up and smiled as he turned her music.

'And if you could, Hannah would come too, wouldn't she?' AliceAnne was saying. 'I like Hannah.'

'Of course you do,' he said, returning his attention to her.

'So will you?'

'Will I what?'

'Will you write to Aunt Sophie and ask her to come at Christmas?'

Thinking about Sophie, Charles had missed the little girl's question. 'I'll think about it,' he found himself saying. 'Now, your turn to read.'

Charles did think about it and the more he thought, the less he wanted to write. Supposing Sophie simply ignored his letter. If that happened he wouldn't even know for sure that she had received it. It would be difficult to explain in a letter how much it would mean to AliceAnne that Sophie should be with them for Christmas. He could tell her that Thomas was missing her and had asked him to write and remind her of her promise, but that, he thought, could well be counterproductive. Sophie, being Sophie, certainly wouldn't come if she thought she were being ordered to do so.

He thought of discussing the idea with Louisa, but was almost sure she would advise against it. She had been delighted when Sophie had taken herself off, back to London. In the end he went over to Treslyn House to consult Matty.

'Do you think she would come if I wrote to her?' he asked his aunt. 'We didn't part on good terms.'

'I don't think Sophie is one to bear a grudge,' Matty replied. 'She was angry at the time, but she may well be regretting the way you parted as much as you do.'

'Well, I do,' acknowledged Charles. 'But the real reason that I'm concerned is because AliceAnne is so disappointed. She was hoping that Sophie would come back for Christmas.'

Matty smiled. 'Of course it is,' she agreed. 'And we must do all we can to make sure AliceAnne isn't disappointed any more.'

'So what do you suggest?' Charles asked when he had explained all the reasons why he was reluctant to write.

'What do I suggest?' Matty thought for a moment and then said, 'I suggest you go up to London and see her.'

'Go to London?' Charles was incredulous. 'How can I go to London?'

'On a train, Charles?'

'Yes, well, I know that. What I mean is, why should I go all that way when she may not even let me into her house?'

'I doubt if Sophie will leave you standing on her doorstep, or shut the door in your face.'

'But she may not be very pleased to see me, even so.'

'No, she may not,' Matty agreed. 'But you won't know unless you go, will you? She might just be waiting for a chance to come back herself.'

'It'll take at least three days,' Charles said. 'I'm not sure I can be away that long.'

Matty laughed. 'Yes, it will, but I doubt if the estate will fall to pieces without you in that time.'

'Well, I'll think about it.'

'You do that, Charles. But I suggest you don't leave it too long to decide or you'll be too late. Now, tell me, how is my father? Is the doctor still pleased with his progress?'

'We haven't seen Dr Bryan for several days now,' Charles replied. 'But Mama says Grandfather seems to be improving. She says he's certainly eating more and his colour is healthier. He's not that chalky-white he's been recently.'

'That's good to hear,' Matty said. 'Tell Louisa and Papa that I'll come over tomorrow for a visit. And what about AliceAnne? How's she getting on with her riding?'

There was no further mention of a visit to London to see Sophie, and Charles had returned from his visit to Matty with his thoughts in turmoil. When he went up to say goodnight to AliceAnne that evening she asked him if he had written to Sophie.

'No, I haven't,' he replied, 'but I'm going up to London to ask her to come. All right?'

He was rewarded with a hug and a beaming smile. 'Oh, Papa, are you? I know she'll come if you ask her!' Charles was not so sure, but his decision had been made and he returned AliceAnne's hug.

Louisa was not in favour of the visit. 'Why you want her to come back here, even for a short visit, I can't imagine,' she said. 'She's just like her mother, nothing but trouble!'

Thomas, however, was delighted he was going. 'Good idea. Sort out the trouble between you and bring her back. When do you leave?'

'In a couple of days,' Charles answered. 'There is business I have to settle here first.'

When Matty arrived on her visit the next day and heard that Charles was indeed going to London to see Sophie, she took him to one side and said, 'If it makes it easier for her to come and stay with me, rather than back at Trescadinnick, tell her she'll be more than welcome.'

Charles had promised to do so and now here he was, braving the London streets, looking for a hansom to take him out to Hammersmith. He walked up the road until he found a cab and having given the cabby the address, settled back, trying to compose his thoughts and wondering just what sort of welcome awaited him.

When the driver set him down, Charles looked up at the house where Sophie lived and had spent her childhood. It was one of a terrace, three storeys high, set back a little from the road behind a low stone wall. Its tiny front garden was winter-bare but neat and tidy. He walked up the path to the green-painted front door with its shining brass knocker and drawing a deep breath, knocked on the door.

It was not Hannah who answered, as Charles had expected her to, but Sophie, flushed and bright-eyed. The words of welcome that had been on her lips died as she saw who stood on her doorstep. 'Oh, Charles,' was all she said.

'Hallo, Sophie.'

For a moment they looked at each other and then Charles said, 'May I come in?'

Sophie stood aside at once and said, 'Yes, of course. I'm sorry, it's just I was so surprised to see you.'

Charles stepped into the house, saying, 'You were expecting someone else.' It wasn't a question, it had been quite clear from her reaction to seeing him there.

'Yes, well, a friend said he might call.' Turning, she called back into the house, 'Hannah, come and see who's here.'

Charles had noticed the word 'he' and wondered who this friend might be, someone whom Sophie had been ready to greet with such a heart-stopping smile.

Hannah emerged from the kitchen and seeing Charles still

standing in the hall smiled her welcome. 'Mr Charles,' she said, 'this is a surprise. Miss Sophie didn't tell me you was coming.'

'Miss Sophie didn't know,' said Sophie. 'It's a surprise to me as well.'

'Well, don't leave him standing in the hallway, Miss Sophie. Let me take your coat and hat, sir. Now, you take Mr Charles into the parlour, Miss Sophie, and I'll bring in some tea.'

Sophie led Charles into the parlour, a small but cosy room, brightened by a wintry sun pouring in through windows that looked out onto the street and the cheerful fire burning brightly in the grate.

'Do sit down, Charles,' Sophie said, waving a hand towards one of the fireside chairs and moving to take the other. 'And tell me why you're here. Has something happened to my grandfather?'

'No, no,' Charles assured her. 'Indeed, he seems to be making a recovery. My mother is very pleased with him. The doctor hasn't been to see him for nearly two weeks now.'

'I see,' said Sophie, wondering whether to tell him why, but deciding against. 'Well, that's good news, isn't it? So why have you come, Charles?' Her voice was calm, almost indifferent.

'I came because AliceAnne wanted me to.'

'AliceAnne!' That did provoke a reaction.

'She misses you very much, Sophie, and she asked me to write to see if you were coming to Trescadinnick for Christmas as she hopes.'

'So, why didn't you?'

Charles sighed. Sophie wasn't making it easy for him, but he had come this far and he persevered. 'Because we parted on such bad terms, Sophie. I wanted to apologize for what I said to you. It was said in the heat of the moment, but it was unforgiveable.'

'Yes, it was,' agreed Sophie, but then she smiled ruefully. 'But I answered you in kind, so the fault is as much mine as yours.'

'I needed to see you, face to face,' Charles said. 'A letter wouldn't have been enough.'

'Well, here you are,' Sophie said. 'It was generous of you to come so far.'

At that moment Hannah came into the room with a tea tray and a plate of cakes. She set it down on the table and then said, 'And how is everyone at Trescadinnick, Mr Charles? They are all keeping well, I hope.'

'Yes, thank you, Hannah,' answered Charles. 'And I'm hoping you'll be coming to see for yourself very soon. I'm here to ask Sophie to come back for the Christmas season. Everyone misses her, but my grandfather and AliceAnne in particular.' He turned back to Sophie. 'I do hope you'll come, cousin,' he said. 'Your Aunt Matty has invited you to stay with her if you'd find that more convenient.'

'That's kind of her,' Sophie said, 'but—' She broke off as there was a loud knocking on the door.

Hannah went to answer it, but Sophie stood up too, her face bright with expectation.

Charles heard a man's voice in the hall, and then the door swung open and Nicholas Bryan strode into the room. Sophie greeted him with outstretched hands and as he took them in his own, his eyes met Charles's startled gaze and narrowed in a smile. Releasing one of Sophie's hands, he led her back to her chair by the other before saying, 'Good morning, Mr Leroy. What a surprise to find you here.'

'The surprise is mine, Doctor,' Charles said coldly as he got to his feet. 'I hadn't realized you and my cousin were on such terms that you visit her in London.'

'Well, it is hardly any of your business, is it?' Nicholas said smoothly. 'I'm sure Sophie doesn't need your permission in her choice of friends.'

'No, indeed,' agreed Charles. 'But is it not unusual for a *gentleman* to call on a single lady alone in her own home, without acquiring the permission of her guardian beforehand?' His stressing of the word 'gentleman' was too marked to be ignored, and Nicholas Bryan's lips tightened.

'And you are her guardian?'

'No, I am not. But her grandfather is, and to my knowledge he has given no such consent.'

'You, Leroy, are a pompous fool,' began Nicholas, 'and I'll have you know—'

'Nicholas, please!' Sophie broke in, jumping to her feet. 'And you, Charles, that's enough.' Sophie glared at them both. 'I wish you would not discuss me as if I weren't here.' She turned to Hannah, who was standing open-mouthed in the doorway. 'Thank you, Hannah. I think Mr Charles will be leaving directly. Perhaps you could find his hat and coat.'

Hannah went back into the hall and Sophie returned her attention to Charles. How she wished he had left before Nicholas arrived. How she wanted him to leave now, so that she could have her last hour with Nicholas alone before he caught his train. She had stopped Nicholas blurting out about their engagement, but now she would definitely have to commit to Christmas at Trescadinnick. She and Nicholas had discussed the idea the previous evening, but had come to no firm decision. The only way to get rid of Charles now was to agree to visit; then she could break the news that she was going to marry Nicholas when she got there.

'Thank you for coming, Charles,' she said. 'You may tell my grandfather and AliceAnne that I should love to spend Christmas at Trescadinnick and will write of my arrival very soon. And please thank Aunt Matty for her invitation, and say that though I shall stay at Trescadinnick, I'm looking forward to seeing her.'

It was his dismissal and Charles, with a curt nod, took it as such. 'Then I'll see you in Cornwall,' he said, and walked into the hall to where Hannah stood, holding his coat and hat. He thanked her politely as she opened the front door, and went out into the street. As the door was closing behind him he heard the sound of laughter coming from within, turning his heart to ice.

Back in the house Sophie said, 'Thank you for the tea and cake, Hannah. I'll call you if we want anything else.'

When Hannah had left the room, Nicholas stepped forward and pulling Sophie into his arms, said, 'We don't have to wait to tell them now.' He ran his hands gently up and down her back and feeling her shudder of pleasure, kissed her hair. 'That pompous ass, Leroy, will be going hotfoot to tell them.'

'Oh, Nicholas, don't speak of my cousin like that,' begged Sophie.

'Well, he is one,' Nicholas said, unrepentant. 'And he's jealous.'

'Jealous?' echoed Sophie. 'Of course he's not jealous. Why would he be?'

'Because he can see you love me, not him.'

'But he doesn't want me,' protested Sophie. 'He told me so in no uncertain terms. And anyway, he doesn't know we're engaged.'

'I think he can guess. He may be a pompous ass, but he's not a fool. I'm sure he'll be telling them back at Trescadinnick about our meeting here and suggesting your grandfather refuses his permission. They've no time for me, you know.'

'Oh, Nicholas, how can you say so? They hardly know you as I do, but they *do* know you're a good doctor and a good man.'

'You know,' Nicholas suggested thoughtfully, 'we could get a special licence, and be married almost at once, before you visit at Christmas. There'd be nothing your grandfather could do about it then.'

'Oh no, Nicholas,' cried Sophie. 'I couldn't do that. It would be dishonest and they would be extremely hurt. There have been too many rifts in the Penvarrow family. I don't want to be the cause of another.'

'You won't be causing the rift, Sophie. If there is one it will be their fault, not yours.'

'Even so, you have to remember that when we are married I shall be living just down the road from Trescadinnick and will be seeing them all the time.'

Nicholas smiled, but made no comment about where they would be living once they were married, simply saying, 'As you wish, Sophie, of course.'

When he had gone, Sophie sat down by the fire and thought about the morning. At least if she spent Christmas at Trescadinnick she would be able to see Nicholas every day. If she stayed up in London, it might be several weeks before he could come and visit her again, and though they could write to each other in the meantime, and had promised to do so, it would not be the same.

Hannah came in to take the tea tray, but before she picked it up Sophie said, 'Come and sit by the fire, Hannah. I've something to tell you.'

Warily, Hannah sat down. 'Are we going back to Cornwall for Christmas, Miss Sophie? Miss AliceAnne will be pleased.'

'Yes, we are, but that's not what I wanted to tell you.' She looked across at her oldest friend, her eyes bright with joy, and said, 'Guess what, Hannah? I'm so happy! I'm to be married.'

'Married?' It was a question, but Hannah wasn't really surprised. She had watched with dismay Sophie's growing attachment to the young doctor over the past few days, and had been afraid she was being wooed for entirely the wrong reasons.

'Yes, Dr Bryan has asked me to be his wife and I've accepted. Isn't that wonderful? Aren't you delighted for me?'

'I'm pleased if it really makes you happy, Miss Sophie,' replied Hannah. 'But I have to say that I think it has all been very quick. Are you really sure?'

'Of course I'm sure,' said Sophie hotly. 'I love him and he loves me!'

'Does he? Or does he just love your inheritance?'

'How dare you, Hannah?' rasped Sophie, her face a mask of anger. 'How dare you suggest such a thing!'

'I dare, Miss Sophie, because I'm afraid it may be the case.'

'Well, I'll thank you to keep such thoughts to yourself. You have no place to tell me what to do.'

'I'm not telling you what to do, Sophie. But as a friend, I am telling you what I think.'

'Well, don't! It has nothing to do with you,' snapped Sophie. 'And I can tell you this, Hannah, you are not a friend, you're a servant, and I'll thank you to mind your own business.'

'In that case, Miss Sophie,' Hannah said, getting to her feet and picking up the tea tray, 'I'll take this out to the kitchen. While I'm preparing the lunch, I shall consider my position.'

Sophie stared at her. 'What do you mean, "consider your position"?'

'Exactly what I say, Miss Sophie. I have known you from a baby, but I haven't never been spoken to like that by anyone and I won't take it now. When you are married you'll have your own household with your own servants and you may speak to them as you choose, but I shan't be one of them.'

'Oh, and where will you be, then?' demanded Sophie.

'I shall be living in my own home with my husband.'

'Your husband!' exclaimed Sophie. 'Who's going to marry you?'

'The man what's already asked me and I turned down to stay with you,' replied Hannah calmly, and with that she went out of the room, leaving Sophie to stare after her in stupefaction.

Chapter 24

Charles spoke little of his trip to London when he returned, simply telling them Sophie would be coming to visit at Christmas as promised. Thomas and AliceAnne were delighted with the news and began planning her welcome.

Louisa heard the news with a sniff. 'I hope you know what you're doing, Charles. As far as I can see, you'll simply have cemented her in your grandfather's affections and he'll never change his mind.'

'Mama, he is never *going* to change his mind,' Charles replied. 'And it seems stupid to try and deny him her company over Christmas in the vain hope that he will.'

'Well, let's hope she makes it a short visit,' muttered Louisa.

When Thomas asked for other news of Sophie, Charles replied that he had found her well and happily settled back into her own home. He made no mention of Dr Bryan and this was a conscious decision. Provided he said nothing, Sophie need never admit that Nicholas had visited her in London if she chose not to. Let Sophie tell the family in her own good time, Charles thought. It's nothing to do with me. Why risk subjecting her to her grandfather's anger by mentioning something that has no substance at all? And in the silent regions of his mind, a quiet voice murmured, And if I speak it aloud, it may become a truth.

He encountered Nicholas the very next morning. The doctor was driving up to the house, and when he saw Charles he raised his hat with a sardonic smile and said, 'Good morning, Mr Leroy. I trust you had a pleasant trip to London.'

Charles, determined not to rise to this gambit, simply replied, 'Good morning, Doctor. This is just a routine visit, I hope.'

Nicholas jumped down from the gig and picking up his bag, said, 'Oh yes, I need to ensure my patient has come to no harm while I've been away.'

Charles gave a shrug of indifference. 'Have you been away?' he said. 'We hadn't noticed.' And with that he turned and walked round the house towards the stables.

Nicholas continued on his way to the front door. Edith opened to his knock and he waited in the hall while she fetched Louisa.

'Good morning, Doctor,' Louisa said as she appeared from the kitchen passage. 'This is a surprise. We weren't expecting you today.'

'I've been away for a few days on family business,' Nicholas said, treating her to his most winning smile. 'So I thought I'd look in to see how Mr Penvarrow is doing.'

'I'm glad to say he's taken a turn for the better,' answered Louisa. 'He has more appetite and has more colour.'

'Excellent,' said Nicholas. 'And I trust you still have enough of the powders I prescribed?'

'Yes, we have,' replied Louisa briskly. 'He's been taking them very sparingly.'

'I'm glad to hear it,' declared Nicholas. 'But perhaps I should take a look at him now that I'm here.'

'Paxton's with him at the minute,' Louisa said. 'He's getting dressed.'

'So early?' The doctor's face was full of concern. 'I do hope he takes a rest later in the day.'

'Indeed, he usually does, Doctor. But I'm afraid he will not wish to be interrupted while he is getting up. At present he is quite well, and I'm sure you have other patients who require your attendance, especially as you've been away. I do assure you that we'll call you immediately should my father take a turn for the worse.'

Louisa saw the flash of anger in Nicholas's eyes before he said, 'As you wish, Mrs Leroy. Let us hope that nothing untoward happens to him.' And with that he strode from the house without a backward glance.

'It was most odd,' Louisa said to Charles over lunch. 'We hadn't called him and yet he took great offence when I sent him away. You should have seen the expression on his face, Charles. He was furious.'

'I don't like that young man,' Thomas said from the head of the table. 'Too big for his boots by half.'

'Well, he's certainly arrogant,' Charles said. 'But with luck, sir, you won't need him again. It seems to me that your health is much improved.'

'And so I told him,' said Louisa. 'But he wasn't pleased. Anyone would think he didn't *want* you to recover, Papa.'

'No visits, no medicines, no payment!' said Thomas, and they all laughed at his cynicism.

Sophie arrived at Trescadinnick the day before Christmas Eve and received an ecstatic welcome from AliceAnne, who was waiting for her in the hall.

'Look, look, Aunt Sophie,' the little girl cried. 'Papa found a tree and Paxton set it up. And now you're here, we're going to decorate it.'

Hannah, coming in behind Sophie, paused in the doorway and when AliceAnne saw her she was immediately enveloped in a hug. 'Hannah! You're here too! Hurrah.'

What a difference in that child, Hannah thought, as she returned the hug. When we came in September, she couldn't say boo to a goose.

'Of course I'm here, Miss AliceAnne, and looking forward to Christmas in the country.'

How nearly Hannah had not come. She and Sophie had never quarrelled before in the way they had over Dr Nicholas Bryan on the day he left London. It had taken several days for them to return to any sort of normality. Words had been spoken that could never be unsaid, particularly by Sophie, and with the strong streak of Penvarrow pride running in her veins she had found it difficult to apologize. But the thought of Hannah leaving her, walking out of the house they had shared for so long and never coming back, filled her with such a deep misery that she had swallowed her pride and made the first move to reconciliation.

'Hannah, will you forgive me for what I said?' she asked. 'It was inexcusable to say you were only a servant and not a friend. You've been the dearest friend to me all my life and no one should speak to a friend as I did to you.'

'Don't worry, Miss Sophie,' Hannah had replied. 'I've forgotten what you said to me already.' Sophie, however, hadn't forgotten what Hannah had suggested; that Dr Bryan was more in love with her inheritance than with her. It was something that still stood between them. Though she could forgive Hannah for saying such a thing if it was said as a friend who truly believed it, she couldn't even begin to consider that she might be right. Nicholas had no idea that she rather than Charles would inherit Trescadinnick, and she knew he would love her even if she were penniless... wouldn't he? She longed to see him again, to feel him hold her close, to know the touch of his lips, gentle against her own. She had two precious letters telling her how much he loved her and how he longed for her return to Trescadinnick.

Neither Sophie nor Hannah mentioned again the idea of Hannah's marriage; Sophie because she assumed it had been said in the heat of the argument and there was nothing in it, and Hannah because it was true and she didn't want to discuss it. Sophie was not the only one who had received a letter from Cornwall. Will was no natural letter-writer, which made his letter asking how soon she could come home all the more dear to Hannah. Home? It would be coming home to be with Will, and she had written back to say they were coming to Cornwall for Christmas.

Sophie and Hannah joined in the preparations for Christmas. As AliceAnne had promised they decorated the tree with garlands and ribbons, and placed a golden star on the top. Candles, carefully placed and spaced, were attached to some of the outer branches, so that when Charles lit them for the first time on Christmas Eve, the hall became alight with magic.

AliceAnne's face was glowing with excitement. 'Isn't it beautiful?' she whispered.

'It is,' agreed Sophie. 'It's going to be a Christmas we'll always remember.'

She had not yet seen Nicholas, but they'd agreed that they would meet at church on Christmas morning. I shall wait until after Christmas to tell them that we've become engaged, Sophie had written. I know Grandfather may not like the idea and I don't want to spoil Christmas Day for everyone else. If you come on Boxing Day we can tell him together.

Sophie had been pleased that Nicholas had agreed to this, but once she was back at Trescadinnick, she found it difficult not to speak of the secret she was hugging so excitedly to herself.

She had settled back into the room she'd had before and when she went up to bed on her first night back, she felt as comfortable here as she did in her room at home. She had paused on the landing outside Joss's room, resting her hand for a moment on the door handle of the locked room, and later, as she lay in bed and watched the firelight glimmer on the old wardrobe, she thought again about what she'd discovered. Should she tell Aunt Matty? Should she be really brave and tell what she knew to her grandfather? Was there any way, she wondered, that she could find out more about what had happened to Cassie and her baby? Would the family want to know?

Sophie was still eager to uncover these secrets, but, immersed in the excitement of her own proposed marriage, she had more important things to think about just now. She had brought all the letters, with some idea of showing them to Matty at least, and being guided by her as to whether she should tell Thomas. But with everything else going on, she decided to wait for the right time, and the letters remained in the drawer of the dressing table.

Christmas Day dawned dank and chilly. Nevertheless, Louisa insisted that they should all go to the church morning service before they sat down to a Christmas dinner of roast goose and plum pudding. 'But not you, Papa,' she said. 'It's too cold, and we don't want you to catch a chill now that you're so much better. It's going to be a busy day. You should stay in bed until we get back.'

One look at the weather had told Thomas that he didn't want to brave the elements and go to church simply to hear the rector maunder on in one of his interminable sermons. He accepted Louisa's decision with little more than a gruff protest at being bossed by his daughter, and stayed where he was.

'Paxton will come and help you as soon as we all get back from church,' Louisa said. 'Edith's staying in the kitchen, so if you need something, just ring your bell and she'll bring anything you want.'

'Tell her to stay downstairs. I shall be perfectly all right without some maid fussing about me,' grumbled Thomas.

'Of course you will,' agreed Louisa, well used to her father's irritability. 'Matty's coming over some time this morning and we'll be back before you know it.' And with that, she left him nursing the cup of tea she had brought him, and went downstairs to join the rest of the family getting ready to leave.

As they neared the church they could hear the bells ringing in the joyous season, and despite the cold wind that swept down from the moor, there was a large gathering of people outside in the churchyard, greeting each other and wishing each other well. Sophie looked for Nicholas and Hannah for Will. Both were among the crowd and as soon as he saw Sophie, Nicholas came up to speak to her as she stood with Charles, AliceAnne and Louisa. It was the first time they had met since they'd parted in London and the sight of him, so tall and handsome, made Sophie's heart beat faster and the ready colour flood her cheeks.

Nicholas, however, showed no emotion at all as he said formally, 'Merry Christmas, Miss Ross.' But, taking Sophie's hand, he pressed her fingers before turning to Louisa and Charles. 'Mrs Leroy, Mr Leroy. Merry Christmas. Mr Penvarrow is not with you?'

'Oh no, Doctor,' Louisa replied. 'It's far too cold for him to venture out this morning. He's staying in bed in the warm until we get home again.'

'Very wise,' remarked the doctor. 'It would be so easy for him to take a chill in this cold weather.'

Hannah, catching sight of Will and his family, had slipped away to greet them and wish them a Merry Christmas. The smile that broke across Will's face as he saw her approach was the only Christmas gift she needed, and her answering smile told him all he needed to know.

'You will come and have your Christmas dinner with us, won't you?' begged Lizzie. 'We've all been given the rest of the day off, once we've served the Christmas dinner at Trescadinnick.'

Hannah beamed at her. 'Of course I will. Miss Sophie won't need me after dinner.'

'And we'll wait until you and Lizzie get there,' promised Grace. 'Molly and Jack are coming with the children, so we'll have a real family Christmas.'

As people began to move into the church Will took her hand and giving it a gentle squeeze, said, 'Merry Christmas, Hannah.' She returned his grasp and then broke away, moving to sit with the other servants from Trescadinnick.

As the five-minute bell started pealing Charles led his mother into the church, followed by Sophie and AliceAnne. They moved slowly up the aisle until they came to the Trescadinnick pew at the front, and the rest of the congregation streamed in behind them, settling themselves into the pews with a rustle of Christmas finery and whispered greetings.

Nicholas, watching them all take their places, did not move into a pew, but remained standing at the back. When the bell finally stopped ringing, a melody was struck up on the harmonium, the rector entered from the vestry and the choir began to sing the first carol. Slowly Nicholas edged back behind the velvet curtain that covered the door to help exclude the cold air and closing the door softly behind him, slipped out of the porch into the chill of the morning. He paused briefly, but no one followed him, and he pulled out his watch. If the rector ran true to form, he knew he had at least an hour or more before the service would end; plenty of time for what he had in mind.

With a quick glance about him to make sure he was unobserved, he hurried along the narrow streets and up the steps to the cliff top where he took the path to Trescadinnick. Below him the sea stretched to the distant horizon, grey and hostile, as tossed by the wind, it surged back and forth against the rocks. He hardly gave it a glance as he strode swiftly along the path. When he reached Trescadinnick's encircling wall he went to the cliff gate that led into the garden. He had reconnoitred the back way into Trescadinnick's grounds on more than one occasion and tall as he was, he was able to swing himself up and over the gate with ease, landing softly on the grass the other side. From there he only had to cross the garden and he would be at the house.

He paused in the shelter of some bushes and looked carefully at the silent house. A faint light glowed in an upstairs window, and a gleam from the kitchen; otherwise the house was in darkness. He wasn't sure if everyone but Thomas was at church, but he was relying on the fact that the front door would, as always, be unlocked. Creeping from his hiding-place, he sprinted across the grass and took cover beside the dark windows of the library. Risking a look inside, he saw that the room was empty, the fire unlit in the grate. Clearly Thomas Penvarrow was not expected downstairs yet. Now for the most dangerous part of his plan.

Nicholas walked round to the front entrance and gently turned the heavy latch. As he had hoped, the door was unlocked and a gentle push eased it open. Once inside, he closed it softly behind him and paused to listen. There was definitely someone in the kitchen; he could hear whoever it was moving about. One of the servants must have been left in the house in case Thomas needed something. Swiftly and silently, Nicholas went up the stairs and crept along the landing to Thomas's bedchamber. Before he went in he glanced at his watch again. Only fifteen minutes had elapsed since he'd left the church. He smiled grimly: plenty of time. He was about to enter the room when he heard a rasping cough coming from within. Clearly Thomas wasn't as well as his family thought.

Nicholas pushed open the door and walked into the room.

Thomas was sitting up in bed, still in his nightshirt. On the table beside him was an empty teacup and a handbell. He turned his head awkwardly to see who had come into his room unbidden. When he saw who it was, he relaxed back against his pillows and said, 'Now what do you want?'

'What do I want?' Nicholas said as he crossed to the bedside and removed the bell from Thomas's reach. 'I want to talk to you.'

'Do you indeed,' retorted Thomas. 'Well, I don't want to talk to you, so you can just take yourself off.'

'No, I don't think so... Grandfather.'

Thomas stared at him, confused. 'Grandfather? Who are you calling *Grandfather*?' And then, with anger, 'How dare you, young man!' He looked up at the man towering over him and for the first time he knew a flicker of fear.

'I dare, Grandfather,' drawled Nicholas, 'because that's who you are. My grandfather. So, I've come to claim my inheritance.'

'Your inheritance! Don't be ridiculous. You're no grandson of mine.'

'Well, that's where you're wrong. Your son, Jocelyn, seduced my mother and then rejected her. Once he'd had his fun with her, his tumble in the hay, he shunned her. Left her shamed and destitute, cast out by her father... and expecting a child... me!'

'I've never heard such nonsense,' Thomas said, but there was a frailty in his voice. 'Jocelyn did no such thing.'

'Oh, but he did,' retorted Nicholas. 'Your son, my father, left her to die in childbirth. Once he had seduced her, he had no more time for the disgraced daughter from a Methodist manse. You knew what he'd done. *You* could have insisted that he did his duty and marry her, but did you? No!'

'You know nothing about it,' Thomas said. But his anger had started a coughing fit and it was several minutes before it subsided, and Nicholas went on. 'You're wrong,' he sneered. 'I know everything about it, because I'm Jocelyn Penvarrow's son. I have as much Penvarrow blood running in my veins as you.

'And I'll tell you exactly how he died,' Nicholas declared. 'He was coming home from the village along the cliff path one night and my Uncle Edwin was waiting for him in the fog. One shove and it was done!'

'I don't believe a word of it,' growled Thomas.

'Maybe not, but I *am* your grandson.'

'Even so,' Thomas said, 'you're a bastard. So you can take yourself off.'

'Oh, I'm not going anywhere,' Nicholas said. 'Not after I've taken such trouble to come and find you... and your grand-daughter.'

'Sophie? You just leave her out of this.' Thomas was frightened now.

'I'm afraid it's too late for that, old man,' murmured Nicholas.

'What do you mean? What have you done to her?'

'Sophie? She's agreed to marry me. She loves me, you see?'

'I'm her guardian,' stated Thomas. 'She can't marry without my consent and I shall *never* give it.'

'I doubt if your consent will be necessary, *Grandfather*!' Nicholas said. 'You won't be here.' Thomas looked up at his grandson, terror in his eyes, as he saw Nicholas pick up a pillow. 'Before you die,' Nicholas said, 'I wanted to be sure you knew just who was killing you... and why.'

Thomas opened his mouth to call for help, but Nicholas, smiling, brought the pillow down. The old man struggled as the pillow was pressed against his face. He was no match for the youth and strength of his killer, and it was not long before his struggles ceased and he was still. Nicholas held the pillow for another minute to be quite sure, and then lifted it and looked down at the old man lying still in the bed.

'Did you really think I wouldn't do it, old man?' he said.

Gently, he smoothed the staring eyes shut, and placed the arms that had tried so valiantly to push him away to rest peacefully at his side; a man who had died in his sleep. A quick glance round the room showed Nicholas that nothing looked disturbed or out of place. He picked up the handbell and placed it by the bed, where it would have been within easy reach of Thomas to summon help, and prepared to leave.

He was just emerging from the room when there came a heavy knocking on the front door. Nicholas froze, trapped on the landing, as without waiting for an answer to her knock, Matty Treslyn pushed open the front door and stepped into the hall. She paused to admire the Christmas tree before opening the library door and looking inside. As she did so, Edith came up the kitchen passage.

'Oh, Edith, there you are,' Nicholas heard her say. 'Has everyone gone to church?'

'Yes, madam,' Edith replied. 'But the fire's lit in the drawing room if you would like to sit in there until they come back.'

'Yes, I will,' Matty said, taking off her cloak and handing it to the maid. 'Perhaps you'd bring me some tea. It's bitterly cold outside.'

'Yes, madam,' Edith said. 'I'll bring it in directly.'

Through the crack in the door, Nicholas watched Matty open the drawing-room door and go in.

Edith moved to return to the kitchen before she turned back to say, 'Excuse me, madam, but of course Mr Penvarrow didn't go to church. He's still in his bed. Mrs Leroy said not to disturb him. Should I bring tea for him as well?'

'Good idea,' said Matty. 'Bring an extra cup, and when I've drunk mine I'll take some up to him and see how he is.' She closed the drawing-room door and Edith disappeared down the passage to the kitchen. For a moment the hall was empty and Nicholas darted down the stairs, across the hall to the front door. Opening it as softly as he could, he slipped out and latched it quietly behind him. Keeping clear of the drawing-room windows, he stole round to the other side of the house, through the stable yard and across to the cliff-top gate. He wrenched the bolts aside and was out on the cliff path in less than a minute. He didn't know how long it would be before Matty went upstairs, but he needed to be back in the church before she arrived there and raised the alarm. Another glance at his watch told him that he'd already taken nearly fifty minutes and the service could be drawing to a close; and so he ran. There was no one to see him running across the cliff, and as he hurried down the steps into the village he found the streets deserted. He paused outside the church to regain his breath and then quietly opened the old oak door and, sheltered by the velvet curtain, slipped inside unnoticed. The congregation was in the process of taking Communion and Nicholas joined the file of parishioners going up to the altar. Sophie and the others from Trescadinnick were already back in their pew, and as Nicholas returned from the altar rail he caught Sophie's eye and they both smiled. He saw that Charles had noticed this exchange and knew a fierce stab of relief. In the unlikely event of there being any repercussion after Thomas's death was discovered, he had his alibi.

As the congregation spilled out into the churchyard after the final carol had been sung, they were amazed to see Edith, the maid from Trescadinnick, running down the road, her cloak flying out behind her, shouting something, her face a mask of panic. People stared at her as she pushed her way through the crowd to where Charles stood, exchanging greetings with Miss Sandra Osell.

He broke off as he saw Edith's face, saying, 'Edith? Whatever is the matter, girl?'

'Oh, sir,' Edith cried. 'Mrs Treslyn is at the house and she says can you come at once and please to bring the doctor with you.'

'The doctor?' demanded Charles. 'What on earth has happened, Edith? Is Mrs Treslyn ill?'

'No, sir, it's Mr Penvarrow. He's been taken bad.' She paused and then said, 'Oh, sir, Mrs Treslyn thinks he's dead!'

There was an immediate stir and buzz of conversation as everyone about them heard her words.

Sophie's hand flew to her mouth, and she saw her own horror mirrored in Charles and Louisa's faces. 'Where's Nicholas?' she cried, looking wildly round, just as he stepped up beside her.

'I'm here. I heard,' he said. 'I'll come at once. It may not be too late. I just need to collect my bag.'

'We'll pick you up on the way,' Charles said, and called to Paxton to bring the pony and trap at once. He turned back to

Sophie and his mother. 'We'll go on ahead. Sophie, please ask
Hannah to bring AliceAnne home.'

AliceAnne happily took Hannah's hand and Hannah said,
'Don't you mind about AliceAnne, Miss Sophie. I'll look to her.'

When they arrived at Trescadinnick, Nicholas jumped down
from the trap and ran in through the front door, quickly followed
by the others. Matty was standing in the hall, waiting for them.

'What's happened, Aunt Matty?' Charles said. 'Where is he?'

'Your grandfather is dead, Charles. I took him up some tea
when I got here and found him, dead in his bed.'

Nicholas led the way upstairs and they all followed him into
Thomas's bedchamber. Thomas was lying on the bed as Nicholas
had left him, his eyes closed, but his arms were flung wide.
Nicholas turned to Matty. 'Did you touch him, Mrs Treslyn? Did
you try and rouse him?'

'I put my hand on his chest, but he wasn't breathing. There was
no rise and fall. I shook him, putting my hands on his shoulders.'
She held out her hands as if to demonstrate. 'But,' her voice broke
on a sob, 'there was nothing there. He was still warm, Doctor. If
I had gone up to him when I first arrived, perhaps I could have
saved him.'

'Don't distress yourself, Mrs Treslyn,' he soothed. 'He may
not have been dead long, but I doubt if you could have done
anything for him if you'd been there sooner. I'll examine him,
of course, but it looks to me as if his heart finally gave out.' He
looked round at all of them. 'You mustn't reproach yourselves.
We all knew this could happen at any time. He has been most
unwell for some months now.' He looked across at Charles and
said, 'Perhaps you'd take the ladies downstairs while I make my
examination, Mr Leroy, and then we can arrange for him to be
laid out properly.'

Charles nodded and shepherded the three women out of
the room and down to the drawing room. When they'd gone,
Nicholas closed the door behind them and opening his medical
bag, gathered up the various medicines, including the arsenic he
had been prescribing over the past few months, the powders, the

linctus and the tablets, and pushed them into his bag. Then he stood and looked down at the remains of Thomas Penvarrow. 'Revenge, Grandfather,' he murmured. 'Revenge is sweet.'

Chapter 25

When Nicholas appeared in the drawing room, Sophie leaped to her feet and ran to his side.

'Oh, Nicholas,' she cried as, unaware of the expressions of surprise on her aunts' faces, she clutched his arm. 'What a dreadful thing! Was there nothing further we could have done for him?'

'I'm afraid not, Sophie,' he replied, gently detaching her hand. 'His heart could have given out at any time.' Nicholas looked round at the assembled group. 'I'm sorry for your loss,' he said. 'I'll arrange for Widow Haller to come up from Port Felec to lay him out.'

He turned, about to leave the room, but Charles stopped him with a question. 'There is no reason you can see, Doctor, for us not to proceed with funeral plans?'

Nicholas looked surprised at the question. 'None at all, Mr Leroy. Your grandfather was an elderly man who'd been unwell for some time. His death was not unexpected. Indeed, he survived longer than I would have predicted in the circumstances.' When this was greeted with silence, he said, 'If that's all, I'll bid you good day.' And turning on his heel, he walked out of the room. Sophie followed him at once.

'Nicholas,' she whispered, 'must you go?'

'Certainly I must,' he replied, but he reached out and took her hand. 'I will come again in a few days and we will tell them of our engagement then. Now is not the time.' He raised her hand to his lips. 'Until then, my love.'

Sophie closed the door behind him and paused to look at the Christmas tree. We should take it down, she thought. There's no place for a Christmas tree in a house of death. In the gloom of the day, with its candles unlit, it seemed a melancholy misfit.

When Sophie returned to the drawing room, her aunt Louisa said, 'Well, miss, and what exactly were you doing chasing after the doctor like that?'

'I was showing him to the front door,' snapped Sophie, 'as no one else seemed to be extending him that courtesy. He came to my grandfather's aid as soon as he was called and you still treat him like... like a servant.'

'Now, Sophie, don't take on so,' Matty said in a conciliatory tone. 'We're all shocked and upset by our father's sudden death. Please let's not make things worse by arguing with each other. Of course we don't treat the doctor like a servant. He is a professional man and we treat him with the respect he deserves, but with Papa's death, well, we are not ourselves.'

'Where's AliceAnne?' Charles demanded suddenly. 'Did Hannah bring her home as we asked? Is she in the kitchen with the Paxtons?'

'I don't know,' replied Sophie. 'I'm sure she did. I'll go and see.' As she walked out of the room the front door opened and Hannah came into the hall, alone.

'Hannah!' cried Sophie, relief in her voice. 'Is AliceAnne with you?'

Hannah didn't answer the question but asked instead, 'Is it true that Mr Penvarrow has passed away, Miss Sophie?'

'Yes, Hannah, I'm afraid it is. But have you got AliceAnne with you?'

Hannah still didn't answer the question but said, 'I need to speak to Mr Charles.'

At that moment Charles, having heard Hannah's voice, came out into the hall. 'Hannah, where is AliceAnne?'

'She's quite safe, sir. I've left her at the home farm with the Shaws, while I came back to see what had happened here.' Charles seemed about to interrupt but Hannah went on, 'If

Mr Penvarrow has indeed passed away, sir, I thought you might prefer Miss AliceAnne to be out of the house for a bit. It's not the place for a little girl while what is necessary is carried out. I've come to ask you if she may have her Christmas dinner with Will Shaw and his family. She knows Lizzie well enough and I could fetch her home again when it's her bedtime.'

Sophie watched as Charles considered what Hannah had said. She could see the sense of Hannah's suggestion and she hoped Charles would too.

'Very well,' he said. 'She may stay there if the Shaws will have her. They are good people. And if Miss Sophie can spare you, I would like you to stay there with her.'

'Of course Hannah should stay,' Sophie said at once.

'And when you bring her home,' Charles said, 'I'll talk to her and explain what has happened.'

'Left her with the Shaws?' cried Louisa when she heard what had been arranged. 'What were you thinking of, Charles? She's his granddaughter. Her place is here.'

Sophie thought at first that Charles was going to point out yet again that AliceAnne wasn't actually Thomas's granddaughter, but all he said was, 'Mama, she's a child of six. If she came home now, she would be sent up to the schoolroom to be out of the way. Christmas Day is already spoilt for her. There is no need to make it any worse.'

'She needs to pay her respects,' persisted Louisa. 'It's only proper.'

'As to that,' Charles said, 'I shall not allow her to see him. Why frighten her with the sight of a dead man, when she can remember him alive and well.'

Louisa was about to speak again, but Charles held up his hand. 'My mind is made up, Mama, and I shall not change it.'

Thank goodness Charles had stood up to his mother and put AliceAnne's welfare ahead of 'propriety', Sophie thought as she rewarded him with a smile. She had not been allowed to see her father after his accident and she knew she was happier remembering him as he had been in life.

The next two days passed in the sombre shadow of death, faces solemn, voices hushed and conversation kept to a minimum. The weather on Boxing Day, Sunday, was as inclement as on Christmas Day itself and there was no question of anyone from Trescadinnick returning to church for the normal Sunday service.

'It wouldn't be seemly to appear in public so soon,' Louisa had announced. 'The news of Papa's death will be the talk of the village by now and I, for one, have no wish to become the subject of idle gossip. We must maintain a proper, dignified distance.' Matty had agreed and thus no one had left the house that day. No further celebration of Christmas was deemed appropriate and on Louisa's instruction, Paxton removed the tree and Edith swept up the sweet-smelling pine needles, leaving the hallway cold and bereft of cheer. The Christmas goose which had been roasted for Christmas dinner could not be wasted and was served cold the following day. Charles and Sophie ate theirs upstairs in the schoolroom with AliceAnne, and gave her the gifts that had previously lain beneath the Christmas tree. A riding habit specially made for her, from Charles; a hat and some kid gloves from Sophie and to AliceAnne most exciting of all, the promise of a puppy from Matty, whose dog Silver was due to whelp in two weeks' time. The atmosphere in the schoolroom, warmed by the stove lit by two oil lamps, and separated from the dank day outside by faded velvet curtains, was so completely different from the chill in the rest of the house that as they sat together Sophie could feel the tension seeping from her body.

'Papa,' AliceAnne said tentatively and then stopped.

'Papa, what?' asked her father with a smile.

'When I was at Mrs Shaw's house yesterday Lizzie was there, and Mrs Smart, who's Lizzie's sister. And she had her children with her, and they're called Alison and Tommy and Sarah, and we played and Mrs Shaw says I can go to the farm whenever I want to and I do want to, Papa, because we played games all round the house and then after tea we did charades and all the grown-ups played too, and we were in teams and Hannah and I were in Mr Shaw's team and we won because we guessed the word which was alligator cos the other team, Mr Smart's team, did Ali short for Alison and then gaiters which Mr Shaw wears on the farm when it's extra muddy, and then Tommy was an alligator and crawled across the floor so we knew what the word was, but they didn't guess *our* word which was kingfisher, even though Hannah crowned Mr Shaw as king and Lizzie did fishing and I flew round as the bird at the end, and so we won the prize and it was a twisty stick of barley sugar and Hannah said I could eat half then and bring the other half home so I've got some for today, or I did have, but she said I could eat the rest of it after lunch, so I did.'

At the end of this torrent of words, such as neither Charles nor Sophie had ever heard from AliceAnne, Charles said rather feebly, 'Well, it sounds as if you had a lovely time.' And Sophie thought, And with far more fun than you'd have had here!

'So can I, Papa?'

'Can you what?' Charles found he had lost the thread of AliceAnne's excited story.

'Can I go to the farm and play with the other children when they come again? Mrs Shaw says she'll show me milking the cows and I can help her feed the chickens, and I do want to, Papa.'

'We'll see,' replied her father cautiously. 'I'll talk to Hannah about it, all right?'

'Oh, Hannah will say it's all right,' AliceAnne said ingenuously, 'cos she likes Mr Shaw. She goes there for tea on Saturdays, so I could go with her, couldn't I?'

'Does she now?' Charles raised an eyebrow. 'Well, if Hannah goes with you I'm sure it'll be all right, but I need to speak to Hannah first.'

When Hannah came up to get AliceAnne ready for bed, Sophie and Charles left her to it and went back down to the aunts in the drawing room, where the temperature and the atmosphere were several degrees cooler. Neither of them spoke of AliceAnne's invitation to return to visit the home farm; sufficient time to apprise Louisa of that idea another day.

Monday morning dawned bright and cold. The bleak grey weather of the Christmas weekend had cleared and Sophie woke to a cloudless blue sky, the pale winter sun giving an illusory warmth to the world beyond the window. She went down to breakfast and found Matty and Charles together in the morning room. They looked up as she came in and Matty said, 'Good morning, Sophie.'

Sophie smiled at her, replying, 'Good morning, Aunt, Charles.'

Charles, who had just finished his coffee, got to his feet and turning to Matty, said, 'Everything is in hand here, Aunt, so I plan to ride out for an hour.' He glanced across at Sophie and asked, 'Would you care to ride with me, cousin?'

'I'd love to,' Sophie said. She had not been looking forward to spending yet another day in this shuttered house of mourning. 'But,' she turned to Matty, 'I suppose it would be considered unseemly and improper with my grandfather still lying upstairs.'

'Charles has to visit the rector this morning to make arrangements for the funeral,' Matty pointed out. 'There is no reason why you should not go with him.'

'But won't you and Aunt Louisa want...?' began Sophie.

'We shall leave all such arrangements to Charles as the man of the family but, in the circumstances, perhaps you should go too.'

Sophie still looked doubtful. 'I'm not sure Aunt Louisa will think so,' she said. 'She's always so concerned about propriety, and,' Sophie looked anxiously at Charles, 'no one but the family knows my grandfather rewrote his will. Everyone still thinks you'll inherit Trescadinnick, Charles.'

Charles shrugged. 'As to that, Sophie, they'll find out soon enough. I shall send a message to Mr Staunton today to tell him what has occurred and ask him to attend the funeral and make a formal reading of the will afterwards.' He gave her a smile and went on, 'Come with me at least to see the rector.'

'Go, Sophie,' Matty encouraged. 'If necessary I'll take care of Louisa... and the fresh air will do you both good.'

Half an hour later Sophie and Charles clattered out of the

stable yard and trotted down the lane towards Port Felec. The brightness of the morning lifted Sophie's spirits and she knew a feeling of release, being out of the house.

'I was very grateful to Hannah for looking after AliceAnne on Christmas Day,' Charles said as they rode together side by side. 'It would have been a dreadful day for her, shut into Trescadinnick with all of us so shocked by Grandfather's death.'

'And no Christmas,' added Sophie. 'Hannah told me that they had all made a fuss of her, to keep her day special.'

'I've spoken to Hannah too, and she says she's happy to take AliceAnne there on occasional visits if I allow her.'

'And will you allow her?'

'I shall certainly consider it,' Charles replied. 'I know you're right when you say AliceAnne needs other children to play with, but I'm not sure how my mother will like it if they are simple farmer's children.'

'But it is your decision,' ventured Sophie. 'You always say she's your daughter...'

'... my daughter.'

They spoke the words together and it made them both laugh. It was the first time either of them had laughed since going into church on Christmas Day. In companionable silence they continued their ride down to the parsonage, where in answer to their knock a maid showed them into a large, cold drawing room. There was no fire laid in the grate and the curtains were half-drawn across the long narrow windows, casting the room into shadow.

The rector's daughter, Miss Osell, came in almost immediately, and addressing herself to Charles, bade him good morning and said her father would be with him at once. In the meantime she invited them to sit and threw back the curtains, allowing sunlight to flood the room.

'I'm so sorry, Miss Ross,' she said, now giving her attention to Sophie. 'The maid's been very slack today, not preparing the room for visitors. My father gave her a half-day yesterday so she could visit her mother and the result is, no work done today.'

'It's of no consequence, Miss Osell,' Charles assured her. 'We have only come to discuss a family matter with your father. We shall not intrude upon you for more than a quarter-hour.'

'But surely you will take some tea? Or a glass of sherry? I know gentlemen often prefer something other than tea,' said Miss Osell, 'and my father considers sherry quite acceptable these days.'

'Tea would be most welcome to us both,' put in Sophie. 'For,' as she said to Charles when Miss Osell had left the room, 'if we do not accept at once, we shall have to accept at last!'

Charles smiled at this and once again Sophie was struck by how much his rare smile became him, lighting his eyes and dispersing his habitual seriousness.

Miss Osell was soon back, followed by the maid carrying the tea tray, and before long they were sitting sipping the unwanted tea, still waiting for the rector. At last the Reverend Osell appeared, full of apologies.

'We shall not keep you long, sir,' Charles said. 'No doubt you have heard the sad news of Mr Thomas Penvarrow's death.'

'Well, dear me, yes. Yes indeed,' replied the rector. 'One heard the rumour, you know, but I was not certain of its veracity.' He glanced at his daughter. 'I'm sure Mr Leroy would prefer to discuss this with me alone, my dear. Perhaps you should withdraw...' he paused awkwardly, '... and show Miss Ross the, er, the garden?'

His daughter got at once to her feet, but Sophie remained firmly in her chair.

'Miss Ross and I would like to speak with you together,' Charles said. And when Miss Osell paused uncertainly at the door, her father waved her out of the room before eyeing Sophie with disfavour and murmuring, 'Most unusual.'

'I am sorry to confirm, Rector, that Mr Penvarrow did indeed pass away on Christmas morning and that Miss Ross and I are here to discuss funeral arrangements with you.'

'But, Miss Ross, this must be most distressing for you,' the rector tried again. 'If you'd prefer...?'

'Thank you, sir,' Sophie replied, 'but my cousin and I prefer to make the arrangements together.'

The rector gave in and with Charles taking the lead in the conversation, whilst referring each decision to Sophie for agreement, the arrangements for the funeral were decided upon within the quarter-hour. There was no need for delay and it was fixed for Friday at noon; plenty of time to bespeak a coffin from Truro, send for the hearse and plumed horses and arrange for the family tomb to be opened in preparation. The rector would, of course, preach at the service, the choir would sing the anthem and workers on the estate would come and pay their respects.

Both Charles and Sophie heaved sighs of relief when they were once again out in the fresh air.

'A ride up to the moor and home that way?' suggested Charles.

Sophie knew they should be going straight back to Trescadinnick, but was unable to resist the thought of a gallop across the country, enjoying the freedom from restraint that riding always gave her. She hesitated, but when Charles simply raised an enquiring eyebrow she smiled and nodded, and they were away up the track and onto the open moor.

As they rode up onto the higher ground, Sophie looked back. Spread out below them was the valley, patchworked with stone hedges, the land muted in its winter colours; the occasional hamlets and farmsteads protected by stands of trees, planted as windbreaks, and beyond the cliffs, the wide expanse of the sea, ruffled silk on this calm winter day. Trescadinnick stood bold and strong amidst its outbuildings and garden, and nestling in the shelter of a hollow between the house and the rooftops of Port Felec lay the home farm.

As they reached the top of the hill, Charles drew rein and they both surveyed the land spread out below them.

'It's a beautiful place, Charles,' Sophie said, 'your home.'

'Not my home any more, cousin,' remarked Charles stiffly.

'It will be your home as long as you want it to be,' Sophie said. 'Who else is going to look after it for me?'

'Thank you, Sophie.' Charles gave her a rueful smile. 'But

when you're married, as you will be some day, your husband may have other ideas.'

The thought had not occurred to Sophie before. When she married Nicholas, surely they would live in his house where his dispensary was and where he held his surgery. 'Time enough to worry about that when the time comes,' she said cheerfully. Looking back at the house, she saw someone moving in the yard. 'Better go back, I suppose,' she said reluctantly.

Charles nodded. He had given Sophie the chance to tell him she was engaged to Nicholas Bryan but she had not, so perhaps his fears in that direction were unfounded. Surely Sophie had enough common sense to see through him; to see what he was after. At least there would be no question of marriage during the period of mourning, following Thomas's death. They headed for home, the horses picking their way down the steep track to the lane that ran to the house.

They turned into the stable yard and once he had seen Sophie safely dismounted, Charles said, 'If you'll excuse me, cousin, I must go in and write to Mr Staunton. Now we have the date for the funeral fixed, I must send Paxton to him with the news.'

He hurried back into the house and Sophie stayed for a few minutes, watching Ned rub the horses down, before leaving the yard and going round to the front of the house. There, to her surprise she was confronted by Nicholas.

He grabbed her by the wrist and said, 'Where have you been? How dare you ride out alone with another man, that man!' His grip on her wrist was fierce and she tried to pull away, saying, 'Nicholas, let go, you're hurting me.'

He did not let go, though his grip eased a little. 'Well, what have you to say?' he demanded.

'Nicholas, this is ridiculous. Let go of me and I'll answer you.'

Nicholas released her and Sophie rubbed her wrist, where the marks of his fingers were plain to see. 'I wasn't with "another man", Nicholas,' Sophie said quietly. 'I was with my cousin Charles…'

'He isn't your cousin,' Nicholas interrupted.

'He is my cousin in every way,' Sophie said. 'He's family and there's no impropriety in my riding with him, especially as we were going to see the rector about my grandfather's funeral.'

'I saw you talking and laughing,' Nicholas growled. 'It wasn't seemly.'

'Nicholas, why are you talking to me like this?' Sophie asked. 'I've done nothing wrong and you know it.'

'It's because you're my fiancée,' he replied. 'I don't like seeing you flirting with other men. I love you too much.'

Sophie softened at once. 'I was not flirting, Nicholas, and I love you too.'

'Well, all right,' Nicholas conceded ungraciously, 'but I don't like it, that's all. When we're married—'

'When we're married, you will have me to yourself,' Sophie said with a smile. 'We shall have each other.'

'Yes,' Nicholas agreed firmly. 'Yes, we will.'

'Why don't you come indoors with me now and we'll tell them we're engaged?'

'I'll come back this afternoon,' Nicholas said, taking her hand again and this time raising her fingers gently to his lips. 'I've a patient to see first. Old Mrs Slater.'

'Of course. Come back later and we can tell them all then.'

Sophie went back into the house. There was no one about and she went upstairs to change out of her riding habit. Nicholas would come back this afternoon and together they would tell the family that they were getting married. She knew a moment's trepidation at the thought, knowing it would not be an easy meeting, particularly in the circumstances, but she hated the secrecy. She wanted everything to be out in the open, for Nicholas to be welcomed not just as the doctor, not just as a guest, but as a prospective member of the family. She wanted him acknowledged as her future husband before the funeral so that he could stand with her in the church, publicly giving her his love and support in her time of sadness.

As she changed her dress, Sophie noticed her wrist still held the marks from his fingers, and she pulled her sleeve down firmly to hide the bruising. Nicholas hadn't meant to hurt her. She thought of him driving over to Tremose to visit old Mrs Slater, and felt a glow of pride at his devotion to his patients. How often had he come to visit her grandfather, concerned about his declining health?

It was when they were all seated at table for the midday meal that Sophie said, 'I have invited Dr Bryan to take tea with us this afternoon.'

'You have what?' Louisa's exclamation was loud and harsh.

'I have invited Dr Bryan to take tea with us this afternoon,' Sophie repeated and went on, 'I feel we owe him a deep debt for the care of my grandfather over the past months, and that we haven't shown how much we appreciate that care.'

'You have no right...' stuttered Louisa, looking round at her sister and her son for support.

'I'm afraid she has every right, Mama,' Charles said quietly. 'Trescadinnick is hers now. Whether you like it or not, she is mistress of this house and may invite whomever she chooses.'

'But Papa is not even in his grave. His will has not been read, and until that happens' – she turned venomous eyes on Sophie – 'I suggest you, miss, mind your place. You may inherit Trescadinnick, but it's not yours yet.'

'Louisa, I understand how you feel about this—' began Matty.

'Do you?' Louisa rounded on her sister. 'Do you? With your own comfortable home to return to whenever you choose and no one to put you out of it? Charles and I have never lived anywhere else, and now? Now it's no longer our home.' She fought to keep the tears at bay, but all of them could hear how close she came to weeping.

'But,' Matty spoke gently, 'Sophie is right. We do owe Dr Bryan our gratitude, and inviting him to take tea this afternoon is a way we can show our appreciation.'

'We're receiving no visitors until after the funeral,' stated Louisa. 'Cards of condolence, yes, but no visitors.'

'I shall receive him,' Sophie said quietly, 'and I am asking all of you to join us for tea in the drawing room.'

'I will not be summoned by a mere chit of a girl to my own drawing room,' muttered Louisa, but Matty simply nodded and said, 'It will be my pleasure to thank Dr Bryan for all he has done.'

Charles made no further comment, but when the doorbell rang later that afternoon he emerged from his study to greet Dr Bryan and lead him into the drawing room, where Sophie and Matty awaited him. There was no sign of Louisa.

They both stood, Sophie stepping forward to take his hand with a smile. 'Dr Bryan, Nicholas,' she said, 'we're delighted to see you.'

Matty also shook his hand and welcomed him. 'Do come and sit down, Doctor,' she said. 'Edith will be bringing in tea shortly.'

Nicholas took the chair she indicated and Sophie, having closed the door, went to stand behind him. In that instant, Charles knew what he was going to hear and a shaft of anguish went through him.

It was Nicholas who spoke. 'Sophie and I wish to tell you, her family, that we have become friends over the past weeks, and when I visited her in London, she did me the honour of accepting my proposal of marriage.'

There was a gasp from behind the folding screen which divided the far corner of the room and to the surprise of all of them, Louisa stepped out into the room. 'Your proposal of marriage!'

'Yes, Aunt,' Sophie said. 'Nicholas and I are to be married just as soon as propriety allows.'

'You are under age,' Louisa said. 'Your grandfather wouldn't have allowed it.'

'We had planned to speak to my grandfather immediately after Christmas,' Sophie said. 'But...' She swallowed. 'But as that is no longer possible' – she looked round at them all, Matty pale and silent, Louisa, white-faced and rigid with fury and Charles quiet and impassive – 'we've come to tell you and to ask your blessing.'

It was Charles who broke the silence and said, 'I wish you well, cousin.'

Sophie turned to him and smiled. 'Thank you, Charles.' And her smile of joy assailed him so that he had to turn away.

'I'm afraid I am unable to stay and take tea,' he said. 'If you will excuse me, cousin, I have to ride to St Morwen. I have a meeting there.'

Sophie watched him walk out of the room, her happiness dimmed a little by his muted congratulations.

The gleam of triumph in Nicholas's eyes was not lost on Matty as she stepped forward to shake his hand and offer her felicitations, and she knew a distinct disquiet at the speed of Sophie's attachment to the young doctor.

Louisa simply glared at them both and walked out of the room, almost colliding with Edith, entering with the tea trolley, and Mrs Paxton, carrying a cake-stand laden with delicate sandwiches and slices of cake. Edith placed the tea trolley in front of Matty. 'Will you pour, Aunt?' Sophie said and as Matty duly filled the cups, Sophie took one across to Nicholas, who remained seated. It was an awkward gathering and one that none of them wanted to prolong. It was Matty who carried the conversation, asking Nicholas about his family.

'Are you a Cornishman, Doctor?' she asked. 'Have you always lived here in Cornwall?'

Nicholas seemed happy enough to answer and as he did so, Sophie too learned more of his life. 'I was born in Truro,' he replied, 'but my parents soon moved to Plymouth where I was brought up.'

'And is your father also a doctor?'

'Both my parents are dead, Mrs Treslyn. Sophie will be my only family.'

'I suppose you went to London for your training,' Matty said.

'Indeed,' Nicholas agreed. 'The best place to learn of modern medical methods.'

'Nicholas chose to come here to Port Felec because he wanted to help poor, country people. He's a very dedicated doctor, driving all over the country to visit patients who cannot come to him. Why, only today he drove to Tremose to visit old Mrs Slater.'

Nicholas gave a brief laugh. 'Thanks for your testimony, my dear Sophie, but all doctors are dedicated, you know.'

'Nan Slater?' exclaimed Matty. 'Is she still alive?'

'Do you know her, Aunt?' Sophie asked in surprise.

'Not really. I once visited her with Louisa.'

When they had finished their tea Matty stood up. 'If you will excuse me, Sophie, Doctor, I promised AliceAnne I would go up to the schoolroom after tea. It's been very difficult for her, well, for all of us, these last few days. But with the funeral now set for Friday at least things are moving forward.' She held out her hand to Nicholas and said, 'I wish you and Sophie every happiness together, and I thank you for all your care of my father.'

When she had quit the room, Nicholas pulled Sophie into his

arms and kissed her. It was an entirely different kiss from any she had received from him before and as he held her tightly against him, his tongue probing her mouth, she found herself curling her own tongue away, disliking the touch of his. Allowing this response for the time being, Nicholas let her go and said, 'So, now they know. Our secret's out and we can be seen together.'

'Oh, Nicholas,' Sophie responded, 'indeed. You must come and go here as you wish. You will always be welcome.'

'My dear Sophie,' he laughed, 'do you really think so? Did you not see Leroy's face when we broke the news? And as for his mother...'

'They were surprised,' Sophie told him. 'They weren't expecting it.'

'And they didn't approve, though your Aunt Matty made a better fist of pretending she did than the other two.'

'They'll soon get used to the idea, Nicholas, and as they get to know you, they'll grow to love you as I do.'

'Will they? We'll see.'

'Grandfather's funeral is on Friday,' Sophie said. 'When you escort me to that, it will tell the world that you are my future husband, even though we have to wait a while for decency's sake, before we can marry.'

This was one of the things Nicholas had not anticipated when he had taken the opportunity to dispatch Thomas on Christmas morning. He'd known there would be violent opposition from the old man to his marrying Sophie, and had decided to deal with it before it occurred. The impropriety of Sophie marrying for at least three months after his death had never crossed his mind.

'And after the funeral,' Sophie was saying, 'which Mr Staunton, Grandfather's solicitor, will attend, there will be the formal reading of the will, and as my fiancé you will of course be present at that.'

'When we shall hear Charles Leroy inherits the estate.'

Sophie was very tempted to tell him there and then about the terms of Thomas's will, but she did not. She was determined that his surprise should be genuine when he heard of her inheritance;

surprise in front of the whole family, so that no one could believe what she knew Hannah thought, that Nicholas was simply a fortune-hunter, after her inheritance.

Nicholas stayed no longer. He knew that despite Sophie's protestations, any welcome he received at Trescadinnick in the foreseeable future would be at best grudging. Before they emerged from the drawing room he kissed her again, less forcefully this time, and felt her warm and compliant in his arms.

There was no one to see him leave except Sophie. Matty had found Louisa in the morning room and together they were talking over the revelation of Sophie's engagement.

'We must put a stop to it,' Louisa announced. 'Papa would never have allowed it.'

'I don't see how he could have stopped it,' Matty replied. 'She'll be twenty-one in March and then she can marry whoever she likes.'

'He'd have found a way,' Louisa insisted.

'Like he did with Mary? If he'd refused his consent, she would simply have waited until she was of age and married the doctor anyway. He'd have lost her as he lost Mary.'

'And good riddance,' snapped Louisa. 'If she doesn't know what's fitting conduct for a Penvarrow, and insists on marrying some nobody, that's up to her.'

'I think,' Matty said slowly, 'that the less opposition we put up the better. They are unlikely to marry immediately, and she may change her mind. She's only known him a few months. As she gets to know him better she may find he's not the man she thought he was.'

'And when they marry,' Louisa went on as if Matty hadn't spoken, 'Charles and I and little AliceAnne will be turned out of our home. That's what he's after. Not Sophie, Trescadinnick.'

'Oh come now, Louisa,' said Matty. 'You don't know that. We can't assume he knows that Papa changed his will.'

'Can't we? He was here when Mr Staunton came, remember? He and Paxton witnessed Papa's signature. He must have known it was on a new will.'

'Even so, he wouldn't have known what was in it.'

'Oh, Matty, don't be so naïve, he'd have guessed! New grand-daughter, new will, new heir!'

When Charles had left the drawing room, he'd taken Hector and ridden away, striking out again onto the moor. The daylight was fading but he just had to get away, from the house and from the news Sophie had just given them. Ever since she had deserted Trescadinnick and returned to London, Charles had gradually realized his true feelings for her. If his grandfather had left matters to take care of themselves, he knew now that he would have grown to love Sophie, wooing her until she came to return his love. If his grandfather had made no demands of either of them, had never told them of his new will, they might have grown together as Charles now wished they could. How he wished he could take back all the unkind words that had exploded from him that fateful day. But now it was too late. Sophie had fallen in love with Nicholas Bryan and she was lost to him.

Chapter 27

Friday morning was cold but dry. The hearse and funeral carriages moved in slow procession from Trescadinnick down to the church in Port Felec. Louisa, Matty and Sophie rode in one, dressed in unrelieved black, their faces discreetly veiled. Charles walked behind the hearse, followed by the pall-bearers.

When the cortege arrived at the lychgate, the rector stepped forward to greet the coffin and the mourners. A crowd had gathered in the churchyard, but they parted politely to allow the ladies from Trescadinnick to pass between them and enter the church. As Sophie descended from the carriage she had caught sight of Nicholas, dressed in sombre black, his head bare, his top hat in his hand. As she walked up the path towards the church door, he fell in beside her, offering his arm. She turned and inclined her head as she rested her fingers on his sleeve. Together they entered the church and took their places in the family pew.

Gradually the church filled up behind them, the Trescadinnick servants, all except Hannah who had stayed with AliceAnne at the house, standing respectfully at the back.

Other landowners from the area had preceded the coffin into the church and taken their seats near the front, and behind these were the people of Port Felec. Will Shaw was there with his mother and so were other men who worked on the estate farms: some miners from the last working Trescadinnick mine; the fishermen who manned the Trescadinnick pilchard boats and seine nets, all there to offer their respects to the old man who had been their landlord or employer all their lives.

As Thomas's coffin was carried into the church, followed by Charles alone, Sophie looked back and saw him, grave-faced with sadness in his eyes. Never one to allow his emotions to show, she knew that despite Thomas's capriciousness and authoritarian attitude, and his apparent rejection of him, Charles had loved his step-grandfather. As he stepped aside to join his family in their pew, Sophie allowed her hand to brush against his. Charles did not turn his head, but the faintest smile touched his lips before he drew his hand away.

'I am the resurrection and the life, saith the Lord: he that believeth in me, though he were dead, yet shall he live: and whosoever liveth and believeth in me shall never die...'

The service was not a long one and as she stood staring at the coffin with its funeral wreath, lying on the bier before the altar, Sophie's mind wandered away from the drone of the rector's voice and she thought about her mother, her father and her grandfather. She had passed almost all her life thinking her parents were her only family and then suddenly she'd found herself part of a wider family, of which she'd known nothing and was the only grandchild. She had shared her grandfather's home for almost two months and had gradually come to know him. She knew she didn't love him as a granddaughter should, but she had developed an affection for him despite his autocratic ways and she sincerely regretted his passing. She had no tears to shed, but, as the rector finally pronounced the blessing and the coffin was carried from the church to its final resting place in the Penvarrow tomb in the churchyard, she knew a deep sadness for all the lost years.

A chilly wind had blown up and after a few moments outside the church, the funeral party returned to Trescadinnick where Mrs Paxton had laid out a collation for the mourners who were expected. Thomas had been something of a recluse at the end of his life, but he had once been a force in the neighbourhood and the other local landowners and businessmen who had come to pay their respects had to be entertained. They were not accompanied by their wives; it was not the custom. Once they had offered their condolences to the ladies of the house, they gathered together in groups and discussed what changes Charles Leroy would make, now that the place was his and he had a free hand. Charles moved from group to group, acting as host, watched by Nicholas as he stood in the hallway, with Sophie at his side. It was not long before the ladies withdrew, Sophie with them, leaving the brandy and the baked meats to the men. Mr Staunton had come from Truro and as he served several of the gentlemen who were there in a legal capacity, he too moved among them, speaking softly with a nod here, a smile there; but all of them knew his real purpose. When they had departed for their own firesides, he would gather the family together and take Thomas's will from his briefcase and all would be revealed.

When Sophie had withdrawn, Nicholas moved into the drawing room. Charles was not surprised. She had told him that she wanted Nicholas to be there at the reading of the will, but it was clear that several of the other guests were surprised that the doctor, once he had paid his respects, had not quietly left the gathering and returned to his own place. He was not their physician and no one engaged him in conversation. He stood alone, a glass of brandy in his hand, noting who was there. They might ignore him now, but it would not be long before they realized his new standing in the community. Master of Trescadinnick. He smiled to himself and waited for them to leave.

At last the door was closed to the final guest and Charles suggested to Mr Staunton that they should all repair to the library for the reading of the will. The ladies, who had been taking tea in the morning room, followed them in; Louisa's face a mask of hostility at the sight of Nicholas, Matty, grave and resigned, and Sophie, smiling as she accepted Nicholas's arm.

The fire had been lit earlier and the room was warm and comfortable. Charles pulled out the chair from Thomas's desk and suggested that Mr Staunton take it as his seat, while everyone else found places on chairs and sofas, waiting to hear Thomas's last will and testament.

As he sat down, the solicitor looked at Nicholas Bryan with interest, recognizing his face, but not knowing why.

Charles, seeing this, said, 'May I introduce Dr Nicholas Bryan, Mr Staunton, my cousin Sophie's fiancé? He is also the family's physician who attended my grandfather in his last illness.'

'Ah, I see,' the solicitor said, and standing up again he extended his hand for Nicholas to shake. 'How d'you do, sir?' Now he remembered why the man was familiar; he was one of the witnesses to Thomas's signature. As he sat down again Mr Staunton opened his briefcase and removing the will, laid it on the desk in front of him. A quick glance at the last page confirmed his memory: *Nicholas Bryan, Physician, Port Felec.*

Looking up again, he cleared his throat and said, 'Ladies, gentlemen. We've come together to hear the wishes of Thomas Jocelyn Penvarrow of Trescadinnick. I shall read the will to you and if there are any questions you wish to put to me, I shall be happy to answer them when I have finished. Mr Penvarrow made a new will recently and there are specific instructions relating to some of the bequests, which I will explain if explanation is required.'

He looked at those gathered, waiting; but as no one spoke, and receiving a nod from Charles, he put on his spectacles, picked up the will and began to read.

'*I, Thomas Jocelyn Penvarrow of Trescadinnick in the county of Cornwall declare this to be my last will which I make this eleventh day of November 1886.*'

He continued to read, naming the executors as Charles and himself. Then followed specific legacies, annuities for his daughters, for AliceAnne and for Charles; fifty pounds to the Paxtons provided they were still in his service at the time of his death, ten pounds to each of the other servants. There was nothing unexpected in all this. Everyone knew that Thomas had changed his will in favour of Sophie, though Nicholas kept his expression neutral, as if he had no such knowledge.

'And now,' Mr Staunton set down the document and looked up, 'we come to the main part of this will. When Mr Penvarrow made it, he included some Trust clauses and Mr Charles Leroy and I are joint trustees of the Trust which is established by

264

those clauses. In the way that we lawyers like to deal with such things the clauses are somewhat technical, so forgive me if I paraphrase. The essence of the Trust provisions is as follows. All the estate not otherwise given away is to be held in trust for Mr Penvarrow's granddaughter, Sophia Alice Ross, until she shall attain the age of thirty years. Under the terms of the Trust she may receive an agreed income from the capital, but will only have access to the capital itself with the consent of the trustees.'

There was a sharp intake of breath from Nicholas, but Mr Staunton continued without pause. 'Similarly, she may have access to the capital necessary to the running of the estate, but again, only with the consent of the trustees.

'The trustees shall appoint an estate manager, who will be paid by the estate and who, in consultation with the trustees, shall deal with the day-to-day running of the estate and any other affairs of business until the Trust is terminated. Miss Ross may live at Trescadinnick whenever she wishes, as may those people already living there when Mr Penvarrow died. However, if there should be any dispute about this while the house is in trust, the dispute will be resolved by the trustees, who have absolute discretion in the matter of occupancy.

'Should circumstances change, by common consent and entirely at their discretion, the trustees may terminate the Trust.'

The family listened in stunned silence to these conditions. None of them, not Thomas's daughters, not Charles, had expected anything other than a straightforward will, naming Sophie as heir. Running true to character, Thomas had not consulted Charles before naming him executor and trustee, and it was with amazement and dismay that he realized he was now, in all but name, Sophie's guardian.

Sophie was trying to understand the conditions that had been dictated by her grandfather, but before she could ask any questions, it was Nicholas who spoke.

'So, Mr Staunton,' he asked, 'what does all that mean?'

All eyes turned on him and then back to Mr Staunton, who replied, 'It means, sir, that Miss Ross is the heir to the

Trescadinnick fortune and the estate that goes with it, but that she is unable to take the reins of her inheritance into her own hands until she attains the age of thirty.'

'Not for another ten years?' Nicholas was incredulous.

'No, indeed,' agreed Mr Staunton. 'But, as is often the case, such Trusts are set up for young ladies to protect them from anyone unscrupulous enough to prey on them and their inheritance. Many fathers... and in this case grandfathers... feel that young ladies do not reach the years of discretion until they are much older than twenty-one.'

'And does it mean she can't marry until she's thirty?' Louisa asked, flashing a look of triumph at Nicholas.

'No, ma'am, it doesn't,' replied Mr Staunton patiently. 'She can marry without consent once she reaches her majority, but that doesn't give her free access to her capital. However, in that case, no doubt the discretion of the trustees could be invoked.'

'And the house?' Louisa asked anxiously.

'It is her house, and she may live in it if she chooses to, but the trustees may use their discretion with regard to anyone else.'

Nicholas said nothing else. Louisa had asked the questions to which he wanted answers, but the answers she had been given didn't please him at all.

Silence descended on the room again and as there seemed to be no further questions, Mr Staunton gathered up the papers and replaced them in his briefcase. 'I'll keep the will to register in the Central Court of Probate,' he said, 'but my clerk will make a copy for your family records. As executor and trustee, I shall also keep a copy in my office.' He looked round at the gathered group before getting to his feet. 'Is there anything anyone else wants to ask?'

'If I choose not to act as executor and trustee?' asked Charles. 'What happens then?'

'Then it will fall to me to act alone as both,' replied the solicitor. 'But as I pointed out to Mr Penvarrow at the time, it is considered better to have two signatures required... it avoids the suspicion of venality.' He looked across at Charles. 'If you are seriously considering refusing to serve as executor and trustee, Mr Leroy, I shall be happy to discuss the matter with you in my office.'

'Thank you,' replied Charles. 'I will certainly give it some thought and then, perhaps after the weekend, I shall call upon you and we can talk everything through.'

'I shall look forward to seeing you either way,' said Mr Staunton. 'Indeed, if you do decide to remain a trustee we should have a meeting in any event. There is much to be discussed and decided upon, particularly with regard to the future of the estate.'

The two men walked out to the front hall where they shook hands, before Mr Staunton left and Charles went into his office.

Nicholas had listened to this exchange, his face impassive, but inside he was boiling with rage. He understood exactly what Thomas Penvarrow had achieved. He, Nicholas, or indeed anyone, could marry Sophie as soon as she was twenty-one. But unless Charles and that solicitor used their discretion, which he was certain they would not, he could not touch a penny of Sophie's money for another ten years. He knew that marrying a woman no longer meant that her property automatically became his. The Married Women's Property Act had changed all that only four or five years ago, but he had, nevertheless, intended that Sophie should sign her property over to him. He would have persuaded her with professions of love and promises to protect her inheritance, to get control of it, but now? Now Leroy would control everything for the foreseeable future, and pompous fool though he was, even he wasn't fool enough to allow Sophie to sign away her fortune. And if Charles actually refused to be executor and trustee, there was still the solicitor, Staunton, standing firmly between Nicholas and what he had come to think of as *his* rightful inheritance.

'So you can't get your hands on Trescadinnick as easily as you hoped.' His thoughts were interrupted by Louisa Leroy, who stood looking down at him with triumph in her eyes. 'Even if you do marry the chit, her inheritance will be protected.'

'I love her and I have every intention of marrying her,'

Nicholas said, getting to his feet and towering over Louisa. 'Heiress or otherwise!'

She looked up into his face, unintimidated. 'Really? You haven't even given her a ring yet. No settlements have been made. As far as I and my family are concerned there is no engagement between you.'

'As far as I am concerned there is.' Sophie appeared at Nicholas's side and slipped her arm through his. 'Ring or no ring. We love each other, Aunt, and whether it pleases you or not, we intend to be married.'

'More fool you,' said Louisa. 'Everyone else can see that it isn't you this man loves, but what you bring with you. It's time you saw it too.' And with this parting salvo, Louisa turned on her heel and stalked out of the library and up the stairs to the privacy of her own room.

'What a sad old woman,' Nicholas remarked as he watched her go. 'Bitter against you simply because she thought her son should inherit and your grandfather didn't agree.'

'Well, he should have,' Sophie said. 'It's been he who has kept the place going over the past few years.'

'But he's not a Penvarrow,' Nicholas reminded her, 'and your grandfather wanted a true Penvarrow to have Trescadinnick. A Penvarrow of the blood.'

'Well,' said Sophie as they walked towards the front door, 'at least I can ask Charles if he'll continue looking after the estate. There'll be no change there even when we're married.' She smiled up at Nicholas. 'And of course they can stay in the house; it's their home.'

This brought Nicholas up short. 'They'll all live with us?'

'No, of course not!' laughed Sophie. 'We shall be living in your house. You'll need your surgery and your dispensary close at hand. Hannah and I will be perfectly happy there.'

'Hannah?'

'Of course Hannah!' exclaimed Sophie. 'Oh, Nicholas, I'm so happy! Aren't you?'

'Happy?' said Nicholas. 'Of course I am, my dearest girl!'

Nicholas strode down the drive. As he passed the home farm Will Shaw waved a greeting, but it went unacknowledged, and Will said to his mother as they sat down to their supper, 'Did you see Miss Sophie on Dr Bryan's arm in the church, Ma? Something happening there maybe, but my, the doctor was in bad humour as he passed by later. Maybe things are not well up at the big house.'

When Nicholas slammed his front door behind him and threw off his coat, his humour had not improved. He went into his sitting room and having stabbed the fire viciously with the poker to bring it back to life, he poured himself a large measure of brandy and dropped into his chair. The anger he had felt as Mr Staunton read the terms of the will had not dissipated; rather, it had built inside him and he had been glad to get away from the house so that he no longer had to wear the mask of concerned love.

How Thomas Penvarrow had tricked him! How he was manipulating everything from the cold depths of his tomb! How even from the grave he'd been able to wreck all Nicholas's carefully laid plans.

Nicholas had listened with growing fury as the solicitor had read the terms of the will. Sophie was indeed Thomas's heir, but there were so many caveats and conditions that she had nothing, could do nothing, without the consent of Charles Leroy and that stick of a solicitor, Staunton.

Leroy's not the heir, thought Nicholas bitterly, but he might as well be. He will control her money, the estate's money, and even decide who may live in the house. That means, without a doubt, he, his mother and that child with the stupid name will continue to live there as if nothing's changed. And nothing will... not for ten years!

If he married Sophie, no, *when* he married Sophie, they would not be able to evict her family from the house unless Charles Leroy decreed they could.

'And Sophie expects us to live in this hovel,' he shouted to the empty room, 'when Trescadinnick is *hers*!'

Chapter 28

Dolly looked surprised and not particularly pleased to see him when she opened her door to Nicholas a few days later.

'Bad penny,' she said, barring his way into the house. 'You can get lost, 'less you've brought the money.' She stared him straight in the eye. 'Have you?'

'Not all of it,' he admitted. 'It's a lot to find all at once. Bit to keep you going.'

'How much?'

'Twenty-five quid.'

'A pony! You're not getting nothing for that, I can tell you. Where's the 'undred you promised?'

'Coming, Dolly! Coming! I'm getting it.'

'Well,' Dolly said, 'you ain't even gonna *see* them marriage lines till I see that money on the table... all of it.'

'Getting that much money, Doll, takes time, doesn't it?'

'I dunno, Nick, do I? Come on,' she sighed. 'Better come in. Luke'll be round for 'is tea in a minute, and I can tell you, he'll be disappointed, an' all.'

'Luke?'

'Well, he knows what you're suggesting. He's my brother, ain't he?' No harm, Dolly thought, to let Nicholas know that she wasn't the only one who knew of his offer. She stood aside to let him in. When she'd fed the three of them and Luke had gone again, Nicholas took her to bed.

Later, as they lay there, Dolly asked, 'So, when *am* I gonna to get my money?'

'Soon as *I've* got it, Doll. I promised, didn't I?'

'So why you bothered to come to London without it? All that way from...' She caught herself in time. Luke had followed Nicholas to Paddington and heard him buy a ticket for Truro, which they had discovered was in Cornwall. 'From the country, just to tell me you ain't got it?'

'And to see you, Dolly,' said Nicholas, reaching for her again. 'And to see you.'

Nicholas hadn't seen Sophie since the day of the funeral and she'd been disappointed when she received a note from him, delivered by one of the fisher boys from Port Felec, telling her that he had been called away to London and would be in town for a day or two.

I'll be back to you as soon as I can, my dearest, he wrote. *But I shall be away at least three days. I shall miss you every minute of every day.*

She was disappointed that he had not called in person to tell her he was going away, but at least she had the note. She said nothing to anyone else in the house. Since the reading of the will the atmosphere had been strained. Mrs Paxton had enquired whether she should be consulting Mrs Leroy about the housekeeping, or Miss Ross.

Sophie said at once, 'Mrs Paxton, please do carry on as usual and speak with my aunt. She has the running of the house.' Though they had a sort of unspoken truce, Louisa still only spoke to Sophie when she absolutely had to. Charles was distantly polite and Matty, after another night in the house, packed up and went home. Sophie was sad that Matty had returned to Treslyn House; she felt in Matty she had some sort of ally.

'Now, come and visit me,' Matty said as she gave Sophie a quick hug. 'Bring the child with you, bring AliceAnne. It's time she was going out and about.'

'Yes, Aunt, I will,' replied Sophie, wondering if Aunt Matty had ever thought of inviting AliceAnne to her house before. 'We'll come and see you before the week's out.'

Sophie resumed the piano lessons she was giving AliceAnne and helped the child with some of her lessons, but still much of the time she felt out of place. The house was hers, but she didn't feel at home in it and there were times when she longed to be back in the little house in Hammersmith.

After the weekend, Charles rode into Truro and went to see Mr Staunton. The solicitor greeted him. 'I wish you the compliments of the season, Mr Leroy,' he said as he led Charles into his office, 'and every good wish for the New Year.'

Charles replied with the same, thinking, as he said it, that the incoming year could hardly be worse than the last one, but fearing that it might.

Mr Staunton sat down behind his desk, waving Charles to a chair opposite. 'I'm glad you have come to see me,' he said without preamble. 'Whatever you have decided, we have a good deal to discuss.'

'I have come to a decision, Mr Staunton,' Charles said. 'I have given the position I find myself in careful consideration. My grandfather has left us with a very difficult situation.'

'He was doing his best to protect Miss Ross's interests.'

'I realize that,' replied Charles, 'but would he not have done better to appoint you as sole trustee?'

'He could have done so but, as I explained the other day, it is usual to have two trustees and he had great faith in your judgement. I am sure you know that he was hoping that you and Miss Ross might marry, and then there would be no question of the Trust being necessary. What he did not want to happen was for Miss Ross to find herself pursued by fortune-hunters.'

'I'm not sure how much fortune there is to hunt,' said Charles wryly. 'Of course, I haven't seen the estate finances in detail, Mr Penvarrow kept those to himself, but I know that the income has dropped substantially over the last few years with the closing of the mines.'

'Indeed it has, but even so, there is a fair amount of money in the funds. The point I am making is that if you are not going to marry Miss Ross yourself, and it would appear that you are not, her inheritance must be protected.'

'I agree,' Charles said firmly.

'And I think as her trustee you would be in the best position to do so. You will be seeing her daily and will be able to judge what she needs herself. She must have an income, and live in comfort. Did your grandfather know that she was engaged to be married? Had he approved the engagement before he died?'

'No,' replied Charles. 'None of us knew of the engagement until after his death. Sophie said they had been going to ask for his blessing after Christmas.'

'And would he have given it?'

Charles sighed. 'I doubt it, not at first anyway. Dr Bryan had been attending him for several months, but my grandfather never had as much faith in him as he'd had in old Dr Marshall. Maybe, if Sophie had persisted in her choice, he would have given in eventually.'

'Did Dr Bryan know Miss Ross was to inherit?'

'I don't think so. The perceived wisdom was that I was the heir.'

'Yes, I realize that,' said Mr Staunton, 'but it was Dr Bryan who witnessed Mr Penvarrow's signature on the will.'

'But surely he had no sight of the content?'

'No, indeed, nor even the certainty that it was a will that Mr Penvarrow was signing, but he may well have guessed, and if he did, he may have also guessed the main beneficiary.'

Charles looked troubled at this. 'And since then,' he remarked, 'Dr Bryan has been a constant caller on Miss Ross.' He told the solicitor of Nicholas's attendance on Sophie in London, where he had called without the knowledge of any of the family, including Thomas.

'He asked a pertinent question on Friday,' Mr Staunton said.

'On her behalf or on his own?' wondered Charles. 'Perhaps he was simply trying to clarify the situation so that he could explain it to Sophie should she not grasp it herself.'

'If I may speak plainly and without prejudice, Mr Leroy,' said Mr Staunton, 'I think you are being too charitable. I think that young man wanted to know exactly what Miss Ross could and could not do without the sanction of her trustees. I think it is exactly for protection from such people that the Trust was set up. Remind me when Miss Ross will come of age.'

'On the twenty-fifth of March this year,' replied Charles.

'Then you have two months to keep watch. After that, with regard to her marriage, she will be her own mistress.'

'Suppose I simply leave the trusteeship to you?'

'I should carry it out as necessary, but I hope you will not. Miss Ross may have great need of you.'

'You believe that Dr Bryan is...' Charles's voice trailed off as he tried to find the words.

'He may be nothing more than a young man who has fallen in love with a beautiful young woman and wishes to marry her,' said the solicitor. 'Who am I to judge? But I would treat him with caution. Something tells me he is not quite as he seems.' Mr Staunton gave Charles a brief smile. 'With regard to the other clauses of the Trust, it would also be much better and easier all round for you to continue as a trustee.'

Charles nodded. 'If that is your advice, Mr Staunton, I will take it.'

The solicitor stood and reached his hand across the desk. 'Thank you, Mr Leroy. I am sure we shall be able to work together most amicably. Now, about the estate itself. Do you think Miss Ross will want to concern herself with that?'

'We should certainly ask her,' Charles said.

'Very well,' agreed the solicitor, 'let us discuss ideas and put them to her.' Pulling a pad towards him, he sat down again and reached for a pen to make notes.

By the time Charles returned to Trescadinnick, dusk had fallen and a chill sea mist was creeping across the cliff. As he approached Trescadinnick he could see the lights of the house, hazy haloes of warmth shining through the mist. It was the only home he remembered and the place where he'd thought he would spend the rest of his life. As he looked across at the house now, he thought again about what the lawyer had said.

'If Miss Ross does marry her doctor in the near future, perhaps you and your family should be looking for somewhere else to live. I assume Miss Ross will want to live at Trescadinnick, and if asked I would have to agree that was fair enough, but I don't imagine any of you will be very comfortable living with a newly married couple.'

Charles had already given this consideration and agreed, but he wasn't looking forward to telling his mother that they should be looking for another home. However, he'd decided he would say nothing on the subject yet; sufficient unto the day. When the time came, he hoped he would have found a suitable house for the three of them, and he could present the move as a change for the better.

How he wished he could turn back the clock to Sophie's arrival at Trescadinnick, before Thomas had started dictating their future together. He had grown to know Sophie and without noticing, had grown to love her; but now it was too late. Despite their partial reconciliation in London, the harsh things he'd said still stood between them. He'd recognized the proprietary expression on Nicholas's face as he'd stood beside Sophie in the church and his heart ached as he realized exactly what he had lost.

He left Hector in the safe hands of Ned and walked into the house. Sophie was just coming downstairs and she greeted him with such a smile of welcome, he could feel tears pricking his eyes.

'Hallo, Charles,' she said, 'you're back. It's very cold out there, but there's a fire lit in both the drawing room and the library, so take your pick.'

'Where are you sitting?' Charles asked as he shed his coat and hat.

'Your mother is in the drawing room,' she replied. 'I was about to join her.'

'You're very brave, Sophie. Mama is not at her best these days.'

'She's disappointed for you,' Sophie said. 'I'm sure she'll

understand in time.' She moved towards the drawing-room door and Charles put a hand on her arm to stay her for a moment.

'I have just been to see Mr Staunton,' he said. 'He is anxious the three of us should sit down together and discuss how things will be best arranged with regard to the Trust. Your income, what we should be doing with the estate. I assume you want to learn what goes on and not simply leave it to us.'

'Indeed I do,' Sophie answered. 'I can't run the estate, that's men's business, but I do want to know exactly what our business interests are and to be kept informed and consulted on any major decisions.'

Charles smiled and nodded. 'Thought so,' he said. 'It's what I told Staunton. We'll get him to call and discuss everything.' Then he stood aside and together they went into the drawing room. Louisa was sitting by the fire and looked up as they came in. For the first time in several days she addressed herself to Sophie.

'Sophie,' she said, 'I told Mrs Paxton we'd eat in the morning room this evening. It's much cosier for just the three of us.'

'A very good idea, Aunt,' Sophie said, taking a seat on the opposite side of the fireplace. 'Perhaps we should take all our meals in there for the time being. The dining room is very cold just now.'

Dinner progressed amicably enough, but after the meal all three of them went their separate ways, Charles to his study, Louisa to her own room and Sophie into the drawing room. She sat down at the piano and after a few scales to loosen the fingers, began to play some of her favourite pieces. As always, the music soothed her, and even as she played she relaxed and let her mind wander over the happenings of the last few days. She was not stupid. She knew why her grandfather had tied up Trescadinnick and its funds, but she was not worried by this. She was certain that once she and Nicholas were married and it was clear to everyone, and to Charles and Mr Staunton in particular, that Nicholas had no designs on her inheritance, they would wind up the Trust, or at least release some of her capital.

She wondered, as she played, why Nicholas had needed to go back to London. He had never explained what had brought him to London the first time, and she, delighted by his visit, hadn't pressed him. She wondered how his patients were managing without him, people like old Mrs Slater, but she supposed he was only going to be away for three days.

From the study, Charles could hear the music drifting through from the drawing room, and he found himself hoping that AliceAnne would continue with her piano lessons and perhaps learn to play as well as Sophie. He hadn't noticed the lack of music in the house after Anne had died, but he'd missed Sophie's playing the minute she'd gone back to London.

Later, when Sophie had gone to her own room and was ready for bed, she reached for the bundle of letters she had brought with her and spread them out on the bed. She picked up and read each one again, and it was then that the name leaped out at her. *Nan Slater.*

Nan Slater! How could she have missed it before? She could hear Aunt Matty saying, 'Nan Slater? Is she still alive?' Aunt Matty had referred to old Mrs Slater as Nan. Could she be the Nan Slater who had helped Jocelyn and Cassie keep in touch? Surely she must be; she would be about the right age, the age that Jocelyn would be if he were still alive. She had known him, certainly, because she had remarked on how like him Sophie was. She had hinted that he had got some girl 'into trouble'. But was she simply repeating the rumour of the time, or did she actually know? Had she known both the girl and Jocelyn and acted as their go-between?

Mrs Slater had asked Sophie to visit her again and having made this possible connection, Sophie decided that it was exactly what she should do. No one needed her in the house, and so, if the mist cleared and the weather proved fine, in the morning she would ride over to Tremose and talk to the old woman again. She gathered up the letters, tied them back into their bundle and placed them on the top shelf of the wardrobe.

Chapter 29

When Sophie awoke the next morning and threw back her curtains she found herself looking at a brilliant January day. Gone was the damp, creeping fog. The sky was a cloudless blue and the polished pewter of the sea, gleaming in the sunlight, reached to a horizon marked with the faintest fluff of white. Sophie went down to the morning room, but found it empty and breakfasted alone. She saw no one as she returned to her bedroom, and changed into her riding habit. She had made her decision; she would ride out to Tremose and visit Mrs Slater. When she was dressed she tucked the letters into her pocket. She didn't know if Nan Slater could read, but she wanted to have something with her to demonstrate her right to some answers.

Not wishing to encounter Charles or answer any questions as to where she was going, Sophie went out through the back door to the stable yard. As she passed through the kitchen, she asked for a loaf of bread and a wedge of cheese to take with her. Mrs Paxton packed them into a basket, and then added a pottery jar with a cork lid.

'Broth,' she said, 'if you're going visiting. Only made this morning.'

Sophie smiled at her. 'Thank you, Mrs Paxton,' she said. 'I'm sure Mrs Slater will enjoy that broth. It smells delicious.'

Sophie took the basket and went out into the yard, where she asked Ned to saddle up Millie.

'Are you riding out alone, Miss Sophie?' he asked anxiously as he led the horse to the mounting block.

'Indeed I am, Ned,' replied Sophie sharply as she handed him the basket to hold while she mounted, 'if it's any concern of yours.'

Ned accepted the rebuke and said no more, simply placing the basket in her saddlebag, but when Sophie had ridden out of the yard and up onto the lane, he went and knocked on the study door to tell Charles.

'Thank you, Ned,' Charles said, 'but I don't think you need to worry about Miss Sophie. I'm sure she's only riding out for some fresh air and exercise and won't go far.'

He tried to sound unconcerned, but Charles himself was worried. Was she going out to meet Nicholas Bryan? As far as he knew the doctor had not called on Sophie since the reading of the will, and Charles tried to tell himself that anyway, it was no business of his if he had. It was no business of his if they had an assignation, but he did worry about Sophie riding out alone. The sea mist which had covered the cliff the previous night had dispersed and the weather looked fair, but he had seen the fluff of low cloud on the horizon. Though he and Sophie had ridden out together on several occasions, he wondered if she would know her way home if the mist returned.

Entirely unaware of Charles's concern, Sophie followed the track across the cliff top and then took the lane they had followed on the day she had driven to Tremose with Nicholas. Once or twice she stopped to get her bearings, but it wasn't long before she recognized the little hamlet, its few houses clustered round the inn. She dismounted outside Mrs Slater's cottage and hitched Millie's reins to the stone wall. She looked about her, but there was no one in sight, the dust-covered village street was empty, so she took her basket from the saddlebag and walked up to the heavy wooden front door.

At first there was no reply to her knock and she was about to knock again, more loudly, when she heard a croaky voice from inside. 'Come in. It's on the latch.'

Sophie pushed open the door and stepped inside. It took a moment for her eyes to adjust to the gloom of the kitchen, but as they did she saw Mrs Slater sitting in her rocking chair at the fireside. She was wrapped in a shawl, wearing fingerless mittens and a crocheted cap set on her thinning grey hair. The room was cold, the fire in the grate little more than a flicker of warmth, and Sophie closed the door quickly behind her to keep in what heat there was.

'Mrs Slater,' she said. 'It's me, Sophie Ross. I visited you before with Dr Bryan.'

'I know who you are,' wheezed the old woman. 'You said you'd come back again.'

'I did,' agreed Sophie, coming further in to the room, 'and here I am. I've brought you some things for your larder.' She moved to the table and unpacked the basket. 'Mrs Paxton sent you a pot of broth. Would you like some now?'

Mrs Slater smiled her gappy smile. 'Is it hot?' she asked eagerly.

'Still quite warm,' Sophie said.

'Then I will have a drop,' said Mrs Slater. 'Just a drop, mind, I'll keep the rest for tomorrow.' She started to haul herself to her feet, but Sophie put a hand on her shoulder. 'Don't get up, Mrs Slater. I'll pour you some.'

The old woman pointed to a bowl on the shelf. Reaching it down, Sophie uncorked the crock, poured a little of the broth into the bowl and passed it across. Mrs Slater grasped it with both hands and tilted it to her mouth.

When she'd finished, she handed the bowl back to Sophie. 'More?' Sophie asked.

Mrs Slater shook her head. 'Saving it,' she said. 'Sit you down.' She waved to the chair at the kitchen table and Sophie drew it towards the fire and sat.

At first neither of them knew what to say, but as Sophie, feeling she must introduce the subject of Jocelyn and Cassie carefully, was about to ask a general question about Jocelyn, Mrs Slater said, 'I thank you for the food you've brought. It was kind of you.' She fixed Sophie with a gimlet eye and added, 'Now, tell me really why you've come after so long.'

'I would have come before,' Sophie said a little mendaciously, 'but I went back to London for a while and only returned to Cornwall just before Christmas.' She sighed. 'And a lot's happened since then.'

'I heard about your granfer,' said Mrs Slater, 'passing on Christmas Day.'

'Did you? Word gets about, I suppose.'

'My son, Edmund, is still away at sea or he'd have come to the funeral,' Mrs Slater said. 'To show respect. Church was full, so I heard. So,' she looked across at Sophie with decidedly sharp eyes, 'why you come a-visiting when there's so much to trouble you at home?'

Sophie took a deep breath and putting her hand in her pocket, drew out the bundle of letters and put them on the table.

Mrs Slater eyed them suspiciously. 'What's all that then?'

'Letters,' replied Sophie. 'Letters from Jocelyn to my mother, in London.'

'Letters?'

'Letters I found in my mother's bureau. In one of them Jocelyn mentions you.'

'Me?' Mrs Slater sounded shocked. 'Why would Jocelyn Penvarrow mention me in a letter to your mother? I hardly knew the man.'

'Didn't you?' Sophie let the question hang in the air, but when the old woman didn't reply she went on, 'I think you knew him very well. I think you knew Cassie well too. Probably far better than you knew Joss.'

'Cassie? Cassie, who's that then?'

'Cassie Drew,' said Sophie, 'and I'm sure she was your friend. Let me read you something.' She picked up the letter from Joss to her mother and finding the place, read: *'Cassie's sister and her husband have taken Cassie in and though her brother-in-law is not happy with the situation, her sister, Henrietta, has talked him round. Poor Cassie is shut away and allowed no contact with me, but we have managed to correspond through her friend Nan Slater, so she knows that I haven't abandoned her.'*

Sophie tilted her head interrogatively. 'That's you, Nan, isn't it? You passed letters from my Uncle Jocelyn to his Cassie.'

Nan Slater looked at Sophie for a long minute and then said, 'More than one Nan Slater.'

'I'm sure there is, but I think this one is you. You knew Jocelyn; you told me so. When Cassie found she was expecting and was thrown out by her father, she took refuge with her sister, Henrietta, in Truro. That's not far from here. You,' Sophie went on, 'were Cassie's friend, so you agreed to carry letters between them. You must have known they planned to marry and to marry well before the baby was due to be born.' Still Nan Slater made no response and after a pause, Sophie went on, 'What happened, Nan? What happened that Jocelyn gave up all his plans and committed suicide?'

'I don't know what you're talking about,' Nan said.

'Oh, I think you do. You were Cassie's confidante and their go-between. Something must have happened for Joss to throw himself over that cliff. What was it, Nan? Did Cassie change her mind about marrying him?' And then, answering her own question, Sophie went on, 'No, he'd never have done that. So, Nan, if it wasn't suicide and it wasn't an accident, what was it?'

For a long moment, Nan didn't answer. Then she said, 'I don't know.' She spoke firmly, but Sophie felt certain that she did know, just wasn't prepared to tell. She left those questions for now and went back to the letters.

'But it was you who carried the letters between them, wasn't it? You were Cassie's friend and Henrietta was sorry for her, shut away in their house. She let you visit because she didn't realize you knew Joss as well. Poor Cassie, not allowed to leave the house, made to stay upstairs when anyone called.'

'What makes you say all this?' demanded Nan.

Sophie picked up the letter again and read: '*Albert is not happy with the situation (I am not allowed out of the house or even out of my room if there is company), but he has agreed to let me stay until my confinement, after which, I understand, the baby will be given away.* She was only there on sufferance,

Nan, and was afraid of losing her baby.' Sophie continued to read: '*I had thought it would be better for him… or her, do you mind which? to be born here among family rather than in lodgings somewhere, so I've been behaving as Albert and Hetty require, but, as I have now learned their plan, dear Joss, do come and fetch me as soon as you can. I will* <u>not</u> – the not is underlined three times, Nan – *give up our child to strangers. I am determined that we three shall be together as a family. Surely your father will eventually come round to our marriage, but if not, well, you will be of age in November, and I am already cast out by my father, so we should be able to marry before the child is born without anyone gainsaying us.* Is that the letter to make a man commit suicide, Nan?'

Nan made no reply, so Sophie went on, 'And finally, a letter that Cassie never received.' Sophie picked up the half-finished letter she had found in the drawer of Jocelyn's desk, and began to read the part explaining that Mary had offered them a home and a place for the baby to be born, and the final sentence, '*I shall come and fetch you from Truro as soon as I am twenty-one and can obtain a special licence for our marriage. What a wonderful day that will be. I think…*

'Cassie never received that letter because Jocelyn never sent it,' Sophie said. 'It was unfinished, indeed, as you hear, he must have been interrupted for he broke off mid-sentence.'

'So, where did *you* get it?' demanded Nan.

'I found it in the drawer of Jocelyn's desk.'

'You found it? After nearly thirty years?'

'Yes.'

'And why wasn't it found before?'

'Because,' Sophie said, 'when Jocelyn died, his father had his room sealed up and no one has been allowed into it since the night Jocelyn left it.'

'No one?' Nan sounded incredulous.

'No one,' repeated Sophie firmly.

'So, how did *you* get into it?' Nan's tone was still aggressive.

'I have the adjoining room,' Sophie said. 'I found a key to the connecting door.' No need, she decided, to go into explanations about moving the wardrobe. 'And as I said, the other letters were in my mother's bureau, so I have managed to piece together much of the correspondence.'

Nan looked at her and seemed to reach some sort of decision. 'Why do you want to know all this now? Why dig it all up again? They're all dead, even your grandfather, who probably is as much to blame in this as anyone. There's nothing to be gained by raking it all over again.'

'But they're not all dead,' Sophie replied. 'What about Cassie? What about the baby?'

'Cassie died in childbirth,' Nan said flatly.

'Cassie died?'

'The baby come early... and that was my fault.'

'Your fault?'

'When the news of Jocelyn's death reached me I knew I had to be the one to break the news to Cassie. The only other person they allowed near her was her brother, Edwin. Nasty piece of work, he was. I didn't want him telling her, nor any of her other family neither. Triumphant, they'd be, pleased he was dead, and serve 'im right. That's what they'd have told her.'

'So you went to tell her.'

'Yes. At first she thought I'd brought another letter, probably the one you found in his desk, telling her what he'd arranged and when he'd be coming to fetch her. She was so pleased to see me and then she realized there was something wrong, and I had to tell her.' Nan's voice broke at the memory of that day. 'I had to tell her he wouldn't be coming for her, ever; that he was dead. She collapsed into a swoon and though the baby wasn't due for another four weeks or so, she went into early labour.'

'And she died?' murmured Sophie.

'The baby was the wrong way round. At first her sister's husband wouldn't let them send for a doctor. He didn't want it to be known that he had given shelter to an unmarried woman about to give birth. I was there, and Henrietta and I struggled to help Cassie for hours, but it was no good. When at last Henrietta went against her husband and sent a maid for the doctor, it was too late. Cassie was exhausted from her struggle and her pain. She had lost a lot of blood. The baby was finally born and though very small, seemed healthy enough, but Cassie never recovered. She developed a fever and died a day later.'

'But that wasn't your fault!' exclaimed Sophie. 'That was the fault of her brother-in-law who wouldn't let Henrietta send for the doctor. Why wouldn't he?'

'He was muttering that the difficult delivery was God's punishment to Cassie for having the baby in the first place. I heard later that her own father said the same.'

'But that is dreadful,' cried Sophie, appalled. 'Was there no Christian charity?'

'They gave her a Christian burial,' Nan replied bleakly. 'That was all.'

'And the baby, what about the baby?'

'He stayed with the family. Henrietta was barren and didn't have no children, and she begged her husband that they should keep the baby as their own. She loved him, but Albert only tolerated him. They moved from Truro to Plymouth, where no one would know them or know that the child was not theirs. He grew up and went to school there. As soon as he was old enough to fend for himself, Albert sent him away to learn a trade to keep him.'

'But where is he now? Do his parents know?'

'His parents are dead. They were caught in a flu epidemic that swept through Plymouth some years ago. I heard he went to London, but after the birth and Cassie's death, I was forbidden to set foot in their house. I knew too much about them all and I've never seen them since.'

'But if they had carried through their plans, Cassie and Jocelyn, they'd have been married before the child was born. He would not have been illegitimate and,' Sophie's eyes widened as the thought struck her, 'and my grandfather would have had a legitimate grandson and a male heir.'

'As to that,' Nan said wearily, 'who knows what that old bugger would have done?'

Sophie felt exhausted, too. 'I don't know what to think,' she admitted. 'It's going to take time to come to terms with all this. Do you think my grandfather knew that Cassie was delivered of a boy?'

Nan shrugged. 'Who knows,' she said again.

'Maybe he did,' Sophie said. 'Maybe that's why he sealed up Jocelyn's room. Because he thought Joss had killed himself and Thomas knew he shared some of the blame.'

A silence fell round them. The last piece of wood slipped into the fire with a shower of sparks and Sophie suddenly realized how dark it had become outside. It was still only the middle of the day, but the sun had disappeared and a chilly wind was rattling the single kitchen window.

'I must go,' she said, starting to her feet. 'I must get back.'

'Have you got what you came for?' Nan asked, the aggression creeping back in her voice. 'Are you satisfied with what you've heard? It's all such a long time ago, I hope you'll leave it alone now, and leave the dead to bury the dead.'

'I suppose we'll never know what really happened to Jocelyn,' Sophie said. 'Perhaps, after all, the Penvarrows were right and it was simply a terrible accident.'

'That's probably it,' Nan agreed, but she didn't meet Sophie's eye. Sophie thought there was more to tell, but she knew she had to go or risk being caught in the incoming mist. 'May I come and see you again?' she asked.

'If you must,' Nan said ungraciously. 'And you can bring me some wood. Food I can manage, but I've nothing for the fire 'cept for the sticks the innkeeper's lad collects me from the wood on the hill an' I'm always cold.'

As Sophie rode away, Nan watched her from the cottage door. There were times as she'd been speaking when Sophie could have been Jocelyn, not just in looks, but in the turn of her head, and the flash of her eyes, the directness of her speech. Nan closed the door and returned to her rocking chair. She had kept faith. She had told the story of Jocelyn and Cassie, but today she too had learned something she hadn't known before. She had been the go-between, but she had never read any of the letters she carried. She might have been tempted to do so, but she'd only had minimum schooling and could scarcely read and write her own name. She had never seen Cassie read one of the letters she brought. Cassie had always tucked them away safely to read when she knew she wouldn't be disturbed and discovered. Nan delivered Cassie's letters to Joss and for every one she brought he gave her a half-sovereign. Nan had never been so well off, and though she had never truly believed that Jocelyn would marry Cassie, she continued to carry their letters. She had been the one to bring the news of Jocelyn's death, but by the time she had learned the truth of it from Edwin, Cassie was dying and Nan had not told her.

As she sat rocking herself before the embers in the grate, Nan wished Sophie had never come, bringing the letters with her and opening old wounds. If Sophie called again, Nan decided, she would say no more.

Chapter 30

Charles spent the morning working in his office. There was so much to consider now that he had the freedom to conduct all the Trescadinnick business. Until recently Thomas had held the purse strings and had the final say, and he had refused to countenance some of Charles's more progressive ideas. He'd known things had to change, but he was reluctant to put such changes into motion. He had capital invested, but as he had grown older he had become less and less willing to take risks with it. When Charles finally looked up from the mass of papers on his desk, he realized that the morning had passed and the brightness of the day with it. Coils of mist were beginning to drift past his window and he suddenly thought of Sophie. Was she back yet? He glanced at his watch and found that it was almost time for the midday meal. He left the study and went out into the hall. He could hear women's voices in the kitchen and sighed with relief; she must be back already. However, just to reassure himself, without drawing attention to his fears, he went out to the stable yard where he found Ned, mucking out one of the stables.

A quick glance showed him that Millie's stall was empty and turning to Ned, he said as casually as he could, 'Miss Sophie not back yet, Ned?'

'No, sir,' Ned replied.

'Did she say where she was going?'

'No, sir, not my business to ask, sir.' Ned scratched his head and added, 'She had a basket with her. Like Mrs Leroy takes with her when she's visiting.'

'I see,' said Charles. But he didn't. Who on earth would Sophie be visiting with a basket? His mother sometimes visited in the outlying cottages, taking gifts of food to the ill and the elderly, but who would Sophie know?

'Saddle Hector for me,' Charles instructed and with that he hurried back into the house. He found Louisa and Mrs Paxton in the kitchen.

'Sophie's not back and the mist's coming in,' he told them. 'Did she say where she was going?'

Louisa looked up in surprise. 'Not back from where?'

'She went out this morning. Took Millie and rode off. The mist's coming down and she may get lost. So do you know who she was going to visit?'

'I didn't know she was out,' said Louisa. 'She doesn't tell *me* what she's doing.'

'Where's Hannah?' demanded Charles. 'Perhaps she'll know.'

'She's up in the schoolroom with AliceAnne,' said Louisa. 'I'll go and find her.'

'Excuse me, Mr Charles.' Mrs Paxton spoke softly as if not wishing to interrupt. 'When Miss Sophie took the bread and cheese, I gave her some broth to take as well.'

'Yes?' Charles spoke briskly.

'She said she thought Mrs Slater would like it. That must be where she went. To visit Mrs Slater.'

'Nan Slater over at Tremose?'

'I assumed so, sir.'

'Thank you, Mrs Paxton,' Charles said. 'I'll ride over that way and see if I can find her.'

As he was mounting Hector in the stable yard, a distraught Hannah came running out from the kitchen. 'Mrs Leroy says Sophie's missing.'

'Not missing, Hannah.' Charles tried to sound reassuring. 'She went riding and now the mist is coming in, I'm going out to meet her.'

'Oh thank you, sir.' Hannah's relief was obvious. 'Bring her home safe.'

'I will,' promised Charles.

But Hannah was still anxious as she watched Charles ride out of the yard, to be swallowed up in the creeping mist.

The sky was already darkening when Sophie had left Nan Slater's cottage and set off back to Trescadinnick. Her mind was a-whirl as she thought of all she had learned from Nan that morning. She'd received answers to her questions, but those answers posed further questions. As she reached the crossroads just outside Tremose, her mind replaying their conversation, she took a wrong track and had gone some way before, looking down at the grey blanket gradually spreading below her, she realized she'd gone wrong and was heading up onto the moor. At once she turned back, letting Millie pick her way down the hill, until she recognized a fallen tree where the paths divided and this time took the right direction. It was only just after midday, but the afternoon seemed to be closing in and though she could still see her way, following the well-worn track, she was aware of the mist beginning to steal around her. She longed to hurry as the mist thickened, but the track was uneven and she dared not even break into a trot, for fear that Mille might stumble, or worse still that they might leave the track and miss their way entirely.

Charles's words of warning echoed in her head; It can change very quickly in this part of the world. Sun one minute, thick mist the next. If that happens seek shelter if you can. If not, let the mare bring you home.

Well, Sophie thought shakily, there's no shelter, so I'll have to keep going and rely on Millie.

It was then that she heard him call, his voice muffled in the shifting mist. 'Sophie! Sophie! Where are you?'

In the fog that now surrounded her it was almost impossible to know from which direction the call came, but she pulled Millie up and listened. When he called again she gave an answering cry. 'Charles! I'm here.'

'Stay where you are,' he shouted, his voice sounding closer now. 'Stay where you are, keep calling and I'll come to you.'

'I'm here,' she called again. 'I'm here.'

Within minutes a shape loomed out of the mist and she could see Charles, mounted on Hector, coming towards her.

'Sophie! Thank God!' Charles rode to her side and she could see the mixture of anxiety and relief in his eyes. 'Are you all right? Where on earth have you been? Hannah's worried sick.'

Determined not to show that she had been afraid, Sophie answered briskly. 'She didn't need to be. Of course I'm all right. As you see, I'm on my way home.' Then, as she saw his expression harden, she added, 'But thank you for coming to find me, Charles.'

Charles reached over and taking hold of Millie's bridle, started to lead her back through the mist. 'Where've you been, Sophie?' he asked as they walked along the track.

'*If* it's any business of yours, I've been visiting old Mrs Slater in Tremose.'

'But why her?' Charles sounded confused. 'What made you go there?'

'I visited her when I went with Nicholas on his rounds that afternoon. She asked me to come back and see her again, so I did.' When this was greeted with silence she went on defensively, 'It was such a lovely day and I had nothing else to do. It seemed a good opportunity. She's a widow and on her own while her son is away at sea in some ship, *The Minerva*, I think she said, and so I took her a little extra food.'

'I see.' Charles's voice was cold, but apparently unaware of this Sophie continued, 'But what she really needs is coal, or anyway, something to burn as fuel. Perhaps we could send Paxton over with some logs.'

'Perhaps,' Charles said. 'But really, Sophie, if you intend to keep riding out by yourself, you should at least let us know where you're going.'

'I don't see why,' Sophie snapped. 'It's none of your business where I go or what I do, is it?'

'No,' conceded Charles. 'All that interests me is your safety.'

He let go of Millie's bridle and moved ahead on the track, leaving Sophie to follow him through the mist, and they rode in silence back to Trescadinnick.

When Sophie went up to her room to change out of her riding habit, Hannah greeted her with a great scolding, as a mother will when a child has put herself in danger. 'Whatever was you thinking about, Miss Sophie, riding out by yourself without a word to no one about where you was going? If Mr Charles hadn't come out to find you goodness knows what might have happened to you in that fog.'

'I was quite safe, Hannah,' Sophie assured her. 'Millie was bringing me home.'

'Relying on a horse!' scoffed Hannah. 'Mr Charles was right worried about you.'

'Mr Charles had no need to be,' retorted Sophie. 'He is not my keeper. I'm a woman grown, not a child.'

'Then it's time you stopped behaving like one,' said Hannah quietly.

Sophie stared at her. 'What did you say?'

'I said, stop behaving like one. It seems to me, Miss Sophie, that this inheritance business has gone to your head,' Hannah said. 'You're getting too big for your boots and it don't become you.'

Sophie felt her cheeks redden and she hissed, 'How dare you, Hannah!'

'I dare, Miss Sophie, because I've knowed you all your life and your ma asked me to look after you. If I don't tell you truths, no one else will.'

Sophie took a deep breath and a firm hold on her temper and said, 'Thank you, Hannah. You can go now. I don't need you at the moment. I am perfectly able to change my dress.'

'Mrs Paxton would like to know when you'll be down for luncheon,' Hannah said. 'I come up to ask.'

'Hasn't she served lunch yet?' Sophie was surprised.

'As you had not said you'd be out for luncheon, she was waiting for you to get home. And Mr Charles, of course.'

'Tell her I'm just changing my dress and that I shall be down in ten minutes,' Sophie said, 'and say I'm sorry I'm late.'

'I think you can apologize for that yourself,' Hannah said. 'To her and to the others what've been kept waiting.'

When Hannah closed the door behind her, Sophie found tears of anger pricking her eyes. How dare Hannah speak to her like that? She hadn't the right. No one had the right. She fought back the tears and started to strip off her riding clothes. She knew, if she were honest, she had been relieved when she heard Charles's voice through the mist. He had come out to find her and bring her safely home. Afraid to seem weak, she had been less than grateful, and now she felt a stab of remorse. Ever since the reading of the will there had been such undercurrents in the house and Sophie had felt isolated. Charles had withdrawn from the easy friendship they'd enjoyed earlier in the year and Sophie found she missed it.

Never mind, she assured herself as she tidied her hair and went downstairs, Nicholas will be back soon and then everything can be sorted out.

Charles was just going into the dining room and, seeing him, she called his name. He turned back and waited for her.

'Charles, I...' She hesitated and started again, 'Charles, I just wanted to thank you for coming to look for me. I remembered what you said and was letting Millie bring me home, but it was a relief to hear you calling me. Thank you for coming.' She held out her hand. 'Don't be cross with me. Pax?'

Charles took her hand and with a rueful shake of his head, said, 'I'm not cross, Sophie. Pax it is.'

Chapter 31

It was three days after that, in the late afternoon, when Nicholas came up the drive to Trescadinnick. Edith opened the door to him and showed him into the drawing room where Sophie was playing the piano. As she saw him come into the room she jumped to her feet and ran to him. Edith retired hurriedly as he pulled her in his arms and kissed her.

'Ever so romantic it was,' she told Lizzie Shaw in the kitchen. 'He's such a handsome man. I wish someone'd kiss me like that!'

'Someone'll give you a clip round the ear, miss, if you don't get on with that silver,' snapped Mrs Paxton. 'We need it for the dinner table.'

Edith returned to the cutlery she had been cleaning, only sticking her tongue out once Mrs Paxton's back was turned.

Hannah had seen Nicholas arrive from the schoolroom window and Charles from the study. Neither of them was pleased to see him, but neither of them could say so, to Sophie or to each other. Hannah had decided that Matty's plan was the best. Opposition would almost certainly be counterproductive, making Sophie even more determined. It was better simply to accept the engagement and hope that Sophie came to her senses before her birthday. Charles felt sure *he* couldn't change Sophie's mind, and simply accepted that all he could do was to protect her and her inheritance to the best of his ability.

Nicholas knew he would be less than welcome at Trescadinnick, but that, he'd decided, was something they'd have to put up with. He had come prepared this time. When he got off the train

in Truro, he'd visited Mr Berg, the pawnbroker, and spending
the last of his ready cash, bought an engagement ring, a slim
band of gold set with a single small diamond. There should be
no further comments about the lack of a ring, and once it was
on Sophie's finger it would show the engagement was official
and she was his.

'I've got something for you,' he said as he released her, and
putting his hand into his pocket, he pulled out a small jeweller's
box. He opened it showing Sophie the ring it contained, then
lifting it out, placed it on the third finger of her left hand.

'Now we are betrothed indeed,' she whispered.

'I wish I could buy you a finer ring,' he murmured, 'but when
we are married, my dearest girl, everything that I have will be
yours.'

'And everything that I have will be yours,' Sophie replied as
she turned up her face to his kiss.

Charles, about to enter the drawing room to greet their guest,
heard these words and went cold. He drew back and crossing
the hall silently, returned to his office. Sophie's promise was
exactly what they'd feared. He looked at his watch. It was nearly
half past four, but if he left now he might just catch the solicitor
before he left his office.

Back in the drawing room, unaware that they had been overheard, Sophie led Nicholas to the couch, and sitting beside him
she asked, 'Was your business successful in London?'

'Yes, indeed,' Nicholas said, though it hadn't been. Edwin
had refused to lend so much cash, calling him a fool for killing
Thomas before he was certain of Sophie. They'd had a row,
Edwin saying that Nicholas should have stuck to his original
plan of bringing the Penvarrows down one by one, and Nicholas
calling Edwin too old and a busted flush, afraid to seize the
offered opportunity. They had parted in anger and Nicholas had
come home empty-handed.

Suddenly realizing that Sophie was looking at him expectantly,
Nicholas continued, 'I have an elderly uncle there. He has need
of me from time to time, and of course I have to go.'

Sophie nodded. How like Nicholas to drop everything and go to his uncle's aid. 'I shall look forward to meeting him,' she said.

'Oh, I don't think that will be possible,' Nicholas replied easily. 'Uncle Edwin's very much a recluse now, I'm afraid.' Then changing the subject he said, 'Now, tell me what you've been doing. How are things in the house? Has your aunt handed over the reins?'

'No,' laughed Sophie. 'Why should she? She's been running the household here for the last thirty years. It's her life.'

'But it's your house now, not hers,' Nicholas pointed out. 'You're mistress of Trescadinnick and she should defer to you.'

'I can't see her doing that in a hurry,' smiled Sophie. 'And I don't want her to.'

'But she and her family will have to move out when we're married,' said Nicholas firmly. 'We can't share our first married home with all your relations.'

'No,' agreed Sophie, 'but as I said to you the other day, we shall be living in your house, won't we? At first anyway. I'm in no hurry to move into Trescadinnick.'

'I've given that some thought, Sophie,' Nicholas said coolly, 'and I think we should start as we mean to go on. Trescadinnick is yours and I think it quite reasonable to tell your trustees that we want the place to ourselves. I don't think either of them could quarrel with that, even though it directly affects one of them.' He took her hand in his and turning it over placed a kiss on its palm. 'When we are married, Sophie, I shall expect you to respect my wishes in such things.'

'And I will,' replied Sophie, 'but there will surely be occasions when we have to agree to differ. All married couples have their differences from time to time, you know.' She glanced up into his face and for an instant saw an expression of anger, before it was smoothed away and he said, 'We shall both have to learn what to expect from each other. Once that is decided upon, I'm sure our life together will be quite harmonious.'

'Well,' said Sophie turning the conversation again, 'I did behave like the mistress of the estate the other day.'

Nicholas smiled. 'I'm very glad to hear it,' he said. 'What did you do?'

'I visited one of our tenants. I went to see Mrs Slater and took her some—'

'Nan Slater!' interrupted Nicholas. 'Why did you go there?'

'Because, when you took me to meet her, she asked me to visit her again.'

'You went on your own?'

'Yes, of course,' answered Sophie. 'I rode over on Millie.' Seeing the look on his face, she asked defensively, 'Why shouldn't I?'

'It's not wise for you to go into the cottages of the poor,' he said.

'For goodness' sake, Nicholas, you took me there yourself.' Sophie sounded exasperated.

'Please don't speak to me like that, Sophie,' he said tartly. 'When I took you there I knew there was no infection in the house, but I haven't seen her for more than a week and the situation might well have changed.'

'She seemed well enough,' Sophie said, 'but cold. I'm going to send Paxton over with some logs for her fire.' She glanced up at Nicholas with a challenging eye. 'I may go with him.'

'No, Sophie, you will not. I forbid you to visit her, or any other of my patients without consulting me first.'

'You forbid?' Sophie's voice was ominously calm.

'That is what I'm trying to explain to you, Sophie.' Nicholas tried to keep his tone reasonable. 'My first responsibility now is to keep *you* safe. In future I hope you will listen to my advice.'

Sophie looked up at him from under her long lashes and said, 'I will if it's sensible advice, Nicholas, I promise.'

For a moment he made no reply, but then he smiled and said, 'Now you're teasing me, Sophie. Come along,' he said rising to his feet. 'I should make my compliments to your aunt and cousin.'

Sophie allowed him to lead her from the drawing room into the hall, where she found Hannah waiting to speak to her.

'Mr Charles has ridden into Truro,' she said. 'He asked me to present his apologies, but he won't be home for dinner.'

'Oh!' said Sophie, surprised. 'Well, never mind. Please would you tell Mrs Paxton that Dr Bryan will be joining us this evening and to set another place at the table.' She turned suddenly to Nicholas. 'You will stay for dinner, won't you?'

'Yes, of course,' he replied. 'Thank you.'

'And will you be served in the dining room or the morning room?' Hannah asked.

'The morning room. The dining room is very cold and with just the three of us huddled at one end of the table, rather depressing.'

'That's more like it,' Nicholas approved when Hannah had gone back to Mrs Paxton. 'You were definitely acting as mistress of the house then.'

'No, I was just following what we've been doing the last few nights. It was my Aunt Louisa's idea not to eat in the dining room at night; and not only because of the cold. I think she misses seeing my grandfather sitting at the head of the table.'

'You're too soft, Sophie,' Nicholas chided gently.

But Sophie answered seriously. 'No, I'm not, not really. Since coming to Trescadinnick I've discovered that I have a strong streak of Penvarrow in me. Do you know, Mrs Slater used to know my Uncle Jocelyn and she says I look very like him. My grandfather said I looked like my grandmother, and I can see that likeness in the portrait in the library, but he didn't mention Uncle Jocelyn. There isn't a portrait of him anywhere except a charcoal drawing of him as a child, in the schoolroom. No picture of him as an adult. Perhaps there wasn't an opportunity to have one painted before he died. That's sad, isn't it?'

'And what else did that batty old woman have to tell you, eh?' asked Nicholas. 'I would take everything she told you with a pinch of salt, I've noticed recently that she's become quite childish in her ways.'

'Oh, Nicholas, don't speak of her in that way. It's not fair. She lives on her own with her son away at sea. She's lonely, and I promised to go and see her again.'

'I hope you were listening, Sophie, when I said I would prefer you did not visit her again.'

Ignoring the chill in his tone, Sophie said, 'I was, but as I have already given my promise, I am bound by that. Don't look so fierce, Nicholas, I shall come to no harm.'

At that moment Louisa came down from her room, and when she saw Nicholas standing with Sophie in the hall she turned back up the stairs.

'Aunt,' called Sophie, and Louisa stopped, but didn't turn round. 'Aunt,' repeated Sophie, 'I have invited Dr Bryan to join us for dinner. We shall not dress, and we'll eat in the morning room, as we have been.'

'Charles is out,' Louisa said.

'Yes, he left me a message to say so.'

'Let us hope he told Mrs Paxton as well,' Louisa said thinly. 'I will join you in the drawing room before the gong.'

Charles reached Truro just as Mr Staunton was leaving his office. Seeing Charles's serious expression, the lawyer turned round and led the way inside.

Charles did not hesitate. 'I am extremely worried about Dr Bryan's intentions,' he said. 'I was about to enter the drawing room where he and Sophie were together, when I heard her promise that when they were married all that she had would be his.'

'We can prevent that for the time being,' Staunton told him. 'Even when they are married she won't have access to her capital without our agreement.'

'Yes, I know that,' said Charles. 'But I don't want her even to marry the man, at least until we find out a bit more about him.' He looked across at the solicitor. 'I don't trust him. We know nothing about him, where he came from, who his family are, what means of his own he has.' Charles gave a sudden bark of laughter and said, 'I'm beginning to sound like my grandfather!'

'Well, they aren't planning to marry until Miss Ross is of age, are they? March, isn't it?'

'Yes,' agreed Charles, 'as a mark of respect to my grandfather.'

'Then we have time to make some enquiries,' Mr Staunton said.

'What sort of enquiries?'

'The sort that answer the questions you have just asked.'

'But how?' wondered Charles.

'We employ an enquiry agent.'

'An enquiry agent?

'Certainly,' replied Mr Staunton, 'and I know just the man. Jeremiah Hawke.'

'But what can he do, this Jeremiah Hawke?'

'He's a man of great experience in such matters,' replied Staunton. 'I have used him before, several times. He will know how to find out what there is to find, about Dr Bryan. I leave such matters to him, but once he finds a trail he'll follow it to the end. Of course, we must supply him with as much information as we can. Have you any idea where Dr Bryan was born? Where he did his medical training?'

'I'm not sure,' answered Charles, 'but I believe he told my Aunt Matty that he was born in Truro but brought up in Plymouth. I don't know about where he trained.'

'Well, those are threads worth following,' Staunton said. 'I'm sure Hawke can take things from there. And I'll suggest he visits Dr Marshall's daughter and find out how he came by the old doctor's practice. If you're in agreement I shall instruct Hawke to start some enquiries at once.'

'Yes, do,' Charles agreed. 'The sooner the better.'

'Indeed. They may take some time, but we shall have to be patient. Even if the marriage goes ahead as planned, we shall have some knowledge to inform any future decisions we need to make with regard to the Trust.'

By the time Charles left the solicitor's office he felt slightly more sanguine. At least they were doing something that might protect Sophie. But what if this Jeremiah Hawke could find nothing?

Chapter 32

Hannah was very concerned about Sophie's engagement to Nicholas, especially since she had been publicly named as Thomas Penvarrow's heir. The news circulated Port Felec very quickly, so Will Shaw had told her, and was currently the chief topic of conversation.

'Everyone's surprised he cut Mr Charles out,' Will said. 'Obvious bloke to inherit, he was.'

'But not a true Penvarrow,' sighed Hannah. 'The thing is, Will, if I'm honest with you and it goes no further, I don't trust Dr Bryan. There's something about him that's not right. He's *too* charming.'

'How can anyone be *too* charming?' asked Will with a grin.

'What are they saying in the village, Will? About the engagement? You say that's all round the place now too.'

'It is,' admitted Will. 'Thing like that spreads like wildfire.'

'And what're they saying?'

'They're saying that he's fallen on his feet. Most folks like him and wish him good luck, but there are one or two who think he's a fortune-hunter.'

'That's it,' cried Hannah. 'That's what I'm afraid of. Ever since the will was read he's changed. He's been coming into the house like he owned the place, marching in the front door before Edith's had time to answer the bell.'

'Well, if he's marrying Miss Sophie, he almost does,' Will pointed out.

'But that's what I'm saying, Will. I think he's only marrying her for her money. Ordering the servants about, almost rude to Mrs Leroy. Telling Miss Sophie what she can and can't do.'

'So, not so charming any more,' teased Will. But he took Hannah's hand, as he could see she was truly worried. 'Listen, love, Miss Sophie's not stupid—'

'She is about *him*,' cried Hannah

'If he's after her money,' Will went on, 'well, he can't get it, can he? Didn't you say there was some sort of Trust that was looking after it for her until she's thirty?'

'Yes,' replied Hannah, 'but that's not for people to know about. Miss Sophie told me and I told you, but I told you too that it mustn't go no further.'

'It hasn't and it won't,' Will assured her.

'The thing is I feel so helpless.' Hannah sighed. 'There's nothing I can do.'

'Well, when they get married, you and I can do the same,' Will said cheerfully. 'It's time you told Miss Sophie we're getting married. You've looked after her as you promised her ma, but when she's safely wed, it's up to her husband to look after her and provide for her.'

'But, Will, what I'm afraid of is that it'll be the other way round; that she'll be providing for him.'

'But you said Mr Charles is a trustee or some such, and if she can't have her money yet without his say-so, Dr Bryan won't be able to have it either.'

'I suppose.' Hannah clearly wasn't convinced.

'Tell you what,' Will said, 'why don't you speak to Mr Charles about it? See what he says.'

'Do you think I can? I mean, it's not for me to interfere. I'm just so worried, that's all.'

'And that's what you tell him, love. He'll understand.'

'If she was marrying Mr Charles, I'd have no fears about us getting married and leaving her.'

Will shrugged. 'Well, she isn't, and there's nothing you can do about that. Even so, you should talk to him. He knows you got Miss Sophie's best interests at heart. He won't think you're interfering.'

'All right,' Hannah agreed reluctantly. 'I'll think about it.'

'An' while you're at it, Ma says to ask him if Miss AliceAnne can come over to the farm, Saturday. Maggie's coming over with the kiddies and they were asking if AliceAnne would be there to play.'

'Tell your mother I'll bring her in the afternoon,' Hannah said. 'I can't see Mr Charles objecting to that.'

Later the same day Hannah took her courage in her hands and knocked on Charles's study door.

'Hannah?' he said when she entered. 'What can I do for you? Is there a problem with AliceAnne?'

'No, sir, Miss AliceAnne is fine. I came to say that she's been invited back to the home farm for a visit on Saturday and I took the liberty of accepting the invitation for her.'

'Did you indeed?' But Charles was smiling and Hannah knew he wasn't angry that she'd acted without asking him. 'Well, I assume you'll be going with her.'

'Yes, sir. Of course I will.'

'Then I have no objection at all,' he said. Seeing Hannah hesitate, he added, 'And so I shall tell anyone who asks me, so don't worry about that.'

'Thank you, sir.'

Still Hannah hovered in the room and he asked, 'Was there something else?'

'Well, sir...'

'Come on, Hannah, tell me what you want?'

'It's Miss Sophie, sir.'

Immediately alert, Charles said, 'Miss Sophie? What about her?'

'I'm worried about her, sir, and...' Hannah hesitated again.

'Just tell me, Hannah,' Charles said gently. 'What is it that worries you?'

'It's her engagement to Dr Bryan, sir. It's all so quick and to me it don't feel right.'

'In what way not right?'

'I don't know, sir,' Hannah answered miserably. 'If I'm honest...'

'You can be, Hannah. I'd like you to tell me exactly what it is that's worrying you.'

Charles listened in silence to what she had to say. He wanted to tell her he was as worried as she was, but that would not have been proper, and he did his best to reassure her that he and Mr Staunton were well able to manage Sophie's affairs so that her inheritance was safe.

'But have you heard anything specific?' he asked, thinking as he did so that Hannah might know something about Nicholas Bryan that could be passed on to Jeremiah Hawke.

'Nothing in particular,' admitted Hannah. 'It's just a feeling I get. You know AliceAnne don't like him.'

'So I gathered, but, Hannah, she's only a child.'

'But not a stupid one,' replied Hannah. 'I don't dismiss her feelings about him.'

'My mother said it was because he gave her some foul-tasting medicine when she had that cough.'

'She did. But I don't think she'd asked AliceAnne if that was why.'

'And have you? Asked AliceAnne, I mean?'

'No, sir, not directly, but I've seen the way she shrinks away from him, and that's enough for me. The child is afraid of him.'

Charles got to his feet. 'I'm glad you came and told me, Hannah. I'll be watching as well, so don't worry.'

It was her dismissal and she left, but as she said to Will the next time she saw him, 'He listened and didn't tell me it wasn't any of my business. He and that lawyer, Mr Staunton, will be taking good care of Miss Sophie's money.'

'Then you don't have to worry any more, love,' soothed Will. 'They'll know what they're doing.'

'But it won't stop her marrying him,' Hannah said miserably. 'Will it?'

'Maybe he feels about her as I do about you,' Will said gently and took Hannah in his arms. Hannah looked up into his face and his expression made the colour flood her cheeks. He kissed her tenderly and added, 'Or as I hope you feel about me.'

'Ah, go on now, Will,' said Hannah, before she kissed him back.

While Hannah and Will were sitting comfortably before the fire in the home farm parlour, Sophie and Nicholas sat together in the drawing room at Trescadinnick. Louisa had taken to sitting in the morning room whatever time of day it was, and though Matty had suggested that perhaps it wasn't proper for the happy couple to be allowed such freedom, Louisa remarked that she had no intention of acting as chaperone.

'Sophie's mistress in her own house now, Matty,' she'd said bitterly, 'and how she behaves with her so-called fiancé is none of my business.'

This afternoon there was no question of improper behaviour. Nicholas was determined to get down to business, business relating to Sophie and her Trust. 'We ought to know exactly how things stand with the estate,' he said. 'We need to be sure that your cousin's managing your affairs properly.'

'I agree,' began Sophie, but Nicholas went on, 'We need to know the state of your finances and how your money is being spent; whether it is wisely invested and what your cousin is doing about replacing income that was lost when the mines closed.'

'I think that's an excellent idea, Nicholas,' Sophie replied, 'and so does Charles. He's already suggested that we get together with Mr Staunton to discuss the terms of the Trust and the best way to carry them out.'

'Good,' Nicholas said briskly. 'The sooner we have it out with them the better.'

Sophie smiled at him a little awkwardly and said, 'Nicholas, dearest, I really do appreciate your care for me, but I think the first time I meet with my trustees I should do it alone. There are several points on which I want clarification and I should feel freer to discuss them on my own.'

'Don't be ridiculous,' snapped Nicholas. 'What can you possibly know about the affairs of the estate?'

'Nothing at present,' replied Sophie calmly. 'That's why I need to learn about them. Charles has promised to explain—'

'I'll bet he has,' interrupted Nicholas.

'And when he has,' continued Sophie, 'I shall at least have some idea of what needs to be done.'

'Your cousin could spin you any line and you'd believe him,' Nicholas said. 'He's out to get his hands on the Trescadinnick estate one way or another.'

'Now it's you who's being ridiculous,' Sophie countered. 'Charles has had the running of the estate for nearly ten years, but always with his hands tied. He never had full knowledge of what money was available for investment.'

'And you believe this because...?'

'Because I asked him about it and he told me so. That's when he suggested that we, he and I, should meet with Mr Staunton and discuss everything.'

'And now he has access to the capital,' scoffed Nicholas, 'do you really think he's going to take direction from you, a chit scarce out of the schoolroom?'

'Is that how you think of me, Nicholas?' Sophie's voice was icy.

'No, of course not, my darling girl,' Nicholas said hastily. 'But you may be sure it's how *he* thinks of you.'

Sophie had no answer to that because she could remember Charles using those very words when Thomas had explained his plans for them. However, she simply said, 'I shan't expect him to. I shall respect his experience and leave the daily running of the estate to him, but that doesn't mean I shan't be interested in things.'

'But, my darling girl,' Nicholas changed tack, 'I only want to protect you.'

'Protect me from Charles?' Sophie laughed, but her laughter died as she saw the expression on Nicholas's face. 'I'm sorry, Nicholas,' she said quickly. 'I'm sure you do and I love you for it, but I'm not one to be coddled. I shall listen to Charles, and if I disagree with anything he suggests I shall tell him so. And of course I shall definitely discuss it with you, so we can decide what we want to do.'

'I'm disappointed, Sophie, that you don't trust me,' Nicholas said coldly. 'Indeed, that you appear to have far greater faith in your cousin, than you have in me.' He paused and then said, 'Perhaps you should be marrying *him* instead of me.' He rose abruptly and walked to the door. Jumping up, Sophie caught his arm and he paused without turning.

'Nicholas,' she said, almost pleading, 'you *know* it's you I want to marry, not Charles.'

'You have a strange way of showing it.' Nicholas still didn't turn round and Sophie slipped her arms round him from behind.

'Please, Nicholas, don't be like this. You know I love you, but Charles is my cousin and I'm fond of him too. But not,' she insisted vehemently, 'like I love you!' When Nicholas still didn't respond she sighed and said, 'If you feel so strongly about it, of course you can be there when we discuss the Trust. I'm sure Mr Staunton and Charles will understand why you should want to.'

Sophie felt Nicholas's rigid shoulders relax and he turned at last, to face her. 'You know I only want what's best for you,' he said, his eyes bright with sincerity. 'I'm sure your cousin is competent enough, but he has to understand that Trescadinnick was left to *you.*'

'It was,' Sophie agreed as his arms tightened round her, 'but in a way it was left to both of us. Grandfather assumed Charles would continue to manage the estate.'

'I'm sure he did,' Nicholas murmured into her hair, 'but it's not an assumption we have to make too.'

'Mr Staunton is coming on Friday next week,' Sophie told him, 'so we can discuss everything then.'

'I see,' replied Nicholas coolly. 'It's already arranged, is it?'

'Charles arranged it with Mr Staunton,' explained Sophie. 'Don't worry, I'll tell them you'll be there as well.'

When Nicholas had gone Sophie was left with a feeling of dejection. She had suggested that he stay for dinner but he'd refused quite brusquely, saying that he had things to attend to at home. They hadn't quarrelled exactly, but there had been a definite coolness in Nicholas's manner when he'd said goodbye with no more than a handshake. Sophie knew that he'd been disappointed when she'd suggested that she meet with Charles and Mr Staunton on her own, and he'd not tried to hide his annoyance.

She called for a pot of tea and when Edith had brought it, sat alone in the sitting room sipping her tea and reliving their conversation. It would be better in some ways, she thought, if Nicholas was involved in the discussion about the Trust, but there were questions she had wanted to ask with regard to his position after they were married, questions to which she wanted answers before she broached the subject with him herself. When she had finished her tea she went upstairs to her room. As she passed Jocelyn's room she touched the door handle; it had become a sort of ritual, as if she were assuring him he wasn't forgotten.

I'll get Paxton to take old Nan Slater some logs, she thought, and I'll go with him and have another chat with her whilst he's unloading them.

With this planned, she changed for dinner and then went up to say goodnight to AliceAnne. She found the little girl full of excitement about the afternoon she'd spent at the home farm. Alison and Tommy had been there and they'd played hide-and-seek in the farmyard and the barn. AliceAnne had never played it before and thought it was the most wonderful game. She was in the middle of explaining to an attentive Sophie just how you played, when Charles came in and she began the whole story all over again. Sophie could see the child's delight at her father's visit and she got up to leave them together, but AliceAnne caught her hand.

'Don't go, Aunt Sophie,' she begged. 'I haven't finished telling you everything yet. When we'd finished hide-and-seek we went in for tea and we all had it together, even Hannah and Mr Shaw. And we had ham and eggs and a jammy pudding. It was such fun and Mrs Shaw says I can come again next Saturday if I want to. Alison'll be there again and she's my best friend and I do want to, Papa, so can I?'

'I expect so,' Charles agreed, with a smile at her enthusiasm, 'if Hannah will take you.'

'Oh, she will,' said AliceAnne with confidence. 'She likes going to the farm like I do. I think Mr Shaw is her best friend.'

Sophie left Charles saying goodnight to his daughter and went slowly downstairs for dinner. Was AliceAnne right? she wondered. Were Hannah and Will Shaw 'best friends'? For some reason the thought made her a little sad.

Chapter 33

Monday morning saw Sophie out in the stable yard with Paxton as he loaded logs into the back of the farm waggon.

'Does Mr Charles know where we're going, Miss Sophie?' he asked. 'Does he know you'm taking firewood to some cottage in Tremose?'

'I told him I intended to do so,' Sophie replied. 'He's already gone out, but there's no reason to wait.'

Paxton was clearly not happy with the situation, but he sighed and muttering to himself, clambered onto the waggon and picked up the reins. He looked astonished when Sophie climbed up beside him.

'Are you coming on the cart with me, Miss Sophie?'

'I certainly am, Paxton. I promised Mrs Slater I'd call again.'

The farm waggon was not like the pony and trap, and they made slow progress as it lumbered up the lane. Sophie was beginning to wish she'd had Millie saddled and ridden on ahead, but because she was already going against Nicholas's express wishes by visiting Nan at all, she had decided not to arouse his anger further by riding alone. At least she was travelling with a trusted retainer from the house and there could surely be no impropriety in that.

As they rumbled along the lanes, Sophie thought back to the previous day. It had not been an easy one and had left her feeling despondent. The family had gone to Sunday service for the first time since Thomas's funeral and Sophie had been very aware that the buzz of conversation in the church ceased as the

Trescadinnick party walked in through the door. Nicholas had been waiting outside and she was on his arm as they walked down the aisle to the Trescadinnick pew. Charles was escorting his mother, who looked neither left nor right as she walked straight-backed at his side. She knew everyone would have been discussing the remarkable news that had seeped out of Trescadinnick over the past two weeks. Everyone would be watching Charles to see if he minded being disinherited; watching Sophie, the new heiress, with the local doctor at her side, whispering behind their hands.

At the end of the service they paused for a few minutes out-side the church to pass the time of day with the rector and Miss Sandra, but it was very cold with a chill wind blowing in from the sea, and was not a morning to linger. Sophie had seen the mixture of jealousy and despair in Miss Osell's eyes and knew it was because she'd had hopes of Nicholas and now they were destroyed.

'Good morning, Miss Ross. I trust I see you well.' She held out her hand to Sophie, but the misery in her eyes belied her words of greeting.

Sophie had shaken her hand and replied in kind, but she felt uncomfortable and was relieved to move away.

The Trescadinnick party hadn't remained there long. It was too cold, and as they walked back up the lane to the warmth awaiting them at Trescadinnick, Sophie had determined that it would be tomorrow and not a day later that she and Paxton took the logs to Nan Slater.

Nicholas was invited to join the family for luncheon, and he accepted, but it did not make for a comfortable dining table. Louisa spoke to neither Sophie nor Nicholas. Charles had made an effort to include everyone, but managed only stiff and formal conversation, and AliceAnne sat in complete silence. They were all relieved when the meal was over and they could escape, each to a refuge of their own.

'You notice how warmly they welcomed me to their table,' mocked Nicholas as he and Sophie returned to the drawing room. 'I hope you can see now, Sophie, that I'm right. It would be quite impossible for us to share a house with them. When we meet with Mr Staunton on Friday it is the first thing we have to agree upon, that the Leroys must find somewhere else and move out. The house should become yours and yours alone on the day you come of age: the day before we are married.'

They had chosen a date for their wedding once Nicholas had reluctantly agreed that it would be improper of Sophie even to consider marriage before three months' mourning for her grandfather were over. After that, he had convinced her, a quiet wedding would be acceptable even to the sternest critic, and so the date had been set.

Now he was angry at the cool reception he'd been given that day. 'I can't stay here any longer today,' he said as he paced the room. 'You must talk to them, Sophie, about their manners. I'll call again to see you in a day or two.'

It had been a brusque farewell and when he'd gone Sophie felt let down. She knew the lunch had been difficult for him, for them all, but there was no need to speak to *her* like that. It was hardly her fault. Perhaps, she thought sadly, it would be better all round if he did visit Trescadinnick less often for a while. Everyone there had to get used to the change of circumstances.

When they reached Tremose, Paxton climbed from the waggon and handed Sophie down. She thanked him and told him to wait while she asked Mrs Slater where they should put the logs.

At her knock the old woman called to come in, and as Sophie opened the door she said, 'Good morning, Mrs Slater. I've brought you some firewood. Where shall I ask Paxton to put it?'

'Miss Sophie?'

'I promised you some fuel for your fire,' Sophie said cheerfully. 'Where shall we put it? Feels as if you need some now.' The cottage was indeed very cold and there was only a glow of embers in the grate. 'I'll get Paxton to bring some in here straight away,' she continued, 'and we'll make up the fire.'

Moments later Paxton had brought in a pile of logs, which he stacked at the fireside.

'There are lots more,' Sophie told her. 'Where shall he put them?'

Mrs Slater, still hardly comprehending what was going on, said, 'There are more?'

'Yes,' answered Sophie. 'Enough to keep you warm for some time.'

'The lean-to, at the back.'

Sophie sent Paxton to unload the rest of the logs and set about reviving the fire. The firewood was dry and it wasn't long before there was a cheerful warmth coming from the grate.

Mrs Slater shook off the blanket in which she'd been wrapped. 'When the kettle sings I'll make us some tea,' she said.

'That would be very kind,' Sophie said, knowing that any of the precious tea leaves would be used several times before they were discarded, but also knowing that to refuse the tea would be regarded as a slight.

The old woman looked up at that. 'You're the one that's kind, Miss Sophie, bringing me logs. I thank'ee for that.'

When the tea was made and they were sitting either side of the chimneypiece, Nan Slater said, 'I hear you're getting married, Miss Sophie.'

Sophie smiled. News certainly travelled fast in this area. 'Yes,' she said, 'I am.'

'To Dr Bryan. Is that right too?'

'Yes.'

Nan took a sip of her tea. 'When did you meet him?' she asked. 'Did you know him before?'

Sophie was surprised at the question. 'Before when?'

'Before coming here to Trescadinnick.'

'No,' Sophie replied carefully.

'So you ain't knowed him long?'

'Long enough,' Sophie said with an edge to her voice. She was getting tired of people questioning her choice of husband and it was certainly no business of cottagers like Nan Slater.

Nan took another sip of her tea, savouring its warmth in her mouth before swallowing. 'So, you know all about him,' she said.

'I know enough,' snapped Sophie. 'Look, I don't think any of this is your concern.'

'My concern is for you, Jocelyn's niece,' said Nan unexpectedly. That brought Sophie up short. 'What did you say?'

'You was asking the other day, Miss Sophie, what happened to Cassie's baby. I thought about what you was asking and when I heard you was to be married, well, you've been kind to me, Miss Sophie, and I thought you should know. Some of the Penvarrows is kind, others, not so.'

'I'm sorry, Mrs Slater, but I don't know what you're talking about.'

'So he hasn't told you.'

'Who hasn't told me what?'

'Dr Bryan... as he's knowed now.'

'As he's known now?' Sophie was quite mystified. 'What are you saying?'

'I'm saying that Dr Bryan hasn't told you who he really is.'

'Please don't talk in riddles, Mrs Slater,' retorted Sophie. 'If you have something to tell me, please do, but say it straight.'

'Straight then,' said Nan. 'Dr Nicholas Bryan is Jocelyn Penvarrow's son. That straight enough for you?'

Sophie stared at her, dumbfounded. 'Say that again?' she whispered.

'Nicholas Bryan is a Penvarrow. He's your cousin. Jocelyn Penvarrow's son.'

'I don't believe you,' Sophie said.

'Believe me or not, it's true,' said Nan. 'He's my friend Cassie's son. He was born Nicholas Drew, but his Aunt Hetty and Uncle Albert took him as their own when his mother died, and he was given their name. Bryan.'

'If that's true, how do you know?' demanded Sophie. 'How do *you* know who he is?'

'Because he come to see me when he come doctoring in Port Felec. Cassie's brother, Edwin, had told him who he really was, making out the Penvarrows owed him, and he come to find them. Edwin told him about me, that I was his mother's friend, so he come to find me too. He told me who he was, but made me swear not to tell a soul as he planned to surprise them all.'

'If he swore you to secrecy,' Sophie looked at the old woman through narrowed eyes, 'why are you telling me now?'

'Because you're planning to marry him, or perhaps I should say, he's planning to marry you.'

'That's the same thing,' Sophie said feebly.

'No, it ain't,' asserted Nan. 'Not at all it ain't. You're kind, like your Uncle Jocelyn. He's more like his Uncle Edwin. Has a right temper on him. You don't want to cross him or he'll make you pay. If you're going to marry him, miss, you need to know who he really is.'

It was all too much and Sophie could scarcely comprehend what Nan was telling her, let alone believe it.

'That Edwin was always a brute,' Nan went on. She shuddered even now as she remembered having to fight him off when her husband was away at sea. 'An' I can see a lot of him in Nicholas.'

Edwin! Well, that was a name she'd heard. Nicholas had told her he'd been visiting his Uncle Edwin when he'd gone off to London so unexpectedly. And surely... wasn't there an Edwin in the letters too?

'How do you know he is who he says he is?' asked Sophie. 'Anyone could pretend to be Jocelyn's son.'

'But why would they?'

'I don't know!' cried Sophie. 'But someone might, hoping for money or something!'

'It's him,' replied Nan. 'He's the spit of his mother. Blue eyes and curly fair hair.'

'Anyone can have blue eyes and fair hair,' snapped Sophie.

'They can, but they don't all have Cassie's face, they don't all tilt their heads the way she did, or sound like her when they laugh.' Nan looked across at her. 'Believe me, he's Cassie's son all right.'

'If all this is true,' Sophie said, 'why hasn't he made himself known to the family? He looked after my grandfather until he died. Why didn't he say who he was?'

Nan shrugged. 'Perhaps he did. But I can't see Thomas Pen-varrow being any too pleased if a bastard grandson suddenly turned up at Trescadinnick, can you?'

At that moment Paxton appeared at the door and said, 'I unloaded all them logs, Miss Sophie, and I got to get back home now.'

Still dazed, Sophie got to her feet. 'I'm coming,' she answered, then turning back to Nan, she said, 'I don't believe any of it.'

'Fair enough,' said the old woman with a shrug. 'But think about it.' And with that, Nan Slater picked up the cup of tea which Sophie had left untouched beside her and downed it in one.

Sophie pulled the cottage door closed behind her and climbed up beside Paxton. They drove back to Trescadinnick in silence, Sophie's thoughts in turmoil. As soon as she reached the house she went straight up to her room and locked the door behind her. She flung herself down on the bed, only to get up again immediately to pace the room. How could what Nan Slater had said be true? Surely Nicholas would have told her. Was his reason for coming to Port Felec in the first place to get to know his father's family, *his* family? If not, why had he come? Had Nicholas told Thomas who he was? If he had and Thomas hadn't believed him, the whole house would have known about it. Thomas was not one to keep his anger silent. And if he hadn't, why hadn't he?

As she paced, Sophie suddenly realized that she was consider-ing all this as if she believed everything Nan had told her. She thought of Edwin, and went at once to the drawer to find the packet of letters and look through them. Yes. There he was. *I am quite well here with Henrietta, and though she is mortified at my disgrace, she will not throw me out like my father and Edwin. (Edwin has since been to see me but was extremely disagreeable and I told him to go away!)*

Cassie had a brother, Edwin, and Nicholas has an uncle, Edwin.

It proves nothing, Sophie thought fiercely. *Nothing at all.* But her more sensible self had to admit that it might be a pointer to the truth.

She read through the letters again, hoping to feel more in touch with the people who had written them. It was easy enough to hear her mother's voice, but the other two were strangers. Nan said Nicholas was like his mother, not only in looks but in mannerism too. Surely she must be mistaken. But why would she make up such a story? What was the advantage in that? But if it was true, Nicholas had kept a huge part of himself secret; secret from her. Why? Because they were first cousins? That would be no barrier to their marriage. Because he didn't trust her? She remembered again Nan's words: *Because you're planning to marry him, or perhaps I should say, he's planning to marry you.*

Sophie had dismissed the distinction at the time, but to Nan it was important and Sophie considered it now. *He's planning to marry you.*

Well, thought Sophie, he is planning to marry me, but that's because he loves me, isn't it?

Her thoughts were interrupted by a knock on the door and Hannah's voice from outside. 'Are you in there, Miss Sophie?' she called.

Sophie unlocked the door and Hannah stepped inside. She took one look at Sophie's face and said, 'Why, Miss Sophie! Whatever is the matter?'

'Nothing,' replied Sophie, trying to sound normal. 'I'm a bit tired, that's all. I don't like sitting by myself in the drawing room or the library, so I came up here.'

'You're pale as a ghost,' Hannah said. 'You're not sickening for something, are you?'

Sophie gave her a wan smile and said, 'No, really, Hannah, I'm fine.'

'That's good then,' Hannah said, though she clearly wasn't convinced, 'because Mrs Treslyn has just arrived and will be joining you for lunch. Mrs Paxton asks if it's all right to serve at the usual time.'

'Yes, of course it is,' Sophie said, 'though I've asked her to refer to Aunt Louisa about things like that.' She paused and then said, 'Hannah...'

Hannah halted on the landing and looked back. When Sophie said nothing more, she said encouragingly, 'Yes, Miss Sophie. Was there something?'

Sophie gave her a smile and shook her head. 'No,' she said. 'No, it's nothing. I'll tell you another time. Please tell my aunts I'll be down in five minutes.'

When Hannah had disappeared downstairs again Sophie closed her door and went to look in the mirror. Yes, she did look pale. She pinched her cheeks to bring some colour, then, having tidied her hair, took a deep breath and went downstairs. She must put the morning's conversation entirely out of her mind while they all had lunch. She had been so tempted to confide in Hannah, to repeat what she'd been told and ask Hannah what she thought, but she realized there was no time for that now. If she did decide to unburden herself to Hannah, it would have to be when there was plenty of time to talk.

Matty was waiting in the drawing room and when Sophie walked in she looked at her in dismay. 'Sophie, my dear, you're looking pale. Are you feeling unwell? I do hope you haven't taken a chill.'

'No, Aunt Matty, I'm just a little tired,' Sophie replied. 'And how are you, Aunt? I didn't realize you were coming for lunch today or I would have been down sooner.'

'I hadn't planned to come,' admitted her aunt. 'But I suddenly decided to come and see how you all are.'

'I'm glad you did,' Sophie said. Then, glancing over her shoulder to be sure she wasn't overheard, she added, 'It's been a little difficult these last few days.'

'I'm sure it has,' Matty said, 'but Louisa will gradually get used to the idea, you know.' Changing the subject, she said, 'How is Dr Bryan? He must be very busy in this cold weather.'

'I think he is,' Sophie said. 'He was with us for luncheon yesterday, but he didn't stay long. He said he would call again very soon.'

Matty stayed for the afternoon and while they were together Sophie seriously considered speaking to her about her visit to Nan Slater, and what she'd learned there, but she held back. It wouldn't be fair to Nicholas to mention it to anyone until she'd had a chance to talk to him, but she found herself having imaginary conversations with him, asking questions that required explanation.

Chapter 34

It was Thursday morning before Nicholas drove up to Trescadinnick and rang the doorbell. He greeted Sophie with a smile and spoke as if they had not parted on uneasy terms.

'I've come to take you for a drive,' he said. 'I thought we could go over to St Morwen and lunch together at the Duke's Hotel there.'

Sophie was pleased to see him, but it was with some disquiet that she accepted his invitation. 'That sounds a lovely idea, Nicholas,' she said, 'but is it quite proper for us to lunch alone in a hotel?' It was the wrong thing to say.

Nicholas's eyes hardened. 'You go gallivanting about the countryside alone with your cousin,' he snapped. 'We, an engaged couple, will be in a public dining room in a respectable hotel. I really can't see the problem, Sophie. Don't you want the treat I planned?'

'Of course I do, Nicholas.' Sophie was immediately contrite. 'It sounds delightful. Just let me find my coat and hat.'

He waited impatiently while Sophie warned Mrs Paxton that she would not be in for lunch and then put on her coat. As they were about to leave, Charles came in through the front door. He had seen the doctor's gig outside and knew he had come to call, but he was surprised to see Sophie dressed to go out.

'Sophie, is Dr Bryan not joining us for lunch?' he asked.

'No, I thank you.' It was Nicholas who answered. 'Sophie and I are going to have luncheon at the Duke's Hotel.' He stepped forward and opening the front door, ushered Sophie outside.

They spoke little on their way to St Morwen. Sophie wanted to discuss what Nan Slater had told her, but she realized that jogging along the country lanes was not the right place for such a conversation. She would wait until they were sitting down together somewhere and she could see his face, but when they were shown into the hotel dining room and seated at a table in the window, they were surrounded by other diners, and it was clear that this wasn't the place to bring up the subject either. Nicholas's mood had eased after the drive and he spoke lightly about what he'd been doing since she had seen him. She did not want to spoil his mood by mentioning she had been to see Nan.

As they were eating their dessert, he looked up and said, 'What time is the lawyer coming tomorrow? I assume you've told your cousin that I shall be there too.'

'Of course,' Sophie replied.

'And he made no objection?'

'No, why should he? I simply said that if we were talking about the Trust, I wanted you there as well, to hear what they had to say.' She did not add that although Charles had made no objection, he had shown some surprise, saying, 'I see. I'll let Staunton know.'

'Mr Staunton is coming to Trescadinnick at two in the afternoon tomorrow,' Sophie told Nicholas. 'Will you come for luncheon first?'

'No, I have my rounds to make,' Nicholas said. It was Friday, the day when he collected his fee from those whom he'd attended in the week. 'I'll come at two.'

The conversation had not flowed with its usual ease today. Sophie was all too aware of what she needed to say to Nicholas, but there never seemed to be a right moment to embark on the conversation and it wasn't until they had returned to Trescadinnick that she said, 'Nicholas, please join me for some tea. There's something else we need to discuss.'

He raised an eyebrow. 'Really? Very well, but I can't stay long.'

Sophie led him into the drawing room and when she'd poured the tea that Edith had brought, she drew a deep breath and said,

'I went to see Nan Slater on Monday. Paxton and I took her some logs.'

'I'm surprised at you, Sophie,' Nicholas said coldly. 'I thought I'd asked you not to go visiting my patients on your own.'

'I was not on my own, Nicholas,' Sophie answered. 'Paxton was with me.'

'Paxton was with you? That makes it all right, does it? When I've particularly asked you not to go?'

Sophie was determined not to be deflected from the main issue and said, 'I had promised Nan that I would bring her some firewood, and—'

'Oh, it's Nan now, is it?'

'Mrs Slater, if you prefer.' Sophie would not be cowed. 'It was you who took me to meet her in the first place, Nicholas,' she said.

'Yes,' agreed Nicholas, 'and I'm beginning to wish that I hadn't. Visiting her with me is an entirely different thing.'

'So I discovered.'

'What do you mean?' For the first time Nicholas sounded uneasy.

'She'd heard we were engaged—'

'So has the entire village,' Nicholas said. 'You can't keep that sort of thing secret.'

'And she asked me a question.'

'Which was?'

'How long I'd known you?'

'Which you told her was none of her business. Really, Sophie, you lay yourself open to such impertinence if you go into the cottagers' homes.'

'She asked if I'd known you before.'

'Before? Before what?'

'Before coming to Trescadinnick. And I said no, and then she said, *So he hasn't told you who he really is then*, and I—'

'My dear girl,' interrupted Nicholas. 'This is all nonsense. You know perfectly well who I am.'

'Do I? That's not what Mrs Slater said.'

'Sophie, my love,' said Nicholas calmly. 'I told you before, old Nan Slater is gradually losing her mind. You should pay no attention to her ramblings.'

'She wasn't rambling, Nicholas. She told me about your mother, her friend Cassie.'

'I believe they did know each other when they were girls,' conceded Nicholas. 'But that was years ago and her memory is very unreliable now, you know.'

Undeterred, Sophie went on. 'She told me about your father too.'

'Nan Slater knows nothing about my father,' stated Nicholas. 'He died some years ago, while I was training in London.'

'She says your father was Jocelyn Penvarrow. What do you say to that, Nicholas?'

'I say that the woman is raving mad,' replied Nicholas gravely. 'What do you expect me to say?'

'And your Uncle Edwin? Your mother's brother.'

'Edwin? Why, I told you about him myself, just the other day. It's what I'm trying to explain to you, Sophie. Nan is confused these days. She knew my mother, I'm aware of that, so she probably knew my uncle as well. But it's all so long ago and she's muddled in her mind.'

'Listen to me, Nicholas,' Sophie said. 'Please?'

Nicholas shrugged. 'Go on then. Tell me what else that stupid old woman is saying.'

'Before I say any more about what she told me,' Sophie said, 'I have to tell you what I already knew.'

'Well, go on.' Nicholas feigned indifference, but he was listening intently. What could Sophie have known before Nan Slater started shooting off her mouth?

'I have letters which confirm much of what Nan says.'

'Letters, what letters?'

'Letters written by my Uncle Jocelyn to my mother in London. They were arranging for him to marry your mother. She was already carrying you and was living with her sister Hetty in Truro.'

'So, you have letters arranging for your uncle to marry some girl who was expecting. But who's to say that she was my mother?'

'Nan was Cassie's friend. She was there when you were born.'

'Let me get this straight, Sophie. You believe that I am the natural child of Cassie, Nan's friend, and Jocelyn Penvarrow?'

Sophie nodded.

'That,' replied Nicholas, 'is utterly ridiculous.'

'You may say so, Nicholas,' replied Sophie steadily, 'but I have come to believe it is true.'

Nicholas finally took refuge in anger. 'You mean to say that you believe old Nan Slater more than me?' he snapped. 'The man you're going to marry?'

'Listen, Nicholas. I also have a letter from Cassie, written to my Uncle Jocelyn. She loved him very much and as soon as he was of age they were going to marry. But he died. He fell over the cliff. He died before they could marry and Cassie died soon after, giving birth to you. Nan says—'

'Nan says! Nan says!' mimicked Nicholas. 'Nan Slater knows nothing!'

'She says that Jocelyn was your father and the letters I have bear that out,' repeated Sophie, 'which means we're cousins.'

Nicholas got to his feet and began pacing the room. 'Sophie, I've listened to you. Now you listen to me,' he said, trying to steady his voice. 'What you're thinking is not true. At least, much of it isn't. It is true that I was born out of wedlock and that my mother died giving birth to me, but do you really think that is something I want the world to know? That I'm a bastard?'

Sophie flinched at the use of the word and he pressed on. 'It is a terrible thing to admit that you don't know who your father is. I was brought up by my mother's sister and her husband, but they would never speak of my mother. They were ashamed of her and so was I. As to my father, the man the world knew as my father, he was my Aunt Henrietta's husband, Albert Bryan.' He glowered at Sophie and said, 'I am *not* a Penvarrow!' And the expression on his face was one she suddenly recognized. She had seen it before, on the face of her grandfather, Thomas

Penvarrow, and she knew he lied. Nan Slater's words echoed in her head. *Some of the Penvarrows is kind, others, not so.*

'So,' Nicholas continued, 'now you know the worst about me. I'm the bastard son of an unmarried mother and an unknown father. I've had to make my way in the world with nothing more than the few pounds my foster-father left me. But *you* know me. I am a doctor, who cures illness and fights sickness. Does it matter who my actual parents were? I was brought up in a God-fearing household and my Aunt Hetty and Uncle Albert were my real parents. Do you love me any the less because my parents were not married?'

As he asked the question, Sophie was aware there had been a shift in her emotions – not because he was an illegitimate child, that was hardly his fault, but because he was still lying to her.

'No,' she said honestly.

'Thank goodness for that.' Nicholas's relief was obvious. 'My dearest girl, you have to understand that Nan is a confused old woman. Such people become childish as they get older and their memories get tangled up. Please don't try and disentangle the truth, Sophie. It's a waste of time.'

Sophie thought of the letters she had in the drawer in her bedchamber. They were the truth and she knew it. Nan hadn't lied to her. It was Nicholas who was tangling partial truths with lies, trying to convince her he was not a Penvarrow. But why? It didn't matter that they were first cousins; that was no bar to their marriage. Why could he not admit that Jocelyn was his father? He must know that he was.

Suddenly Sophie wanted him to go. She needed to be alone, to think things through and to decide what she should do. She stood up and walked to the window. Nicholas followed her and put his arms round her, pulling her close. She stiffened and he felt it.

Releasing her, he murmured, 'Don't turn from me, Sophie. You're mine. I love you and you're mine. Don't you believe that, Sophie?'

She looked up at him, her eyes full of tears. 'I don't know

what to believe any more!' And with that, she turned aside and left him in the drawing room.

Nicholas stared after her for a moment before he walked swiftly out of the house and climbing into the gig, set off at a smart trot to Tremose.

Chapter 35

While Sophie and Nicholas were having their luncheon at the Duke's Hotel, Charles rode into Truro to see Mr Staunton. Sophie had told him that she wanted Nicholas to be present when they were going through the details of the Trust and he was not at all happy about it. Without refusing, he had been noncommittal when she had suggested it, but he was going to see Mr Staunton in the hope there might be some legal reason to refuse her request.

When he arrived at the solicitor's office, he was shown straight in and was surprised to find another man sitting at his ease across the desk from Mr Staunton.

As Staunton's secretary held the door for him, the lawyer rose to his feet, his hand outstretched in welcome. 'Mr Leroy,' he said, 'how fortuitous that you have called. Mr Jeremiah Hawke is here with some news.'

Jeremiah Hawke stood up and turned to meet Charles. He was a big man, tall and broad, his waistcoat straining across the barrel of his chest. His large head was circled with a fringe of shaggy black hair, and deep-set eyes peered out from under almost continuous eyebrows, above an eagle's beak and a jutting chin.

Hawke extended a huge hand to grip Charles's in a painful handshake. 'Howdy do, Mr Leroy?' he rumbled.

Charles returned the greeting, thinking as he did so that Jeremiah Hawke was not a man he'd want to cross, or meet in a dark alley.

Staunton pulled up another chair for Charles and said, 'Mr Hawke has been working on our behalf and has just this minute come into the office to make his report.'

Charles sat down and having turned down the offer of refreshment, came straight to the point and asked, 'What have you discovered, Mr Hawke?'

'Not a great deal, as yet, sir,' Jeremiah Hawke's voice was sonorous and slow, 'but I'm on the trail, on the trail.'

'So where did you start?' asked Staunton. 'And where does your trail lead?'

'First off I went to visit the daughter of Dr Marshall. Miss Daisy Marshall. She weren't hard to find, because so many people knowed her father over the years. Miss Sandra Osell, rector's daughter in Port Felec? She told me Miss Daisy had gone to live with her sister Perranporth way.'

'And what could she tell you?' Charles was itching to hurry the man's report, but Mr Staunton was used to dealing with him and knew that the quickest way to discover what Hawke had learned was to let him speak in his own ponderous way.

'That's what I'm telling you,' Hawke said. 'Your Dr Bryan come to visit her about nine months ago, not long after her father died. She was still living in her father's house at Port Felec then. He come along and said he was new-qualified and wanted to set up in practice. Said he wanted to buy her father's house and dispensary. She asked him how he'd heard about her father's practice and he said he'd been born in Truro, and that someone in the town had told him Dr Marshall had passed on and there was now no doctor in Port Felec. Your man told her that he wanted to come back to Cornwall and work in a country parish and that Port Felec would just suit him.' Hawke paused and as Charles drew breath to ask him a question, Staunton gave a slight shake of his head, and Charles sat back and waited for the investigator to continue.

'He said he had money and could pay her cash. She being anxious about money at the time, accepted his offer. Enough it was, she said, to let her move to her married sister's up

Perranporth way with something over to live on. I asked her if he showed her anything to say he was a doctor and she said he had some sort of certificate. Didn't have her spectacles on, she said, but she was sure the large print on the top said St Thomas's Hospital. He was such a charming young man, she said, and she was pleased that her dear father's place was going to be filled so soon with a new young doctor from London. All the new ways, she said, all the new doctoring.'

'So,' Charles was losing patience, 'where does that take us?'

'It took me, sir, to St Thomas's Hospital in London. I got a contact there's helped me before. For a small fee he looked up the records and found that your Mr Bryan had enrolled to learn doctoring, but had disappeared after about nine months. My friend said lots of their students don't finish learning and this Nicholas Bryan was one.'

'You mean he's not even a qualified doctor?' Charles was aghast.

'Looks that way, sir.'

'Anything else that can help us, Mr Hawke?' asked Staunton.

'He told her he was born in Truro, so that's another trail I can follow.'

'And where will *that* take you?' asked Charles.

'Don't rightly know yet, sir,' replied Hawke. 'Can but wait and see.'

'I don't know how much time we have to wait and see,' said Charles in frustration, and he told them of Sophie's request that Nicholas should attend their meeting the following day.

'Not what I'd choose,' Staunton said. 'But if she invites him to be there, we can't really say no. He is her affianced husband and as such it would be reasonable for him to be there. I expect he will want to be assured that her interests are being properly served.'

'I'm sure he does,' growled Charles.

Mr Staunton gave Charles a sympathetic smile. 'You think he's after her money, and on balance I do too, so we shall do our best to ensure he don't get it. Within reason, we can deny him access to her inheritance.' Turning to Jeremiah Hawke, he went on, 'Back to London for you then, Mr Hawke, and telegraph me any more information you can discover.'

When the investigator had left the room, Charles said, 'So what do we do now? Do we face him with the fact that he's not even a doctor? Surely that must be enough to make Sophie think again.'

'We could, but I'm sure there is more to discover and I think we should keep our powder dry until we hear from Hawke again.'

'But it's not just Sophie's concerns here,' Charles pointed out. 'He's practising as a doctor with almost no training. Surely he can be prosecuted for that. He attended my grandfather with no training at all. His doctoring may even have precipitated his death.'

'Which is why we need to tread carefully,' replied Staunton. 'We need concrete evidence of wrong-doing. We only have the word of Miss Daisy Marshall that the certificate she saw was from St Thomas's. Hawke told us that she didn't have her spectacles, and if that is the case she could have been mistaken about which hospital it was.'

'Or whether it was a certificate at all!' snapped Charles.

'Indeed,' answered Staunton. 'But there may be one from a different hospital, so I still think that for the moment we should wait.' He saw the look on Charles's face and said, 'If we're going to catch him, we have to be certain of our facts. It's no good accusing him of something for which we have no proof. We need proof. If he knows he's being investigated he may take fright and disappear.'

'That's exactly what I want him to do!' cried Charles. 'I *want* him to disappear, anywhere, away from Sophie.'

'I know,' Staunton said, 'but it's better to keep him under our eye for now. If he disappears he could well set up the same trick somewhere else. He has to be stopped. I know it's frustrating, but we do have time. They aren't getting married until the end of March. Hawke will cable from London in the next few days with more information and we can decide then what to do next.'

'Suppose he finds nothing else?'

'He'll find something,' Staunton promised. 'I told you, I've used him before. He has useful contacts everywhere and he's never failed me yet.'

Charles returned to Trescadinnick even more worried than when he'd left. Sophie was home again, but she was upstairs in her room and he didn't see her until they met at the dinner table. She looked pale and seemed very subdued. Was that something to do with Nicholas Bryan? Charles came very close to telling her what Jeremiah Hawke had discovered, but he held back, the words of Mr Staunton echoing in his head. 'We need proof.'

Instead he asked, 'Did you enjoy your luncheon, Sophie?'

'Yes, it was very pleasant.'

But Charles didn't believe her. He had never seen her so cast down. Something must have happened. After dinner he stood aside to let her follow Louisa into the hall and when his mother had disappeared upstairs, he touched Sophie on the arm to stay her and asked, 'Sophie? Is something wrong? Is there anything I can do?'

Sophie fixed a smile to her lips and shook her head. 'No, Charles. There's nothing wrong, really. But if you'll excuse me, I think I'll have an early night.'

'I'll wish you goodnight then,' Charles said and watched as she picked up her candle and started upstairs. At the turn she looked back, and he thought he caught the glint of tears in her eyes as she asked, 'What time will Mr Staunton be coming tomorrow?'

'He will be here at two. I thought we might meet in the library. I've asked Mrs Paxton to make sure the fire is lit first thing so that room is really warm. I should have asked you first. I'm sorry.'

Sophie gave him a tremulous smile. 'You don't have to ask, Charles. This is still your home, you know.' And with that she turned away and continued up the stairs.

It was not long before Hannah came knocking on her door to see if she was all right. 'You're looking right peaky, Miss Sophie,' Hannah said. 'I'm worried about you.'

'You needn't be,' Sophie replied. 'I just need an early night.'

'When you was little and something was wrong,' Hannah said, her back to Sophie as she poked the fire into a blaze, 'you used to come to me and tell me.' She replaced the poker and turning round, continued, 'I've knowed you all your life, Miss Sophie, and I can tell when you're upset or worried. Can't you tell Hannah what it is that's troubling you now? You know it won't go beyond these four walls.'

Sophie was on the verge of tears and Hannah's kindness brought them even closer, but Sophie fought them back and said, 'I need to go home, Hannah. I can't stay here. I need to go back home for a while, give myself time to get used to... well, everything.'

Hannah was no nearer knowing what was wrong, but she said at once, 'Then we'll go, Miss Sophie. The change will do you good.'

'Really? Do you think we really can? Just go home, to London?'

'You tell them tomorrow that we're going and I'll get everything packed up. We can be on the train on Saturday.'

Relief flooded through Sophie and at last she gave way and allowed her tears to fall. Hannah put her arms round her as she had when she was a child. 'There, there,' she soothed, 'don't take on so. It's been a difficult time, but we'll be home again before you know it.'

Sophie didn't sleep well and in the morning she looked, if anything, paler than the day before.

'I shall be going back to London for a few days,' she announced at breakfast. 'I know we have our meeting with Mr Staunton this afternoon, Charles, but Hannah and I plan to leave on Saturday.'

'That's all very sudden,' remarked Louisa, looking up from her plate. 'What's happened?'

'Nothing, Aunt,' Sophie replied. 'But if I am to come here to live, there are things I have to deal with in London.'

'It's up to you, of course,' sniffed Louisa, and turned her attention back to her bacon.

'I quite understand,' Charles said with a smile. 'But I'm glad we're still meeting with Mr Staunton this afternoon.'

Nicholas arrived at the house ten minutes before Mr Staunton. Sophie was waiting for him in the hall. He greeted her cheerfully, as if the conversation they'd had the previous afternoon had never happened, and asked, as he shrugged himself out of his coat and handed it to Edith, 'Is the lawyer here yet?'

'No, not yet,' Sophie said, and she led him into the drawing room. She closed the door behind them and turned to face him. He moved forward as if to kiss her, but she put up a restraining hand. 'I've changed my mind, Nicholas. I have decided that at first I shall see my trustees on my own—' she began, but was interrupted by Nicholas.

'Now, Sophie,' he said sharply. 'We agreed. It's important that I'm there too.'

'And you will be.' Sophie spoke firmly. 'But not until I've spoken to them first.'

'And what will you say that I'm not allowed to hear?'

'I shan't say anything,' replied Sophie. 'I shall listen to what they have to say to me.'

'So, why am I to be excluded?'

'Because,' Sophie said, 'I want to hear them without interruption. I want—'

'What do you mean, without interruption?'

'Exactly what I say. Listen to yourself, Nicholas. If you don't happen to agree with what's being said, you interrupt and shout it down. You don't listen. If you want to wait in here and come to join us in the library when we're discussing what we plan to do, that's fine, but I will hear them alone first.'

'Sophie, this is quite ridiculous,' snapped Nicholas. 'You need to have another pair of ears listening to what they say. If I've heard everything myself, I shall be able to explain it to you afterwards, so there are no misunderstandings. You won't know what questions to ask.' Seeing her rigid expression, he softened his tone. 'My dearest girl, I only have your best interests at heart. I just want to be sure—'

It was Sophie's turn to interrupt. 'To be sure that I'm not going to tell them of the discussion we had yesterday afternoon. About your being a Penvarrow? Well, I'm not, but you'll just have to trust me for that.'

Just then the front doorbell rang and glancing out of the window, Sophie said, 'That'll be Mr Staunton.' Without further comment she walked out into the hall to greet him. Nicholas followed, pale with rage at her decision. Charles was emerging from the study and when Staunton was divested of his coat he led him towards the library door.

Nicholas stepped forward and said, 'I'm afraid I shall not be able to join you this afternoon after all. As I've just been explaining to Sophie, I have an extremely sick patient to visit beyond Felec Head, and her son has sent for me, so if you'll excuse me...?' He retrieved his coat from Edith and with a curt nod went out of the front door.

If Sophie wasn't going to allow him to hear all that the trustees said, then he wouldn't stay at all. He was angry, as angry as he had been the night before.

When he had got home the previous evening, he had poured himself a large brandy and considered what Sophie had faced him with. All his instincts had been to deny everything, to dismiss Nan as being senile and refuse to listen to any evidence that Sophie had. He had been to see Nan and there would be no further interference from that quarter, but he had been so stunned by Sophie's assertions that he hadn't considered his answers carefully enough. He had begun his denial in such vehement terms he couldn't go back on it. What he should have done was to acknowledge that he was indeed Jocelyn's son. He should have said that he'd only recently learned of his connection with the Penvarrows.

'You see, Sophie...' he spoke aloud as he paced his parlour, rehearsing the conversation he should have had with her. 'I understood that they might not be pleased to recognize me as Jocelyn's son, so I decided the best thing was to become acquainted with them slowly, before I claimed any kinship. I was just getting to know your grandfather, my grandfather, when you first came to stay at Trescadinnick. When I saw you, Sophie, it was love at first sight. I've never believed in that before, but it does happen, and the day you stepped down from the trap, it happened to me.'

Yes, Nicholas thought, he'd been stupid. *That* was how he should have handled her revelations. He should have admitted them and brought her in on his side. A version of the truth would have served him better than denial. Calming down a little he'd refilled his brandy glass and planned his next move. After the meeting with her trustees, he would speak to Sophie privately. He would apologize for lying to her, saying he'd been afraid of her reaction. He'd tell her he was trusting her now with his deepest secret, their secret. No one else need ever know that Jocelyn had been his father.

That had been his plan and he was sure it would have worked. Sophie doted on him, and he could have talked her round, but now, suddenly, she had shut him out, publicly shut him out and he'd had no chance to speak to her. He was furious, but he had walked away on his own terms. He could play the waiting game. It had worked well before. He would stay away from Sophie for a few days and then go back and make his admission. She had told him she wasn't going to mention the question of his parentage to her trustees and he believed her; nor had she denied his excuse for leaving, allowing him to make a dignified exit. So, he decided, as he climbed up into his gig and set off down the lane to his imaginary patient, he was still angry, but all was not lost.

Chapter 36

Sophie and Hannah took the train back to London on Saturday morning and arrived in Hammersmith late in the evening. As the hansom carried them through the familiar streets where gaslights threw pools of hazy light, and lighted windows poured their brightness into the road, or lit bright curtains with indoor warmth, Sophie knew a deep feeling of homecoming. The house, so familiar, standing in darkness, a darker shape against the blackness of the night sky, was cold when they went inside. But it wasn't long before the lamps were lit and Hannah had the kitchen range alight and a fire burning in the parlour. Mrs Paxton had packed them a basket of food for the journey, including some of her chicken broth, thick with vegetables and wonderfully warming, and they were soon sitting down to steaming plates of the broth and some home-made bread and cheese.

Sophie stretched out her toes to the fire. 'Isn't it lovely to be back, Hannah?' she said. 'How I miss the cosiness of our little home in that great house.'

Hannah had to agree. She had learned to fit in at Trescadinnick, but she was certainly more at home in the comfort of the Hammersmith house... or better still the large warm kitchen at the home farm.

She had slipped out on Friday evening and hurried down to the farm to tell Will they were going back to London. 'I don't know what the problem is,' she told him, 'but Miss Sophie's real upset about something. Won't tell me what it is, but maybe she will when we're back in her own place.'

'Trescadinnick's her place now,' said Will.

'Well, it don't feel like it to her,' Hannah replied.

'Reckon she'll come back?'

Hannah shrugged. 'I suppose so. She's getting married in a couple of months. She'll be back before then, won't she? Getting ready.'

'Suppose she will. That's good,' Will reached for her hand, 'cos you'll be coming with her.'

'Oh, Will.' Hannah sighed. 'I wish I didn't have to go, but she needs me.'

''Course she does, love. 'Course you must go.' He put his arms round her. 'But when you come back, I'll be waiting for you. I need you, too.'

'I've been wondering if she's been having second thoughts,' said Hannah as she nestled against his comforting warmth.

'Second thoughts?'

'About getting married. Maybe she's been rushed into it and wishes she hadn't.'

'Well, she can change her mind, can't she?' said Will.

'She can, I suppose, but it's not that easy. She knows people think that she's made a mistake, but her pride may not let her admit it.'

They had parted with a kiss but as Hannah began to settle back into the Hammersmith house the next day, she knew for sure that it was no longer her home.

Sophie hadn't seen Nicholas again before she left. He probably didn't even know she'd gone. When he'd walked out of the house on Friday afternoon she went into the library to sit with Charles and Mr Staunton, and listened to the various things they proposed. The first was an income for her, paid every quarter.

Sophie's eyes widened at the suggested amount. She'd never had that much money before and said so.

'Well, that's for your own personal use,' Charles explained. 'Then there will be monthly housekeeping, which is needed for such household expenses as the servants' wages, kitchen expenses, food, fuel and such. Anything major, maintenance work that needs to be done and suchlike, well, you simply ask us and we'll deal with the matter.'

Charles also described how the estate was being changed. 'We can't live on income from the mines any more, so in recent years we've bought some seine nets and boats, to take advantage of the autumn pilchard shoals, and we employ men to man these when the pilchard shoals come in. It's a seasonal harvest, but the shoals are so huge that there're plenty for everyone and they produce a fair profit.

'We still own several farms, but I'm inclined to sell them to their tenants and use the capital for other investment. Your grandfather was against that, so it shouldn't be something we rush into. Our best investment was made three years ago, when I persuaded him to buy a part share of a small coastal ship *The Minerva*, which plies between Liverpool, Plymouth and London. She carries a general cargo and is certainly paying her way.'

The Minerva, thought Sophie. Surely that was the ship Nan Slater's son was aboard. The thought of Nan turned her mind to what Nan had told her about Nicholas, and for a minute or two Sophie stopped listening to what Charles was actually saying, as she wondered whether she should, after all, tell them what Nan had said. No, she resolved, yet again. She hadn't believed his version of events. She knew he was lying, but she hadn't yet decided what she was going to do about that. She gave her attention back to Charles and found he was still explaining where the Trescadinnick income came from.

'She brings in a steady income,' Charles was saying, 'and I would like to invest in another ship. Steam is the way forward and another share in such a ship could bring us great profit.'

'At what risk?' Sophie's question was a shrewd one and Charles smiled his appreciation.

'Good question,' he replied. 'Of course, there're always risks when you're challenging the sea, but steam ships are better able to survive bad weather, being less reliant on the wind.'

Sophie listened as the two men discussed this and other possibilities, and Charles was charged with working costs and returns so that they could make an informed decision at some time in the future. Mr Staunton had left it to Charles to explain his ideas, but he agreed that such an investment was worth looking into now that there was so little return from the land and the pilchard fishing, though lucrative, was very seasonal.

Nicholas was mentioned only once, when Sophie asked about living in Trescadinnick.

'I don't want to turn you and your family out, Charles,' she said, 'but I know Nicholas wants to live here at Trescadinnick when we are married. I think it would be difficult for us all to live together—'

'It would be impossible,' Charles said quickly. 'I have already made enquiries about a number of properties in the area and hope that we shall have settled upon somewhere suitable before very long.'

Sophie gave him a grateful smile, a smile that made his heart contract, and he said, 'You shall have the house to yourselves, I promise you.'

'Thank you,' Sophie said. It would be a relief to tell Nicholas that much at least. 'But you won't be far away, will you? I mean, I want to be able to see you and AliceAnne and my aunt, all of you, very often.'

When Mr Staunton left, Sophie went upstairs to see AliceAnne. The little girl was in the schoolroom. Sophie wanted to spend the last evening with her and together they played Snap and Beggar-My-Neighbour until Hannah came upstairs to put her to bed.

'Aunt Sophie says you're going away again tomorrow,' Alice-Anne said. 'I thought we were going to play at the home farm. Alison is coming, and Tommy. Now I can't go! It's not fair.'

'Tell you what,' Sophie said, 'I'll ask your papa if Lizzie may come and fetch you after lunch and bring you home again before it gets dark. She's a sensible girl.'

At that moment Charles came into the room and AliceAnne rushed to him, crying, 'Aunt Sophie and Hannah are going away tomorrow, so Hannah can't take me to Mrs Shaw's so I can play with Alison and Tommy, but Aunt Sophie says can Lizzie fetch me because she lives there too, Papa, and so she knows the way and would look after me and bring me home again before it gets dark. So can I go with Lizzie to the home farm?'

Sophie watched Charles's face. It seemed incredible that he was the same man who had hardly a word to say to his small daughter just three months ago.

'We'll see,' began Charles, but AliceAnne interrupted him, something she would never have dared do before.

'Oh, Papa, that means no!'

'No, it doesn't,' answered her father. 'It means we'll see.'

Later, at the dinner table, he asked Sophie what she really thought of the idea.

'I think AliceAnne will be very disappointed if she doesn't go,' Sophie said. 'And Lizzie could quite safely take her there and back. She's used to her sister's children and deals with them very well.'

'I'm not sure about Lizzie. Perhaps I should take her there myself.'

'Don't be ridiculous, Charles,' interposed Louisa. 'I can't imagine any other father taking his daughter to somewhere like that. If Hannah isn't here to take her,' and as she said this Louisa glowered at Sophie, 'then the child can't go! No reason for *you* to act the nursemaid.'

'I think she'll be disappointed,' Sophie murmured.

'I expect she will,' agreed Louisa, 'but she'll have to learn to cope with far greater disappointments in life than not visiting a farm. Goodness knows what manners she's picking up there!'

No more was said at the table, but as they moved into the drawing room Charles said, 'Don't worry about AliceAnne. I'll take her. I need a word with Will Shaw anyway. I'll tell her in the morning when you've gone, and with luck it will cheer her up.' He smiled at her and went on, 'We'll all miss you while you're away, but I'm sure it won't be for long.' He looked over at the piano and on impulse asked, 'Will you play for us tonight, cousin?'

'Of course,' Sophie replied, though she had hardly touched the piano since her grandfather had died. She crossed the room and pulled out the piano stool. A Chopin nocturne was on the music stand and she ran her hands over the keys. Charles watched her, seeing the graceful movement of her hands and arms, and the lamplight on her hair, and cursed himself for a fool.

When Sophie woke up on Sunday morning it was to the familiar sounds of a London street, wheels on cobbles, footsteps on the pavement and an occasional voice calling; so different from the quiet of the Trescadinnick countryside. Church bells were ringing in the distance, but as she lay in the warmth of her bed she decided she was not going to church this morning. Hannah brought her a cup of tea and said she was going to the market, leaving Sophie sitting up in bed, drinking her tea. Though she was back in Hammersmith, Sophie's thoughts were still in Cornwall. Would Nicholas be standing, waiting for her outside the church in Port Felec? If so, he was probably angry that she hadn't appeared. She knew she should have sent him a message to say she was leaving, but all she'd been able to think of was getting away to a place of refuge, a place where she could think. She thought of Charles and hoped that he had kept his promise and taken AliceAnne to the home farm yesterday afternoon. She smiled as she thought of how close he and AliceAnne had become. At least something good had come from Mama's deathbed letter. Dear Charles, so strong and steady; she had come to love her cousin dearly and still wished with all her heart that Thomas had not made her his heir. Then she and Nicholas could have married without Nicholas being regarded as a fortune-hunter. She thought of her aunt, Louisa, so bitter against her for stealing Charles's rightful inheritance, and knew that would never change. She thought of Aunt Matty in her house at Treslyn, well away from all the family unpleasantness. She had welcomed Sophie into the family, and had offered her a place to stay if she ever needed one. Perhaps she should have gone there instead of coming home. Perhaps she could have confided in Aunt Matty, told her what she had learned about Jocelyn, Cassie and the baby. But she knew Matty would have been angry at her intrusion into Joss's room, and might have blamed her for reopening a matter that had been laid to rest over twenty-five years ago.

When Hannah returned to the house she found the fire lit in the parlour and the kettle singing on the kitchen range. Sophie was sitting at her mother's bureau, writing a letter. It was clear that she'd come to some sort of decision for she looked relaxed and some colour was creeping back into her cheeks. The smile on her face and the happiness in her eyes belonged to the old Sophie.

Sophie posted a letter to Nicholas, and waited over the next few days for a reply. In the meantime she and Hannah began packing up the house. If she were going to live at Trescadinnick permanently there were things from home that would have to be sent down to Cornwall. In her letter she had told Nicholas she was buying mourning clothes and so decided to make that the truth. There had been no reply from Nicholas by Thursday and so she thought she would go out. Flush with her new allowance from the Trust, she set off to Madame Egloff's salon. Hannah was far less worried about her going about town alone than she had been about her riding alone in the country, and watched from the window as she set off down the street. She was pleased that Sophie was much more her old self. Whatever it was that had so upset her down in Cornwall seemed to have resolved itself. Perhaps, Hannah thought, it was simply that she had found the big old house oppressive. If that were the case, she wondered, how would Sophie manage living there permanently? Only time would tell, she supposed, but she was still worried about Sophie's proposed marriage with Nicholas Bryan.

It was an hour later that there came a knock at the front door. Hannah went to answer and found herself facing a thin, scruffy individual, wearing a coat several sizes too large for him and oversized black boots.

'Well?' she said discouragingly.

'Come to see the lady of the 'ouse,' replied the man.

'She's not at home,' said Hannah and began to close the door.

The man planted one of his huge boots into the doorway and said, 'She'll want to talk to me.'

'Take your foot out of the way.' Hannah fixed him with a gimlet eye. 'She's not here and she *won't* want to talk to you.'

'Know Nicholas Bryan, does she?'

'What?'

'Know Nicholas Bryan?' The man gave her a toothy grin. 'Fought you'd know that name.'

'I don't know what you're talking about.' Hannah tried to sound firm, but her face had already registered her shock at the mention of Nicholas Bryan's name.

'She needs to know about 'im,' said the man. 'I got somefink to show 'er.'

'What have you got?' demanded Hannah. 'Show me.'

'You gonna let me in?'

Hannah looked up and down the street. There was no one else in sight. The man seemed to be on his own.

'I ain't come stealing or nuffink,' he said as he read her mind. 'I just got somefink your lady did ought to see, but I ain't going to show you standin' on the doorstep.'

Reluctantly Hannah stood aside. She was decidedly nervous about letting the disreputable man inside, but if he had anything to do with Nicholas she wanted to be the one he told, not Sophie. He followed her indoors and she took him straight to the kitchen.

'Well,' she said, standing, hands on hips, 'who are you and what do you want?'

'Luke,' he replied. 'I come from my sister, Dolly. Dolly Bryan.'

'Dolly Bryan?' echoed Hannah. 'Who's she when she's at home?'

'My sister, what's married to Nicholas Bryan.'

'Married to...'

'To Nicholas Bryan.' He pulled a paper from his pocket and thrust it at Hannah. When she reached to take it, he pulled back. 'Oh no you don't,' he snapped. 'You can look at it, but I keep hold of it.' He held it up for Hannah to read.

She stared at the names written there: *Nicholas Bryan, Bachelor* and *Dolly Mangot, Spinster*; the date, *6th January 1883*; place, *St John's Church Waterloo*.

'So,' she said, 'what has this got to do with Miss Ross?'

'Miss Ross, is it? We heard Nicholas wants to marry her.' Luke folded the certificate and put it back into his pocket.

'Really? Who'd'you hear that from then?'

'From the horse's mouth.'

'Well,' Hannah said, 'I don't know which horse you was talking to, but it ain't got nothing to do with Miss Ross. Far as I know, she ain't marrying anybody. You want to leave that certificate with me, just in case I'm wrong?'

Luke edged towards the door. 'No,' he said, 'but I'll be back. I come round before, but you was all away. Want to talk to the organ-grinder, not the monkey.' He paused when he reached the front door. 'He's offered good money for this certifticate, he has. Me and Dolly thought it might be worth a bit more to your lady, seeing as *she's* worth a bit.'

Hannah reached past him, opened the door and gave him a push. 'Out!' she shouted. 'Out, before I call the police and you gets taken up for blackmail.'

'All right,' Luke said with a shrug, 'but you talk to your lady. If you change yer mind send a message down the Drummer Boy in Southwark.'

As soon as she'd closed the door, Hannah went to the bureau and wrote down all she could remember from the certificate; names, date, place: St John's Church. She put the paper under her pillow and then, putting on her hat and coat, set off to the telegraph office.

Chapter 37

The telegram reached Charles that same evening. Thinking it must be from Jeremiah Hawke, he told the boy to wait in case there was a reply, and he took it into his study to open. Pulling it from the envelope, he stared in amazement at the message it brought: *Sir, come at once STOP Sophie needs you STOP Hannah.*

What could have happened that Hannah felt the need to summon him by telegram? He quickly wrote a reply: *On my way STOP Arrive Paddington Friday STOP Leroy.*

'A telegram from Hannah!' Louisa had been incredulous. 'What is Sophie's maid doing sending you telegrams?'

'She's told me to come at once,' replied Charles.

'She's *told* you to come?' Louisa looked outraged. 'And you're jumping to her bidding?'

'She says Sophie needs me,' Charles said simply. 'And if she needs me, I shall go.'

'Sophie's chosen her own path,' snapped his mother. 'She's not your responsibility. Has Hannah sent Dr Bryan a telegram as well?'

That's an interesting question, thought Charles. If not, why not? And why has Hannah telegraphed me?

'I've no idea, Mama,' was all he said. 'But I do still have some responsibility for Sophie's welfare, so I shall go.'

Before he left in the morning a second telegram arrived: *Meet Paddington STOP No reply please.*

He was at Truro Station for the first train to London, and

when he arrived at Paddington he found Hannah waiting on the platform.

'Hannah, what is all this about?' he cried. 'What's happened to Sophie?'

'Nothing yet, sir,' she replied, 'but there is news that I needed to tell you face to face,' adding, 'before you see Miss Sophie and without her knowing.'

Intrigued, Charles led her to the station restaurant and sat her down with a cup of tea and a piece of fruit cake. 'Now then,' he said, 'you'd better tell me what all this is about.'

So Hannah told him about the visit from Luke Mangot with the certificate recording the marriage of one Nicholas Bryan with Dolly Mangot.

'I sent him packing, but he said he'd be back to talk to Miss Sophie herself. He's asking for money.'

'But you saw the certificate?'

'Yes, sir, and I've written down all I can remember from it.' Hannah pulled out her piece of paper and handed it to Charles. 'Of course,' she said as he looked at it, 'we can't be sure it's the same Nicholas Bryan.'

'Oh, I think we can, Hannah,' Charles said. 'Tell me again exactly what this Luke Mangot said.'

'He said that Nicholas had told them he would pay this Dolly for her marriage certificate, and then they would no longer be married.'

'And she believed him, do you think?'

Hannah shrugged. 'I don't know, sir. Maybe all she wanted was the money.'

'And her brother came to show you the certificate, wanting to sell it to you for more than Nicholas was paying.'

'Well, not to me, sir. He wanted to see Miss Sophie. Only I didn't want him to be the one to tell her that Dr Bryan's already married... if it's true, that is.'

'You were quite right to send for me,' Charles said. 'Have you any idea where I can find this Luke Mangot fellow?'

Hannah shook her head miserably. 'No, sir, not unless, well, he did say something about sending a message to a public house in Southwark, the Drummer Boy, if we changed our minds.'

'When did he come?'

'Thursday morning, sir.'

'And he hasn't been back since?'

'No, sir. Though he threatened to. I've stayed home all the time till I come to meet you.'

'Where does Sophie think you are now?'

'I'm on my afternoon off, sir.'

'Good. Well, the first thing we have to do is find a telegraph office, and then I'll go straight to the house in Hammersmith. And if this Luke Mangot shows his face again I'll deal with him. You come home in an hour or so and you'll be surprised to see me at the house.'

They parted company and Charles immediately sent a telegram to Mr Staunton, alerting him to developments and telling him to set Jeremiah Hawke on the new trail: Dolly Mangot, St John's Church, Waterloo, and the Drummer Boy, Southwark. With that all done he took a hansom to Hammersmith, deciding to tell Sophie that he'd come to town for a business meeting with Herbert Hawthorne, the other part-owner of *The Minerva*.

The cab dropped him outside the house and Sophie saw him from the window. She ran to the front door and threw it open, greeting him with a wide and welcoming smile.

'Charles!' she exclaimed. 'What are you doing in London? How lovely. Come in, come in, and I'll put the kettle on. Hannah's out for her free afternoon, but she'll be back soon. You will stay for supper, won't you, or do you have somewhere else to go?'

'Nowhere this evening,' Charles said, taking off his hat and coat. 'Tomorrow I have to meet with Mr Hawthorne, the other owner of *The Minerva*, to discuss our plan for buying another ship. I'm hoping he may want to invest with us again.'

When Sophie had made tea, they sat together beside the parlour fire in companionable conversation.

'Did you take AliceAnne to the farm last Saturday?' Sophie asked.

'Yes,' replied Charles. 'I said I would, didn't I?'

'You did.' Sophie smiled. 'And you're a man of your word. I'm sure she was pleased.'

'She certainly seemed so,' answered Charles, remembering AliceAnne's delighted smile when he told her she could go, and that he would take her.

'The other thing I should tell you, cousin, is that I have found a suitable house for us in Kenwyn, just outside Truro. My mother, AliceAnne and I will be moving there in the next month. It's much smaller than Trescadinnick, of course, but that makes it a much easier place to run. Mama says we can easily manage with just the Paxtons to look after things.'

'The Paxtons!' Sophie hadn't thought about what servants she would need at Trescadinnick; she had just assumed that they would all stay on.

'When Mrs Paxton heard we were moving out, she asked if she and Paxton could move with us. She said they were getting too old to learn new ways, and of course my mother was delighted.' He smiled across at Sophie's stricken face. 'I'm sure you'd rather choose your own servants, Sophie, though I expect Edith and Ned will want to stay. Oh—' He paused and Sophie said, 'What? Something about Ned?'

'No,' said Charles. 'Well, yes and no. Ned brought some news home yesterday. Old Nan Slater over at Tremose has been found dead in her home.' He saw the colour drain from Sophie's face and said, 'I'm sorry, Sophie. I'd forgotten you'd visited her just recently.'

'How did she die?' whispered Sophie.

'They found her out by the woodshed. She must have been fetching firewood and fallen. I heard that she'd died of cold.'

'When?'

'No one's quite sure,' replied Charles. 'They found her on Tuesday. She'll be taken to the church today.'

'Her son is away at sea,' Sophie said. 'He won't even be at her graveside.'

'The people of Tremose will be there, Sophie. She won't go unattended to her grave.'

The cheerful atmosphere in the little parlour vanished and Sophie shivered. 'Poor Nan,' she said, 'dying alone in the cold.' Moments later the door opened and Hannah arrived home.

Nicholas had decided not to meet Sophie outside the church the previous Sunday. Let her find that he was not waiting, dancing attendance on her. And if people gossiped, well, that was her fault.

Thus it was that he heard nothing of her absence until her letter arrived from London. When he realized where she was he was irritated. She should have told him she was going. Still, he thought, at least she seems to be preparing for the wedding. Sorting out the house and buying mourning clothes, she'd said, so the trustees must have given her some money when they met the previous Friday. He could have done with some of that. He still wanted to ensure that there was no tangible evidence of his marriage to Dolly five years ago.

Sophie had said she wasn't sure when she'd be home, but she would write again soon with all her plans. She suggested that he went to see the rector about having the banns read. That, however, did not help him with his money problems. He was glad Sophie had made no further mention of his father and his Penvarrow blood. He could only hope she'd decided to believe him. Once they were married he would find the letters she'd mentioned and burn them; then there'd be nothing to prove he was anything to do with the Penvarrows.

That afternoon he sat down and wrote back to Sophie, telling her he missed her and couldn't wait until they were man and wife. When he'd sealed the letter he found himself imagining their wedding night, the night he would take possession of her and do with her as he chose. Hot with excitement at the very thought, he needed a woman now, and so he took horse and rode into Truro. He knew just the place to go.

*

With Hannah acting as chaperone, Charles was persuaded to stay at the house in Hammersmith. Hannah prepared Mary's room for him, and they spent a quiet evening before the parlour fire.

The postman arrived soon after breakfast next morning and Charles was pleased to see he had a letter from Mr Staunton. He took it upstairs to his room to read it in private.

It was a long message from Mr Staunton, telling him that Jeremiah Hawke was on his way back to London.

When we received your telegram Hawke took the afternoon train to London. He plans to visit St John's Church Waterloo to look at the marriage records for January 1883, and then to go and find Luke Mangot at the Drummer Boy in Southwark. He suggests you should meet him there at midday on Saturday.

Hawke had moved fast and Charles was determined to keep the appointment in Southwark; far better to meet Luke Mangot away from the Hammersmith house. Until they knew exactly what he was after, Charles didn't want him anywhere near Sophie.

'It's as I thought,' he told her when he returned downstairs. 'I have to meet *Minerva*'s other owner at midday.'

'Can I come too?' asked Sophie. 'I'm interested in our ship.'

Charles shook his head apologetically. 'Not this time, Sophie,' he said. 'This is very much an exploratory meeting. Mr Hawthorne is an elderly man and would be uncomfortable doing business with a woman. I have to talk to him alone, but I promise you I'll tell you everything that was said, when I get back.'

Sophie looked disappointed, but she was sensible enough to know that what Charles said was right, and she didn't want to put the other man against the deal because there was a woman involved. 'Come back this afternoon, and tell me what he said.'

Charles took a hansom to Southwark and as he crossed the Thames he looked out at the narrow streets snaking their way from the main thoroughfare. The cabby drew up at the kerb and Charles, looking out and expecting to see the public house, found he was facing Waterloo Station.

'Sorry, guvnor,' the man said. 'It's in an alley off of Cons Street. I don't take my cab into them streets. You'll have to get out here.'

Charles got down and paid his fare. 'Round the back of the station,' said the cabby, 'an' keep yer wits about yer if yer really going to the Drummer.'

After several false starts Charles finally found the tavern, seeing its grubby sign hanging out into the alley. He was just walking towards the door when he heard a call behind him and spinning round saw Jeremiah turning into the narrow lane.

'You got the message then,' the big man said.

'Yes. How did you get on this morning?'

'I'll tell you about that, soon enough. Better get inside here before some likely lad thinks we're ripe for plucking.' As they reached the door, Jeremiah Hawke paused and said, 'Leave the talking to me.'

When they entered the pub Charles wasn't at all certain that they were any safer than they had been in the street, and he was glad to have the reassuring bulk of Jeremiah at his side. The bar was dark and smoky, furnished with scarred wooden tables standing on a sawdusted floor. Heads turned as they entered but Jeremiah, ignoring all the other customers, walked up to the bar counter and ordered two pints of ale from the drudge standing behind it.

A large man, the landlord, moved up beside her as she drew their beer and said, 'Haven't seen you gents in 'ere before, 'ave I?'

'No,' replied Jeremiah easily. 'Come to meet someone.'

'Who's that then?'

'Luke Mangot. Got some business with him. In here, is he?'

'Wouldn't know,' replied the landlord.

Jeremiah took out a half-sovereign, laying it on the counter but keeping his hand over it. 'Help you to look?'

The man's eyes glinted at the sight of the coin, and he cast a glance round the room, before giving the slightest nod towards a young man seated at a table in the corner, a half-empty glass in front of him.

'Refill for him then,' Jeremiah said, and waited for it to be pulled before leading the way over to where the young man was sitting.

He looked up as Jeremiah and Charles approached. He was older than Charles had first thought, probably about twenty-five, thin-faced, with straw-coloured hair and close-set faded grey eyes. Jeremiah set the refill down in front of him and hoiking a stool from under the table with his foot, said, 'Luke Mangot?'

The man didn't touch the glass but stared up at him. 'Who wants to know?'

'My friend and I just wanted a word with you.' Jeremiah sat down on the stool, placing his own glass on the table, but Charles remained standing, effectively blocking the way to the door.

'Oh yeah? 'Bout what?'

'About a visit you paid to a lady what lives in Hammersmith.'

Luke's eyes narrowed, but he said, 'Dunno what you're talkin' about. I dunno any ladies in 'Ammersmif.'

'Then I've made a mistake,' Jeremiah said. 'It must've been someone else what called, wanting to do some business. I'll bid you good day.' And downing his pint in one long swallow, he got to his feet.

'Just a minute,' cried Luke. 'Maybe I do remember visiting someone in 'Ammersmif. But what's it to you?'

'More importantly, Mr Mangot,' replied Jeremiah Hawke, 'what's it to you?'

'I was just trying to 'elp the lady, but she weren't there.'

'Help her? In what way?'

'Just wanted to tell her somefink. Somefink I fought she'd wanna know.'

'And there was no thought of asking for money... or anything like that?'

'Just a bit of business,' Luke said. 'That's all. 'Ad sommat I thought might interest 'er.'

'I see.' Jeremiah sat down again and Charles, drawing up another stool, sat down beside him. 'And what was that?'

Luke gave him a crafty look and said, 'That's between me an' 'er.'

'No,' Jeremiah said firmly. 'It ain't.' He stared the young man down, until he looked away. 'It's between you and us now. We're the ones what've got the money to buy things, and we might, just might, be interested in what you're selling. But of course, if you don't wanna deal, that's down to you. I'm sure Mrs Dolly Bryan might prefer us to deal direct with her.'

At the mention of his sister's name, Luke looked anxiously round the bar and said, 'Well... all right. But not in 'ere.'

'I suggest we go and visit your sister,' Jeremiah said. 'Don't you? At 14 Clayton Street?' Luke's eyes flickered at the mention of Dolly's address, and Jeremiah added, 'I'm sure you want the best deal you can get for your sister.'

Luke jerked his head at Charles and said, 'Who's he then?'

'He,' replied Jeremiah Hawke, 'is the man with the money.'

Luke stared at Charles for a moment before saying, ''Ow do I know I can trust yer?'

Jeremiah, already getting to his feet again, said, 'You don't. Shall we go?'

The three of them left the bar, watched by the landlord, but no one else seemed to have taken any notice of the encounter. Hushed, private business was often conducted at the Drummer Boy.

When they arrived at Dolly's house she stood at the half-open front door, not allowing them inside.

'What you want, Luke? And who's these?'

'We come to talk business, Doll. 'Bout you know who?'

'I don't wanna talk about 'im,' Dolly snapped. 'Told yer before, I don't want no trouble wiv 'im.'

'Don't be stupid, Doll. This bloke's got money. He's ready to buy.'

'I ain't stupid,' retorted Dolly, 'an' it's because I ain't stupid I don't wanna talk to them, whoever they are. You think I want Nicholas round here, beating me up?'

'Mrs Bryan,' Jeremiah said, 'please don't be alarmed. We just need to speak with you. I have a suggestion to make which might suit us both.'

Dolly was still about to say no, when Luke said, 'It can't hurt, Doll, just to see what they've got to say. Come on, girl, let us in. Don't wanna be seen wiv them on the doorstep, do yer?'

Reluctantly, Dolly stood aside and they all trooped in to the house. From the tiny hallway a flight of steep stairs ran up to the first floor, and behind that was a door leading into the only downstairs room, a cramped kitchen-cum-living room. Dolly didn't sit down or ask her visitors to. She turned to face them and stood, arms akimbo, and said, 'Well?'

'Mrs Bryan,' Jeremiah said, 'I have, this morning, been to St John's Church, Waterloo, where I looked at the marriage records kept in the vestry there, and in those records I found one dated 6th January 1883.' He gave her a serious look and said, 'Does that date have any significance for you?'

'What d'yer mean? Significance?'

'Is that a special date in your life?'

When Dolly didn't answer, Jeremiah went on, 'You see, there is a marriage registered for that date between Dolly Mangot and Nicholas Bryan. Now, I believe that you are the Dolly Mangot mentioned and that you are still married to Nicholas Bryan.' When Dolly still said nothing, he added, 'Is that true?'

'Course it is,' cried Luke, unable to keep silent any longer. 'Tell 'im, Dolly!'

'Thank you, Mr Mangot, but I'd prefer Mrs Bryan to answer for herself. Now, I'm working for two gentlemen who look after the interests of a certain lady, who thinks herself engaged to marry Nicholas Bryan. Obviously, she cannot marry him if he is still married to you. Have you got the marriage certificate?'

'No,' said Dolly, speaking for the first time. 'I ain't.' But her eyes flicked to her brother and Jeremiah caught the glance.

'That's a pity,' Jeremiah said, 'as this gentleman needs proof for his client. We wouldn't need to take it away. We just need a sight of it.' He let the idea hang for a moment and then said, 'Would a half-sovereign help you find it?'

Luke's hand went straight to his pocket. 'Been looking after it for her,' he explained. 'Just in case Nick come back for it.' Still holding on to the certificate, he showed Charles and Jeremiah what was recorded on it. And when he'd noted the details, Jeremiah parted with the coin which, like the certificate, vanished into Luke's pocket.

'Now there's one more thing we need you to do,' Jeremiah said, turning to Dolly.

'Another way we can arrange things to your advantage. We need you to come with me to visit a lawyer and swear an affidavit to the effect that you married Nicholas Bryan on 6th January 1883 at St John's, Waterloo, and though estranged, are still married to him.'

'What's an affi... affi-thing?' asked Luke

'It is simply a statement made on oath, before a special lawyer. Your sister would go with me to make this statement, which could be used in court should the occasion arise.' Jeremiah spread his hands. 'There would be no need for Nicholas Bryan to know anything of this arrangement. He would only be informed that there is evidence in the form of the church records of your marriage. The affidavit would simply be kept on record in case of need.'

'No,' Dolly said firmly. 'He'd come and find me.'

'It seems to me that you, and your brother, might be happier living somewhere else. My friend here,' he indicated Charles, 'would be happy to defray the cost of moving.'

Luke was interested. 'What d'yer mean "defray"?'

'What he means,' Charles said, speaking for the first time, 'is that if your sister would like to move away from London and start a new life, I should be more than happy to help her do so.'

'You mean pay cash,' said Luke, anxious that there be no doubt of what was on offer.

'I mean pay cash,' agreed Charles. 'Not to get her to swear the affidavit, but to help her move somewhere more congenial when she has done so.'

'How much?' asked Luke.

'I was thinking two hundred pounds,' Charles said, hoping that this would be enough.

'That's double what Nick was gonna pay yer!' Luke said to Dolly. 'Set us up for life, that will.'

'Nick'll find us,' Dolly said bleakly.

'No, he won't. Not if we go to Australia!'

'Australia!' echoed Dolly incredulously. 'Why would we wanna go there?'

'Cos then he won't find you! An' there ain't nothing for us here in London, is there?'

'What I am suggesting, Mrs Bryan,' Jeremiah explained, cutting into this argument, 'is that you come with me to the lawyer on Monday. Once I have the affidavit you'll have the two hundred pounds in your hand and you can go anywhere. By the time Nicholas Bryan is confronted with his attempted bigamy, you will have disappeared to your new life.'

'Come on, Dolly,' urged Luke. 'This is a chance we'll never get again.'

Dolly looked at Jeremiah and said, 'An' he'll never know I told yer?'

'He won't know,' said Hawke. 'But if he ever did come looking for you, you'd be long gone... without, I'm sure,' he added, 'having told anyone where.'

At last she was persuaded, and Jeremiah Hawke and Charles left the tiny house with the promise they would come back on Monday morning to take her to a Commissioner of Oaths and then provide her with the funds for her new life.

And so it was that three days later Dolly Bryan and her brother walked out of the house in Clayton Street, carrying their worldly possessions in two cardboard suitcases, and disappeared. Luke kept the marriage certificate safely in his pocket. They hadn't had to part with it, so if Nicholas did ever catch up with them, Luke pointed out, they could show it to him to prove that they had not sold it to a higher bidder.

Chapter 38

Charles and Jeremiah Hawke met with Mr Staunton in his office four days later, the affidavit safely signed, and lodged it in the solicitor's safe.

'What are we going to do now?' Charles asked. 'We have proof that he's married, but he can still maintain that Dolly was married to a different Nicholas Bryan.'

'Difficult to maintain when our original information came from a man who followed him from Dolly's house where he'd spent the night, to Sophie's where he spent the day,' pointed out Mr Staunton. 'Hannah can testify to Luke Mangot's visit if necessary.'

'I think it is unlikely that he'll contest what we can put before him,' Mr Staunton continued. 'If we let him know we have traced the marriage to St John's, Waterloo, and that you, Mr Hawke, have made a copy of the entry in the register, certified by the rector as a true one, he's unlikely to dispute it. If it went to court he could end up in prison. If we confront him privately, Dr Bryan can simply disappear without anyone but us being any the wiser.'

'Of course he's not a doctor, is he?' Hawke reminded them. 'He only spent a few months at St Thomas's.'

'You're quite right, but I think that the fact that he's married is more important just now. He mustn't be allowed to make a bigamous marriage with Sophie,' Charles said.

'I agree,' said Mr Staunton. 'And we need to make further enquiries before we can be sure he is *not* a qualified doctor. However,' he went on, 'I think it would be wise to watch him carefully in case he does go back to Clayton Street to find Dolly. That would be further proof. I would like you, Mr Hawke, to continue to follow him until we are sure that he has given up all thoughts of marrying Miss Ross. I think Mrs Dolly Bryan was right to be concerned about her safety.'

'That can be arranged, Mr Staunton,' agreed Jeremiah. '"Course, I can't keep watch twenty-four hours a day. I'll have to call in my assistant, Rufus.'

'Whatever it takes, Mr Hawke,' replied the solicitor.

'Before we confront him,' Charles interposed, 'we shall have to break it to Sophie.'

'If you would like me to undertake that, Mr Leroy...' began Staunton.

'No, thank you, Mr Staunton,' answered Charles. 'That is something I must do myself. My cousin will be distraught when she hears what we've discovered, and I must be the one to explain.'

Stepping into the street, Charles had sighed as he left the lawyer's office, having a fairly good idea what Sophie's reaction would be to his news. But he was relieved they had some concrete evidence that would end Nicholas Bryan's plans regarding marriage to her.

And so Charles returned to London the next day, not at all looking forward to his errand. He didn't warn Sophie that he was coming, and he was glad that Hannah was alone in the house when he arrived so that he was able to tell her of the discoveries they had made.

'So it was true,' she cried in dismay. 'What a wicked, wicked man, to lead her on so!'

'She may not believe me at first,' Charles said. 'And she's going to wonder how we came to hear about it.' He looked at Hannah ruefully. 'So, I'm afraid that's going to implicate you.'

'Don't you worry about that, Mr Charles,' Hannah said. 'She may be angry at me at first and call me interfering for sending for you, but in the long run she'll believe I did it for her own good.'

'She is going to be very upset,' Charles said, 'so I know she'll need you, Hannah. It's you she'll turn to.'

'And you, sir,' asserted Hannah. 'She'll turn to you as well.'

'I doubt it,' said Charles with a sigh. 'I think in my case she'll want to shoot the messenger. Where is she today?'

'Gone to that Madame Egloff for a final fitting of her new clothes. Oh, Mr Charles,' Hannah cried as she realized what she'd just said, 'how are we going to tell her?'

'I'm afraid there's no easy way, Hannah.'

Charles was quite right. When Sophie got back from Madame Egloff's she was full of bubble. The fittings had gone well and she would be able to collect the completed garments at the end of the following week; black for immediate wear and pale grey and lilac for later in the year when, though still in mourning, she was married. She was delighted when she found Charles drinking tea in the parlour.

'Have you got another meeting with Mr Hawthorne?' she asked as she joined him beside the fire.

'No, not yet. As I told you before, these things take time. But I do think that eventually he will join us in the purchase of another ship. No.' Charles sighed. 'I'm afraid I've come to talk to you about something entirely different.'

Sophie waited a moment before saying, 'And that is...? From your face I think it must be something bad. Has something gone wrong at Trescadinnick, or on the estate? Are my aunts both well?'

'They are quite well, thank you. No, it's nothing like that.'

'Well, what then?'

'Sophie, it's very hard for me to tell you this...'

'Then just tell me,' said Sophie. 'That's always the best way with bad news.' She cocked her head at him in the way he so loved. 'Don't you think?'

Charles nodded and drawing a deep breath, said, 'Sophie, I'm afraid we've just learned that Nicholas Bryan is already married.'

The colour drained from Sophie's cheeks and he reached out to take her hand, but she shook him off. 'We?' she demanded. 'Who's we?'

'Mr Staunton and I—'

'You and Mr Staunton? How did that happen? What were you doing? Why were you checking up on Nicholas? You were, weren't you? Don't you dare deny it!'

'We certainly made some enquiries, yes,' Charles began.

'There, I knew it. How dare you check up on *my* fiancé?'

'We felt it our duty,' responded Charles. 'It was with the best of intentions—'

'The way to hell is paved with good intentions!' snapped Sophie. 'Your duty indeed!'

'Whatever you think about that,' Charles said, 'it wasn't we who were told that he was already married.'

'Oh, and who was it then?' cried Sophie. 'Because I don't believe a word of it!'

'A man came to the house, here, one day when you were out. Hannah answered the door and he said he had information about Nicholas Bryan. She didn't believe him at first, but he showed her a marriage certificate naming Nicholas Bryan as the groom. He was married to this man's sister, Dolly.'

'And he was asking for money, I suppose.'

'Yes, he was,' admitted Charles, 'but that didn't make his information wrong. He didn't give Hannah the certificate, of course. But he showed it to her and she remembered the names of the couple, the name of the church and the date, 6th January 1883. She sent me a telegram, asking me to come to London.'

'Hannah sent you a telegram? I don't believe it!'

'Well, she did and I came at once.'

'And that's why you were here last week? It had nothing to do with Mr Hawthorne or whatever he's called, did it?'

'Not at the time, though I've an appointment with him in a fortnight.'

'I don't care about your appointments with him,' Sophie retorted. 'How do you know it's *my* Nicholas Bryan? There could be a hundred others.'

'We know because this woman's brother followed Nicholas from her house to yours. Nicholas had been with Dolly trying to buy her silence. He offered to buy the marriage certificate so that there'd be no evidence to link him with his wife. Unfortunately for him, there is other evidence that can be produced, church records and the like.'

Silence fell round them, broken by the crackling of the fire. 'And there is no doubt?' Sophie said at last.

'I'm afraid not. Nicholas and Dolly were married on 6th January 1883. Dolly is still alive and they are still married.'

The tears which had been flooding her eyes overflowed and began to course down her cheeks as she wept. At a loss to know what else to do, Charles pulled out his handkerchief and she took it blindly to staunch her tears.

'Does Hannah know?' asked Sophie as at last her tears subsided.

'Yes, I told you, it was she who sent for me...'

'But does she know it's true?'

'Yes,' replied Charles. 'I told her when I got here. I wanted her to know that she'd been right to call me.'

'She should have told *me*, not you.' Sophie sniffed.

'Maybe, but I think she did the right thing. She couldn't have made the enquiries we did, she didn't have money at her disposal to get rid of the man, and she didn't want you to know anything about it unless it proved to be true. Imagine how you'd have felt if she'd told you and it had all been a hoax.'

'But it isn't, is it?'

'No,' Charles replied gently. 'I'm afraid it isn't.'

'Have you told anyone else?'

'No, of course not, and we won't. We shall try and deal with everything as discreetly as possible. Now you know, we can confront Nicholas with what we've found out.'

'Oh no,' Sophie said, some of the old spirit reasserting itself. 'I'm going to be the one to confront him.'

'Dear Sophie, I'm not sure that's wise,' Charles said. 'I think he is a man of very uncertain temper. He could become violent. His wife was afraid of him.'

'Well, I'm not,' declared Sophie. 'I shall have it out with him.'

'If you're determined to do so, I think you should have someone with you.'

Sophie shook her head. 'No,' she said. 'It's not the sort of
thing you can do in front of an audience.'

Charles did not stay at the house that night. He could tell
that Sophie did not want company and he took himself off to the
hotel he'd planned to stay in the previous week. Before he had
dinner, he took an omnibus to Waterloo Station and from there
followed the way Luke had led them to Clayton Street. When he
reached the end of the road he walked along the pavement and
was pleased to see that number 14 was empty. It was clear that
no one was living there; Dolly and Luke had moved on.

That evening Sophie called Hannah into the parlour. 'Sit
down, Hannah,' Sophie said. 'We've got to talk.'

Hannah took the chair that Charles had been seated in earlier.
It was warm beside the fire and had anyone seen the two of them
through the window, they would have thought them best friends
sitting together for cosy chat. The atmosphere between them
was strained, however, as Hannah waited for Sophie to speak.

'Hannah, I wish you'd told me about that man who came to
the door about Nicholas,' Sophie said at last. 'Rather than go
straight to my cousin.'

'I'm sorry, Miss Sophie,' Hannah answered, 'but I did what
I thought was best. I didn't know if what that man told me was
true. I knew I couldn't find out but I thought Mr Charles might.'

'I know,' sighed Sophie, twisting her engagement ring round
and round her finger. 'And it does seem to be true. Oh, Hannah,
what am I going to do?'

'Well, I think you should give him his ring back and say that
as there is no question of marriage between you, you'd prefer not
to see him again.'

'What will everyone in the village say?' wondered Sophie
dismally.

'It doesn't matter what they say. It's none of their business,
and as soon as something else happens it'll all be forgotten. No
one will know why the engagement was broken off. They may

speculate, but Mr Charles isn't going to tell them the reason, is he? Nor are you and I, and you can be sure Dr Bryan isn't. They will just think you changed your mind, which I might add you are quite entitled to do.' She smiled across at Sophie. 'Be brave, Sophie. Chins are being worn very high this year!'

That brought a faint smile to Sophie's lips before she said, 'But poor Nicholas will have everyone wondering why.'

'Poor Nicholas has only himself to blame, Miss Sophie.'

'You've never liked him, have you?'

'I've never trusted him,' Hannah answered honestly. 'And this has proved me right. He's a liar. If he's been lying to you about this, what else has he lied about? What other secrets is he hiding?'

'Hannah,' Sophie began and then stopped. She knew another secret Nicholas was hiding but could she, should she, finally confide in Hannah about his parentage? It would mean explaining how she had broken into Jocelyn's room and found his letters, leading her on to searching her mother's bureau for the replies, and then the meetings with Nan Slater. She thought of the old woman lying there dying, in the cold of winter, when she'd gone out to fetch firewood. Would she still be alive, Sophie wondered, if I hadn't taken her that firewood? But that was ridiculous speculation; it was simply dreadful misfortune that she had slipped on the icy surface of the yard while fetching some wood indoors.

All these things flitted through her mind as she sat by the fire, and Hannah, seeing that she was having some sort of battle with herself, simply waited.

At length Sophie said, 'Hannah, if I tell you something, you have to promise me that it goes no further. Will you promise?'

'It rather depends on what you're going to tell me, Miss Sophie. Of course I want to help you in whatever way I can, but please don't burden me with a confidence that I can't keep.'

Sophie stared at her for a moment. In the months since her mother had died, Hannah had changed. She had been there all Sophie's life, a friend and comforter, offering sensible counsel when she was asked; occasionally speaking her mind, but always softening her comments with a smile or a word of affection.

Recently, however, she had been a good deal more forthright, criticizing Sophie for her behaviour when she thought it justified, and Sophie recognized a difference in their relationship. She knew Hannah loved her just as she always had, but as an adult not as a child. She could see the sort of love she'd received as a child was now given to AliceAnne, but she also realized that neither of them was actually the centre of Hannah's world.

Still, she needed Hannah's no-nonsense counsel now, so she said, 'Well, I'll tell you anyway, but I hope you'll feel able to respect my confidence.'

Hannah nodded and waited while Sophie composed herself.

'You remember when you found me moving the wardrobe in my bedroom at Trescadinnick?'

Hannah laughed. 'Indeed I do, Miss Sophie. What you thought you was up to I do not know!'

'I wanted to explore my Uncle Jocelyn's room. I wanted to know why it had been locked up for so long, why he had been shut away for all those years, rather than being remembered as a loved member of the family who had died young.'

'I recall you said something of the sort,' said Hannah.

'Well, I did manage to get into his room and it was just as he had left it the day he died. There was a half-written letter in his desk, but more than that, there were letters from my mother and also from a girl he was in love with and wanted to marry. She was carrying his child.'

'You never read his letters, Miss Sophie.' Hannah sounded shocked.

'I did,' admitted Sophie, 'and I discovered a great deal about him and his fiancée, Cassie. She was expecting Jocelyn's child and as far as I can tell his father, my grandfather, refused to give his consent to their marriage.' Sophie looked up. 'Just as he did with my parents.'

'Not quite the same,' Hannah interposed. 'Your mother and father simply wanted to get married. There was no question of illegitimate children.'

'No, but listen, Hannah, till you've heard the whole story.'

And Sophie went on to tell her everything that she had discovered, including her conversations with Nan Slater, culminating in the revelation that Nicholas Bryan was the fruit of that relationship.

'He's my grandfather's grandson,' Sophie said. 'If Jocelyn hadn't fallen to his death in the fog, they'd have married and my grandfather would have had a legitimate heir.'

Hannah was silenced for a moment as she tried to take in what Sophie was telling her. Then she said, 'So he came back to Trescadinnick to try and claim his inheritance? Is that what you're saying?'

'That's what I thought, but when I told him what I'd found out, he denied it all. He admitted he was an illegitimate child, brought up by his aunt and uncle when his mother died giving birth to him, but obviously he didn't want that known. He said he loved me and he wanted to marry me. I believed him, but now? I don't know. Was everything a lie? Everything has changed and now I have to confront him with the fact that he's already married. I don't know what's true and what isn't. Ever since I first met him, he's paid me special attention, made it clear that he wanted to be more than just a friend. I fell in love with him and he loved me. At least I thought he did. Oh, Hannah, why has he led me on when he knew we could never marry?'

'He didn't think anyone would find out, Sophie, and it was pure chance that we have. If we hadn't he'd have married you.'

'Would he? Do you really think that?'

'I know it, Sophie,' Hannah replied gently.

'But why? It would be no marriage at all.'

'No.'

'So why?'

'You're asking what I really think?'

'Yes,' Sophie replied. 'Of course I am.'

'He was marrying you to get his hands on Trescadinnick. Now I know he's an illegitimate Penvarrow, I'm certain.'

'You think he doesn't love me,' Sophie said.

'That I don't know. Perhaps he does in his own way, but from what you've told me it seems to me that he came to Trescadinnick, not to claim an inheritance that would never have been given to him, but to have some sort of revenge on the family. They'd refused to accept his mother, which made him a bastard.'

'You don't know that!'

'No, I don't, not for sure, but why else would he come? He must have known Thomas Penvarrow would never acknowledge him as a grandson.'

'What sort of revenge?'

'I don't know,' confessed Hannah. 'But whatever it was, I think it changed when he met you. Once you arrived on the scene, young, beautiful, available as a wife, what better revenge than to marry you, and claim what he considered as rightfully his?'

'But he didn't know I was the heir!' cried Sophie.

'Sophie,' said Hannah patiently, '*everyone* knew, or at least they guessed. Once that lawyer had been, it was clear that old Mr Penvarrow had changed his will and that you, a true Penvarrow, would inherit Trescadinnick. Didn't Dr Bryan witness his signature?'

'Yes, but he couldn't have known what was in the will.'

'Your grandfather didn't like him, did he? Maybe he saw which way the wind was blowing. He may not have known exactly who Nicholas was, but he made very sure that whoever you married couldn't get his hands on the Trescadinnick inheritance.'

'He wanted me to marry Charles.'

'I know,' said Hannah. 'And if he had left well alone, that might have happened.'

Sophie gave a short laugh. 'I don't think so, Hannah. Charles made it quite clear that he wouldn't consider the idea. He said if he wanted a wife he would choose his own, and it wouldn't be a chit from the schoolroom. He really was most clear on the subject.'

'So I heard,' said Hannah wryly. 'But maybe he's had time to change his mind. You seem to get on very well.'

'That's because there's absolutely no expectation of anything more than friendship between us,' declared Sophie. 'Charles doesn't want me, even if I wanted him.'

'But he does protect your interests,' pointed out Hannah, 'which brings us back to this question of Nicholas already being married.'

'Charles is coming again tomorrow, and I shall tell him I'm going back to Trescadinnick to have it out with Nicholas.'

'Sophie, I think you should tell Charles everything else you've found out about Nicholas,' Hannah advised. 'I think that is all part and parcel of why he came to Trescadinnick in the first place.'

Sophie sighed. 'Maybe,' she conceded. 'I'll sleep on it and decide in the morning.'

Chapter 39

When Charles arrived back in Hammersmith next morning, Sophie led him into the parlour and asked him to sit down.

'I've been thinking about all you told me yesterday,' she said, 'and we need to talk. But first I have to tell you something else about Nicholas and you have to promise to listen and say nothing, no interruptions, until I've finished. Can you do that?'

Charles smiled at her earnest face and said, 'Yes, I should think so. What's on your mind?'

What was on her mind? Everything. She had hardly slept as everything she had heard the previous day churned around in her head. How could Nicholas have proposed to her when he was already married? He must have counted on the fact that no one would ever discover that he already had a wife, and why should they? This Dolly lived in London and if Nicholas had left her and moved to Cornwall, it was unlikely that she would learn that he'd got married again.

If we had married, Sophie thought, Nicholas would have been betraying both of us. Me and Dolly. How could he? He'd said he loved me and all the time he was married to someone else.

Tears of misery and rage filled her eyes and her throat ached with wanting to cry, but she would not. She would not cry for someone who had told her nothing but lies! He was a liar and a deceiver and she'd never forgive him!

And was Hannah right about his motives for coming to Port Felec in the first place? She was right that he could have expected nothing from Thomas Penvarrow. He was not the man to welcome a bastard grandson into the family. But if Nicholas had no ulterior motive, surely he wouldn't have denied it so violently when she'd taxed him with being Jocelyn's son.

All Nan had told her whirled round in her head, forcing her to accept that Nicholas had been quite happy to deceive her and had intended to go on doing so. *Has a right temper on him*, Nan had said. *You don't want to cross him or he'll make you pay.* And Sophie remembered the marks of his fingers when he'd gripped her wrist, angry that she had ridden alone with Charles. Yes, Nicholas had a temper, but she had excused it because she loved him.

She lay in bed, staring up at the ceiling, seeing the dark familiar shapes of her bedroom furniture, the shadows cast by the street lamp beyond her window. She closed her eyes, willing herself to sleep, but her brain wouldn't relax, couldn't relax, and it wasn't until the first grey fingers of a false dawn crept into the eastern sky that she finally drifted off into a fitful doze, bedevilled with muddled dreams of Nicholas, Nan, her mother, her grandfather.

She awoke pale and unrefreshed when Hannah brought her tea in the morning, but as she slept her decision had been made. She would tell Charles everything.

Now, sitting by the fire in the parlour, she did just that. She told him everything from the moment when she had broken into Jocelyn's room and found the letters, to the last time she had seen Nan Slater and been told that Nicholas Bryan was Jocelyn's illegitimate son. She left out no detail, including Nicholas's reaction when she had faced him with what she had learned from the letters and from Nan.

'He denied it completely,' Sophie said, 'and he was angry, so angry. Nan had warned me that he had a temper, but that was the first time I had really seen it.'

Charles, good as his word, listened to her without interruption, but his expression was a mixture of incredulity and anger. When Sophie at last lapsed into silence, he said quietly, 'Is that it?'

'Isn't it enough?' cried Sophie.

'More than enough,' Charles said. 'And when we add it to what else we've found out about him, it takes on an even more serious aspect.' He shook his head reproachfully. 'Sophie, why on earth didn't you tell us what you'd discovered? About Jocelyn, I mean?'

'Aunt Matty made it clear that I was never to mention Jocelyn or ask any questions about him. She said his death had been an accident when they actually thought he'd committed suicide. Having read those letters, Charles, I am quite sure it wasn't suicide. Jocelyn was planning to marry his Cassie as soon as he was of age. But if I'd told anyone what I had found out, I'd have had to admit breaking into Jocelyn's room and everyone would have been furious with me.'

Charles gave a grim smile. 'You're right there.'

'So I said nothing. I thought it was better to leave things as they were. It's only since I found out that Nicholas is *their* child that I've told anyone. Hannah thinks he's taking some sort of revenge by marrying me,' Sophie went on. 'Using me to get his own back on the Penvarrows. Getting his hands on Trescadinnick.'

'Hannah's almost certainly right,' Charles said. 'And the only person who might have stopped you marrying him was our grandfather.'

'And he died.'

'And he died.'

'Well, I shan't be marrying him, shall I? Not now we know he's already married. So he won't get his revenge, if that was really what he was after, and he won't get Trescadinnick.' She thought for a moment and then asked, 'Are you going back to Trescadinnick today?'

'Yes,' replied Charles. 'I have to. I'm catching the late-morning train to Truro.'

'Then I'm coming with you,' announced Sophie. 'I need to face Nicholas with this and the sooner I do, the better.'

'But not on your own,' said Charles. 'He's a man with a temper.'

'I told you, I'm not afraid of him.'

'Maybe not,' Charles said. 'But there's no knowing how he'll react and no point in taking chances.'

'If I see him at Trescadinnick, with other people in the house...?' suggested Sophie.

'If you see him in the drawing room and I'm in my study,' Charles said reluctantly, 'I suppose you can come to no harm.'

Before they left for the station Charles wrote an account of everything Sophie had told him and sent it to Mr Staunton. *I think it best if we have this account kept safe,'* he wrote.

...and perhaps Hawke can make further enquiries based on this information. It strikes me that it is possible that Bryan may have had a hand in two deaths, that of my grandfather, Thomas Penvarrow, and possibly also that of Nan Slater who was found dead of cold in her backyard soon after Sophie had told Bryan what she had learned from her. I have made no suggestion of these thoughts to Sophie and I doubt anyway there would be any way of proving that Bryan had a hand in either death, but I am concerned for Sophie's safety. I think Bryan will be a man bent on revenge.

When they arrived at Trescadinnick, late that evening, Sophie went straight up to her room, exhausted. As he had promised, Charles said nothing of their discoveries about Nicholas Bryan to anyone else. They had agreed that Sophie would send a note to Nicholas to say she was back at Trescadinnick and then wait for his visit. Until she had challenged Nicholas about his marriage to Dolly, there would be no mention of Sophie breaking off the engagement, and even then no reason would be given, simply change of heart.

Next day Ned was dispatched with a note, and he returned with a message saying Dr Bryan would call that afternoon. Sophie spent the morning with AliceAnne, helping her with her schoolwork, trying to keep all thoughts of the impending interview with Nicholas out of her mind, but it was impossible, and several times AliceAnne had to recall her attention to what they were supposed to be doing.

At the midday meal Sophie ate almost nothing, causing Louisa to ask, 'Are you not well, Sophie? You're very pale and you've eaten nothing.'

Sophie managed to smile and answer, 'No, Aunt, thank you. I am quite well, just a little tired after the journey yesterday.'

'Well, your Aunt Matty is coming over this evening, so I hope you'll look a bit brighter for her.' Turning to Charles, she said, 'What are you doing this afternoon, Charles? I have nothing planned and I wondered if you could take me to see this house you've found. Matty's sure to ask about it when she gets here.'

'I'm sorry, Mama,' Charles replied, 'but I shall be working in my office this afternoon. I have several letters to write.'

'Surely they can wait until tomorrow,' said his mother. 'I particularly wanted to go today.'

But Charles was adamant. 'No, I'm sorry, Mama, but if you would like to go tomorrow, I shall be happy to take you... and Aunt Matty too, if you like.'

Louisa subsided into disgruntled silence and as soon as possible, Sophie excused herself and left the table. Charles found her in the drawing room, pacing the floor as she waited for Nicholas to arrive.

'Don't close the door completely,' he said, 'and my door will be open. Call me if you need me.' To her surprise he bent forward and kissing her lightly on the cheek said, 'Be careful, cousin,' before returning to his study.

Sophie stared after him, her fingers going to the place where his lips had touched her cheek, before giving herself a shake and going to the window to watch for Nicholas.

It was not long before she saw his gig coming up the drive and she found her heart was pounding in her chest. The time had come to confront him with his duplicity, and suddenly she wasn't ready. She saw him get out of the gig and hitch the reins to a fence post.

It was a cold, bright day and the sun struck golden lights in his fair hair. As he turned for the house she could see his face, as handsome as ever, and for a moment she saw him as she had seen him that first day, a good-looking young man whose admiration for her had been apparent in his eyes. *Was that a lie too?* she wondered bitterly.

She heard the knock on the front door and Edith coming to let him in and take his coat. She heard Charles's voice as he wished him good afternoon, and then saying, 'I think you'll find Sophie in the drawing room.'

The door opened and Nicholas strode in, a broad smile on his face. 'Sophie,' he cried, his hands outstretched to her. 'You're home. How I've missed you, my darling girl.'

'Have you, Nicholas?' she replied, her hands firmly by her side. 'And do you miss Dolly when you're away from her?'

Nicholas stopped in his tracks, his face rigid with shock, before he said, sounding confused, 'Who?'

'Dolly, your wife.' There, it was done. 'You forgot to tell me about her, Nicholas. Or were you going to let me into the secret when we were married?'

'Sophie, my dearest—'

'But I'm not your dearest, am I, Nicholas? You have a wife and surely *she* is your dearest.'

'Sophie, please, you've got it all wrong. Let me explain—'

'Explain how you forgot you were married?'

'Explain about Dolly.'

'All right.' Sophie sat down in an armchair and then wished she hadn't as Nicholas came towards her, towering over her. But she raised her chin and looked him in the eye. 'Explain about Dolly.'

'Listen,' Nicholas said, 'I don't know where you heard about Dolly, but you've got it all wrong. I do know a Dolly, in London. I met her and her family while I was training at St Thomas's. We became friends and for a while, I have to admit to my shame that I lived with her as man and wife. I was young and impressionable. Dolly was young and sweet. I know it was wrong, but we were only together for a few weeks and then she met someone else.

I know it was wrong,' he repeated, 'but I promise you there was never any question of marriage. I was a poor student. I couldn't afford to get married.'

'So the record of your marriage with Dolly at St John's Church, Waterloo, on 6th January 1883 is wrong, is it?'

Nicholas, taken aback at her knowledge of this information, thought fast. Shaking his head, he said, 'I don't know what you're talking about, Sophie. Really. Maybe Dolly married someone else,' he suggested. 'Our life together was long over by then.'

Sophie suddenly got to her feet, making Nicholas take a step back. 'Nicholas Bryan, you are a liar,' she declared, her voice icy. 'You lie about everything. I know who you are and you know it, but you still lie. You're married to this Dolly, we both know it, but you still deny it.' She tugged the engagement ring off her finger and placed it on the table. 'I can't marry you, Nicholas, because you are already married and there is written proof, but I wouldn't marry you even if you weren't. You are a liar and you have lied to me from the start. You told me you loved me and I believed you—'

'But, Sophie, I do love you—'

'Stop it!' Sophie cried. 'Stop it. You don't! All you ever wanted was Trescadinnick. Why else did you come here in the first place?'

Nicholas made a grab for her hands, gripping her wrists so tightly that she couldn't break free.

'Sophie, listen to me—'

'Let me go!' she shrieked. 'Let me go! Just get out of here! I never want to see you again.'

At the sound of her cries Charles erupted into the room and swung his fist full into Nicholas's face. Nicholas let go of Sophie as he staggered back, blood streaming from his nose.

'I think you were just leaving,' Charles said through gritted teeth.

'I am, but don't think this is the last you'll see of me. You'll regret this,' Nicholas warned, 'all of you. I won't be made a laughingstock.'

'Oh, don't worry,' Sophie retorted. 'I won't be spreading your grubby little secrets. You can simply let it be known that I've changed my mind and I'm not going to marry you after all.'

'Now get out,' growled Charles.

Nicholas gave him a look of pure loathing. And with one hand holding a handkerchief to his nose, with the other he snatched up the engagement ring and stormed out of the house.

'Are you all right, Sophie?' Charles asked anxiously. 'He didn't hurt you?'

'No,' Sophie replied a little shakily. 'But thank you for coming so fast. I'm so glad you were there.'

'So am I,' Charles said, looking ruefully at his split knuckles, before adding with a smile, 'but Nicholas isn't!'

Later that afternoon Sophie again took Hannah into her confidence and told her what had happened. Hannah looked distressed at what she heard. 'Oh, Miss Sophie, I wish you'd let Mr Charles deal with him.'

'That might have been even worse,' Sophie said. 'If Charles had confronted him, Nicholas would still have come to me. It was better that it came from me and I told him straight out. Anyway,' she went on, 'he won't be coming back. My cousin and I have decided to tell no one what we have learned about him. There is no need to open up old wounds and it would even now invite unwanted scandal for the family over something that happened long ago.'

'Don't worry, Miss Sophie,' Hannah promised. 'I'll be as silent as the grave.'

That evening, as they sat at dinner, Sophie told her aunts that she had broken off her engagement to Dr Bryan. 'I felt I was being rushed into it,' she said, 'and I don't think we're suited after all.'

'Hhm! Thank goodness you've come to your senses,' retorted Louisa.

'I think it's a sensible decision, my dear,' was all Matty said.

'And now we shan't have to move to that pokey little house at Kenwyn after all,' Louisa went on.

'That is something we shall have to discuss with Sophie,'

Charles said, giving his mother a quelling look, 'and not over the dinner table.'

'No discussion necessary,' Sophie said at once. 'There's no need for any of you to move. I hope you'll stay here at Trescadinnick for the foreseeable future.'

'And will you live here too?' asked Matty.

'I certainly will for now,' Sophie said. 'Things will be as they always have been.'

She'd made that decision earlier when talking with Hannah. 'I don't want him to think that he's frightened me away, Hannah. We may go back to London from time to time, you and I, but we shall stay here for a while now. Will you mind?'

Hannah had smiled and said that she didn't mind at all.

Chapter 40

For the next few weeks life at Trescadinnick settled back into its normal routine. Charles asked Sophie not to go out alone for a while. He didn't really think Nicholas would hurt her, but he still didn't trust him, and though they had seen nothing of him since he'd stalked out of the house, they knew he was still in Port Felec.

Will Shaw told Hannah that the news of the broken engagement had quickly spread round the village.

'Dr Bryan's no gentleman,' he said. 'He's saying that Miss Sophie has jilted him; that she considers herself too superior to marry a simple country doctor now that she's inherited Trescadinnick.'

'That's ridiculous,' retorted Hannah.

'Maybe,' agreed Will, 'but the sympathy is all with him.'

'She had a change of heart, that's all,' Hannah said, wishing she could at least explain to Will what had happened.

Will nodded acceptance of this. 'Better now than after they're wed,' he said, 'but you should warn her what story is going round. She may find things difficult till it all blows over.'

'I will,' said Hannah, and spoke to Sophie that very evening.

'Dr Bryan is brazening it out,' Hannah warned her. 'The blame is being heaped on you; typical Penvarrow, too proud to marry beneath her.'

'They can say what they like,' Sophie said. 'Anyone who knows me, knows that it isn't true.'

Even so, Sophie had to hold her head high the following Sunday, when several people with whom she would normally chat outside church cut her and turned away. Nicholas was not there that day, so they had no occasion to meet, and as Sunday succeeded Sunday and there was no sign of him, she began to wonder if he had only attended morning service to be seen with her. Surely that couldn't really be the case, but whatever the reason for his absence, it was a relief not to have to avoid him every Sunday morning.

It was after the service one Sunday, when Sophie was just about to start walking home with Charles and AliceAnne, that Miss Osell came up to sympathize with her about her broken engagement. 'So uncomfortable for you, a broken engagement,' she said, her voice consoling, her eyes alight with malice. 'So close to your wedding day as well.'

'Thank you for your sympathy, Miss Osell,' Sophie replied sweetly. 'But the wedding was still some way off, you know, and really it was all for the best. I doubt if I'd have made a good doctor's wife.' Adding with a questioning look, 'I thought that was probably more in your line?'

Sandra Osell coloured and gave a tinkling little laugh. 'Oh no, Miss Ross. I shall never marry. My calling is to look after my dear papa. Whereas you, no doubt, may take your pick of suitors. Plenty look for a wealthy wife, do they not... irrespective of her character?'

Sophie held on to the rags of her temper and smiling, said, 'I really couldn't say, Miss Osell. But I beg you not to give up hope of a husband yet. Surely someone will marry you... in the end.' And leaving the rector's daughter standing speechless, she inclined her head and walked away.

'What was all that about?' asked Charles as Sophie came up beside him.

'Sympathy,' said Sophie succinctly.

'Sympathy?'

'Disguising her jealousy. She wants Nicholas, but he's never given her the time of day.' Sophie gave a self-conscious laugh and said, 'I have to admit it wasn't a very charitable conversation for a Sunday, though, on either of our parts.'

'Never mind her,' Charles said, offering her his arm. 'Let's get back home.' And with AliceAnne skipping along beside they walked companionably up the hill to Trescadinnick.

Back at the house, Sophie went upstairs to tidy her hair for lunch. As always, her fingers brushed the handle of Joss's room as she passed. The door remained locked. Charles had been determined that they should not tell Louisa or Matty of Sophie's discoveries, and Sophie agreed with him. But one day, she had promised herself, when she was truly mistress of Trescadinnick, that room would be opened and Joss's memory should be allowed to drift out through the house that had once been his home.

It had been suggested that perhaps Sophie might like to move into the tower bedchamber, which had been Thomas's. It had been cleaned and polished, its windows thrown open to the fresh sea air, clean curtains fluttering beside them, and fresh hangings on the large old oak bed, but to Sophie it would always be the room her grandfather had died in.

'Such a fuss about that,' scoffed Louisa. 'The tower is the oldest part of the house. Generations of Penvarrows have been born and died in that room. My father was simply the last of many.'

Sophie knew that Louisa was right, but even so she chose to stay in her own room, the room that had been her mother's. It had become her refuge, a place away from her Aunt Louisa, who had a caustic tongue and was still bitter about her inheritance, and from Charles, for whom she recognized she was developing more than cousinly love. She found she was listening for his voice about the house, watching for him to come home, looking for the rare smile that lit his face and made him look so much younger and less careworn. Of course, she knew that he had no such tender feelings for her, still simply regarding her as a cousin he was fond of, but no more, so she was careful not to betray any change in her feelings for him. She didn't want his pity and was determined not to leave herself open to rejection by him a second time. She realized now that what she had felt for Nicholas was nothing more than infatuation, the infatuation of a young woman meeting with the admiration of a handsome man for the first time, swept away by his good looks and easy charm. She could see now that there was no depth to Nicholas Bryan. He was guided solely by his own selfish desires and she blushed at the thought of how easily he'd manipulated her, and for how she had allowed him to dictate to her with no thought of what she wanted or how she might feel.

The comforting presence of Charles in the house must be enough until, of course, he found someone he wanted to marry, for surely such a man wouldn't remain a widower for ever, but that, she hoped, was in the distant future. Sophie was determined not to look beyond the next few months. She would spend the summer at Trescadinnick and then decide whether she was going to return to London or make her permanent home in Cornwall.

Gradually the house began to feel like a home once more. Louisa continued to manage the household, but Sophie took on AliceAnne's education. She enjoyed teaching the little girl and AliceAnne was an eager pupil, longing to learn more about the world beyond Trescadinnick. Together they pored over the old atlas on the schoolroom shelf, and read from a tattered history book with stories about William the Conqueror, Henry VIII and Bonnie Prince Charlie. AliceAnne had a quick brain, and both of them enjoyed the lessons and the time they spent together. Sophie also gave her daily piano lessons and it was clear that AliceAnne had some aptitude. It wasn't long before she could play simple pieces, delighting both her and her father when she played them for him.

Spring was in the air, but winter had not given up its last grasp on the world and there were days when the wind came in strong gusts off the sea, scurrying dark storm clouds before it – days to stay indoors in the warm, learning to make bread with Mrs Paxton, or to sew with Hannah.

It was late on an afternoon such as this, when the rain was battering the windows and the noise of the wind had risen in a crescendo, that the air was split by an echoing boom, quickly followed by two more, all clearly heard in the Trescadinnick schoolroom. AliceAnne gave a cry of fear. 'It's the bangs!' And she buried her head in Sophie's lap.

Sophie felt a jolt as well. Charles had told her long ago that if the maroons summoned the lifeboat men, he always went. Would he really venture out in this dreadful weather? She gave AliceAnne a hug and trying to keep her voice steady, she said, 'Let's go downstairs and see what's going on.' Taking her hand, she led the little girl down into the hall, where they found Charles hurriedly pulling on tarpaulin jacket and trousers over his clothes.

'Are you going?' Sophie asked.

'I must,' replied Charles. 'I could be needed.'

'Don't go, Papa,' AliceAnne cried, rushing over to him and clinging on to his arm. 'I don't want you to go.'

Charles kneeled down beside her and put his arms round her, drawing her against him for a moment. 'I have to go, sweetheart,' he murmured, 'but I'll be back soon.'

'Promise?'

Charles looked at Sophie over his daughter's head. 'I promise, I'll do my best,' he said, and got to his feet. 'Now you be a good girl and stay with your Aunt Sophie,' adding with a meaningful look at Sophie, 'I know you'll look after her, Sophie, if... if I'm gone long.'

Sophie, understanding only too well, nodded, and said in a tremulous voice, 'Come back safe, Charles. We all need you here.'

For a moment their eyes met. 'I love you, Sophie,' he said, as he opened the front door and without a backward glance, vanished into the storm.

Had she heard him right? Had he really said he loved her? For a moment Sophie stood transfixed and then she rushed to the door, heaving it open against the strength of the wind, and ran out into the rain, but he had disappeared into the night. Slowly, she turned, her hair dripping about her face, her clothes already soaked by the torrential downpour, and went back into the house. AliceAnne was standing where she had left her.

'That was silly of me, AliceAnne. Now I'm all wet. I think I'll have to go and get changed. Why don't you run and ask Hannah to bring some tea and pikelets into the drawing room and we'll have them by the fire?' Sophie didn't want tea or crumpets, but it gave the child something to do while she went upstairs to put on dry clothes.

I love you, Sophie. Charles's words echoed in her head. Had he really said them? Did he really mean them? Joy flooded through her, only to be dashed to nothing by the thought that he was going to risk his life in a small open boat in a heavy sea, to try and save the lives of others. Of course, he might not have to go. Surely they'd have a full crew, with men from the fishing fleet. All the other volunteers would go, people like farmer Will Shaw and postman Fred Polmire, and if necessary she knew Charles would too, in the hope of saving lives.

Will Shaw! Poor Hannah! She must find her straight away.

Charles hurried along the cliff path to the village. The wind tore at his clothes and the rain drove into his face, making it difficult to see where he was going. But he knew the path well enough and it was far quicker to go that way than down the lane. When he reached the stone steps down into the village he joined others who were hurrying to the harbour, not only the lifeboat men, but those alerted to the disaster by the maroons who'd come to hear the news.

Martin Penlee was standing in the doorway of the inn, and for a moment Charles took shelter from the rain beside him. 'What's gone down?' Charles asked.

'Distress flares nor-norwest out beyond Felec Head,' Martin replied. 'Coaster driven onshore by Brea Head, I shouldn't wonder. Be rough going out that way in this gale.'

Together the two men followed the other lifeboat men hurrying from The Clipper to Anvil Cove where the lifeboat, *Lady Margaret*, waited in her stone boathouse. Cork life jackets were handed out and the crew put them on, securing them firmly over their waterproofs. Coxswain Joe Fraser was counting heads.

'Where's Dan Martell?' Joe Fraser demanded. 'And Alfred? Alfred Dawes?'

'Couldn't rouse neither of 'em, Skipper,' answered Peter Daniels, the second coxswain. 'Banged on their doors, but no lights came on, and Davy Knight's got a broken leg. He won't be comin'.'

'So we're at least two short, if not three,' growled Joe.

Charles stepped forward. 'I'm here, Joe, if you want me.'

'Give Mr Leroy a life jacket, Peter,' ordered Joe, and moments later Charles had struggled into the jacket, fashioned from rings of cork, and joined the group hauling *Lady Margaret* out of the boathouse on her launching carriage.

He didn't hear a second volunteer offer his services. Joe Fraser looked at the man and realized it was Dr Bryan.

'You got any sea-going experience?' he asked. The last thing he wanted was a totally inexperienced man who might be more of a liability than an asset in the boat.

'No,' admitted Nicholas, 'but I am a doctor. I could be useful, and I'll follow your orders in the boat.'

There was no time to lose and they were still a man short, so Joe made his decision. 'Grab a life jacket,' he said, 'fast as you like.'

Nicholas had volunteered on impulse. He had come to the harbour to see why the maroons had been fired and he was not dressed for an open boat at sea, but following the crowd heading to Anvil Cove he got there in time to hear Charles Leroy volunteer and the germ of an idea took root. Even before he had thought it through, he had volunteered to go as well. Who could tell what accident might happen in an open boat in a heavy sea? Moments later, he too was equipped with some waterproof clothing and a cork life jacket and was back on the beach.

Willing hands had rolled the *Lady Margaret* down the slipway towards the tumult of the sea and she was ready to launch. Open to the seas, she was double-banked with space for twelve oarsmen. The masts had already been stepped, and the sails were ready to unfurl the instant they were clear of the rocky shore and out on clear water.

The crew scrambled aboard and took up their positions at

the oars. The pounding waves splintered and shattered on the rocks that surrounded the cove, flinging spray and spume into the darkening sky, but most of the men were old hands and they had the launch of the *Lady Margaret* down to a fine art. The launching party pulled the boat off the trolley and she hit the waves bow on, to be tossed high on an incoming roller before slamming down into a trough beyond.

Charles had never been launched into such a wild sea and he feared that unless they could pull away quickly from the beach they would be wrecked themselves.

At a roar from Fraser, the oars were shipped and the crew began to heave in unison, trying to pull the boat clear of the incoming sea before she was turned broadside on and overturned, drowning them all. Charles gripped his oar and keeping time with his pair, pulled until his arms ached, struggling to keep the rhythm as the boat pitched its way forward. Cresting the breaking waves, and rowing into the teeth of the gale, was one of the most dangerous parts of the launch. Joe Fraser roared at them, his voice hoarse, in his determination to be heard above the thunder of the waves, and they laboured at their oars, pulling for dear life to get beyond the rocks and broken water and out towards the open sea.

Nicholas saw the seas piling up round them, breaker after breaker threatening to bury them as they struggled to pull free, and terror welled up inside him. He was going to drown. He couldn't swim. He was wearing a life jacket, but in the roiling sea about them he knew it wouldn't keep his head above water. Only Will Shaw, chanting the rhythm of the oars beside him, kept him in time with the rest of the crew. The oar was heavy and slippery in his hands and he longed to let it go, but inexperienced as he was, he realized that would be disastrous and had to keep pulling. Suddenly they burst out of the cove, rising on a wave, surfing down its back into a valley of green water, only to rise on the next wave to be buffeted by the wind. But for now they were clear of the rocks and headed out to sea.

Immediately the boat passed Anvil Rock and the dark needles of rock just below the surface that surrounded it, Fraser gave the order to hoist the sails. With the oars shipped inboard and the lifeboat now under sail, the coxswain stood in the stern, clinging to the rudder lines as he did his best to steer a course through the mountainous seas to take the *Lady Margaret* and her crew out towards the distressed ship.

Charles watched the expert seamanship of the coxswain and his second as they ordered the reefing of the sails, leaving mere rags of canvas to carry them along. The boat carried swinging storm lanterns, giving minimal light for the coxswain to check the compass as they headed out to sea. As the darkness deepened, their swinging circles of light cast moving shadows across the faces of the men as they strained to see out over the heaving water. At first Charles thought he must be mistaken, but as the lantern swung again he saw and recognized the man seated two thwarts in front of him, and it was only then that he realized Nicholas Bryan was also aboard. He sat beside Will Shaw, his face a deathly white beneath his sou'wester, his body rigid with fear.

He must be another extra volunteer, thought Charles. He's clearly not one of the regular crew.

As if he'd felt eyes upon him, Nicholas turned stiffly and looked back along the boat, his expression hostile when he saw who was watching him, and then looked away.

The rain had eased a little, but the wind was still as strong and the sea as rough. Ahead of them there was another burst of flame that burned for several minutes, illuminating the drifting ship, before it was quenched by the sea. She was a small cargo ship and it was clear that the storm had damaged her superstructure. One mast was snapped off, its cross-trees smashed across the deck, and they could see that she must already be holed as she was listing heavily. Unable to steer away from the lee shore, she was being driven by wind and tide towards the cliffs that dropped sheer into the water, and it wouldn't be long before she was cast up on the rocks at their feet.

The *Lady Margaret* was making good headway now, and her crew heard a ragged cheer go up from the sailors, as they saw her lights and ran to lean over the rails and call for help.

'We'll try and go alongside,' called Joe Fraser. 'Ready the lines.' The regular crew knew the drill and stood by to throw lines to the waiting sailors, but the sea was too rough to get close enough. Joe took *Lady Margaret* round again, and as they passed under her stern Charles saw the name *Minerva* painted in curved gold letters on her stern, and his heart missed a beat. Their ship! And she was going to be a total wreck. They'd be lucky if they could save anything of her cargo, even if she stranded within reach of the shore rather than the reef that ran out from the cliff. But then, at this rate, he'd be lucky to survive himself!

He put the fate of the cargo and the *Minerva* herself out of his mind. The priority now was to take the crew off and carry them safely back to Port Felec, and that, Charles could see, would be no easy task. *Lady Margaret* was in great danger of being smashed against *Minerva*'s hull as the seas threw them together. Even as they approached a second time, the *Minerva* gave a shudder, and sank lower in the water, and the cries of her crew came in desperation across the water.

Joe Fraser ordered the sails to be lowered, and this time when they approached the wreck the oars were shipped, and they rowed the lifeboat as close as they dared in a desperate attempt to hold the boat steady on the swell of the sea and effect a rescue.

'Ready the lines,' cried Peter Daniels.

Again men were ready to toss ropes to the men on the stricken ship, and though this time they were closer, the lines still fell short. Another rumble came from within the belly of the ship and her bow dipped deeper into the sea. Suddenly one of *Minerva*'s crew tied a rope round his waist and without warning jumped into the sea, disappearing into the water between the two boats. At first Charles thought he must have jumped to his death, but suddenly Martin Penlee, holding one of the lanterns over the side and peering into the water, gave a cry. 'There he is!' He picked up a cork lifebelt and fastening a line to it, tossed it towards the man struggling to swim in the surging water. He grabbed it and clung on tightly as they pulled him through the water to the side of the boat and heaved him aboard. He was gasping for breath, and while he vomited seawater over the side, Peter Daniels grabbed the line from round his waist and started to haul on it. Fred Polmire tail-ended the rope and together they pulled it inboard, bringing in the heavier rope attached to it, which they made fast round a thwart. With a shout and a wave, they signalled to the *Minerva*'s crew to slide down this rope to the safety of the lifeboat. The rope pulled taut as the sea pulled the lifeboat away, but with a yell the first crewman swung himself onto the rope and clinging on for dear life above the surging water, he swung down and was gathered into the arms of Peter Daniels.

'How many more?' Daniels demanded.

'Six,' gasped the man. 'The rest...'

Another shout and the next man was on his way down, clinging to the rope with hands and feet, swiftly followed by the rest. The *Minerva* continued to drift and the crew of the *Lady Margaret* struggled manfully to keep her on station as each man slithered down the rope. As the last man began his descent the *Minerva* began to roll. The rope stretched to breaking, snapped with a sound like a gunshot and with a scream the last crewman fell into the sea.

'Pull!' bellowed Joe Fraser. And they pulled, heaving on the oars to carry *Lady Margaret* away from the sinking ship. The sea boiled round them as the *Minerva* rolled slowly over until she was on her side, and then with a strange sucking sound she slipped beneath the waves and disappeared, leaving only a whirlpool swirling behind her.

They could feel the lifeboat being drawn back into the vortex *Minerva* had created as she sank into her grave, and they pulled for their very lives until at length they were clear and Joe Fraser called for them to rest on their oars. There was no sign of the man who had fallen in and everyone aboard knew that there never would be.

The coxswain ordered the sails hoisted again and they began the long beat back to Anvil Cove. The rescued sailors huddled together for warmth, frozen in the chill of March. They had been on the drifting ship for several hours, not daring to go below for fear of being trapped and drowned.

Peter Daniels spoke to the man who had risked his life jumping to bring them the line attached to the rescue rope. 'What happened?' he asked.

'We hit a rock coming round Brea Head. Though we sailed on, we were holed below the water line and began taking on water. The cargo shifted and we began to list. We were getting the sails down when the mast snapped, just like that!' He snapped his fingers. 'Broke clean away and landed on the deck. Two men killed outright and another two swept overboard, but we could do nothing for them.' He buried his head in his hands. 'Good men all,' he said.

'It was your jump that saved the rest of you.' Daniels rested a hand on his shoulder. 'We couldn't get close enough to throw you a line.'

'You, Dr Bryan,' Peter Daniels called to Nicholas. 'See what you can do for these men. They're all in a pretty bad way.'

Nicholas did what he could for the rescued men, who huddled together in a vain effort to keep warm, but had little to offer them apart from a mouthful of brandy each from the supply kept for just this purpose. All the way back to Anvil Cove, they were drenched by the sea breaking over the *Lady Margaret*'s bow, slapping the crew and nearly swamping the boat. Every man prayed as he clung to his thwart to avoid being washed overboard by the fearsome waves.

By the time they were in sight of the beach, the rain had ceased and a half-moon sailed out from the ragged clouds still being driven across the sky. As they rounded the headland they could see lights on the beach, and the crowd of people gathered there.

They still had to run the boat in through the breakers and onto the beach and that, they all knew, was going to be a rough ride. Joe Fraser went head to wind so they could furl the sails and unstep the masts. With the rescued men aboard there was little room to manoeuvre, and Charles moved out of the way of the crew who were dealing with the sails and stood in the waist of the boat, waiting to resume his seat. The moon had disappeared behind a cloud and in that instant of darkness Nicholas, who had been waiting his chance, came up behind Charles and punched him violently in the kidneys. Charles gasped and staggered, clutching at air as the boat heaved on an incoming wave and he felt himself falling. A second punch followed the first and then Charles was hoisted off his feet and over the gunwale. In desperation he kicked back at his attacker, bringing his boot up hard into his groin even as he fell into the icy cauldron of the sea. He didn't hear the agonized screech that Nicholas gave as he doubled up in pain and falling against the side of the boat, vomited into the sea. At that moment the *Lady Margaret* was inundated by a mountainous wave that broke over the boat, its waters cascading over the crew and sweeping Nicholas over the side.

'Man overboard!' cried Fred Polmire, who had seen the wave take him. He rushed to peer into the heaving water, but he could see nothing. The *Lady Margaret* had swung round on the tumult of the sea and Nicholas had disappeared. 'Man overboard!' Fred shouted again. Peter Daniels grabbed a storm lantern and held it aloft, straining to see the bob of a head above the water, but there was nothing. Two of the crew grabbed the other two lanterns and leaned out as far as they dared, swinging the lanterns to try and catch sight of someone in the water, but there was nothing to see but the swirling waves.

'Too late for him now,' cried Joe Fraser. 'Ship oars.'

The crew followed his orders and the *Lady Margaret* negotiated the dangerous run into the mouth of the cove, running aground on the beach. The incoming waves still lifted her stern, but there were plenty of strong arms ready to haul her clear of the waves. They were home. The crowd surrounded her, wives and mothers reaching for their loved ones who staggered out onto the beach, returned safe home from the sea. Willing hands helped the rescued crew of the *Minerva* out of the boat and led them, cold, wet and shaking, along the path to the harbour and the welcome warmth of The Clipper.

Joe Fraser and Peter Daniels stood with Fred Polmire beside the lifeboat, and from habit Joe counted heads. Were there two missing, or had he miscounted with all the people milling about on the beach? Yes, that had to be it. It was bad enough to have lost one man to the sea, but he was sure he hadn't lost two.

He turned to Fred Polmire. 'What happened out there, Fred?' he demanded.

'Not sure, Skipper, but the doctor suddenly gave a shriek. For some reason he was leaning over the side. Then that big wave broke over us and when we steadied again, I realized he was gone.'

'But what was he doing?'

'Think he was being sick. It was pretty rough out there and he's not a sailor, is he? 'Less you're used to a sea like that, it can bring your guts up.'

'You think he was leaning over the side to be sick?'

'I don't know, Skip, it was all so quick. One minute he was there and the next he was gone.'

'And no sign of him in the water,' Joe said bleakly.

'Tide's on the ebb. He must've been sucked under and dragged out.' Seeing the coxswain's agony, he added, 'But don't you blame yourself, Skipper. No more you could do by then and it was your job to bring the rest of us in safe. If we'd gone broadside to they rollers, we'd all have been done for. He had a life jacket on, didn't he? So, maybe he'll swim ashore somewhere.'

'If he can swim,' said Peter Daniels gloomily. 'But Fred's right, Joe, you made the right call. There was not much we could do for him once he was in the water in the dark. You were right to make sure everyone else in the boat was safe. No point in rescuing the others to lose them coming into the beach.'

Joe Fraser knew they were right, but it didn't make it any easier. Until now, in all their attempted rescues, he'd never lost a man from his crew. Nicholas Bryan was the first and he felt the full weight of that responsibility.

Chapter 41

Will Shaw was in The Clipper, warming himself at the fire with a glass of brandy in his hand before he went back to the farm. They were safely home with seven rescued men, after braving some of the worst seas he'd ever been on, but in the most unlikely way they'd lost one of their own. The usual euphoria that filled the bar when the *Lady Margaret* returned to the village was muted. Oh, the wives and families of the crew were overjoyed to see them safe, but the loss of one man was one man too many, especially as he was an extra volunteer, not regular crew. The rescued men needed the proper services of a doctor, but it was the doctor who was missing.

Will thought he'd have one more glass and then he'd go home to dry out properly. At that moment the door to the bar opened and Hannah appeared. She paused on the threshold, but seeing there were plenty of women there as well as men, she stepped inside and looked for Will. As she saw him standing by the fire her face broke into a beam and she hurried across to him.

'Oh, Will, thank God! Thank God you're safe. I didn't know!'

'Didn't know I was safe?' grinned Will, putting his arms round her and holding her close.

'Will!' she murmured. 'We're in public!'

'So we are,' Will agreed and kissed her gently on the lips before letting her go.

'No, I mean I didn't know you were lifeboat crew. I thought they was all fishermen. When Miss Sophie told me you'd have gone out with the lifeboat, I thought she'd got it wrong.' Suddenly realizing something else, she looked round the room again and then said, 'Where's Mr Charles?'

Will looked at her, surprised. 'Isn't he at home?'

'No,' replied Hannah. 'Not yet. I thought he might be in here.'

'I didn't see him after we landed,' Will said. 'We'd picked up six men from the stricken ship and were almost home safe and sound when we lost a man overboard.' He took Hannah's hand as she gasped, 'Not Mr Charles?'

'No, no, not Mr Charles. Dr Bryan.'

'Dr Bryan?' echoed Hannah. 'What was he doing in the life-boat?'

'Crew was two men down. Mr Charles has been out with us before and he volunteered. Skipper was happy enough to take him. Then Dr Bryan turned up, and the next thing you know he's paired with me.'

'What d'you mean, paired?'

'*Lady Margaret* is double-banked. Six oars on either side. We have an oar each, so we're sitting next to the man with the opposite oar. He was sitting next to me. It'd usually be Davy Knight, but he broke his leg t'other day; fell off his roof mending his chimney he did, and Dr Bryan had his place.'

'So what happened to him?'

'We were coming home, preparing to make the run in through the breakers, taking down sails and masts before rowing in on the waves. Tricky coming in when it's rough, specially if the tide's on the turn. Anyway Fred Polmire saw him being sick over the side. Not surprised at that, he looked pretty green about the gills the whole time. And while he was leaning over the side a freak wave broke over us, almost drowning us all, but he was swept away. It was dark and with only light from a couple of storm lanterns we couldn't see much, but there was no sign of him in the water.'

'And you just came in without him?'

'It was getting dangerous out there, Hannah. Skipper's responsible for everyone and he had to make sure the rest of us was safe. It was close to the shore and the doctor was wearing a life jacket, so he'll probably be all right.'

'And you think this Skipper was right to leave him?'

'I do,' Will said firmly. 'And Mr Charles'll say the same, I'm sure.'

'But where is Mr Charles?' wondered Hannah. The crowd in the bar was thinning out now as the crew went home to dry out and to get some sleep. 'He hadn't come home when I left.'

'Which way did you come?'

'Down the lane. I wouldn't cross that cliff top in the dark in weather like this.'

'That'll be it then,' said Will. 'He'll have taken the cliff path and you'll have missed each other. He's probably tucked up in bed now, glad to be safe on shore. Come on,' he said, 'it's very late. I'll walk you home.'

Charles was certainly not tucked up in bed. When he'd hit the water the chill of it numbed him completely. His life jacket brought him back to the surface but he knew he was going to die. For a moment he struggled to keep his head above water, but as he turned his face from the incoming sea and kicked out with his feet, he found that with the buoyancy of the cork he could fight against the pull of the waves. For a couple of minutes he allowed himself to be carried where the sea took him; he could no longer see the lights of the *Lady Margaret* and hoped he was beyond the needle rocks that lined the shore. The tide should carry him towards the harbour.

Suddenly he felt something grab at his legs. He kicked out, trying to pull free, but desperate hands gripped him and began to pull him under. Kicking and struggling, he managed to break free and was being carried away by the tide when a head burst up through the water, and by the pale light of the moon he saw who it was. Nicholas Bryan was flailing about in the water and Charles realized with a sinking heart that the doctor's life jacket had been ripped away, leaving a single ring of cork about his waist. Charles swam towards the struggling man and reached out a hand.

'Hold fast!' he called. 'Don't panic and we can reach the shore.'

Nicholas clutched the outstretched hand, trying to pull Charles closer. Charles could see the naked terror in his eyes and he called again, 'Don't panic, Nicholas, turn your face from the waves!'

But Nicholas was beyond reason. He fought to cling on to Charles and was in danger of sinking them both. Once more Charles managed to break free from the clutching hands, and struggling himself to keep his own head above water turned back again to shout, 'I'm coming back for you. Don't struggle. You'll drown us both.' But even as he shouted, another huge wave swept him further away, and when he looked again there was no sign of Nicholas Bryan.

By the light of the moon Charles could see the shore. The tide continued to sweep him along with little he could do about it. He could see the lights of Port Felec and the entrance to its tiny harbour, but he was too far out to swim ashore.

I'm going to drown.

The thought passed through his head but somehow it didn't seem important. The sea was carrying him under the cliffs, and above him he could see more lights. That must be Trescadinnick, he thought. At least Sophie and AliceAnne are safely inside.

It was then that he heard again Sophie's last words to him, echoing in his mind. 'Come back, Charles, we all need you here.'

AliceAnne needed him; Sophie needed him. Sophie needed him. Sophie needed him. Suddenly the words penetrated his brain, and he remembered his own reply. 'I love you, Sophie.'

The moonlight gleamed on the sand of the tiny cove below the house and Charles realized that he still had one chance to save his life. Forcing himself to turn into the waves, he kicked out in one last effort to swim for the shore.

★

When Will and Hannah reached Trescadinnick they were greeted by a worried Sophie, waiting by the front door. 'Hannah, did you find him?'

'I found Will, Miss Sophie.'

'I didn't mean Will, Hannah. I meant Charles. Where is he?' She turned to Will. 'Didn't he go with the lifeboat?'

'Yes, Miss Sophie, he came with us. We were two men short and he and—' Will caught himself just in time. 'And he volunteered.'

'So where is he now? Surely everyone is back. Is he at The Clipper?'

'No, Miss Sophie,' replied Will. 'I'm afraid he's not. Are you sure he's not home?'

'Of course I'm sure,' snapped Sophie. 'I've been waiting up for him. He couldn't have come in without me seeing him.'

Will looked concerned. 'How's about I go and talk to the coxswain straight away, Miss Sophie? See if he saw him after we landed?'

'Something's happened to him. I know it has,' Sophie cried.

'I'll go and see what I can find out,' Will promised. 'You stay here with Hannah and I'll be back as soon as I can.'

Will set off back to the village and went straight to Joe Fraser's house on Fore Street, just beyond The Clipper. A heavy bang on the front door brought the coxswain to answer and when Will told him what he wanted to know, Joe Fraser paled beneath his weather-beaten skin.

'I counted them in,' he said. 'But there was such a crowd on the beach, I couldn't be sure. 'Cept of course I knew Dr Bryan had been lost. Once I did think there was another man missing, but in the hubbub I thought I'd just miscounted.'

'But when could he have gone overboard? Surely someone would have noticed him fall.'

'Fred says that the doctor was leaning over the side. He thought he was being sick, but maybe he saw Mr Leroy fall over and was looking for him when that wave nearly took us all.' He reached for his coat and calling back into the house to say he was going out again, came out into the street. 'Come on, Will,' he cried. 'We better go and see Fred Polmire.'

Fred, already in his bed, was summoned by his wife and came bleary-eyed down the stairs to see them. 'I only saw the doctor,' he insisted. 'Perhaps he was looking for Mr Leroy in the water, but he never called *man overboard* and the simplest man knows to do that.'

Will returned to Sophie and Hannah, waiting by the dying fire in the drawing room at Trescadinnick. One look at his face told them the news wasn't good.

'No one's seen him since we came ashore at Anvil Cove,' Will told them. 'Of course, we can ask about again tomorrow,' he said. 'Someone may have taken him in for shelter.' But they all knew that was unlikely in the extreme. Why would Charles seek shelter in someone else's house when his own was just up the hill?

Despite Hannah's insistence, Sophie didn't go to bed that night. She sat in the drawing room and waited. She would be there to welcome him when he came home, but her heart was breaking. He had told her he loved her and she had not replied. She had been too proud to let him know how she'd come to feel about him over the last few weeks, and now it was too late. He had given up his life in a bid to save others.

Before he'd left he'd charged her with looking after his daughter. 'I know you'll look after her, Sophie, if… if I'm gone long.' Had he had some premonition that he wasn't coming back?

'Oh, Charles!' she cried in despair and buried her head in her hands. The fire long gone out, the room grew colder and colder, and eventually Sophie dozed, sitting on the sofa. That was how Hannah found her when she went down to see her later.

Let her sleep, Hannah thought. *Tomorrow's going to be a difficult day.* And tucking a blanket around her, she left her to sleep.

★

Charles had used every ounce of his energy to swim towards the little beach that those at Trescadinnick used for their picnics in the summer months. It was here he'd learned to swim himself, but never fully clothed nor in such cold rough water. The life jacket stopped him sinking but did not keep his head above water. His heavy clothes weighed him down. He'd managed to kick off his boots, but however hard he swam he seemed no nearer the beach. In despair he gave one last thrust with his legs as a wave swept over him, and this time it carried him forward, exploding into foam around his head and leaving him cast up on the sand. Almost immediately another wave broke over him, but without the strength of the one that had beached him. Instinct made him bury his fingers in the wet sand, literally clinging to the beach with his fingertips. He was ashore, but he was bitterly cold and he knew that he had to move, or he would die. Sophie was waiting for him in the house at the top of the cliff. All he had to do was climb up the path to reach her. The path he had climbed so many times without a thought now seemed a mountain, but Sophie was waiting at the top. With immense determination he dug his feet into the sand and began to drag himself clear of the sea.

Chapter 42

The storm had blown itself out when Frank Davies left his cottage in Port Felec the next morning. It had stopped raining and though it was still very windy, pale sunlight was lighting the sky. He'd heard the maroons go off, but neither he nor his wife had been prepared to brave the fury of the storm to watch the launch of the lifeboat. Now he trudged up the hill and took the path across the cliff to Trescadinnick, wondering what damage the bullying winds had done to his garden. As he neared Trescadinnick he saw something lying in the path. For an instant he stopped stock-still and stared, then realizing what he was looking at, he hurried forward.

'Mr Charles!' he cried, and kneeling down shook the lifeless figure on the ground. He got no response to his shaking and put his hand on Charles's face. It was stone cold.

Getting stiffly to his feet again, Davies almost ran to the house, to bang on the front door and tell the news. 'Oh, Miss Sophie,' he croaked, when she opened the door to his frantic knocking. 'Oh, Miss Sophie. He's dead. On the path.'

Sophie grabbed at the old man, himself almost collapsed on the doorstep, and shook him. 'Who's dead. Where is he?'

'It's Mr Charles. He's lying on the cliff, stone cold.'

Sophie gave a shriek that brought Hannah running. 'He's dead!' she sobbed. 'He's dead.'

Hannah pulled Frank Davies into the house and pushed him onto a chair. 'Tell me,' she ordered. 'Tell me what you've just told Miss Sophie.'

'Mr Charles lying dead on the cliff,' he wheezed.

Sophie was already out of the door and, leaving the old man sitting in the hall, Hannah rushed after her. Together they ran out onto the cliff and there they found Charles, lying at the top of the path that came up from the beach.

Sophie flung herself down beside him, putting her arms round him, her face against his cold skin. He was still wearing his bulky cork life jacket and his tarpaulin waterproofs, but his feet, hands and head were bare. Hannah kneeled down beside him and took one of his hands in hers. It was icy cold, but she pressed her fingers to his wrist in search of a pulse. At first she could find none, but moving her hand under his chin she thought she felt a flutter.

'Get up, Sophie,' she cried. 'He's still alive. We have to get him to the house. Run back – send Ned for Will. Tell them both to come here and bring blankets.'

For a moment Sophie stared at her and Hannah shouted, 'Go, Sophie!'

Sophie was on her feet and running, while Hannah threw off her own cloak and wrapped it round the motionless Charles. Had she imagined a pulse? She felt again at his neck. No, it was definitely there, very faint, very slow, but beating.

'Come on, come on,' she muttered as she waited for help to arrive. She took Charles's hands in hers and tucked them under her cloak, wishing there was more she could do to fight the cold that was taking him. It seemed an age before Sophie was back with a blanket and the promise that Will and Ned were right behind her.

'Shouldn't we take this cork thing off him?' she suggested as she kneeled beside him, trying to tuck the blanket round him.

'No,' said Hannah. 'I think it might be keeping him warm.'

'But he's freezing,' cried Sophie in despair.

There was a shout from the path and they looked round to see Will and Ned arriving at the run.

'We'll get him back to the house,' Will said. 'You run on ahead and get his bed warm. Light the fire in his room. We need to fight the cold.'

Sophie and Hannah ran back to the house and several minutes later Ned and Will arrived, carrying the inert figure of Charles. They took him straight upstairs to his room, where the fire was just catching in the grate and Edith was running a warming pan between the sheets. Louisa, wearing a dressing gown over her nightclothes, was waiting in the hall, her face pale as she followed the two men carrying her son upstairs.

'Now then, Miss Sophie,' said Hannah, taking charge, 'you go downstairs and get Mrs Paxton to make us all hot drinks. Tell Edith to bring up plenty of hot water. Will and I can do what's needed up here.' She gave her a little push. 'Go on now, we'll look after him.' She turned to Louisa. 'Mrs Leroy, please, will you wait downstairs?' Louisa seemed about to say something, but changed her mind and did as she was asked.

Will and Hannah closed the door and set about getting Charles out of his cold wet clothes. They removed the cork jacket.

'That's what saved him,' Will murmured. 'Not just in the sea, but from the cold as well.' They stripped the sodden clothes away and patted his freezing body dry with warm towels, trying to get the blood flowing again. They bathed him all over with warm water and then rubbed him dry again, before putting him into a warm, dry nightgown and nightcap and tucking him into the warmed bed, the blankets up to his chin. All the time they watched for any flicker of life, but there was none. Hannah felt for the pulse yet again, and still it was there, but the figure in the bed could have been carved out of marble.

'We've done all we can here,' Will said. 'He needs a doctor. We should send Ned to Treslyn to fetch Miss Matty and her doctor. In the meantime he must be kept warm. I've seen a man come back from this, so we mustn't give up hope.'

'How did he come to be out on the cliff top, d'you think?' Hannah wondered.

Will shrugged. 'Could have collapsed coming home last night,' he said. 'But he was so wet, I think he came out of the sea. Must've gone overboard in the wave that took the doctor. Currents would carry him this way. Maybe he got ashore, managed to climb up the path before he was too exhausted to go further. Whatever happened, he'd be a dead man now if Frank Davies hadn't found him and raised the alarm.'

'I'll tell Miss Sophie and his mother that they can come in now,' Hannah said, 'and I'll send Ned to fetch Mrs Treslyn.'

Sophie and Louisa came into the bedroom and looked at the still figure in the bed. 'We must keep him warm,' Louisa said. 'And someone must sit with him.'

Sophie was already at the bedside. 'I'll stay with him,' she said, 'until he wakes up.'

Louisa seemed about to protest, but seeing the look on Sophie's face said, 'We'll take it in turns.'

When Matty and Dr Crown arrived from Treslyn, the doctor went straight upstairs to visit his patient and Sophie, sent out of the room during his examination, came downstairs to greet her aunt.

'He's still alive,' she said. 'I won't let him die!'

'That decision is not yours to make,' said Louisa. 'We can only pray for him now.'

'If he has something to live for perhaps he will pull through,' Matty said soothingly. 'He's young and he's strong and is safely in his own bed.'

Dr Crown echoed her words when he came back downstairs. 'You have done exactly the right thing,' he said. 'Now that his body is gradually warming up, he should regain consciousness. I advise constant attendance, so that if he wakes up someone is on hand to give him sustenance. A little water, a sip of brandy, perhaps a spoonful of broth. Warm drinks, not too hot, but regular.'

Matty stayed the rest of the day, but she left Louisa and Sophie to sit at his bedside. Dr Crown had been carried off by Will to attend the rescued men who were still recovering at The Clipper.

Sophie sat by Charles's bed and held his hand. He seemed to be a little warmer now, and his breathing became a little steadier.

'Come back to us, Charles,' Sophie murmured softly as she stroked his hand. 'Come back to us. We all need you. What will

AliceAnne do if you die? Your mother is praying for you to recover. And I? I can't imagine my life without you at the centre of it. You said you loved me before you left. Was that true, my dearest? Come back to all of us. Come back to me. It's me, Sophie, calling you because I love you and need you and want you.'

It was later that evening, as she continued to sit by his bed, that Sophie noticed a difference. The sound of his breathing changed and the faint shallow breaths sounded stronger. The light of the lamp, shielded from his face, showed a slight movement beneath the covers. Sophie leaned forward and suddenly his eyes flicked open for a second.

'Charles?' she breathed, 'Charles, can you hear me? It's me, Sophie. Are you awake?' She grasped his hands so that he would know she was there, and his eyes opened again, and this time stayed open.

'Sophie?' he croaked, his voice husky and dry. 'Sophie?'

'I'm here, Charles,' she whispered. 'I'm here... always.' And leaning forward, she touched his cheek with her lips.

For a moment a beatific smile spread across his face before he lapsed back into sleep.

Sophie felt a surge of joy welling up inside her as very gently, she tucked the hand she'd been holding back under the covers, and went to tell his mother that Charles had turned the corner and he was coming back to them.

Epilogue

It was almost a week later that the body of Nicholas Bryan was discovered, battered and broken, at the foot of the cliffs. His life jacket was gone, his clothing ripped to shreds on the jagged rocks. He had been cast up at high tide, so much flotsam, and lay face down in a rockpool just yards from where his father had been found over twenty-five years earlier. He was seen from a passing fishing boat and a rescue party clambered down the steep cliff path to bring what was left of him up for burial in the churchyard.

Charles's memories of exactly what had happened on the fateful night of the lifeboat rescue had at first been patchy, but, as he recovered, so what had happened came back to him. On Dr Crown's instructions and Sophie's determination that they should be adhered to, Charles had remained in bed for several days after his brush with death. Sleep was his healer, but Sophie sat with him whenever he was awake and they talked to each other as they had never talked to anyone else before.

AliceAnne was allowed to visit him night and morning, and her delight in his gradual recovery added to it. 'You're getting better every day,' she told him. 'But Aunt Sophie says you must stay in bed until the doctor says you can get up.'

'And I shall do exactly what Aunt Sophie tells me,' Charles promised meekly and then gave his daughter a huge wink, which sent her off into hoots of laughter. 'Oh, Papa,' she cried, 'you are naughty!'

When Charles heard that Nicholas's body had been found,

he had already remembered the vicious punch that had pitched him into the sea and realized that it must have come from Nicholas. 'He tried to drown me,' he told Sophie. 'But how he came to be in the water as well, I don't know.'

Sophie told him what Will had told Hannah, that Nicholas had been washed overboard by a freak wave, and on hearing this Charles asked to see Will.

The farmer came up to the house, and Charles heard from him how Nicholas had been swept away. 'It's a sobering thought the thin line between life and death,' Will said. 'One minute a living breathing man, the next a soul gone and a body floating in the water.'

Charles remembered the panicking Nicholas clinging on to him, pulling him under the surging water before another wave had broken them apart, Nicholas to his death, Charles to struggle for his life. He remembered his battle to reach the shore and the nightmare climb as he inched his way up the cliff path, clutching at the rope beside the path and hauling himself upward until he finally reached the top.

'I must thank you and Ned for bringing me in so quickly,' he said. 'I should have died out there on the cliff if you hadn't carried me home.'

'Lucky old Frank Davies found you,' Will replied.

'I know, I've already spoken to him, but I survived because you knew what needed to be done to save me.'

'Seen a man taken from the water cold like that before,' Will said. 'We've learned what to do.'

Seeing Sophie's happiness in her promised future with Charles, Hannah decided that at last she could broach the subject of her own forthcoming marriage.

'Since you're going to marry Mr Charles,' Hannah said, 'I can now tell you that Will and I are going to be wed as well.'

'Hannah, you dark horse,' cried Sophie, giving her a hug. 'You and Will! AliceAnne said that she thought you were "best friends". How right she was!'

Hannah laughed. 'Is that what she said, bless her. I always

said she was nobody's fool. Let's face it, she was the first person to take against Dr Bryan.'

'Well, Hannah, dear Hannah, I wish you every happiness. And even if you are leaving me, you'll be close by at the home farm and AliceAnne and I can come and visit you whenever we want to.'

'I wouldn't have left you if you'd married *him*,' Hannah said. 'And so I told Will, but now I have no worries about you. I've kept the promise I made to your ma and I can leave you safe in Mr Charles's care.'

Sophie hugged her again. 'Hannah, I don't know how I would have survived without you after Mama died. You were more than a friend to me, and I shall never forget how you stood by me. Be happy with your Will, you deserve him.'

After some discussion, Sophie and Charles decided there seemed no point in making public Nicholas's attempt on Charles's life.

'The man's dead,' Charles said. 'To most in the village he'll be a hero, a volunteer who took a place in the lifeboat and lost his life in a tragic accident.'

'You're very generous with your forgiveness,' Sophie said as she reached up to kiss him. 'More than I am.'

'What was between us has died with him,' Charles said, his arms tightening round her. 'I have everything to live for. I have you. I have AliceAnne. And we have a future. He has none. Let him rest in peace.'

SIGN UP FOR MORE BOOKS NEWS FROM

DINEY COSTELOE

For exclusive previews, behind-the-scenes content, book extracts, interviews and much more, simply email:

Diney@headofzeus.com

HEAD *of* ZEUS

www.dineycosteloe.co.uk